W9-CAL-494

She swore she could never love him,
but anything can happen ...
when an angel falls.

Phyllis

"I'D LIKE A WALTZ, LISSA," IVAN SAID WITH A WICKED SMILE.

"It'll be a cold day in—" Before she could even finish her oath, he had taken her by the waist and in moments they were dancing among his guests.

"You are an arrogant, self-serving, licentious, dissolute . . . rakehell!" she whispered furiously.

"Try bastard, sweet. That word always works well."

"Only because you work so hard at being one," she hissed.

"Believe me, it takes no effort at all." His hand tightened at her waist possessively and he swept her toward the balcony. When she tried to pull away he caught her. "Don't fight me any more," he whispered.

She shook her head. "Ivan, we'll destroy each other."

"So let's destroy each other," he answered huskily before claiming her mouth in a soul-searching kiss.

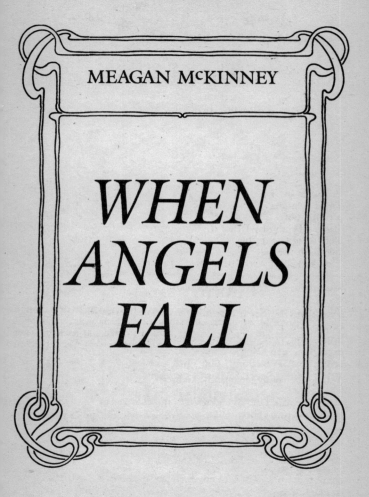

MEAGAN McKINNEY

WHEN ANGELS FALL

A DELL BOOK

Published by
Dell Publishing
a division of
Bantam Doubleday Dell
Publishing Group, Inc.
666 Fifth Avenue
New York, New York 10103

Interior design by Jeremiah B. Lighter

The trademark Dell® is registered in the U.S. Patent
and Trademark Office.

ISBN: 0-440-20521-2

Printed in the United States of America
Published simultaneously in Canada

February 1990
10 9 8 7 6 5 4 3 2 1
OPM

During the Regency period, Parliament standardized titles of the peerage, thus changing the title of marquis to marquess. Those families, however, who had possessed the title of marquis for centuries still retained personal use of that title, and do so to this day, such as the Marquis of Queensbury and the Marquis of Winchester.

PROLOGUE

OCTOBER 1855

*Revenge
is a dish
best served
cold . . .*

✻

The gentleman's house on Piccadilly was elegant, expensive, and aristocratic. But far from awestruck, Holland Jones merely stood before the baroque wrought-iron gates of No. 181, shaking his head.

It was the perfect dwelling for the eleventh Marquis of Powerscourt. The Sir John Soane red brick Georgian had become renowned for its gatherings of wits and beauties, poets and antiquarians. For three years the marquis had lived there, had thrived there, so it would seem. And for three years the marquis had been happy—that is, Holland thought, if happiness could ever be described as passing over the implacable features of Ivan Comeragh Tramore, the eleventh marquis.

Through the bars, Holland took one last look at the house. His position as Powerscourt estate manager had been his birthright, but Holland still found himself dreading any kind of meeting with his relatively new yet already notorious master. The marquis was always civil with those in his employ, but Holland, for his own personal comfort, preferred to avoid the icy pauses and black, brooding stares that the marquis was known for. Holland particularly wanted to avoid them this day because for the first time since he'd been with the new marquis, he had bad news. Resigned to his duties, however, Holland Jones had no other choice but to enter No. 181 and inform the marquis of the current situation of his estates.

The marquis was expecting him. As the majordomo held the door for him, Holland heard bells ringing belowstairs—for brandy, no doubt. Looking up, he saw an abovestairs maid lighting the gasoliers for the evening.

"I suppose he's in the library?" Holland faced the majordomo and wearily rubbed his eyes beneath his spectacles.

"Hrrrrumph . . . Ah, yessir," the majordomo answered, clearing his throat and lifting his chin in one practiced motion.

"Then don't bother to show me the way, my good man." Holland looked toward the mahogany library door. "I shall face the beast alone," he added under his breath as he stepped across the black marble floor. Pausing, he ran a finger along his starched collar, shrugged his shoulders, and entered the marquis's bastion.

The light and the bustle in the hall had no impact on the library whatsoever. Rows upon rows of leatherbound tomes covered the entire four walls, including the back of the door through which Holland had entered. Heavy red velvet draperies were closed against the drafts from the windows. The only light came from a small, lusty fire in the hearth. The flames lit up the huge gold tassels on the pelmets and, also, the unsmiling face of the marquis.

Unwittingly, Holland was once more struck by the incongruity of the marquis to his surroundings. Ivan Tramore was the sort of man one would have expected to find jousting at a medieval tourney, not sitting in a room full of books. He was better suited to armor, and German armor at that, Holland thought unkindly, recalling the particularly evil-looking armor he had once seen at the Queen's Exhibit. Yes, black steel would have befitted Ivan Tramore far better than the dark trousers and civilized silk paisley waistcoat he was wearing. Holland knew he himself was more suited to a gentleman's lifestyle than the grand marquis. This thought brought him little comfort, however.

"Very good to see you, my lord." Holland waited for a nod before he went to the club chair next to the marquis's. At the hearth, two huge brindled mastiffs raised their heads from the carpet to stare at the visitor. Noting their unwelcoming stance, Holland took special care easing himself into the chair.

Typically the marquis dispensed with any greetings and proceeded directly to the business at hand. "You've been there, then?"

"Yes," Holland answered, a wariness to his eye.

"And?" The marquis shot him a glance.

"And . . ." Holland straightened, forcing himself to meet his master's fury head on. "And as expected the castle is in ruinous condition. Being the Powerscourt estates manager, I heartily advise you against removing yourself there."

Holland peered at the marquis through his smudged spectacles. The marquis did look as if he was taking the news rather well. Ivan Tramore was quiet for a long while, and, as Holland had seen him often do while deep in thought, he rubbed his right cheek. Some time in his past he had acquired a neat slash of a scar there, and, watching his hard, aquiline profile, Holland didn't doubt the rumors of the widows and the debutantes who had thrown themselves at Tramore's feet, so enamored were they of that particular scar. Such women had probably read too many penny gothics, he surmised, for he didn't doubt, either, that the marquis's fierce countenance had sent just as many women scurrying away.

"How much will it cost, do you think? To put the castle in order." The marquis's deep voice startled Holland out of his musings.

"Too much, my lord. A king's ransom. As we speak, there are rats gnawing at the tapestries—"

"Have I that much? Have I a king's ransom to restore the castle?"

"My lord, your fortune has at least tripled since you inherited. I think it was your investment in iron that really—"

"So I have enough," the marquis stated impatiently.

"Aye, my lord." Holland put his spectacles on his

forehead and pinched the bridge of his nose as if to ward off a headache.

"Good." The marquis stood and rested his arm on the mantle after motioning Holland to remain seated. "There's another matter I want you to take care of for me."

"And what is that, my lord?" Holland lifted his head and let his spectacles fall back onto his nose.

"Miss Alcester. I want her cut off. After next month's allotment, she is to receive no more money."

Holland could barely believe what he was hearing. "But, if I may, my lord, you just sent me to Nodding Knoll to check up on her."

"I sent you to check up on Powerscourt." The marquis's statement was adamant.

"Yes, of course, my lord. But Nodding Knoll sits right at the foot of the castle. I assumed you wanted me to make the usual discreet inquiries into Miss Alcester's welfare—"

"And in what condition did these inquiries find her?"

Holland looked at Tramore, but something in the fire had caught the marquis's interest and his head was turned.

"Elizabeth Alcester is doing fine. Just fine, from what I could gather from the gossip." Holland's blue eyes narrowed. "If I may ask, my lord, why must you cut her off? Though I've never formally met the girl, nor her family, I must say it's been quite noble of you to help her out. Especially since you've not seen her in five years—"

The marquis's head snapped up. "It's not your place to speculate upon my relationships."

"No, my lord," Holland placated, "I don't speculate at all, particularly since I know Miss Alcester was barely a young woman when you last set eyes upon her."

"That's right."

The statement was brittle, yet the undertone, for some reason, struck Holland as oddly poignant.

He began again, this time more slowly. "But if you

will pardon me, my lord, I know the Alcesters have a rather disgraceful past; and it's true that the neighbors gossip about Elizabeth Alcester like little foxes; but, still, for the three years that I've been doling out her money, Miss Alcester has spent it only on her family. Why, I'm positive the girl hasn't bought a new gown in years."

"All very well," the marquis answered succinctly, "but I want you to write her a note and tell her that poor 'Great-aunt Sophie' has died in Paris and left all her guineas to the Museum of Practical Geology, or whatever you like. Tell her that after next month, her pension ends."

"My lord, I'm sure you have good reasons for cutting off Miss Alcester. But there is her family to consider. Her brother is merely a lad. And have you forgotten that Miss Alcester's sister is blind?"

"I haven't forgotten anything about Elizabeth Victorine Alcester, nor her family. Of that, I can assure you." The marquis's dark eyes flashed. When he seemed to have calmed down a bit, he changed the subject. "When will the castle be ready?"

"There is a lot of work to do on it," Holland said. "It may take months . . ."

"In the will, when did the tenth marquis say that I may live at Powerscourt?"

"Three years after his death, my lord . . . as you well know." Holland crossed his arms. It was common knowledge that Ivan Tramore was a bastard. And it was common knowledge that for the past twenty-some years of Tramore's life he had made his way as a stableboy, and at a neighboring estate at that. Tramore had even been denied the dubious honor of being a servant in the shadow of Powerscourt. The previous marquis had treated his only offspring like a beggar to be thrown out of one's path on market day. But still, in spite of this, Tramore had always cut too terrifying a figure to be pitied.

Holland still found it disconcerting that Tramore never referred to his father as anything but the tenth marquis. Not even now did he admit to his lineage, three years after he had inherited everything the marquis's legitimate son could have been due. Possessing wealth and position, Tramore had then lacked only one thing: knowledge. And it was said that the first thing he had done when he had inherited was to read every book in his father's library. It was as if he wanted to make sure there was nothing the tenth marquis knew that the eleventh marquis did not.

"It has been three years and then some, hasn't it?" The marquis's face tightened with some repressed emotion.

"Yes, my lord," Holland answered uneasily.

"Jones," Tramore baited, "remind me, will you, why was it stipulated that I wait three years?"

Holland met the marquis's level gaze. If Ivan Tramore abused one aspect of his vast power, it was his ability to make people uncomfortable. There were times when Holland swore the man enjoyed that more than he would enjoy a woman. Now was just such a time.

"I find it hard to believe that such a thing would have slipped your mind, my lord."

Tramore remained silent.

Seeing no way out, Holland began haltingly. "Your fath—excuse me, I mean the tenth marquis, stipulated three years, for he did not want you, I believe the words were, 'to walk upon his grave until it was sure to be cold.'"

The marquis let out a black laugh. His dark, handsome face lit up with a passion that Holland was sure would never cross his own proper English schoolboy features. And for that, he didn't know whether to be envious or relieved.

"I ask you, man, when you were up at Powerscourt, was the grave cold then?" Tramore's eyes glittered darkly.

"Yes, my lord. Quite frigid, in fact, considering the weather they've been having up north." Holland rose from his seat, hoping that this unpleasant visit had come to an end.

"Then I want the work done on Powerscourt right away. I plan to reside there in one month." The marquis went to the door to hold it open for Holland's exit.

"One month! My lord, I cannot be sure it can be done in that amount of time!"

"The tenth marquis is not getting any warmer in his grave, Jones."

Holland prickled. "Yes, my lord." Tramore *was* a bastard, he thought ungraciously as he stepped into the light of the hall. And not about to let *anyone* forget it.

"Jones." The marquis stopped him before the majordomo opened the front doors. "Your family has been estate manager for the Powerscourts for how long?"

"Six generations, my lord." For the second time that day Holland wondered if he should have pursued becoming a chemist like his brother.

"I see. Then you're the only man qualified to do this for me, Jones. You'll get the job done and when you do, there'll be hearty compensation, I promise you." Suddenly the marquis smiled and shook his hand. "See you at Powerscourt in one month's time."

"Yes, my lord." Dumbfounded, Holland was ushered out the door. The tides had abruptly turned. Instead of threatening him, the marquis had done something even worse. He had placed his faith in him. Holland knew now he would have to give Powerscourt back its old glory in an absurd four weeks or dishonor himself.

Wondering how he would ever accomplish the task before him, he picked up his stride and walked grimly down Piccadilly heading for Pall Mall and the Carlton Club.

As Holland left, he was unaware of the eyes that watched him. In the library, the marquis had shoved aside one panel of velvet to peer through the window. His breath clung to the cold panes until Jones was hardly a shadow beneath the streetlamps. Only then did the marquis let the drapery fall back, closed once more.

As if agitated, Tramore ran his knuckles over the scar on his cheek. His hand dropped immediately, however, when a soft knock came upon the door.

"Who is it?" he asked brusquely.

"Mrs. Myers, my lord." The frilly-capped head of a plump housekeeper appeared at the door with a tray.

"Take it all away, Mrs. Myers. He's gone already and I've no need for refreshment."

"Oh, I'm so sorry, sir. You see, the girls were all cleaning the lamps and there was no one to serve. That's what took the brandy so long. I had to come myself instead of sending the parlormaid." In contrition, the housekeeper shook her head so hard that if not for the fat ribbons beneath her cherubic chin, her cap would have flown off her head.

"It's all right." As if he were used to her performing contrary to his wishes, the marquis didn't even look up when she entered the library. She moved past him with a tray of decanters and glasses. Underneath her evening black dress and starched white apron, her horsehair crinoline crackled with every step she took to the hearth. When she reached the pair of club chairs, she set the tray upon a mahogany drum table.

"There. I'll be leaving the drink with you nonetheless. Just in case you'd like a spot." She turned. "Anything else before I go?"

"Yes." The marquis slowly met her gaze. "I'd like to dine in my rooms this evening. And I shall be having an evening companion, so I should like service for two."

"Very good, sir." But Mrs. Myers's expression proclaimed that it was not very good at all.

"Indigestion?" the marquis inquired.

The housekeeper's jaw dropped, then she abruptly remembered herself. "Nothing of the sort, my lord! I shall see to your service immediately!" She headed for the door.

"You don't approve, do you?"

Hearing the unexpected question, Mrs. Myers whisked around to face him.

"What?"

"You don't approve of my . . . lady friends, do you?" The marquis eased his large frame upon a nearby sofa done in the current Gothic taste.

"It's certainly not my place to disapprove of anything you do, sir."

"But come now, if it were your place, you would not approve, would you?" He crossed his arms over his chest with an air of nonchalance, yet his dark stare pinned the housekeeper to the floor.

"I believe in marriage, my lord."

"I see." The marquis thought on this for a while.

"Will there be anything else, sir?"

"Would you be surprised to find that I share that same sentiment?"

"What sentiment, my lord?"

"That I believe in marriage too."

"No, my lord. I would believe it." Mrs. Myers lowered her head. "Your mother's situation still pains you, if only you would admit it."

Tramore stiffened at the housekeeper's frankness. "That's enough, Mrs. Myers. You go too far."

Though she should have been chastened by the marquis's reply, the housekeeper instead burst out with another unwanted opinion. "Perhaps you're right, Lord Ivan, but I've known you all your life and I remember when your mother died. And I've seen how tough and silent a little boy becomes when he finds he has no other home but the streets." When she was finished, she watched for the marquis's reaction.

"I see," Tramore uttered with difficulty.

The housekeeper finally looked chastised. "Forgive

me, my lord," she whispered. She then looked around the room to see if he needed anything. "Would you like the girl to bring more coal for the fire, or will that be all?"

"No, you may go." He shot her one last disapproving look, then turned away.

"Thank you, sir." Mrs. Myers made her way to the door, but before she exited, she paused and looked as if she wanted to speak.

"Is there something you've forgotten?" Tramore acknowledged her.

"Aye, my lord. 'Tis not been my place to say such things . . . but if I may, you're not a bad man. That's what I tell everyone. You're not a bad man and I hope someday you'll find a ladylove who can convince you of that." Suddenly, as if she remembered what such an outburst could cost her, she brought herself upright and said, "I beg your pardon, my lord."

"Don't be absurd." The marquis's face was so tight from unexpressed emotion it looked as if it were hewn from marble.

"If I may be excused?"

"Of course."

The silence in the room was leaden and Mrs. Myers's brow cleared considerably when she was finally able to close the door behind her.

But in the library, the marquis's brow furrowed more deeply. Something was on his mind. He ran his knuckles down his scar, but only twice. Then he stood and strode out the door himself.

He went up the staircase, taking the steps two at a time. He passed the second floor where the chambermaids were already setting his apartments to rights for the evening. He passed the third floor where most of the house servants had their rooms. Yet he didn't stop until he was in the enormous fourth-floor attic. He discreetly pulled the attic door closed behind him.

Tramore looked around, his only light from a candle

he had picked up from the servants' landing. It didn't take him long to find the path he sought. Through a maze created of tattered French chairs, rotting Elizabethan chests, and fractured gilt mirrors—an entire history of the old owner—he followed his own previous footprints in the dust to reach the article he wanted. It was a huge canvas; the top rail of its frame easily met with Tramore's chin. A great linen lay over it, and when he snatched it off, a cloud of dust sent the candlelight shimmering over the portrait of an exquisitely beautiful woman.

She was young, but not so young as to be unaware of her effect upon people, particularly those of the opposite sex. Her eyes were eloquently expressive. They were crystalline blue and heavily lashed, but it was not coyness they held, never that, for her expression was much too artless. Rather it seemed as if they held a promise, or a secret that even she had yet to discover fully, much less practice upon the world around her. But someday when she did understand this secret she would bring men to their knees.

But not the eleventh marquis.

He stood before her, his features taut in the sputtering candlelight. The inscrutable expression on his face was as close to hate as it was to love, as close to joy as it was to pain.

Slowly he reached out his forefinger and began tracing the girl's firm, sweetly curved jawline. His finger moved higher to her nose, which was slightly haughty yet also gamine. His thumb brushed her flaxen-haired temple and he traced one silvery blond curl to the level of her lips, where his forefinger once more took up its quest. His last touch was upon the rose-petal curve of her lower lip, and as if this were almost too much for him, he closed his eyes.

"Lissa," he uttered in a tight voice. His eyes flew open but he was held captive, marveling at the girl's femininity. For she was as vulnerable in it as she was made powerful by it.

He bent down and wiped the dust off the brass plaque

on the frame's bottom rail. The fair-haired girl's name was engraved upon it in heavy ornate script. It said: *Miss Elizabeth Victorine Alcester of Nodding Knoll 1850.*

He straightened and gave the portrait one last glittering stare. Then, as if he were fully aware of his own madness, Tramore tipped back his dark head and laughed. He ended this strange self-indulgence by violently whipping the linen covering back over the portrait. He left the attic without a backward glance.

Some time later that evening the gold-painted calèche from Fanny Kimbel's pulled up in front of the marquis's door. A fine mist had begun to fall just after eight o'clock, but as Fanny always saw to it, her girls were well shielded from the weather. When this particular beauty emerged from the leather-upholstered, satin-hung interior, all she had to do was pull her fox mantle a little bit closer to keep warm. The trip to the door was only a few steps, and soon she was inside the well-lit hall, being attended to by the marquis's majordomo.

Upstairs the marquis was waiting in his apartments. Attired for the evening in a black cutaway and trousers, Tramore looked the quintessential peer, rich and disciplined. A deep-blue silk cravat tied around his wing collar broke some of the severity of his dress, as did a matching blue foulard waistcoat that showed along the edges of his coat.

He waited in the anteroom, nursing a small brandy and lounging in an old-fashioned wing chair. When he heard the footfall of visitors, his head turned to the door.

Mrs. Kimbel's most expensive girl entered Tramore's apartments with a sweep of crinoline and perfume. Roseanne was a gorgeous creature, from her perfectly set glossy brown ringlets to her costly white satin slippers. Her powder-blue watered silk gown made her a vision of elegance. Its bodice was alluring yet tasteful, the waist tiny yet not artificial.

"My name is Roseanne, my lord. Mrs. Kimbel said

you had need of companionship." Roseanne tilted her head to the marquis. Tramore's mouth lifted in an arrogant half-grin and he stood to greet her. With one look from him, Biddles, the majordomo, immediately closed the door and left them in private.

"I hope the weather didn't make your journey too tedious." Tramore put down his drink.

"Nothing could be tedious this evening, my lord." Roseanne's gray eyes narrowed. She was obviously pleased with Tramore's dark good looks, and even more so with his lean, broad-shouldered figure.

The marquis also stared assessingly at her. But his eyes were more dispassionate; the gleam of lust lent them their only sparkle. "Fanny has excellent taste," he finally commented.

"Mrs. Kimbel was determined to send a girl who would please you." Roseanne walked up to him and put a finger to his finely hewn lips. "And I shall."

Tramore looked away, desire and, yet, disinterest etched on his Adonis-like face.

Unhappy with his sudden aloofness, Roseanne then kissed him. She stood on her tiptoes, placed her soft hands on either side of his rigid face, and pulled him down to her lips. Though Tramore was just barely cooperating, it was still a most intimate kiss. Afterward, at least Roseanne looked quite hungry for more. The marquis only stared at her, his eyes heavy-lidded yet watchful.

She whispered, "There's no need for you to be so distant, my lord. Not on a rainy night such as this. I promise you, it will be far better to let me keep you warm than to go to your cold bed alone."

He looked down. Roseanne was already unbuttoning his waistcoat. Her hands then worked beneath his cravat to unfasten his shirt. A warm palm slid beneath the linen and massaged his hard, hair-covered chest.

"You're a greedy little one, aren't you?" he stated

flatly. Tramore placed his hand over hers and made her stop. He did not, however, remove it.

"As you should be, love." She licked her soft, full lips. "Fanny said she hasn't sent over a girl in months, my lord. Months . . ." She whispered hotly, "Has it truly been that long? My God, what a raging bull you will be . . ."

She watched him. Tramore just looked on, as if he were actually trying to divorce himself from her charms. The heat in his eyes was the only thing that told her he was not altogether successful.

She began whispering again.

"Do you know that I begged Fanny to be the one to come tonight? Rachel who was here three months ago has never forgotten her night with you, my lord. She still murmurs that it was exquisite." She repeated breathlessly, "Exquisite."

Tramore's gaze left hers and wandered down to her bosom where several mahogany curls rested in teasing disarray. He picked up one curl and rubbed it between his strong fingers.

Watching, Roseanne smiled slyly. Her cold lover was beginning to thaw.

"My lord, I dressed my hair just for you. Does it please you?"

Tramore smiled cynically.

"It's scented, my lord. I rinse my hair in rosewater. Here, put it to your nose." She guided the hand that held the curl to his nose. After a moment she sighed. "Does that not please you?"

"It does." He dropped the curl.

"So you like my hair?" Roseanne would have continued, but she found the marquis beginning to unhook the back of her dress. When she looked up again, he caught her mouth in a fierce, impatient kiss. Though her attire was quite complicated, it did come off, piece by tortuous piece. And she gasped with pleasure every time Tramore's hands came closer and closer to her skin.

Soon they were both naked on the marquis's splendid full-tester bed. A crackling fire in the hearth kept them warm, but still Roseanne shivered, for she felt a delicious chill run down her spine as her hands roamed the marquis's hard, muscular body. In a moment of playfulness, she pinched one of Tramore's flat nipples. She wanted to see him smile, and when one corner of his mouth turned up in a grin, she was so ecstatic that her hand involuntarily went to touch his cheek, the one that was scarred.

He caught her hand in midair. His grip was iron-hard.

"What is it, my lord?" she whispered fearfully, seeing the light die out of his black eyes.

"Don't."

"If I cannot touch you there, then where?"

"Here," he groaned, guiding her hand downward.

"I see," she said softly, wrapping her hand around him. She presented him with a coy, mysterious smile for she knew flirtation was her art, but she was bewildered by his reaction. Even though they were entwined in a most intimate embrace, the marquis now seemed impossibly distant and utterly unreachable. With only one intent apparent on his features, he kissed her. Though his tongue stole the breath from her soul, Roseanne suddenly had the awful feeling that the notorious Lord Powerscourt was wretchedly disappointed that it was she beneath his hands and not some other woman.

PART ONE

We should doubt whether the woman who is indifferent to her own appearance be a woman at all. At all events, she must either be a hardened character, or an immense heiress, or a first-rate beauty—or think herself one.

HONORÉ DE BALZAC
The Quarterly Review, March
1847

CHAPTER ONE

✤

If she had to wear the puce-colored spencer one more time, she would weep. Lissa Alcester turned her azure eyes toward the odious jacket-bodice that was now laid out on her bed. She reached for it, but then pulled her hand back as if she actually dreaded putting the garment on.

Once it had been extraordinarily fine. Fashioned out of a costly French bombazine, the jacket's workmanship had been exquisite. But it had been given to her in the days when words like "costly" and "exquisite" had no real meaning to her. When luxury had so dominated her life, she had hardly noticed it, never imagining she would one day be without it.

Now Lissa could hardly remember when the spencer had been made. But she suspected it had been a long time ago, for she wryly noted the many let-out seams where the bustline had had to be increased. She noted also the frayed collar and the black machine-made lace that had been tacked to it to hide its wear. To further the insult, the spencer's sleeves were too short and the waist, while still fitting well, rode up in the back, and she was constantly forced to reach around and check that her cotton chemise was not peeking out.

Lissa turned away in despair. Her thoughts brightened a bit, however, when she thought of the reason why she and Evvie were going out that morning. Great-aunt Sophie's post had most likely arrived at Bishop's Mercantile. And perhaps this month, like so many months before when they'd been in need of something, they would receive just a bit extra. Enough for a new spencer, she mused.

"Lissa! Come see! Have I got it on right?" She heard her sister's voice call up from the parlor. Without further deliberation, Lissa pulled the worn spencer over her chemise and buttoned its horn buttons down to the tip of its pointed front. Then she made her way down the narrow stairway of the cottage.

Lissa's younger sister, Evelyn Grace, was sitting on a well-worn blue sofa before the stone hearth. When Lissa entered the room, she smiled softly at her. Evvie looked up, but her gaze never quite found her. It was obvious she was blind, but Evvie's eyelids didn't droop, nor did her head tilt back at every sound like those born with no sight. Her tragedy had struck after her girlhood and that was why her eyes were now opened wide, sparkling with anticipation, searching for something she would never see.

"Oh, Evvie, it looks marvelous!" Lissa sat down next to her on the sofa and studied her sister's handiwork. Evvie had placed a small violet-covered bonnet most artfully atop her brunette head. Her dark, lustrous hair had already been coiled and pinned, then neatly tucked into a matching black snood.

"They're wearing them a little bit back this year, I believe." Lissa studied her a moment longer, then pushed the bonnet back a half inch toward her nape. With that, the small curled brim smartly framed Evvie's pretty oval face.

"Oh, Lissa, we shouldn't have bought it . . . but do I look—?"

"Gorgeous! You look gorgeous! And it was worth every tuppence." Lissa squeezed Evvie's fingers. She did look gorgeous. Her only wish was that her sister could be able to see for herself in the mirror.

"It was quite dear in price," Evvie mentioned.

"Nonsense," Lissa told her. "Besides, I have a feeling Great-aunt Sophie is going to be especially generous this month. We'll do just fine."

"Oh, I hope so. You need some things too, Lissa." Evvie frowned while she put on her gloves. "Are you wearing . . . the spencer?" she asked, as if that were the most horrifying thought in the world.

Lissa laughed. "Yes, but I'm sure I'll be getting a new one soon." Not wanting to make Evvie feel any more guilty about the new bonnet, she hastily changed the subject. "Where do you suppose she is right now?"

"Who?"

"Great-aunt Sophie." Lissa pulled on her own black leather gloves. Her expression turned dreamy. "Will the solicitor say she's traveling down the Nile? Or sipping *café au lait* in a Parisian café? Oh, what adventures she must have! I wish we'd met her or at least heard about her before Mother and Father . . ." She paused. How she hated to mention *that*. "Passed on," she finished.

"You think about Aunt Sophie a lot, don't you?"

Lissa met Evvie's sightless eyes. "Not that much," she managed.

"Why don't we write her solicitor again and ask him if she might be free to visit us this winter?"

Lissa shook her head and handed Evvie her shawl. "We've done that a hundred times, and you know it. Sophie has never answered any of our letters. I suppose she must feel the time she has left is precious, and that's why she's been off all these years seeing the world."

"But wouldn't it be grand if she'd visit us. Just once!" Evvie exclaimed, flipping the points of her shawl across her arms. "She must have some fondness for us. After all, she has sent the pension."

"Yes, she has sent the pension. But I don't imagine she'll ever make a trip to boring little Nodding Knoll. If she were to come, I'd ask instead to meet her in London." Lissa's cheeks suddenly flamed with excitement. "Wouldn't it be wonderful if she took us traveling with her?"

"Traveling? Where would we go?"

"We could go pig-sticking in India or ride a gondola in Venice or—"

"Or be anywhere instead of living spinsterish lives in Nodding Knoll," Evvie finished sheepishly. "I wish Sophie would come and at least take you away, Lissa. You deserve it, you know, what with all the sacrifices you've made for George and me."

Sobering, Lissa picked up her reticule. "I'm not a spinster, Evvie. I'm only twenty-one."

"And I'm only nineteen and yet, I daresay, I live a spinsterish life. It must be worse for you."

"No, it's not worse for me. I like our life here. In some ways it's much better than when we lived at Alcester House."

"I suppose. But things are so difficult for you sometimes. And I wish so much that I could do something, but there's nothing—"

"You do everything. You keep George and me going." With that truth unleashed, Lissa led her sister out the door. She was not going to let Evvie bemoan the fact that they both were still unmarried. Besides, she felt guilty enough for all that had happened in the past, and she didn't want Evvie to feel guilty too. Her blindness wasn't the cause of their spinsterhood anyway. Everyone knew it was The Scandal.

Putting her arm through her sister's, Lissa resolutely lifted her head to the sunny day. Already she felt much more cheerful. Now it was up to her to make Evvie more cheerful also.

"Pig-sticking indeed!" she finally said. "What nonsense! I'd probably spend the whole rout persuading the hunters to leave the poor things alone. Great-aunt Sophie would be disgraced." Lissa laughed warmly. She recounted the coins in her reticule, then looked at their list for the market.

"But it should have been your right to have the world in your palm. And instead you've been left without." Evvie again grew serious.

Lissa was not about to let this conversation go further. She said simply, "It should have been both our rights, I suppose, but then, such is fate. Now are we going to stand here until the arcade has sold out of lamb for

George's dinner? He's only a little boy, you know. I'd hate to see him miss a meal because his sisters became prostrate with grief and couldn't move from their threshold."

"Oh, you ninny! Let's be off then. I shall never be so serious again." Evvie shook her head, then walked briskly at her sister's side in the cool October morn.

The village of Nodding Knoll was not far away. Their cottage—astutely named Violet Croft for in May their lawn was like a carpet of purple—sat on the edge of the old Alcester estate, and it had been built on the side closest to Nodding Knoll. The old estate house sat almost a half mile behind the cottage in a grove of gnarled oaks. Unkempt and abandoned, it was now owned by Brandts, Limited, in London, which for years had been unsuccessful in selling it.

Lissa disliked walking by the gates of Alcester House. She did so only when she was feeling particularly melancholy. Then she would stand at the rusting ornate gates and survey the weeds and crumbling marble that had once been her home. Alcester House sat like a withering old woman ready for the graveyard, and usually the sight of it only depressed her further.

But sometimes, usually late in the summer, she would take heart. Among the weeds and mustard, she would find a single perfect rose—a staunch reminder of the grand garden that had once grown there—a reminder of everything that had once been. It was a sign of endurance—as she and Evvie and George had endured. And when she would see that tiny blush-colored bloom, her whole outlook would change and she would find the courage to continue.

Now as Lissa walked with her sister on the wide cobbled path that served as the village's only road, her mind was on something else entirely. She was chagrined to note how busy the road was this morning. Wagons rolled by leaving behind the scent of linseed oil, which was used in painting, and freshly cut lumber. Of course, she knew where the wagons were headed. Several dark-green hansom cabs, obviously hired from London, went by also, and she speculated that they were probably filled with skilled workers brought up from the city. They were headed for the castle that loomed behind them, where the sandstone turrets towered above the brilliant autumn elms.

She'd known about the new marquis's coming for several days now, but for some reason she hadn't been able to summon the nonchalance she needed in order to tell Evvie about it. But now as one vehicle after another filed past them on the narrow road, her sister brought up the subject.

"What is the bustle about, Lissa? I've never heard so many carriages and wagons on this road." Evvie slipped on a cobble and clung to Lissa's arm for support.

Lissa clutched her sister, perhaps a bit too tightly. She wished she didn't have to tell Evvie now, for she would want a full description of all the activity. Evvie would also ask too many probing questions, and those she couldn't bear to answer. But there was no avoiding it now.

"The marquis is returning." There. She'd said it.

Evvie was speechless. When she did find her tongue, she gasped out, "You mean Lord Powerscourt? The new marquis?"

"Yes." The word caught in her throat. Unable to stand another second of the conversation, Lissa continued along the road so briskly that Evvie was practically running by her side.

"Oh, Lissa . . ." Evvie finally moaned. "When?"

"In two weeks, I hear." That thought alone terrified her. She silently begged Evvie to cease her questioning. Evvie did.

"Shall we get to market before the butcher sells all of his mutton?" Lissa refused to acknowledge her sister's shocked expression. When Evvie nodded, they continued on their way without another word.

Nodding Knoll's arcaded market was not too crowded, Lissa noted thankfully, for the housewives had already been there at dawn to haggle down the prices with the sleepy shopkeepers. They strolled along the stalls, stopping to admire some pink satin ribbons and a pair of fine calfskin gloves. As usual, gypsies possessed several stalls at the end of the arcade where they sold charms and dried lavender. Their dark looks and wild ways intimidated many of Nodding Knoll's citizens, but Lissa had always felt drawn to them. Today was no exception. Now as she discreetly met their gazes, a little thrill went down her spine. And though she was loathe to admit it, she supposed she was remembering another such gaze, one that she knew was best forgotten.

After leaving the gypsies, they made all their domestic purchases and stopped last at a fruit stand. Lissa couldn't help but be attracted to the rare oranges the seller had stacked in a pyramid near his money box. She took the top orange down and held it to Evvie's nose. Both girls reveled in the precious, exotic scent.

"Two for a quid, ladies." The fruitseller smiled jovially as he courted the two pretty Alcester girls.

"Harry McBain, now you know we can't afford to pay almost half a guinea for one orange," Evvie exclaimed.

"The price is right steep." Harry looked over his shoulder. His elderly mother was sitting on a stool knitting. When the two ladies had walked up, Mrs. McBain had stared right at them, frowning.

Harry turned back to Evvie. "Me mum thinks to get it from the gentry. They'll pay a quid—and more—for oranges."

"But not us, I'm afraid." Lissa reluctantly pried her gaze from the pyramid of oranges. With trepidation, she watched Harry's mother rise from her seat.

"Anything else for you, ladies?" Harry had seen his mother coming. When Lissa put in her order for a dozen baking apples, Harry's mother grudgingly resumed her seat.

"Here you go, Miss Alcester." As he brought them

their apples, he leaned over the wooden counter to drop
them in Lissa's basket. But as he did so, he left one apple
out. With sleight of hand, he pulled an orange from the
front of the pyramid and immediately replaced the hole
with the apple. The costly orange then dropped into their
basket.

Lissa started to thank the kindly man, but she immediately silenced herself, for his elderly mother was already
stomping to the front. She was sure Mrs. McBain hadn't
seen the orange go into her basket. However, Harry's
mother had long ago made it clear she didn't want her son
to fraternize any longer than necessary with the Alcester
girls. And she supposed that was exactly what Mrs. Mc-
Bain was thinking now.

Her suspicions proved all too correct. As they left,
Lissa overheard Mrs. McBain whisper to her irritated son,
"They haven't a quid more than we do, and besides, you
know what *her* mother did!"

The "her" in question had to be herself, Lissa knew,
for much to the townspeople's chagrin, she had grown to
look shockingly like her late mother. She was grateful that
Evvie had somehow been kept out of the gossip, probably
because of her affliction, and also because her quiet, dis-
arming beauty put everyone in a respectful mood. But she
herself had had no such luck.

Though Lissa always kept to herself, her looks alone
seemed to bring out the worst kind of suspicions in people. It pained her every time she was likened to Rebecca
Alcester. While she had loved her mother and hated to see
her memory so despised, Lissa knew only too well that she
had never really known Rebecca. Her mother's life had
been parties and London and ballgowns, not her children.
Despite this, Lissa had adored her; adored her as she
would an angel who, from time to time, would descend
upon her daughter's dull little life and make it sparkle if
only for a day. Rebecca Alcester had been too glorious to
touch, too ethereal to hold. Her father, William Alcester,

had ultimately been the one to pay the price for loving such a creature.

Now no remaining Alcester was ever going to be allowed to forget their mother's chronic infidelities, particularly Lissa, who had turned out even more fatally beautiful than her mother. That was why Lissa did without, saved every tuppence she could, so that one day they would be able to get away from picturesque little Nodding Knoll. Every day the town choked her just a little bit more, and she ached for the day they could afford to move.

Wishing away Mrs. McBain's words, Lissa pictured again the imaginary little town where the Alcesters would make a new start. She then looked at Evvie, praying all the while that her sister hadn't heard the old woman's parting words. But there was no such hope. Evvie's face had turned pinched as it often did when someone said something cruel and there was nothing she could do about it.

But Lissa's spirits sagged only for a moment. She looked behind her. As Harry kept an ear on his mother's admonitions, he turned to her and gave her a saucy wink. Harry McBain had a weakness for the ladies, but he still made her feel much better and she renewed her pace with much more vigor.

"Come, Evvie, Bishop's Mercantile next. Let's see what Great-aunt Sophie has for us this month. Then we'll come back and buy all of those wretched oranges!"

Evvie gratefully kept up with her sister's steps.

Lissa loved Bishop's Mercantile. The tiny little store sold everything from rye flour and Chinese tea to cashmere shawls and pruning shears. This was where she had bought Evvie's bonnet—shamefully on credit, but Mr. Bishop would not take no for an answer—and where they came to pick up their mail in the tiny village of Nodding Knoll. Lissa also loved the fact that the little store boasted no less than nine resident felines. The Bishops were notorious for putting up strays.

Mr. Bishop was a neatly groomed, short man, and his

wife—whom Lissa suspected as the cat lover—was as kind-hearted as she was plump. The Bishops made an odd couple, for Mrs. Bishop outweighed her husband by at least six stone. But anyone who ever met Mathilde Bishop was immediately taken in by her warmth, and Mr. Bishop, Lissa had surmised, had long ago fallen under his wife's spell. He adored her.

"Good morning, ladies." Mrs. Bishop, her gold-gray hair neatly arranged in sausage curls, sailed toward them. She immediately grasped Evvie's hand and patted it.

"Mrs. Bishop," Evvie acknowledged, smiling brilliantly.

"We're going to browse, I think. But we've come for Sophie's post though. Is it in?" Lissa inquired.

"Yes, it is, my dear. I shall get Mr. Bishop to fetch it for you this minute." The woman released Evvie's hand. She then added enticingly, "We have a few new toilet waters, girls. Why don't you dears look there first?"

Lissa needed no prodding. She was already leading Evvie to the dark oak counter where the perfumes were displayed. Both girls loved the Mercantile even if, now, most of their purchases were made with their imaginations rather than their purses.

Lissa gently moved a fat gray tom from his sleeping quarters on the counter and handed an open bottle to Evvie. "Smell this. It's 'Passel's Oil of Cloves.' What do you think?"

Evvie took one whiff and wrinkled her nose. Even the tom made a face and backed away.

"Too strong?" Lissa replaced the bottle onto a blue willow platter crammed with vials. "How is this? This is 'Linsey's Violet Water.'"

"Too sweet!" Evvie turned that one down too.

"This is it. 'Gray's One Hundred Roses.'"

"Yes, this *is* the one. Much better." Her sister brought the bottle to her nose a second time, but she was stopped when Lissa put a warning hand on her arm.

"Oh, Evvie, don't start but there's a man watching you," she whispered.

"A man?" Evvie blushed quite prettily. "There are other customers in here?"

"He just walked in. He's browsing by the gent's coat catalogs, but I daresay, he doesn't buy his frock coats from them. He's much too well dressed." Lissa tightened her grip on her sister's arm. Her glance darted across the store, then she whispered, "Oh, Evvie, don't move. He's staring quite boldly now. *Quite* boldly."

Evvie colored profusely. "Oh, Lissa, he must be staring at you, not me! I'm the mousy one . . ."

"Pooh! You're a beauty. And he is staring at you. Let me look again." Casually she took a perfume bottle and lifted it to her nose. Her sparkling blue eyes slid to one side and she took another covert glance at the mysterious gentleman who seemed so interested in them.

"What does he look like?" Evvie whispered.

For Evvie's sake, Lissa made her description as detailed as she could. "He's rather handsome. Quite handsome actually. He's tall and wears spectacles, but those make him look very intelligent and dignified. He possesses a rather classic Englishman's face. He has blond hair. Let me see . . ." She stole another glance. "And he hardly looks forty but I would guess that to be his age for he does possess some lines around his eyes and mouth."

"I wonder who he is. You've never seen him before?"

"Not that I can remember. However, something does seem familiar about him. Perhaps Mother and Father knew him. I don't know." She took another peek at the gentleman but this time he was conversing with Mr. Bishop.

". . . so sorry. I regret they've not come in yet. But I promise to have them before the marquis arrives at Powerscourt. You have my word, Mr. Jones." Mr. Bishop's voice boomed clear across the shop.

"Did you hear, Lissa?" Evvie grasped her arm and whispered. "Jones. He must be the gentleman who is Powerscourt's estate manager. He's here seeing to the castle. And Mother and Father surely must have known him for they knew the old marquis quite well. That's why he seems familiar. Lissa?"

But Lissa didn't hear her. The very name Powerscourt stabbed at her heart. It brought up all kinds of emotions that she preferred stayed buried.

"Lissa?"

"Yes?" She turned her attention to her sister.

"Are you thinking of . . . Ivan?" Evvie gently prodded.

"No."

"I see." Somehow Evvie found her sister's cheek and patted it comfortingly.

Feeling almost ill, Lissa put down the perfume bottle and said, "Let's get Great-aunt Sophie's post and go home. George will be home from school before we've made him supper."

"Yes, that's a grand idea." Evvie followed her.

The man named Jones remained in the store, ostensibly looking at cutlery displayed in an old mahogany case. Mr. Bishop was free at this point, however, and when he met Lissa's eye, he immediately came up to her with their post.

"Came in good time, ladies. I suppose Old Sophie must be done with her travels for the year." Mr. Bishop's baby blue eyes twinkled. "What is she, ninety? Where does she get all that spunk?"

"She's an Alcester, Mr. Bishop. You should know that!" Evvie laughed nervously and squeezed her sister's hand. Gratefully Lissa squeezed back.

But behind them, the man named Jones was hardly finding the situation amusing. In fact, if anyone had bothered to scrutinize him, they would have seen his countenance turn grim. His gaze was pinned to the letter Mr. Bishop held so confidently, and he seemed to be hanging on to every word of their conversation.

"So what's the old girl up to now, Miss Alcester?" Mr. Bishop handed Lissa the letter. "The tales you girls tell of her are the only excitement we get here in Nodding Knoll."

Eager for some good news, Lissa smiled at him, then tore at the wax seal.

As if unable to watch, Jones abruptly turned his back to the group. He feigned an interest in a steel fish-boner, but all the while his eyes were closed as if he were in pain.

Lissa's expression soon matched his. She read the letter and, with it, her entire world seemed to fall out from under her.

"Miss Alcester, whatever is the matter?" Mr. Bishop frowned as she forced herself to read the letter for the second time.

"Lissa? Is something wrong?" Evvie reached for her.

"There's been a tragedy. Great-aunt Sophie is dead," she uttered bravely. Though her voice shook with every syllable, she continued. "Mr. Fennimore, her London solicitor, says she died in her sleep in Vienna. He has enclosed one month's pension for us, but after that, there is to be no more."

"Oh, Lissa, no," Evvie whispered. Behind them, unnoticed, Jones was shaking his head.

"Oh, my dears, not another tragedy! How unkindly life has treated you!" Mrs. Bishop cried out from behind a counter, obviously having overheard the conversation too.

"We didn't know her well, Mrs. Bishop," Lissa confessed. "In fact, we didn't know her at all. We didn't even know we had a Great-aunt Sophie until three years ago . . . but we owe her a great deal for our upkeep these past years."

"Whatever will you do now?" Mrs. Bishop's brown eyes filled with tears.

"I don't know," she answered numbly.

"Let's go home." Evvie grasped her arm. "We'll get along. We've always found a way before."

"Yes, we'll manage. Thank you, Mr. Bishop, Mrs. Bishop."

Lissa grasped the letter in her gloved hand and they moved to the door. It was opened immediately by the man named Jones, but Lissa hardly noticed the concern on his face. Her mind was elsewhere, already looking ahead to a grim future.

CHAPTER TWO

❈

"I must see him, at once." Holland's voice was firm as he pushed his way past Biddles. Agitated, he barely paused in the hall of Tramore's London town house to demand, "Where is he?"

"His lordship is in the breakfast room finishing his coffee," the majordomo said icily. "If you would be so kind—Mr. Jones!" he called as Holland started for the breakfast room.

Holland didn't hesitate. He threw open the mahogany double doors just as a footman was serving the marquis another helping of black pudding. Shocked by the intrusion, the footman looked up.

Tramore did not.

Holland noted that he merely took another sip of coffee from an exquisite Wedgwood creamware cup. He then placed the cup back on its saucer and continued with his breakfast.

"I've come about the Alcesters," Holland stated coldly.

"I don't remember your being announced, Jones."

Tramore let the words hang in the air before he finally looked up. With a nod he instructed the footman to retreat to the kitchens.

"Damn being announced. I was there, I tell you. I

was there when they got that letter and a damned bloody sight it was too!" Holland's face reddened with anger. "Why must you cut them off? Couldn't you have at least given Miss Alcester more time to adjust?" He took a bold step further. "Or did you want it to be like this? Do you want them to suffer all because of what happened in the past?"

"And what happened in the past? You tell me, if you're such an expert on the Alcesters." Powerscourt sent him a piercing stare.

"I don't know everything that happened between you and Elizabeth. But I do know how you were treated in that village. And I suspect you have some twisted notion that if you wreak your vengeance on Elizabeth Alcester— set her up as example—you'll have somehow gotten even with the whole of Nodding Knoll."

The marquis was quiet for a moment, as if he were pondering his accusation. He then blithely announced, "You're wrong, Jones. Go back to your tasks concerning Powerscourt. You've only two more weeks." With that, he seemed to have finished his breakfast and the conversation. He stood and began to walk past Holland.

Holland wasn't through, however. "I resign."

"What?" Tramore shot back.

"I said I resign. I shall no longer work for the Powerscourts. You shall have to find another estate manager." He turned to go.

"And what is it that has you so upset, Jones? You quit a position that has been in your family for centuries all because I've cut off a woman's support that was not my responsibility to provide in the first place? I don't understand your motives," Powerscourt finished coolly.

"You're the enigma, not I!" Holland shouted, his voice filled with frustration. "You do these inexplicable things, which will have tragic consequences. I will not continue on!"

"Ah, but you will continue on!" Tramore suddenly

commanded. His angry voice boomed across the room. "If only for the reasons that throughout your lifetime the Powerscourts have seen to it that you've been well fed and finely clothed; they've paid for you to attend Cambridge and they gave your parents a respectable burial. So you will remain my estate manager, Jones. You will stay because you owe it to me!"

Holland listened to this outburst, his face becoming as white and rigid as a piece of Roman sculpture. He wanted to throw the words back in Tramore's face, but all at once guilt wouldn't let him. He tried to stop himself, but the memory of his languid days at Cambridge came to mind, as did the memory of Tramore's working in a stable like the meanest of paupers. Worse was the remembrance of his comfortable and pleasant childhood. As the son of the mighty estate manager of Powerscourt, he had wanted for nothing, while Tramore, the actual heir of the estate, had buried his mother along the roadside and scrounged for his very existence in the street.

Holland met Powerscourt's dark stare, but not another word passed between them. After a moment's pause, Tramore promptly quitted the breakfast room. In angry silence, Holland watched him go.

His conscience told him there was no way to avoid returning to Powerscourt and the disagreeable tasks that awaited him there. But as he made to leave the opulent London manse, Holland consoled himself with one thought. Perhaps by being at Powerscourt, he could change the marquis's mind and avert disaster for the Alcesters.

Perhaps.

"We must sell Violet Croft, Lissa. That's the only way," Evvie stated as she bent over her knitting.

Lissa watched her purl and sighed. They'd been discussing their future for almost two weeks now and not once had they agreed on what would be best.

It was a cold afternoon and the two women were sitting in the parlor, warming themselves before the peat fire. Lissa was too agitated to knit, so she sat on the sofa, tapping her fingers on the sofa's worn, doily-clad arm. George was due home from the Nodding Knoll school any moment, and they both looked to his arrival to cheer them up.

"We cannot sell the cottage. We could never afford another. Besides, it's all we have left of Mother and Father's estate." Lissa shook her blond head.

"But Violet Croft is what's been keeping us here all along, and it's been miserable. We've never belonged in Nodding Knoll, not since The Scandal." Evvie's needles stopped clicking. She grew quite sober. "I know how they talk, Lissa. I may be blind, but I'm not deaf."

"It's not been so bad," Lissa refuted, though only halfheartedly.

"Not been so bad! It's been torture and I know it!" Evvie looked toward her sister and implored her, "Don't you think I know old Widow Tannahill crosses the street every time she sees us? You've been telling me she's been nodding in greeting these days, but why don't I feel her footsteps pass? Why don't I hear her crinoline sway? Why do I feel you tense whenever she's about?"

A tiny furrow lined Lissa's brow. She'd always wanted to protect Evvie from the scorn of the little town, and she'd obviously done a poor job of it. "She's never really said anything since the funeral. I can live with her avoiding us. In fact, I think I prefer it."

"She said you'd turn out just like Mother."

She couldn't bear to hear Evvie's words. Her hands shook with anger at the old widow's cruelty. "But I haven't. Isn't that enough? Let's not talk about it."

"But she won't let it go, Lissa. The town won't let it go. So let *us* go."

Lissa shook her head. "We can't. We'd get a pittance for this cottage, and then live a mean existence indeed, for we could never afford to let another cottage for long." She released a long, drawn-out sigh. The weeks of worry since they'd received Great-aunt Sophie's post were beginning to show. Pale lavender smudges had appeared beneath her eyes, a sure sign that she hadn't been sleeping well. "I do have another idea, however," she mentioned hesitantly.

"And what is that?"

"Wilmott Billingsworth."

Evvie let out a terrible groan. "I shall not listen to you speak that vile man's name ever again! And to have you talk about sacrificing yourself to that—"

"He's not so terribly bad," Lissa interrupted. "And you know he's always had a fancy for me . . ."

"A fancy for you! He's a lecher, sister. Pure and simple. And his watch fob is made out of human hair."

"You make too much of that. I shouldn't have told you. Besides, it's all the rage now. Even Arabella Parks wears earbobs made from her own red hair."

"Delightful," her sister exclaimed sarcastically. "That makes it all so much better. Now I won't have to worry that you'll marry him and wake one day to find yourself bald, and his two daughters wearing necklaces made out of your blond tresses. Oh, Lissa, don't let's talk about it!"

"But we must talk about it! That might be the only way to save ourselves from utter ruin!"

Lissa stood and began pacing, her heavy gray wool skirt swooshing as she walked. The whole situation was impossible. It was hard enough to think of marrying a man such as Wilmott without being forced to fight her sister all the way to the altar. She must get her support! Without Evvie holding her up she would never get through it.

"And if Wilmott Billingsworth isn't bad enough just by himself," Evvie continued, "there are his two lovely daughters. You remember Honoria and Adele?"

"Yes, and they will make fine stepdaughters." Lissa bit her knuckle to keep from laughing.

"Fine stepdaughters! They're both one hundred and fifty years old!"

"Oh, they are not." Lissa finally giggled.

"They are, and I shudder to think how old that makes Wilmott. Lissa, you must stop thinking about marrying him. It's all wrong."

Lissa looked at her sister. Her smile disappeared. It certainly was all wrong. Wilmott was greedy, lecherous and altogether repulsive, and those were probably his better attributes. Besides, she had always dreamed that someday a strong, noble-hearted man would come for her; a man who she could give herself to with her whole heart; a man who needed her love as desperately as she needed his. Unwittingly she stared past Evvie and found the spires of Powerscourt through the mullioned window of the cottage. But what could dreams do for her now? The answer was all too brutally clear.

"I must do it, Evvie," she whispered, all the while pondering her responsibilities. Her brother had to be raised. And Evvie had to be taken care of. The thought of losing either of them made her quake with fear. George and Evvie meant everything to her. It was up to her to keep the Alcesters together. And if she had to sacrifice her own happiness to do so, then so be it.

She released a brittle laugh and said, "Besides, what else is left for us? I have no other suitors."

"You could write to Ivan."

Lissa whipped around. "Why would I do that?"

"My vision didn't go until I was sixteen, Lissa, remember?" Evvie said quietly.

"And what does that mean?"

"It means I recall quite vividly how taken Ivan was with you."

Lissa fought down the panic that always rose in her breast whenever Ivan Tramore's name was mentioned.

And she beat down another emotion as well, one she refused to acknowledge.

Evvie took note of her silence but continued. "I just think that if you're going to sacrifice yourself to a man, that Ivan would be the best—"

"And why would he want me? He cares nothing for us, and you know it. We haven't seen him in five years," Lissa stated, her voice painfully even. "He's been living quite a luxurious life in London and, I daresay, he never gives us a moment's thought. Nor should he," she conceded, "for we're peasants in his eyes now. Things have changed. And everything that once happened . . . was so long ago . . . and . . . everything's different now . . ." Her voice trailed off. She became silent as she looked out the window at the brown foliage that had once been pink petunias in the window box.

Ivan Tramore. She could hardly think the name, let alone say it. Damn him anyway! Why did he have to come back to Powerscourt just when they'd been cut off! Lissa closed her eyes. She could already picture his smug satisfaction at finding them destitute. If anything, he'd most likely be delighted to make their situation worse. And why was he coming back? Was it for her? Was it for revenge? She opened her eyes. Beneath her dark lashes, her blue eyes glittered with fear.

"I shouldn't have mentioned him," Evvie finally said.

"No, it's all right." She turned to her sister once more, her face a beautiful mask of control. "He's coming back. So we must deal with his presence eventually— though I doubt, because of our station, we will see much of the grand Marquis of Powerscourt." Lissa let out a well-rehearsed laugh. "So perhaps our poverty is a blessing in disguise."

"You would have made a splendid match—"

"Father was not about to see me married to my stable-boy, especially one," she said, lowering her voice, "who was born on the wrong side of the sheets." Her brow furrowed. "So now let's not speak of it further. It's in the past. And Wilmott Billingsworth is in the future."

"No, Lissa, no," Evvie groaned again. But this time their contentions went no further for George abruptly burst through the door, arriving home from school.

Their little brother was a handsome boy. Lissa knew he would devastate the ladies once he became a man. Just nine years old, he already had Alice Bishop, the Bishops' granddaughter, completely smitten with him. Alice was quite free with the horehound candy from her grandparents' store whenever George was about. And though George tried to be manly and aloof, he was inevitably taken in by a sweet, toothless smile and the offer of candy.

As if she were his mother, Lissa went to him and took his school bag. She ran her hand lovingly through his coal-black hair, so different from her own blond tresses and Evvie's brunette ones.

"So how was school today? Are you hungry?"

"It was fine," George answered glumly, then he brightened. "But I read about Africa. Did you know there are tribes there who can kill you with a poison dart? And they stretch their lips like this . . ." He walked to the tea service, pulled out his lower lip, and tried to place a tea saucer inside it.

"No, George. Not with Mother's Copeland Spode." Horrified, Lissa immediately took the precious saucer from his grasp. "Eat something," she ordered.

She gave him some tea she and Evvie had made earlier. There were some scones on a plate, and he eagerly reached for two.

"Any teasing today?" Evvie asked lightly.

George scowled. His heavily lashed, dark-brown eyes darted to Lissa.

"Well?" Lissa probed.

"No." He began swinging his legs.

"No one said anything. Not even Johnny Miller?"

"No." His legs swung harder.

"Well, that's a relief." Evvie began to knit once more. The clicking of her needles was soothing, but Lissa frowned, her gaze on George's swinging legs. She looked him in the eye, but when she did, he sheepishly looked away.

Brave child, she thought, then sighed and watched him devour a third scone.

The next morning Lissa was out in the side yard hanging laundry. She was hurrying for she needed to go to Bishop's to price fabric. Though they could hardly afford the expense—particularly now—she had convinced herself that she would need a new gown in order to call on Wilmott. Evvie was still in despair over her plan to marry the elderly man, but Lissa was determined to go forward.

It was a blustery fall day that held the threat of storms. However, once washed, the linens had to be hung, so Lissa quickly pinned the sheets, all the while glancing balefully at the sky, as if she were daring it to rain.

Without her crinoline, her long blond hair tucked in an old purple kerchief, and the sleeves of her faded pink calico pulled up to her elbows, she certainly felt as plain as an old washwoman. But the wind had chaffed her cheeks, making them a rosy pink, and her eyes sparkled vibrantly from their seductive azure depths. Many a gent had tipped his hat passing Violet Croft while she was in the yard. Unaware that they found her a fetching sight, Lissa merely nodded back demurely, uncomfortable with their attention.

She was almost done with her task when a commotion drove her to the front yard. Down the lane, the Johnsons were all stepping from their cottage, excitedly pointing in the direction of town. Several travelers on the road bade their horses pause as they, too, watched the bustle.

A coaching party, consisting of scarlet-liveried outriders, blue-and-silver bedecked postillions, satin-clad coach-men, eight Irish Thoroughbreds harnessed with silver fittings, and last, a gleaming black-lacquered coach bearing the silver-and-black Powerscourt crest on its door, made its way through town, ultimately heading for the castle up the knoll.

Peering toward the main thoroughfare of the village, Lissa gasped at the magnificent sight. Then she felt her heart lurch in her chest when she realized what it meant.

Ivan had returned.

How she had dreaded his arrival—dreaded it like a specter that had haunted her for five years. And now he was here. That thought left her almost in a swoon, but as she continued to watch the glorious entourage wind its way up to the castle, she couldn't help the small thrill of pride that ran down her spine. Her stableboy had come home triumphant. And somehow, by fate or simply by sheer dint of will, he had shown them all.

Suddenly she had the urge to laugh. Her terror now seemed absurd. The man who possessed this elaborate con-veyance was not likely to spend his time seeking the com-pany of two pauperish spinsters.

She thought of him sitting inside his coach as it rocked and swayed. Even now she found her imagination trying desperately to picture him. Was he still handsome? Did his eyes still twinkle when someone made him laugh? Did his face still bear—

"What is all the bustle about?" Evvie called to her from the front door. "I could hear the Johnsons ex-claiming in the parlor."

Lissa could hardly speak for the emotion caught in her throat. "Lord Powerscourt has arrived."

All at once she felt tears of panic and guilt spring to her eyes. Acting like a madwoman she rushed past her sister into the house. There she began to change her clothes for a trip to Bishop's. Suddenly her courtship with Wilmott could not wait.

It was several hours later when Lissa came trudging home from the Mercantile. Disheartened, she had looked at every bolt of silk Mrs. Bishop could dig out for her, but there was not a yard in one of them that she could afford. There was always linsey woolsey, or worse, hopsacking, but she needed something appropriate for tea or, perhaps, a quiet dinner at the Billingsworth estate. And even the least expensive machine-made horror was still beyond the price she could pay.

So with this dismal revelation, she walked through the village, her mind all the while scouring her wardrobe in hopes of finding a gown that could be modernized with some lace or cording. When she turned the corner to go home, she had just decided that her gray-blue serge could be refashioned. Her thoughts elsewhere, she absently looked down the path to her cottage. There, to her horror, she saw the coach.

She stumbled forward in disbelief. It had to be some terrible mistake! The coach in the distance could not be the same one she had seen hours earlier. But, running, she soon confirmed that it was indeed the same. There were the postillions sitting idly on the Thoroughbreds, their silver-corded coats glinting in the fall sunshine. Two coachmen were leaning on the back of the cab, polishing their silver buttons and laughing, no doubt over some bawdy joke.

Bewildered, Lissa came to a halt, then put her hands to her flaming cheeks. Panic again welled in her breast. This couldn't be happening! It couldn't, she told herself as she neared Violet Croft.

But it was happening; the coachmen told her so as they met her arrival with a long, perusing stare; the weather told her so as she felt several drops of rain bring her back to reality. Ivan Tramore was at her house. Her entire world spun before her.

Slowly she walked to the door of the cottage and grasped the heavy iron knob for support. Her hand went to her waist to make sure her spencer was properly pulled down. When she was sure her chemise was hidden, her hand then went to her throat. Dismally she felt the scratchy machine-made lace at her collar. How she'd wished she'd worn anything else this day! She closed her eyes and took a deep breath. There was nothing she could do about it. Resigning herself, she twisted the doorknob and entered her home with utmost trepidation.

Evvie was on her feet the second she walked to the parlor door. Unable to breathe, Lissa dared not look around. Instead her gaze fixed on their mother's pink and green tea service, which was laid out on a linen tea cloth Evvie had blessedly used to cover the scratches on their old rectory table. Feeling a bit more brave, she looked at Evvie, who was pale in spite of the glitter of hope in her eyes. Too terrified to move farther into the room, she simply looked at her sister and waited for her to speak.

"Lissa, dear," Evvie began nervously. "You'll never guess who's come to call."

But she knew, all right. Lissa suppressed the overwhelming desire to flee and just continued to stare at her sister. She was unable to let her eyes search the room for *him*.

"Come and have tea with us." Evvie held her hand out in the direction of the parlor entrance. "Ivan . . . uh, I mean, of course, *Lord* Ivan, has just been telling me of his trip from London."

When Evvie mentioned his name, the man Lissa had dreaded seeing for five long years finally rose from his seat. His chair had been facing away from the parlor entrance, so the first glance she had of him was just the top of his dark head.

When he finally faced her, Lissa turned fearful eyes upon him. As she dared to look at him fully, she almost gasped at how much he'd changed and yet how much he had not. He was taller than she remembered, his shoulders broader. Though she had never seen him so attired, his fine masculine form looked quite at ease in the expensive marine-blue topcoat. His hair was still as dark as a raven's wing, but now he wore it cropped in a fashionable style. His eyes were just as beautiful; gypsy eyes she had once called them, and though most believed Ivan Tramore's eyes to be black, Lissa knew all too well that they were blue, as dark and mysterious as the sky at midnight.

Her gaze swept his face, and she found it even more devastatingly handsome than the day he had left her. There was only one addition to it, however, and seeing it, her heart skipped a beat. She saw the scar on his left cheek, a white, angry scar. In morbid fascination, she stared at it, mesmerized.

Deep in her thoughts, she barely heard Evvie clear her throat. It took all her effort to tear her gaze from the scar, but she was finally able to. She then turned to Evvie and said as graciously as she could, "Isn't this an unexpected delight." Yet even to her ears, the words sounded forced.

Uncomfortable beneath Lord Ivan's dark perusal, Lissa nervously made her way to the sofa. When she took her sister's hand, Evvie released a little laugh, unable to bear much more of the tension. To Lissa's horror, her sister blurted out to their guest, "Lord Ivan, your silence dismays me. Could it be that my sister is not as beautiful as I remember her to be?"

Hardly believing that Evvie would ask such a thing, Lissa blushed furiously. With Tramore still scrutinizing her, she felt horribly self-conscious. Nervously she reached around and pulled on the waist of her spencer.

"She's more so."

With Powerscourt's unexpected words, she was brought upright. Unwillingly she met his stare, and as her azure eyes locked with his, she saw the shadowy glimmer he held in them just for her. Feeling as if a knife had passed through her heart, she suddenly knew, without any doubt at all, that he'd come back for revenge.

If she had been the type to faint, she would have fallen right then to the floor in a glorious heap of skirts and crinoline. But she was not the type to faint, so instead she took a deep breath, put on her iciest façade, and sat down to tea.

"Please sit, Lord Ivan. More tea?" she asked him coldly, taking over the role of hostess from Evvie.

Lord Powerscourt gave her a sardonic smile and sat also. He nodded to the tea, then his gaze took liberties with her figure that no other man had ever dared.

She knew that arrogant stare only too well, and she endured it as best she could. But when she couldn't stand it a second more, she blurted out, "So what has brought you calling on Evvie so soon after your arrival . . . ah . . . my lord?"

"I thought it my duty to offer your sister my condolences. I was quite sorry to hear about her 'difficulties' in the time I've been away."

Lord Ivan watched her pour out. She damned his look of satisfaction when he saw her hand shake.

"Shall we have more biscuits?" Evvie suddenly stood. She put her hand on the empty biscuit plate. Picking it up, she frowned worriedly in Ivan's direction, then made her way through the maze of furniture to the kitchen.

As Lissa watched her go, she regretted those long painstaking days when she had taught Evvie how to get about in the house. She had always been so proud that her sister was able to take care of herself at Violet Croft, even so far that she could make and serve tea to their few guests. But now she damned all the lectures to George about keeping the chairs out of Evvie's path, she damned all of Evvie's bruised shins, and mostly she damned herself for teaching her sister self-reliance to the point that Evvie was the one allowed to leave this terrible scene for more biscuits, and not herself.

Lissa worriedly put down the teapot. Alone, she faced her nemesis. There was no need for pretense now.

"Why have you come back, Ivan?" she demanded in a whisper.

With his frame more than filling the large easy chair, he leaned back and touched his fingertips together. He stared at her over his hands. "I've come for the country air . . . you see, Nodding Knoll left me with such pleasant memories."

Liar, she wanted to say, then her gaze skimmed over his scar and she thought better of it. "You could have come back sooner, I daresay," she accused.

"So you've missed me?" He leaned forward and grasped her hand, which was resting next to the teapot. Shocked by the warmth of his calloused palm, she immediately wanted to pull back. But he wouldn't let her. He held her hand tightly. Although he didn't hurt her, she could not pull free.

"I haven't missed you," she whispered, tugging futilely at her hand.

"But maybe you have. Shall we go to the stables and see?" The corner of his lips lifted in a smile.

"You cad," she hissed, this time violently shoving on his arm.

"Here we go! Freshly made this morning!" Evvie breezed into the parlor with a plate full of biscuits. Immediately Ivan released her. Not expecting it, Lissa was thrown against the tea table.

Quickly she scurried back on the sofa as far from Powerscourt as she could get. As Evvie brought her a cup and saucer, she regained some of her composure.

"Will you be staying at the castle long?" Lissa asked, once more striving for polite conversation.

"Long enough," Ivan stated. He smiled sardonically as he leaned to retrieve his teacup.

Now most definitely rattled, Lissa struggled for a reply. Trying desperately to think of one, she looked all around the room, everywhere but at Ivan; for every time she looked at him, all she could see was that vicious scar and the promise of revenge in his eyes.

Trying to look as cool as possible, she lifted her tea-cup to her lips, but, of course, she had forgotten to pour herself tea. Caught in the act, a small furrow appeared in her brow.

"Your sister makes a good cup of tea, don't you think, Miss Alcester?"

Her gaze met with his. Wicked amusement sparkled in his eyes, but she was not about to let him unravel her further.

"Yes, Evvie always does." In an attempt to ignore his stare, she almost took another sip from her cup. Appalled, she turned to Evvie, hoping that somehow, she would sense how things were going and start up some conversation. But to her dismay, her sister only sat silently beside her, half frowning, half smiling; panic and joy written all across her features.

Lissa swallowed hard. She turned once more to their overwhelming guest. "So, Lord Ivan, how do you find Nodding Knoll? Has it changed much in five years? Or have you been away four? It's so hard to keep track of time when you live in a little village as we do." She smiled, but it was a bit too bright.

"It's been five. And yes, it has changed." His glance flickered over the shabby interior of the cottage. She colored with embarrassment.

"But not so much that you don't recognize us, my lord?" Evvie finally chimed in, trying desperately to cheer things up.

"No, not that much." He looked at Lissa. She looked away.

"Well, the next time you come to tea . . . t-that is," Evvie stuttered, "if there is a next time . . . that is, of course you're certainly invited anytime, my lord, anytime . . . that is . . . well, when you do you must tell us all about your life in London, isn't that right, Lissa?"

"Yes, of course." She reassured Evvie with a touch on her arm. "But I'm sure Lord Ivan has better things to do with his time than dazzle us with his social triumphs, isn't that right, my lord?" She gave him a glittering stare.

He suppressed a smile. "On the contrary, I invite you both to Powerscourt anytime to hear about my triumphs."

Or *be* one of them, Lissa thought unkindly.

"But now, I'm afraid you must excuse me," he announced.

"Leaving so soon, Lord Ivan? I had hopes you'd stay for dinner." Evvie stood and held out her hand.

Lissa looked up at her sister as if she'd gone mad. She for one wasn't about to serve this man shepherd's pie at their tiny kitchen table.

"A gracious offer, made by a gracious lady." Lord Powerscourt stood, then reached for Evvie's hand and took it in a warm grasp. "However, I must refuse. I have another engagement."

"Miss Alcester," he said to Evvie in farewell. Lissa watched her sister return his smile. To her bemusement, Evvie actually looked sorry to see him go.

Powerscourt then turned to her. Filled with sudden trepidation, Lissa stood, still keeping hold of her empty teacup.

"Miss Alcester." He nodded to her coolly. But before she could respond in kind, his eyes suddenly filled with some unnamed emotion. He raised his hand and ran one strong finger down her left cheek, exactly mirroring the path of the scar on his own. Paralyzed by his touch, Lissa closed her eyes and wondered if she was capable of fainting after all. Her heart stopped in her chest and she gasped for breath. Her hand immediately went to her cheek and held the spot that still tingled from his touch. In her state, she was unaware as her teacup slid from her grasp and fell with a dull thud to the carpet.

At Evvie's gasp, she opened her eyes. But by this time, Ivan Tramore was gone.

CHAPTER THREE

❈

"Mr. Billingsworth! How . . . charmingly . . . forward you are!" Lissa exclaimed the next day as she sat in the Billingsworths' parlor. She smiled and tried to ignore the liver-spotted hand that rested on her knee. But she was successful for only about three seconds before she nervously rose from the tufted loveseat and stood by the mantel.

"Lizzy, old girl, there's no need for shyness now! I know you didn't come here to visit my daughters. It's clear you've reconsidered my suit. And by God, I won't make you sorry you did! So come now and sit beside me. I want to converse." Wilmott Billingsworth patted the ruby-velvet upholstery next to him.

At one time, most definitely in the century past, he had been a handsome man. He still sported a hopelessly old-fashioned "parricide" collar, and she couldn't help but remember the fable about a boy who had worn such a high, pointed collar, he'd accidentally slit his father's throat. But despite Wilmott's passé attire, one could still consider him handsome, in a grandfatherly way. The look he gave Lissa now, however, was far from grandfatherly.

He smiled coyly at her. Wilmott's teeth were a bit yellow from age, but at least, Lissa told herself, he had all of them. Just like an old wolf's, she couldn't stop herself from adding. Quickly chastising herself, she daintily smiled a refusal. Already she had a headache.

"Lizzy!"

Her azure gaze slid over to the loveseat where Wilmott sat. She despised that name: Lizzy. It made her sound like a barroom serving wench.

She closed her eyes and wondered how she was going to endure this courtship. Her honor wouldn't allow her to be anything less than a devoted wife to the man she married—no matter whether she loved him or not. Yet how was she going to give Wilmott her unwavering devotion when she could barely stand to be in the same room with him? Whatever made her think she could do this?

Ivan.

Unconsciously her hand swept her left cheek. Then as if she'd just realized what she had done, she angrily opened her eyes. She wasn't going to allow that gypsy to disparage her. She might not be rich, but she wasn't so poor that she had to stand by impotently taking all of his smug looks. And that . . . that . . . *pity* in his eyes! She silently moaned, remembering how Ivan had looked yesterday as his gaze had swept Violet Croft's interior. He certainly wouldn't pity her if she were mistress of Billingsworth Manor!

Her black thoughts turned to that very morning. She had readied herself with a vengeance to call upon the Billingsworths. Deaf to Evvie's pleas, she had put on her old dark blue tartan dress printed with pink rosebuds. She chose the gown not so much because it was her best, but because it was of a modern design that hooked down the front—and she was able to dress without her sister's unwilling assistance. Fastening the last hook at her throat, she had pulled on her white muslin undersleeves. When her *engangeants* were snugly tied around her elbow, she gathered her mother's old sovereign purse and walked downstairs, all without hearing one word of Evvie's pleading. She had been out the door before George had even left for school.

Her visit to the manor had been ostensibly to see Honoria and Adele, Wilmott's daughters. But it was obvious from the moment she was shown into the ladies' parlor that the two Billingsworth spinsters did not appreciate her coming to call. As Lissa already knew, Honoria and Adele were as tight with the family money as two wealthy penny pinchers could be. And from the time of their mother's death, the two spinsters had always made it clear that they had no desire to share the Billingsworth guineas with a usurper.

When Wilmott finally joined them, Lissa was already desperate to leave. Honoria had been kind enough to call for refreshments, yet Adele—like one vulture recognizing another—examined their guest as if measuring her for a coffin. Needless to say, Lissa barely touched her tea.

Honoria and Adele made their exit only after several meaningful looks from their father. With his daughters out of the room, Wilmott brazenly took a place right next to her on the tufted loveseat. She had tried to continue their conversation, but Wilmott was too busy sneaking an arm around her shoulders to respond. Now was the fourth time she'd felt compelled to stand at the mantel. Watching Wilmott rise to join her, she found she could take no more.

"Good heavens, look at the hour!" she exclaimed, nodding to the longcase clock out in the foyer. "I am sorry to be leaving so soon but I do have a previous engagement." She scurried past Wilmott and retrieved her gloves and purse from a giltwood console near the doors. "Do tell your delightful daughters that I shall call upon them again soon."

"Lizzy! I insist you let me take you home!" Wilmott took her arm and led her into the foyer. There he barked out orders to his butler to summon the Billingsworth carriage.

"You shouldn't trouble yourself, sir, I can find my way back to Violet Croft." Nervously she put on her gloves. If Wilmott had tried to maul her in the parlor, what would he attempt in the confines of his carriage cab?

"Far from being a trouble, it is a pleasure!" Wilmott bade her wait on a small silk-covered bench beneath the grand staircase. She fiddled with her gloves, a small frown marring her perfect brow. She had to think quickly of an excuse to walk home.

"While we're waiting, my dear"—Wilmott's voice intruded upon her thoughts—"I'd like to speak with you about something."

Startled, she looked up. Was he going to propose so soon? Good God, she would be debauched before the carriage could even get to her cottage door!

"Certainly, sir. What is it?" she whispered despairingly.

"The castle. There's to be a small soirée there week after next. Of course, Honoria and Adele will be along," he added fretfully as if this were actually not a point to be rejoiced upon, "and I would very much like you to accompany us. I'd like to show you off to old Powerscourt."

Powerscourt. She rubbed her temple with her gloved hand. Would that name not go away? Somehow she could already picture the amusement on Ivan's face when she arrived at the castle on Wilmott's arm.

"Oh, dear, I don't think—"

"Father!" A hushed voice from the staircase interrupted her. Looking up, Lissa saw Honoria glide down the staircase like a wraith, her long, skinny frame and tight, graying bun only accentuating her ghostly appearance. An embarrassed flush colored her face, and she seemed hesitant to speak in front of their guest, but the matter must have been of some import for she began anyway. "Father, before you go, the cook is out of mutton and we must go to market and buy some."

"Mutton be damned! Can't you see I'm busy!" Wilmott snapped.

"Yes, I quite see," Honoria said meaningfully, making Lissa color. "But, nonetheless, we must have some dinner."

"That cursed cook! That pilfering witch! I've given her the household allowance! How can she need more!" In his anger, Wilmott's face turned beet red.

"You don't give her enough, Father, that is why we run out before the month is over." Honoria was blushing furiously now and Lissa began to feel sorry for her. It seemed her father was even more of a skinflint than she was.

"I'll be right back, my dear," Wilmott said to Lissa, resuming his pandering tone. He patted her hand and walked to the library with Honoria. Lissa could hear his lecturing until they disappeared down the passage, but long afterward, phrases like "the sinfulness of flagrant spending" and "the purity of the thrifty home" still made their way to the foyer.

Thoroughly chagrined, Lissa sat in the huge marble foyer until the carriage arrived. When she heard the steely creaks of its wheels on the cobbles, she immediately stood and allowed the butler to help her to the conveyance.

It was clear she was to wait for Wilmott to accompany her, but she had made no such promise. When the butler stepped back into the manor, Lissa leaned out the window and asked the driver to take her to Violet Croft cottage. She gave the elderly gent such an imploring look that barely five seconds passed before the carriage took off.

That same morning, George Alcester stood by a pond and skipped acorns on its wavy surface. It was a splendid autumn day with a crisp breeze that rustled the brilliant oaks now at the peak of their glory. The little boy's hair was ruffled, but he gave his appearance not a whit of concern as he hurled the acorns into the pond. A dark look was upon his face, and it became blacker still when he heard far away the Nodding Knoll school bell faintly peal the noon hour.

From a distance, Ivan Tramore watched the little boy. George scowled, threw his last acorn, and settled himself upon a fallen poplar to brood. But then, as if from years of school-day discipline, the boy took out his dinner pail and began his midday meal. Seeing this, Ivan almost smiled.

Tramore had been surveying the estate, having taken

a glossy bay steed from his stables. He had just come into the pond clearing when he saw the lad. Concealed by a clump of yews, he now bent to his two mastiffs who sat obediently at his mount's flanks.

"Pups," he whispered to them, "seek!" He nodded in the direction of the young boy. Immediately upon their master's command, the two huge canines scrambled for the edge of the pond. They skirted the water and were upon their target almost before the lad had time to look up. Startled by the enormous dogs' approach, George leaned backward, his dinner pail clutched to his chest. However, the mastiffs politely seated themselves at his feet, wagging their whiplike tails, their eyes glued to George's delectable dinner pail.

After giving the dogs several distrustful looks, George relaxed a bit. Once convinced they meant him no harm, he dipped into his tin pail and took out a piece of sausage. The mastiffs' tails wagged furiously when he offered them each a morsel. As he went to give them another piece, the dogs tried licking his face. Soon he tumbled from the poplar and was on the forest floor squealing with laughter as the dogs playfully competed for a dry spot on his cheeks.

"Good pups. Now sit." From the forest, the mastiffs' owner appeared on his steed. Hearing his voice, the dogs immediately complied and again sat in unison at the stallion's flanks.

George looked up at the tall, unsmiling man and scrambled to his feet. With his mouth open, he stared at the wicked scar on the man's face. Caught in the act, he guiltily looked away, then darted uneasy glances at the intruder as he dismounted.

"What are you doing here, lad?" Ivan asked, his dark gaze resting on the boy's face.

George wiped his wet cheeks with the back of his hand. "I was having my dinner," he answered.

"I see."

"Is this your pond?"

"Yes, it is." Ivan crossed his arms in front of his chest disapprovingly. "I daresay, lad, you should be having your dinner in the schoolroom."

George looked away. "Are the dogs yours too?" he evaded.

"Everything is mine. All that you see for miles on end. Now I ask you again, shouldn't you be in school?"

George scowled. "I'm never going back there again!"

Ivan cocked one of his jet eyebrows. "If you don't go to school people will think you're stupid. Would you like that?"

Taken aback by this statement, George scrutinized him. "I'm not stupid!" he exclaimed.

"Perhaps, but the only way to prove that is in school."

"I'll prove it another way!" he retorted.

"The other way is far more difficult."

"Did you go to school?"

The question took Ivan off guard. His face tensed almost imperceptibly. Slowly he answered, "No, I did not go to school."

Perplexed by this answer, George could only stare at him. Finally he asked, "Are you stupid then?"

Ivan released a black laugh. "I say, lad, you'd best watch your tongue." With that one statement, George appeared suitably chastised. But perhaps because he seemed so, Ivan felt compelled to answer him. "It may be that I'm not stupid now, but a long time ago, many people thought I was. Poor and stupid go hand in hand, I'm afraid."

George looked thoroughly confused now. "But you're not poor either. You said you own everything for miles."

"I was poor then, and not going to school only made things worse." He nodded his head to the tin dinner pail flung aside near the fallen poplar. "Go fetch your things, lad, and I shall take you back to school."

"I'm not going back there! I don't care if people call me stupid! They call me worse things already!" George stomped away and once more took up skipping acorns across the pond. The mastiffs watched the acorns fly, their sad, ugly faces tilted to one side in fascination.

"Think of your sisters, Alcester. Won't they be upset to hear that you're skipping school?"

George spun around to face Ivan. "How—how did you know who I was?"

"I know who everyone is in Nodding Knoll." Now it was Ivan's turn to skip acorns across the pond. His, of course, went farther and faster. George was visibly impressed.

"What's your name?" he finally asked.

"Ivan."

George took in this bit of information, then he became wary. "My sister Lissa knows you." He put his hands on his hips and brazenly stared up at the dark, awe-inspiring man. "But I don't think she likes you."

"Oh?" Ivan said flatly. "And why is that?"

"I'm not sure." George scowled and skipped another acorn. "But I think it's because she didn't have any suitors."

"Any *what?*" Ivan asked, unable to hide the amusement in his eyes.

"Any suitors. She said once that if she had some suitors then Ivan Tramore could go to the devil." George looked hopeful. "Perhaps you aren't Ivan Tramore?"

"I'm afraid I am."

The boy looked thoroughly disappointed. It was obvious he had begun to like this man who was skipping acorns with him. Reluctantly he said, "I suppose I shouldn't be speaking with someone my sister wants to go to the devil."

"I suppose not."

He brightened. "But perhaps it would be all right because she has a suitor now."

"She does?" Ivan narrowed his eyes. "And who might that be?"

"Old Moneybags Billingsworth. I don't like him very much. He smells kind of musty, but Lissa says we won't be poor any longer when she marries him." George turned thoughtful. "I don't mind being poor though. I'd rather Lissa not marry him, but she says it's for the best."

"Old 'Moneybags' eh?" Ivan said, chuckling, and skipped his best acorn yet.

George looked at how far the acorn went before sinking into the pond. "I think Lissa should marry you," he said abruptly. "You skip acorns much better than old Mr. Billingsworth ever could, I'm sure."

The corner of Ivan's mouth tipped in a smile. "We shall see, lad, but now you really should return to the schoolroom." Noting George's stormy expression, Ivan tempered it by coaxing "If you let me take you back and you promise not to miss school any more, I shall let you come to Powerscourt to visit the pups."

"Truly?" George seemed tempted.

"Truly. You may come to the castle anytime—anytime, that is, when you're not supposed to be attending class."

George thought upon the offer for a moment, then he finally succumbed to the bribe. He went to fetch his dinner pail and his books. As if they were his prize, he covetously patted each dog's head. "The pups—what are their names?" he asked.

"Finn and Fenian."

"What strange names . . ."

"Not so strange to the Irish," Ivan answered. "Finn was a most famous Irish king, and many a story has been told of the Fenians—they were legendary Irish warriors."

"And how can you tell them apart?" The boy looked at each dog. They were obviously brothers; even their black and gold fur seemed marked with the exact same pattern.

"I tell them apart this way." Ivan commanded, "Finn, down." One dog immediately lay down. "Now you try."

"Fenian, down," George said, and the other dog went down also.

"Shall you have them escort you back?"

George nodded.

"Come, pups." The mastiffs immediately went to their master and stood at his side. "Come along, Alcester." Ivan gave him the reins of his stallion and they started back to Nodding Knoll, but before they left the pond, George couldn't seem to stop himself from asking one last question.

"How did you get that scar on your face?"

The back of Ivan's hand immediately went to his left cheek. He lowered it, and slowly he answered, "I got it in a fight."

"Did you win?" George asked.

"That hasn't been determined yet" was the only answer Ivan supplied before nodding his head toward the path back to town.

CHAPTER FOUR

❁

George's schoolteacher seemed truly concerned when she told Lissa the news later that week. "Miss Alcester, the entire situation is really quite puzzling. More tea?" The elderly widow held out the pot.

"No, thank you." Lissa covered her cup with her gloved hand. "However, I am curious as to why you asked me here." She looked around at George's classroom. The children were already gone for the day. Empty, the room smelled only of chalk and lavender—lavender water being Miss Musgrave's favorite fragrance.

"I really don't know what's been going on." The

widow indulged in another cup, then put the teapot back on the iron coal stove. "You see, George has been skipping school."

Lissa's hand tightened around her teacup. She had suspected as much, but now she wished fervently it wasn't true. How could George go to Cambridge as their father had if he was missing school? Without pondering the financial improbability of that thought, she became angry. George had lied to her! She'd known something was going on; she'd known it for weeks. But every time she'd questioned him about it, he had never indicated it was this bad. Now he was being truant. That little shameless liar had even told her what they'd been studying in school. Africa indeed!

Hearing Miss Musgrave's embarrassed cough, Lissa once more gave her her attention. The schoolteacher hesitantly continued, "I think the problem is, of course, that George is teased about your . . . situation." The widow gave her a knowing, sympathetic look. "And because of this I'm afraid to admit that I've been hard-pressed to punish the lad. I almost don't blame little George for wanting to skip class.

"However"—the widow straightened—"we both know the boy must keep up. A brighter boy I've yet to meet. It won't do for him to turn into a hooligan—and that's just what boys become when they miss school; they become hooligans."

"He won't miss class any more, I promise," Lissa said. Already she was pondering his punishment.

"Oh, I know he won't. And that's what's so terribly odd about this situation." Miss Musgrave took a tiny sip of tea. "You see, several weeks ago, he was missing school almost every day, then Tuesday he returned just after the dinner hour and hasn't missed a minute since." The widow smiled sheepishly. "You see, Miss Alcester, I would have informed you earlier about all this; however, for some reason I was led to believe that George was home helping you take care of your sister, Evelyn Grace."

"What made you think that?" Lissa asked.

"Well, that's what the little hooligan told me! He said he was helping you with Evelyn, and I didn't want to press him for details for fear that your sister was terribly ill. But then, imagine my shock, Miss Alcester, when Mrs. Bishop told me today that Evelyn has been in the Mercantile nearly every day this week! I was absolutely astounded. That's hooliganism for you!" Miss Musgrave lowered her voice. "We must stop it now, Miss Alcester. We cannot delay. For George's sake."

Lissa stood determinedly. The lies had gone far enough. "He won't miss another day. I shall see to it myself."

"But I still wonder what made him decide to come back on his own, don't you? I suspected you had talked to him, but I see now—"

"He probably imagined what a fury I would be in if I found out." Lissa's cheeks reddened with anger. How could George have done this to her? And worse, how would she punish him for it, when she understood better than anyone his reasons for not wanting to attend school? She clutched her silk purse in her hand and nodded to Miss Musgrave. "I do thank you for telling me. You've always been so fair and so kind to George. Now with all the trouble he's caused, he hardly deserves your regard."

"Nonsense, Miss Alcester," the elderly lady said, walking out of the schoolhouse with her. "George is a bright and handsome lad, and I daresay he has me quite under his thumb. But we must be firm here. The boy should go on to university, and he won't unless he stays in the classroom."

"Thank you so much. You're too kind. I shall speak to George as soon as I return home." She squeezed Miss Musgrave's hand and bid her farewell. With deflated spirits, she began the walk back to Violet Croft.

She didn't get far, however, before she spotted the subject of her ire walking ahead of her up the castle road. In the distance, she could barely make out his form through the elms, but she knew it was her brother. There was no mistaking his dark hair, nor his gait, which was more swagger than walk.

The late-afternoon light was already beginning to fade and an icy wind swept through the countryside. A leaden sky had threatened snow all day, but even now all it produced was a few flurries. She pulled her dove-colored mantle closer to her neck, then quickened her step. Her eyes were trained on George but he never looked back. He seemed quite intent on going to the castle. She found this odd and would ask him what he was doing when she caught up with him. She would ask him a lot of things when she caught up with him.

But how would she discipline the boy? Somehow, no matter how painful, she and Evvie would have to think of a way to do it. George had been indulged his entire life. His sisters had desperately tried to make up for the loss of their parents and for The Scandal that had occurred in the wake of their deaths. But now they would have to be firm, they would have to be—

A cry escaped her lips. From out of the elms, two huge, terrifying mastiffs came galloping down the lane toward George. In the whipping wind, George didn't even hear her cry of warning before the animals were upon him, knocking him down and mauling him.

Numb from fright, she began running toward her brother, determined to save him from death, even if she had to pull the savage canines off of him with her own hands. Upon hearing George's squeals, she found she had to suppress the desire to faint dead away. Terrified, she ran without paying due attention to her cumbersome crinoline. Immediately it caught in her toe and tripped her up. She almost took a brutal fall before two strong arms went about her waist and lifted her up.

In the back of her mind, she registered that it was Ivan who held her, but she was too intent on rescuing George to do anything but cry out, "Help him! Help him!"

She tried to pull from Ivan's grasp and continue running toward her baby brother, but much to her horror, Ivan not only did not help George, he refused to let her go. She reached toward her little brother and clawed at the steely arms around her, but they held her like manacles. Finally, in agony, she cried out, "Release me! They're going to kill him!" She didn't expect the soothing baritone response she received from her captor.

"Only if affection is lethal."

"My God, what—what are you saying?" she cried, still terrified for her brother. But before her question was answered, George answered it himself. She watched as he scrambled from the road, his blue tweed jacket ripped at the shoulder, his checked trousers covered with dust. Yet he was laughing joyously nonetheless, and the two mastiffs bounced alongside as he ran farther up the castle road.

"George! George Alexander!" She practically screamed at him. Hearing her voice, George spun around, but his brow turned stormy as he looked at his sister with Ivan Tramore's arm wrapped intimately around her waist.

"Come here at once!" she demanded before twisting to face her captor. When she met Ivan face to face, she gritted her teeth and said stiffly, "Unhand me, my lord, if you would be so kind." He was holding her much too closely. She had gone to see Miss Musgrave without having donned a corset, and she was mortified to feel Ivan's large, strong hands sweep down her unbound waist. His breath warmed her cheek and she could see every blue fleck in his irises and every taut movement of his lips. For one wild moment, she even thought that he might try to kiss her, but instead she was released and he allowed her to stumble backward on the road. She shot him a furious look for being so unchivalrous, then she hurried over to her brother.

"Lord in heaven, look at you," she whispered as she knelt at George's feet. Her gloved hand touched a bruise near his eye, then she fingered the tear in his tweed jacket. Shaking with rage, she stood and faced Ivan. "Are these your mongrels that did this to him?"

"Mongrels? My dogs are no mongrels," Tramore countered, a ghost of a smile on his lips. He seemed about to dispute this further, but she was in no mood to let him. She had everything to fear from the Marquis of Powerscourt, but when her family's safety had been jeopardized, her own concerns were cast aside. She lit into the marquis as if he were once again her stableboy.

"How could you let these animals roam free? They're a menace to society, and I shall see them properly restrained or I shall report them to the authorities—why, *especially* when they take to knocking over children—and—and—"

"No, Lissa!" George pulled at her skirts. Behind him, the mastiffs were seated, their tails wagging only harder the more angry Lissa became.

"—and mauling them!" She grabbed George to her and looked accusingly at the mastiffs' owner. Her fury increased when Ivan seemed to be laughing at her.

"The pups have nothing to do with Alcester's condition," he answered leisurely, his dark eyes glittering with amusement.

"The *pups*?" she sputtered incredulously. She waved a hand at the huge canines who appeared to be listening to her with rapt facination. "You call these carnivorous . . . *beasts* pups? Why, look what they've done to him!" She pushed George out in front of her.

Ivan only nodded to George's burgeoning black eye. "You believe that just happened? I think not," he stated. Ignoring her then, he turned to fetch his steed, which he'd left abandoned behind him.

Begrudgingly she watched him walk away, his collected stance infuriating her more. She noted he was again dressed like a gentleman, attired discreetly in Nankeen trousers and a heavy morning coat of black flannel. He seemed so superior, even the blustery wind didn't seem to dare whip at his hair as it did her own, which in her flight to aid George had come loose of her bonnet and hairpins.

She pulled a silvery-blond lock from her face and watched Tramore. Unruffled, he walked his spirited mount back toward them. Only the slight puckering of the scar on his cheek proclaimed he flinched against the cold at all. Lissa was sure that, in contrast, the Alcesters looked like a pair of miserable wretches indeed: She shivered like a matchgirl beneath her threadbare mantle and George scowled belligerently as she tried to touch his bruised brow.

"Did the dogs attack you then?" she finally asked her brother.

"Finn and Fenian wouldn't, Lissa. We're chums," George answered emphatically.

"Finn and Fenian?" she repeated, then shot Ivan a distrustful glance. It was now obvious George and Ivan's "pups," as their master was wont to call them, were well acquainted. "Well, if not the dogs, then who ripped your jacket and blackened your eye?"

George's mouth took on a stubborn set. He hid his hands behind his back and when she grabbed one, she saw his knuckles were as swollen and bruised as his face.

"You've been fighting, George, and you must tell me with whom. They will have to be disciplined. Was it a few of the lads at school today?" In concern, she ran her palm over her brother's dark locks.

"I hate them," the boy burst out passionately.

"Such harsh words." She knelt again to face him. "But why do you speak them?"

He again resumed his silence.

Disheartened, she held George's cold little hand in

her warm gloved one. "Don't fight them any more. Promise me? There's nothing they can say about you that can hurt you. You know what I told you about sticks and stones."

"But it wasn't me they were calling names today," he uttered, his lower lip beginning to tremble.

"Then there's even less to quarrel about—"

"They made fun of you, Lissa! And I won't let them do it! They say you're just like Mother. They call you 'Lusty Lissa,' and I hate it!" Seeing the look of horror pass over his sister's beautiful face, George quickly dispensed with his manly demeanor and wrapped his arms around her neck. "I won't let them call you that any more," he vowed.

Her hand touched his back. Shocked beyond belief at the schoolchildren's cruelty, she could hardly give George the hug of reassurance he so desperately needed. She knew, in the back of her mind, that somehow she had to laugh the entire episode off and inform George that she didn't need his protection, especially at the cost of a blackened eye. But that required a monumental effort indeed when her cheeks were as red as a fire iron and their one spectator was Ivan Tramore.

She refused to meet Ivan's eyes as she got to her feet. From the perimeter of her gaze, she could tell he had yet to remount. He merely stood by, reins in hand, listening to the discourse. When she recovered some of her composure, she took off her mantle and put it around George's shivering body. She certainly didn't need it when her entire body burned with shame and humiliation. Still unable to meet Ivan's stare, she said to George, "I think we should get back. Evvie has promised to make us a chicken pot pie, and we shouldn't be late."

George acquiesced, then unnervingly asked, "What does 'lusty' mean, Lissa? Why do they call you that?"

She stiffened and her cheeks burned anew. Unable to avoid it this time, her eyes met Ivan's. But there was certainly no solace to be found there. The expression in his eyes seemed to ask the same question: Why *do* they call you that?

Beneath that stare, she wanted to clutch her little brother to her and thank him for trying to shield her. And if she could have, she would have sobbed on his shoulder, telling him that she did want his protection. Desperately.

But she knew she couldn't. She was a woman now, not a child. She was the protector now, not the protected. And when she did her crying, she knew all too well she would do it alone in her bed at night.

"We'll speak of this later, love," she told him in a voice husky with unshed tears. "Right now we should get back to Evvie."

"Do allow me to escort you both home, Miss Alcester," the marquis offered.

If she had looked up then, she might have seen the barest glimmer of empathy in his eyes. She might have seen the marquis's face hardened with anger that the townfolk of picturesque little Nodding Knoll were still so abominably cruel. Looking up, she might have seen these things, but she did not look up. Ivan's presence alone mortified her. Meeting what she thought would surely be that dark, mocking gaze would completely undo her. So instead she backed away, saying "No—no, thank you."

"I insist."

Still without meeting his eyes, she gave him the only excuse she could think of. "I cannot be seen with you alone, Lord Powerscourt. It isn't proper, surely you understand that."

"Of course," he answered sarcastically. "You wouldn't want your reputation further besmirched by being seen with *me* in public, now would you?"

Angry, she finally looked up at him. "If I might remind you, Lord Powerscourt, I am an unmarried woman and am presently out here with you unchaperoned. Society deems it improper for you to see me home, not I."

His smirk told her what he thought of her answer. "Pray, do tell me, Lissa. When *did* the Alcesters become so concerned with their reputations?"

"I do believe, my lord, that it all began five years ago. In fact," she said furiously, "if I recall correctly, it was the night *you* left town."

"Ah, yes, it comes back to me now," he snapped.

"Very well then. We understand each other." She nodded smartly, unable to bid him even a polite farewell. Then she took George in tow and walked quickly down the castle road, eager to seek refuge anywhere that was out of sight of Ivan Tramore.

CHAPTER FIVE

❊

Lusty Lissa.

Groaning into her hands, Lissa tried to forget the name as she had tried to do a hundred times since George had told her about it the day before. But it would not go away. The children's cruel nickname kept echoing in her mind until it had become her scarlet letter. Now she felt it might as well have been written on her forehead for all her efforts to erase it from her thoughts.

She had certainly tried to make light of it in front of George. Later the previous evening, when they'd returned from the castle road, she'd explained to her brother what lusty meant—in the most gentle of terms, of course. She'd told him that the children were only saying that his sister found men attractive, and that it was nothing so terrible that he must fight them over it. She told him blithely to ignore their taunts, and she felt he almost believed her. Yet there was still that familial bond that proved them siblings. Even young George could see past his sister's brittle smile and find the pain that made it so. Lissa knew this, and it only made the situation worse.

To further her torture, Wilmott had insisted on escorting her to the soirée at the castle. He'd sent a note earlier that day stating that the Billingsworth coach would pick her up at eight o'clock that evening. It was now five minutes of that hour, and though she had dressed, she still wasn't sure she could go through with it.

How would she bear the humiliation? she asked herself blackly. The thought of having to look upon Ivan Tramore's smug countenance was more than she could endure. She would look into those dark eyes of his and all she would find there would be disdain. He probably thought her a trollop. But she was as spinsterish as a woman of eighty! Her entire experience with men could be reduced to one single kiss. The terrible irony was that Ivan himself had given her that kiss, five years ago in the Alcester stables. Though Ivan's kiss had hardly been chaste, it had most definitely been her last. Dowerless and scandal-ridden, she was not a prize catch. Men wanted her, she knew, but she was not one to dally outside the protection of marriage. Thus no respectable offers had come her way.

But now there was Wilmott. With him there was hope. And for that reason alone she would endure this soirée. Determinedly Lissa looked into the mirror and pinched some life back into her pale cheeks.

"Are you all right, Lissa? You've been so quiet all evening." Evvie sat on the edge of her bed dressed in her finest apparel—a white wool gown with stripes of brilliant violet silk woven through it. The basque waist and ruched sleeves still fit her though the gown was made when she'd been only fifteen. Evvie looked quite enchanting with her sable hair dressed and curled and the matching white-and-violet pelerine wrapped snugly about her shoulders.

"I'm just fine," Lissa stated evenly as she clipped on a pair of Berlin ironwork eardrops.

"Don't let's go," Evvie suddenly implored her. "Wilmott will be so displeased to see me. He doesn't know you intend for me to chaperone."

"I've my right to a chaperone. Those wicked children's nicknames haven't so soiled my reputation that anyone will begrudge me some respectability." Lissa again pinched her cheeks. They were abominably pale.

After picking up her lavender crepe shawl, she self-consciously covered her chest with it. Evvie had been blessed with a cooperative figure. Unfortunately Lissa had found it was highly inconvenient to blossom out of one's dresses when there was no hope at all of buying new ones. Physically she was like their mother in all respects, including being endowed with their mother's generous bosom. She practically spilled out of the slate blue taffeta neckline. Looking down at the sight she made, she was reminded of an old gent who'd come to one of her parents' parties. Scandalized by the low necklines some of the women were sporting, the gent had told their butler upon leaving that he hadn't seen anything like *that* since he'd been weaned.

Coloring, she wrapped her shawl well around her bosom and bared shoulders. She would claim she had a chill and not remove the shawl all evening.

"I hear a carriage," Evvie said in a worried voice.

Lissa looked out the tiny, frost-covered window to the road below. By the light of the carriage lanterns, she watched the vehicle come to a halt at their cottage door. Immediately the driver jumped from his seat and helped Wilmott disembark.

"They're here." Lissa took her sister's hand and made her rise from the bed. She gave Evvie's attire a final assessment, and, ignoring Wilmott's loud knocking, she leisurely clipped a dangling thread from Evvie's pelerine. Giving herself and her shawl a last look in the glass, she pinched her cheeks again before leading Evvie down the stairs and out the front door.

The carriage ride was unpleasant. Wilmott made no

effort to hide his displeasure at seeing Evvie. Only when Lissa shot him several icy looks did he finally quiet. But almost in retaliation, he took his seat right between herself and Evvie, crushing their skirts beneath him. Lissa looked over and saw Evvie's lower lip tremble. She then looked at Wilmott, smiled a tight smile, and promptly vowed to ignore him for the rest of the ride.

Her attention turned to the two women who sat facing her. Honoria and Adele were appropriately attired in brown satin. Each wore a necklet of pearls and garnet earbobs. Their hair was dressed as hers was, in a chignon pinned to the back of their heads. However, the Billingsworth sisters favored the old-fashioned look of wearing several fat curls in front of their ears. As Lissa watched them, Adele shot her a smug look, but Honoria almost seemed sympathetic to her plight. She didn't quite smile, but she did seem less disapproving than usual, and her lips pursed in a rather friendly way.

Lissa spent the rest of the short trip looking out the window. She dreaded the evening ahead of her. She was sure Wilmott's abrasiveness only foreshadowed what was to come. Shivering, she clutched her thin shawl to her arms.

The short trip to Powerscourt was soon over and the Billingsworth coach rattled over the drawbridge, through the barbicans, finally to stop in the castle's bailey. Lit with torches, not gaslights, a hundred flames illuminated the courtyard and turned the sandstone a brilliant shade of gold. It was a heathen touch indeed, and Lissa had forgotten how primitive Powerscourt actually was. The castle was said to have been built in the twelfth century, given to the Irish Tramores by Richard *Coeur de Lion* for their help in storming the city of Acre. To the north the castle still retained the weathered ruins of the original keep.

There had been many a marquis who had fortified its ramparts in ages past, but none of them had apparently done much to Powerscourt's interior. Lissa recalled her visits to the castle with her parents, and she remembered quite clearly not liking the damp corridors and particularly the smoke-blackened Baronial Hall where Ivan's father, grim and humorless, would receive callers. Thinking of how somber the old castle had been, something sad pulled at her heart. Now another marquis had come to embrace Powerscourt's dark interior, to brood upon past injustices, and to perhaps become just as grim and humorless as his notorious sire.

Already Lissa could picture Ivan sitting in his bleak dark Hall, never to laugh or marry, hug his children or love his wife. Things might have turned out differently. She'd spent nights dreaming of Ivan, imagining him as her husband in the innocent ways only a naive sixteen-year-old can. Now her dreams were not nearly so innocent, nor, unfortunately, her possibilities so endless.

She looked at Wilmott as he escorted Honoria and Adele to the doors carved with Powerscourt's ornate heraldry. Would they ever have children? She doubted it. Wilmott was far too old. Would she ever love him? A frown passed over her brow. Perhaps eventually she would find some fondness for him. But Wilmott *would* make her happy, she vowed. Married to him, she would be able to take care of Evvie and George. In return, she would be a faithful wife. Though she might always be cursed by dreams of another man, a man with eyes as dark as the midnight sky, she would give Wilmott no reason to complain.

And if that was all that heaven allowed, it would have to suffice.

"Lissa, what does the castle look like? Is Ivan here? What is he wearing? Does he look as handsome as I picture him?" Evvie whispered in her ear.

Shrugging off her pensive mood, Lissa whispered back, "They're just opening the doors, love. We haven't got to the Hall yet. And I daresay the marquis doesn't answer his own door." Suddenly she exclaimed under her breath, "Good heavens!"

"What is it?"

Lissa couldn't answer. When the huge carved walnut doors finally opened, she was overcome by surprise. Looking up from the great limestone stairs in the vestibule, she discovered the dark, shabby Hall was gone and in its place was a sparkling majestic chamber. Hidden for centuries by dirt and smoke, overhead more than a dozen quatrefoil stained-glass windows sparkled like jewels cast upon the ceiling. French medieval tapestries depicting the entire history of the Capetian kings hung over the triple fireplaces at each end. With six blazing hearths, gone was the perpetual chill, and now the Baronial Hall seemed almost as cozy as Violet Croft's parlor. Five enormous carpets of Portuguese needlework warmed the stone floor, and four heavily upholstered couches covered with an invitingly thick Bordeaux-colored velvet lined each wall.

If the sumptuousness of the decor didn't sufficiently impress Powerscourt's visitors, then the army of footmen that came to assist their entrance did. Each man was attired in full livery, their breeches of chamois, their coats of azure satin with long black shoulder-knots hanging to the elbow. There was even a "flash," or black bow sewn to the back of each man's collar—a vestige of olden times when men sported queues.

One footman courteously reached for Lissa's shawl. She gave a start, then shot the man an apologetic smile. Hugging the shawl to her, she discreetly moved from the footman's reach and feigned interest in the Hall's interior. Great pains had been taken to make the temperature quite comfortable and there was obviously no need for a shawl, but suddenly Lissa was overcome with insecurity. Watching Evvie remove her pelerine and hand it to a nearby footman, she panicked. What were they doing here? They were in Ivan's domain now and she knew better than anyone how merciless he could be. With "Lusty Lissa" again reverberating through her mind, she knew she had given him more than enough ammunition with which to hurt her.

"Right this way, my dear." Wilmott held out his arm. She looked behind her and found Evvie being escorted by a dapper elderly footman. Having no choice, she lightly touched Wilmott's arm and they were led to the castle's drawing room.

Powerscourt's drawing room was the grand dame of Victorian delights. It was done in the modern Grecian style; ladies perched on saber-legged chairs and men sat on scroll-end couches. Carved in the marble overmantel, a lifelike Orpheus played his lyre for the Muses. Sea-green shadow-striped satin covered the windows in swags and jabots and framed the archway that led to a sumptuous glass and iron conservatory.

Already feeling like a churchmouse in a cathedral, Lissa hugged her crepe shawl to her and looked at the ladies in the drawing room. In her pitifully plain taffeta, she was overwhelmed by the scallops, poufing, cording, piping, fringing, passementerie, and tassels that ornamented their sophisticated gowns. Arabella Parks, an old chum from days long past, looked particularly fetching in a peach satin oversewn with gilt fringe. It was all Lissa could do not to run the other way.

But by then she had met Ivan's eye. He stood by the mantel looking every bit as handsome as Orpheus himself. He wore a severe black cutaway relieved only by his brilliantly white shirt. Even his barrel-knotted tie was an unheard of black silk, but it complemented his coloring magnificently. Though she was terrified, she would die before she would show it.

Meeting his cool gaze, she allowed Wilmott to escort her to their host and exchange pleasantries—if that was possible with the eleventh Marquis of Powerscourt. Yet seeing how changed the castle was, she was beginning to think anything was possible with this wickedly attractive man. Anything at all.

"Who would have ever thought, old boy!" Wilmott congratulated Ivan on his newfound wealth as if he were still the stableboy he remembered him to be.

With all eyes on them, Ivan chivalrously bent down and brushed Lissa's hand with his lips. His touch felt at once like fire and ice, and her fingers curled into her palm as if to protect them from the strange sensation.

"Yes, who would have ever thought," he answered meaningfully, his assessing gaze darting between her and Wilmott. His hidden meaning not lost on her, she colored, then despised herself for doing so.

Numbly she watched him greet her sister. After he kissed Evvie's hand and she was blushing prettily, Tramore greeted the two Billingsworth sisters in the same manner, though perhaps a bit more dispassionately. He next proceeded to introduce his company. The group was small. Arabella sat next to her mother and father, and much to Lissa's relief, the Bishops were there also.

Lissa turned to meet the stranger in the group. Yet he was no stranger, not really. He was the man who had been in the Mercantile that terrible day they received the news of Great-aunt Sophie's death. He looked quite dashing now in doeskin trousers and a gray cutaway. His cravat was blue, and as bright as his eyes, which were now trained on herself and Evvie.

"This is my bailiff—if you will—Holland Jones," Ivan said, introducing the stranger.

Mr. Jones bent to kiss her hand. His manners were assured, but Lissa could have sworn his hand shook when he touched hers. When he was introduced to Evvie, he made the same elegant gesture, and his eyes seemed to warm at her sister's sweet appearance.

When the introductions had been made, the ladies were served sherry and seated. A short half hour was spent in idle conversation while Lissa self-consciously fingered the corners of her shawl.

There was only one terribly uncomfortable moment when Mrs. Parks bubbled with enthusiasm over the castle's new appearance. Thoughtlessly she exclaimed, "I've never seen this old place look so grand! Why, the last time Mr. Parks and I were here, one could hardly see to the end of the Hall in the gloom. It's quite extraordinary—can you believe it's the same place, my lord?"

A booming silence reverberated around the room and Lissa knew all too well the reason for it. There wasn't a person in the room who hadn't been to tea at Powerscourt —except, ironically, the very person who now owned it. Everyone knew Ivan had been barred from the castle like a leper.

"I wouldn't know," Ivan answered, as solemn as death.

His words immediately put everyone to shame. Mrs. Parks, remembering whom she'd been talking to, seemed to go into apoplexy. She fanned herself most hysterically while the silence in the room became almost unbearable. Everyone suddenly seemed to find their drinks or shirt buttons so much more interesting than the conversation at hand.

Only Lissa seemed to find the courage to look at Ivan. It had been thoughtless of Mrs. Parks to inadvertently bring up his father's cruelty, and if Lissa had found even the tiniest glimmer of hurt in Ivan's eyes, she surely would have been beside herself trying to ease it. Yet typically, Ivan seemed to relish his guests' discomfort and suddenly she was angry. How like him to fight back in this manner, she thought. But he was not going to destroy everyone around him and he was most definitely not going to destroy her.

Abruptly she stood and walked to the mantel. Joining Ivan, she daringly met his gaze and said, "I daresay the marquis has been the lucky one, then, not having had to

endure tea in that gloomy Hall with the former Lord Powerscourt."

A few of the men released chuckles, and quickly the
tension was dispelled. Lissa knew there wasn't a visitor in
the room who didn't remember all the awful calls made to
Ivan's father. For years an invitation to Powerscourt had
been like an invitation to hell. Certainly one did not ignore it.

With the company again at ease, conversation began
once more. Heartened, Lissa looked about the room. Her
gaze was caught by Mr. Jones's. To her surprise, Ivan's
bailiff looked at her with open admiration, as if she had
done something he'd wanted to do for years. She smiled at
the nice gentleman, then took a sip of her sherry.

"How well I remember that unchecked boldness,
Lissa," Ivan whispered for her ears only. Shocked by his
comment, she stared up at him. As if it were yesterday, she
recalled his kiss in the stables, but then the phrase "Lusty
Lissa" echoed once more in her mind. He had obviously
seen the look that had passed between her and Jones. Was
he accusing her of something? He now appeared thoroughly displeased. With a sense of foreboding, she took
another sip of her sherry.

Thankfully dinner was announced at that point, and
all the ladies were escorted to the dining room. Lissa was
pleasantly surprised to find Mr. Bishop her companion for
dinner, for Wilmott had been forced upon Mrs. Parks. Yet
for some reason she was perturbed to find Ivan holding
out his arm for Arabella. She had no doubts they made a
fine couple. Arabella's flaming locks were perfectly complemented by Ivan's darkness. But the picture of them together jarred her.

She'd always thought of Ivan as a loner, not as some
well-bred young lady's socially correct escort. In the past,
Ivan's very aloofness had only fed the flames of her terrible
attraction to him. Now, thankfully, perhaps those days
were no more. The old Ivan was gone. In his stead was a

man she hardly knew—a devastating marquis who obviously knew how to court women. And if the old Ivan was gone, it just might be possible that her attraction to him was gone too. That it had diminished with time.

She allowed a footman to seat her. Once settled, she looked down the long banquet table and stole another glance at Ivan, who sat at the head. His strong fingers neatly unfolded his napkin. With the appearance of the sommelier, Ivan nodded to his wineglass. The essence of a smile played upon his fine lips and with it, Lissa found herself captivated. His smile had always been so elusive. As a girl, she'd spent days wagering against Evvie to see who could make their somber stableboy smile first. Somehow Evvie had usually won, because she was so sweet and guileless. But Lissa hadn't minded losing, especially if the reward was one of Ivan's smiles. Even Michelangelo couldn't have painted a more handsome youth.

Unexpectedly Ivan raised his eyes. His gaze shot down the length of the table and locked with hers. He'd caught her staring like an awestruck maiden, and she couldn't hide the blush that seeped up her bosom and stained her cheeks. Unnerved, she immediately looked away. She spent the time before the soup was served fiddling once more with her shawl. And worrying that perhaps instead of diminishing with time, her attraction to Ivan had only ripened.

Dinner was served fashionably *à la Russe,* whereby each dish was carried round in succession to all the guests. Lissa could hardly name all the dishes for each course, but she was glad there was so much to take her attention away from the man who sat at the end of the table. The wine was sweet and heady, and before she knew it, she felt brave enough to turn her head again in Ivan's direction. This time, unfortunately, her gaze was caught by Wilmott, who was also sitting at that end of the table. The old man smiled at her and wiggled his fingers in what he hoped was a discreet wave. Lissa acknowledged him with a smile but

quickly averted her eyes, only to turn once more to the
marquis.

Yet now Lissa found Tramore's attentions elsewhere.
They weren't on Arabella as she expected, but rather the
marquis was leaning back in his chair, his arms crossed
upon his chest, studying Wilmott. The object of his scrutiny, however, didn't seem to notice for Wilmott was
again trying to catch her eye. Old Billingsworth brazenly
winked this time, and she had to stifle the urge to giggle.
The entire situation was so absurd! She longed to tell Evvie all about it, but her sister was sitting at the opposite
end of the table engaged in a lively conversation with Mr.
Jones.

When dinner was over cordials were served in the
conservatory for the ladies, and the gentlemen retired to
Ivan's library for brandy. Though the conservatory was a
most glorious setting for cordials and cakes, Lissa found
the humidity quite unbearable. There was a huge porcelain
stove in the middle of the room, and while the oleanders
and palms thrived on the heat, she felt wilted and op-
pressed. She took a lime cordial and sat gingerly on a
wrought-iron chair next to Evvie. She opened her shawl a
bit and listened in on the conversation the other ladies
were having.

"How delightful that dinner was. The trifle was excellent." Mrs. Parks plunked herself down on a baroque-
revival bench.

"Yes, but if only I were young and slim like the girls
here, I wouldn't feel so uncomfortable in my stays right
now." Mrs. Bishop ran her hands down her hefty sides
and smiled warmly at the company.

"It was quite decent of Ivan to invite us here. Why do
you suppose he did so?" Arabella bit into a pink petit-four.

"He only invited us because of Father's new business
deal with him. Lord Powerscourt is buying some of Father's lands," Honoria stated.

Lissa looked at her abruptly. Was it true? Ivan and

Wilmott doing business together? She suddenly had an awful thought. Did that have anything to do with her? Was Ivan somehow . . . ? Realizing surely she was over-estimating her own importance, she quickly abandoned the idea, yet still it tickled at the back of her mind. Finding the humidity cloying, she patted her temples with a handkerchief. Though she longed to take off her shawl, even in this company she felt it would be too scandalous.

"But no! Lord Powerscourt invited us all simply because he is a generous man," stated Mrs. Bishop. "A far cry from his father."

"Ah, but he's more like his father than anyone could have predicted." Adele spoke up from the corner. "He is quite the Gothic character—with his dark looks and tragic past."

Lissa turned to Adele and could have sworn she saw passion in the woman's eyes. Adele almost seemed smitten with their host. But Lissa could hardly speculate on that possibility as she watched the steam cling to the crystal panes of the conservatory. She wondered vaguely if she were about to have heat stroke.

"And that scar—where on earth did he acquire it? It has me utterly captivated!" Arabella practically swooned.

Now Lissa most definitely felt sick. Turning to Evvie, she took her arm for support.

"That wicked thing. He didn't have it before when he was a stableboy. I swear he didn't," Mrs. Parks insisted.

"He acquired it in a fit of passion—as all Gothic characters do," Adele stated assuredly.

"My God, Evvie," Lissa whispered, "I must get some air." Abruptly she stood and headed for the drawing room. She knew the other ladies were taken aback by her rudeness, but she had to get to the passage. She had to go somewhere cooler, where she could walk off the wine she had drunk and gather her thoughts.

Once in the darkened passage, however, she felt little better. She took off her shawl and leaned her bare shoulders against the cool granite stones of the wall. Her head spun abominably and she regretted every sip of wine she had taken. Forcing herself to walk, she wandered down the corridor, but every nook and cranny made her think of Ivan. She pictured him everywhere, looking at her with disapproval, his scar white and angry, jagging down what once had been a most handsome cheek.

She backed against the wall and closed her eyes, trying desperately to get the picture out of her mind. In her state, she barely heard the opening and closing of the door down the passage and the murmurs of male voices, nor did she hear the footsteps as they approached her.

"Lizzy! What are you doing there?"

Her eyes flew open and she found herself face to face with Wilmott. Instinctively she clutched her shawl to her bosom.

"I—I was freshening up and was looking for the conservatory. I suppose I got lost. What are you doing here, if I may ask?" Wilmott was standing far too close. And that gleam in his eye was not a good sign.

"Looking for old Powerscourt. He wandered off, saying something about getting us another bottle of port and not bothering the servants. We haven't seen him since."

"I'm sure he'll return. But I think the conservatory is back this way and I suppose the ladies are wondering what has become of me, so—"

"Old girl, why don't you come in here and sit down a moment. You look a bit flushed." He took her arm and opened one of the doors in the passage. She could see a tiny salon, almost like a morning room. It was a pretty room, but it contained far too many couches for her to go in there with only Wilmott.

"No, really, I must get back to the conservatory." She gently pulled from his grasp. Seeing the elderly man's gaze dip to her décolletage, she tried to cover herself with her shawl.

"You do look . . . fetching tonight, my dear." Wilmott came closer. "But the reason you're so flushed is that shawl. It's far too warm in here for you to wear it. Here, let me take it." He reached out but Lissa pulled back.

"Oh, no! I actually feel a chill. And I must return to the conservatory—"

"Come on, Lizzy, do as I ask. What kind of wife are you to become if you cannot obey your husband? Give me the shawl and we'll rest in here. Come along now." He reached for her arm but she sidestepped him. He reached again, she sidestepped again. Then he began to laugh.

"Why, you coy minx, you're flirting with me, aren't you?" With that, Wilmott practically lunged at her. He grabbed the back of the shawl just as she was fleeing. She scurried away, leaving her only means of modesty in Wilmott's grasp.

"Come back, Lizzy old girl!" he called to her. When all she did was shoot him a withering look, he laughed all the harder, then began to chase her.

For his age, Wilmott had a pretty good set of legs. She was amazed at his endurance as he followed her through one room after another, then back out into the passage. She did get enough ahead of him at one point, however, to duck into a room at the far side of the passage. With her hair atumble and her dress practically falling from one shoulder, she shut herself in with the hope that Wilmott would give up his search for her and return to the library.

Watching the door as she heard footsteps pass on the other side, she backed farther into the dim room and bumped squarely into what she thought was a huge table. But as her hands met the baize that lined its top, she realized she was in the billiard room.

"You could hide behind the drapery, but may I suggest the settee instead? It's so much less obvious."

Recognizing that awful voice, she spun around and searched the room for her new tormentor. It was Ivan, of course, and he stood at the other end of the room by the window seat, nursing a brandy.

"You!" was the only foolish word that could escape her lips. Her eyes met with his and it was all she could do not to run back out to the passage.

With excruciating slowness, he studied her. He seemed to take note of her disheveled hair, then his gaze slid down her dress, only to raise again and rest at her heaving, well-displayed bosom.

"You seem to have misplaced some of your clothing since dinner," he stated dryly, his eyes flicking from her bodice to her face.

Before she could answer, a voice rang out in the passage. "Lizzy! Come on out, Lizzy old girl!" When she heard Wilmott checking all the rooms in the passage, she tensed. If he found her in there with Ivan, no doubt he would be most displeased—displeased enough, perhaps, to decide not to marry her. But then, the thought of hiding from him in front of Ivan was too humiliating even to consider.

Standing in indecision, she listened as the doors banged in the corridor. It was obvious Wilmott was getting angry, and with each successive empty room, his fury seemed to increase.

"Lizzy!" he shouted in the room next to them.

"There's a key in the lock. Turn it," Ivan stated. She looked at him as if he were mad. It was a terrible decision. To have her family's future ruined because she'd angered her fiancé, or to willingly lock herself in a room with Ivan Tramore—her nemesis.

Her eyes turned to the key. If only Wilmott would miss this room! But as his footsteps neared, she knew she couldn't be so foolish as to rely on that. So, feeling more than seeing Ivan's look of triumph, she tiptoed to the door and turned the key. The bolt shot home with an almost imperceptible noise, and Wilmott was shaking im-

potently on the handle before she could even take a step
back from the door.

"Lizzy? Are you in there, old girl?" Wilmott called
out to her through the doors. Wild-eyed, she turned to
Ivan. Would he say something? Would he further ruin her
by calling out now, letting her be found locked in a room
with him?

Her eyes pleaded softly with him. And for some reason, Ivan complied.

Soon Wilmott's footsteps moved on. The banging of
doors continued down the passage, and Lissa knew she
would always be grateful that Powerscourt was such an
enormous castle.

As she leaned on the billiard table, weak from relief,
Ivan stepped nearer. He'd put down his brandy and came
to stand squarely before her. His lips twisted in a sarcastic
smile. Suddenly his hand pulled at one fallen shoulder of
her gown.

"I see Billingsworth was out for a little slap and tickle.
Did he get any?"

Furious, she shoved his hand away. "Of course not,"
she answered icily before making her way to the door. But
just as her hand was about to take the key, she found Ivan
holding it.

Disconcerted, she said, "I thank you for helping me.
It was . . . uncharacteristically chivalrous of you. But
now Wilmott is gone and I must return to the conservatory."

She put her palm out, expecting him to hand her the
key. Yet to her horror, she watched him place it on top of
the billiard cue cabinet completely out of her reach.

"What are you doing?" she asked incredulously.

"Waiting for old 'Moneybags' to move farther down
the passage," he answered calmly.

"Old *what*?" she asked, mortified. How on earth had
he found out that she and Evvie called Wilmott that
name?

"You think you're going to marry him, don't you?" His eyes narrowed.

"Wilmott's not asked me to in so many words, but I daresay he will. But in any case, he's long gone by now. And I must go." Summoning her courage, she walked past him toward the cue cabinet. The key was way above her head but she would attempt to reach it anyway. As she stretched toward the top of the mahogany and glass cabinet, Ivan came up from behind her. Before he could exclaim her surprise, she found his arm around her waist, and herself spun around to face him.

"I thought since we're trapped here we could discuss your clothing—or lack of it—until it's safe to leave." When she tried to pull away, he grasped at her skirt.

"Wilmott is gone. It's safe for me to leave now," she told him struggling with his iron grip.

"He might return. I suggest we wait awhile longer."

"I should think it will be safer for me to go than to stay." She snatched her skirts from his grasp and ran to the other side of the billiard table. To her chagrin, her struggles had loosened her hairpins completely and now her hair tumbled free down her back in a long cascade of silver-gilt curls.

Anxiously she searched the room for another means of escape. But the room had only one door, which only Ivan could unlock. With his great height, he would have no problem retrieving the key. She watched him go to the cue cabinet. In mute dismay, she saw him take out a billiard cue and begin to chalk it.

"Shall we play while we wait?" He tossed the cue to her. She barely caught it.

"I don't know how to play billiards, and besides, I must insist that you open—"

"I shall teach you. The game's quite simple." With that, he took out another cue. He chalked it and placed three balls on the table—two white ones and a red. He positioned the white ones at one end of the table and the red one at the other end. With that task completed, he easily bent and made a shot from the top of the table. In amazement, Lissa watched as his ball first struck the red one, then made a four-cushion carom.

He straightened. "You see, it's quite easy. All you need is a good stroke and follow-through."

Fascinated, yet terror-stricken, Lissa watched him walk to her side of the table.

"You understand?" he asked.

Vehemently she shook her head.

He bent and demonstrated again. When he straightened, he gave a cynical little laugh. "That's all it takes—a good stroke and follow-through. But you'd be surprised the number of men who can't quite pick up the game." He looked down at her meaningfully, an amused glint in his eye. "Billingsworth, for example. Yes, let's take old Billingsworth. You can just look at the chap and see he hasn't a good stroke and follow-through."

"How dare you speak like that . . ." she whispered, his meaning all too clear.

He ignored her. "Now you try," he said, nodding toward the billiards.

She gripped the cue. She didn't dare bend over the billiard table, and he knew it only too well.

"Come along, my dear proper little Miss Alcester, it's really quite easy. You just lean forward like this and—"

It was all she could do not to smash the cue over his handsome head. Yet with heroic self-restraint she placed the cue on the table. He was baiting her. He wanted a reaction. She wouldn't give him one.

"That's not going to do it, Lissa." He shook his head. A whisper of a smile touched his lips. "You're giving up much too easily. Where's that spirit I remember? Where's that girl who met every challenge?"

She tried to control her ire, but it was not easy. "That girl," she said evenly, "has grown into a lady—a lady who will not be fooled by your licentious little games."

"But come now, I'll make it worth your while."

With widening eyes she watched as he sauntered around the table. He picked up her cue and without warning thrust it back into her hands. His gaze then flickered down to her neckline and he said huskily, "Love, I'll wager you a thousand pounds to play with me. Just for one game."

Her temper began to flare. What he wanted her to do was bad enough, but that he should offer money for her to do it was beyond insult.

"And pray where, my lord, would I get a thousand pounds with which to pay you should I lose?" She tried to put down the cue but his hand wrapped around hers and she couldn't release it.

"You won't need it. I can almost assure you a complete win."

"And why is that?" she snapped.

He leaned forward. She stiffened and watched the corner of his mouth lift in a cynical grin. His knuckles grazed the swell of flesh that rose over her neckline and he whispered, "Because I never play well when I'm distracted."

Her control snapped. Angrily she turned away, and even managed a step or two before he caught her from behind. The cue fell to the carpet with a dull thud while his arms took her by the waist. He was at her back and though her legs kicked out, she was fighting only with the air.

"Why are you tormenting me like this, Ivan? What do you want from me?" she cried out in frustration. Forcibly she pulled at his hands but they held like steel.

"Everything. I want everything from you, Lissa. And then when you've nothing left to give, I want some more." He turned her around and forced her head up to look at him. Appalled, she felt his hands run down the sides of her bodice. He seemed to finger every whalebone stay in her corset.

She finally saw the anger in his eyes. "You won't get it. I promise you that," she whispered harshly.

"And why won't I?" He laughed bitterly. "I have everything else. I have Powerscourt and land as far as the eye can see. I even own those miserable little shops in the village—so what's one more conquest?"

"You'll never have me. You'll never have Violet Croft."

"You dare me?"

She stared at him, hurt and anger filling her eyes. So he did truly hate her. The thought whipped at her heart like a quirt. Yet, however much his hatred might be justified, she couldn't allow him to destroy her. If she challenged him he would win every time. Her only defense was to stay clear of his path and hope that he would find livelier prey elsewhere.

"Do your best to ruin me, Ivan," she said in a brittle tone, "for I have my own plans to thwart destruction. Wilmott, for one." She looked down at his hands spanning her waist, then gave him a dispassionate smirk. "So, if you can bear to part with my company, I have more desirable companions to seek out this evening."

Disgusted, he dropped his hands. He gave her a brutally assessing look, then he went to the cue cabinet and retrieved the key. Hardly able to believe he was complying with her wishes so easily, she watched him walk to the door and unlock it.

Her hands immediately flew to her hair and as she made for the door, she tried to fix her chignon. She hadn't enough hairpins, however, and when her hand reached for the doorknob, her hair once more fell down her back.

Bother it! she told herself, and pulled on the door. She just wanted to be free. She would find some discreet nook in the passage where she could fix her hair. With her mind on her appearance and not on her task, it took her a moment to figure out that the door was not opening.

Quickly she fiddled with the key in the lock. The door was unlocked. Why was it not opening?

Then she saw why. Ivan's foot was resting at the threshold, easily keeping the door closed. Her eyes traveled the length of his body until they clashed with his own.

"Please let me pass," she said, desperate to keep her voice cool and uncaring.

"If you think you're going out there in that absurd little dress, think again." His gaze again raked over the low décolletage of her gown. She had to fight back the urge to cover herself with her hands.

"This dress is made of French taffeta. It's not at all absurd," she countered.

"It's a child's dress. Made for you when you were a child. You're no child now, Lissa." His words were harsh, yet her name on his lips was as seductive as a caress.

"That's right, I'm no child, but a woman who has the right to leave. Wilmott is surely going out of his mind—"

"I could kill Billingsworth for taking just one glance at you in that dress, did you know that?"

She swallowed and tried to move away. His arm went up and blocked her in against the door.

"I'll not have every man gazing upon you like this," he whispered. "I'll not give them the pleasure. For that pleasure will be mine and mine alone." •

"No, Ivan, no . . ." she murmured when she felt his hand stroke her hair. Her eyes rose to his face. He suddenly seemed so solemn. His hand ran down her hair once more. Its color seemed to mesmerize him. His strong fingers wound through its silvery gold length and his lips tightened, but from pain or pleasure, she couldn't tell.

Then her gaze rested on that terrifying, magnificent scar. That scar that reminded her of so many unleashed passions. It slashed down his cheek like a sleek bolt of lightning—and like lightning, it was just as dangerous. So dangerous, in fact, she felt if she touched it, she would burn. Forever.

He had stopped caressing her hair. His thumb stroked the rose satin of her cheek until his hand moved beneath her chin and tipped her head back. His lips moved closer until she felt his breath, hot upon her cheek. All she would have to do was sigh and they would meet. She would feel his lips upon her again, as she had dreamed so many times since the night he'd left. But this time perhaps they would be tender and sweet. This time she might be able to comprehend the feelings they aroused, and this time she might be able to handle them. She was a woman now, as even he had pointed out. She was capable of being kissed.

But not by Ivan. Never by Ivan. The memory of one stormy night in the stable came back to haunt her. His touch upon her cheek at the cottage also rose like a specter before her. He hated her. His punishment would be to ruin her. He was already on the path to doing so. First with a kiss, then with a caress. That had ruined her mother. She would not be so foolish.

Her head turned away and she was brought back to reality by his harsh words.

"Disenchanted, my love? So soon? Does this disfigured face repulse you?"

"My God, no, Ivan. No." She looked up at him. Anger burned into his every feature. The scar had whitened and her only instinct was to touch it. She raised her hand to caress his ravaged cheek, but just as she did so there were suddenly noises in the corridor. Her head turned to the door. Immediately Ivan laid his hand across her mouth. Her own hand dropped to his arm. She looked at him with frightened eyes.

His finger went to his lips.

"Where could she be? And Lord Ivan's not to be found anywhere?" Adele's voice echoed in the passage. Footsteps came nearer.

"Ivan went for more brandy." Wilmott's voice echoed back. "But it's Lizzy I'm worried about. She's obviously gotten lost in these damned passages."

"No doubt when we find Lord Ivan, Lissa Alcester shall surely turn up too."

"Adele! What you're implying is improper indeed," Honoria answered faintly.

"Perhaps, but it's nothing you've not heard before. You remember those two. Lissa and her handsome stable-boy. There was talk even back then that she—"

"Shush, you witch. You'll not speak about Lizzy that way," Wilmott broke in.

"Yes, Father," Adele sniped.

"Come along. Perhaps she wandered back into the Hall. We'll ask some of the footmen if they've seen her." Wilmott led his daughters out of the passage and soon the corridor was silent again.

Lusty Lissa. Her eyes closed to Ivan's stare. Her cheeks burned with humiliation. Would she ever escape all the ugliness the world had thrust upon her? Had she been cursed at birth?

Ivan's hand dropped to his side. They weren't touching at all now. Her hand swept to the doorknob. She pulled it open five inches but immediately it was slammed shut.

"Let me out of here, you cad," she whispered harshly.

"And how many fights will George have to fight to-morrow because of his sister's indecent dress here to-night?" he answered back just as harshly.

Horrified, she backed away from him. Her hands helplessly covered her chest and her hurt-filled eyes stared at him in disbelief.

"That was cruel of you," she said, her lower lip trembling.

"But no less true." His sober gaze flickered once more to her attire.

"Then you plan to keep me locked in here forever?" she asked sarcastically.

He looked at her as if the idea of keeping her locked up in his castle had most definitely occurred to him before. Her mouth dropped open in surprise but before she could say another word, he opened the door and left her, locking the door behind him.

Just when Lissa was sure she was about to lose her mind, a maid knocked at the billiard room door. Wiping tears of frustration from her cheeks, she looked up just as a little servant let herself into the room with the key. The housemaid held Lissa's shawl in her arms, and the only thing the girl claimed was that Lord Ivan had thought Miss Alcester might need it.

Wrapping the shawl snugly around her shoulders, Lissa thanked the maid. She smoothed her newly pinned chignon and wiped the last bit of moisture from her eyes. With a great deal of trepidation, she walked to the passage and made her way back to the conservatory.

The looks she shot Wilmott and Ivan were more lethal than poison. Wilmott shrank back in his seat when she entered the room, but Ivan, as she expected, seemed immune to her venom. He stood watching her, an amused gleam in his dark eyes. When she murmured her excuses for being so tardy, saying something about losing her shawl, the light in Ivan's eyes only danced more.

She refused to look at him for the rest of the evening. She and Evvie said their farewells early, claiming they could not leave George unattended at the cottage for too long. They bid the Bishops and the Parks a fond good-bye, yet when they turned to Ivan Lissa was as cold as a snowflake. He ignored her mood entirely, however, and bent to kiss her hand. She hoped to give him frostbite, but she doubted she could, especially in light of the heated tingle that remained on her hand long after she left in the Billingsworth's poorly sprung carriage.

"Next week Powerscourt's having a card game for the gents, Lizzy. Would you like to come with me? Just to watch, of course! I know how you ladies like an evening out." In the dim vehicle, Wilmott looked at her hopefully.

She merely shot him another withering look and pretended not to have heard him. She then turned her eyes to the window and remembered how he'd behaved in the passage. It wouldn't do to offend Wilmott overly much, but for tonight she just couldn't bring herself to keep up the pretense of politeness.

As if accommodating her foul mood, Wilmott kept his mouth shut for the rest of the ride to Violet Croft. They arrived there shortly, and Lissa quickly said their farewells. Once they assured themselves that George hadn't caused too much mischief in their absence and was now properly in bed asleep, they both collapsed onto the parlor settee.

"Shall I make us some warm milk?" Evvie asked wanly.

"Wretched stuff. No, don't bother. I won't sleep tonight anyway," Lissa murmured.

"Nor shall I—at least not until you tell me where you disappeared to after dinner. I was terrified when you didn't return." Evvie sat up. She reached for her sister.

"Wilmott cornered me in the passage. And then . . ." Suddenly Lissa couldn't find the words to explain to Evvie her encounter with Ivan in the billiard room.

"And then what?" An awful thought seemed to occur to Evvie. "Wilmott didn't . . . ?"

"No! Certainly not! I was with Ivan!" Lissa blurted out before she could stop herself.

"Ivan? He was with you?"

Lissa touched her sister's cheek to reassure her. "I was trying to avoid Wilmott and while I was doing so, I had the misfortune of running into Ivan. It was all quite innocent."

"What did Ivan think of you and Wilmott? Did you inform him of your pending engagement?"

Lissa paused. "Yes. He was delighted, of course." Ivan *had* been delighted, she reassured herself. It was a perverse delight but a delight nonetheless.

"I see," Evvie answered flatly.

"Now enough about me!" Lissa gently shook her. "Tell me about Mr. Jones. He seemed quite taken with you. You both seemed to be having the most interesting conversation at dinner." She stood up and swung the kettle over the coals at the hearth for tea.

"Lissa, is Mr. Jones really as handsome as you said he was at the Mercantile?"

"More so! He was quite dashing tonight! He was surely the most handsome man at the soirée!"

"No," Evvie refuted, "he couldn't have been. Not while Ivan was there."

A small furrow appeared on Lissa's brow. "But, Evvie, you forget, Ivan's face has been . . . marred."

"And that notorious scar seems only to have made him more handsome. After you left, Lissa, Adele couldn't stop talking about his dark, dangerous looks. I suppose in some ways I'm lucky God has taken my sight. Oh, Lissa, can he truly be so terrifying?"

In the background, as if demanding an answer to the question, the kettle began its shrill whistle and Lissa rose to attend it. With her thoughts very far away and not on the task at hand, she reached for the kettle stand, forgetting the need for a pad. The hot swing scorched her palm. She clutched her wrist and moaned in pain.

"What is it?" Evvie asked, coming up to her.

"I've burned myself," she whispered, her eyes welling with tears for the second time that night.

"Oh, dear. I'll get some butter from the pantry." Evvie disappeared and Lissa stared at her red palm. With vivid clarity, she remembered how she had tried to touch Ivan's cheek in the billiard room.

Now she felt as if she had.

CHAPTER SIX

❋

Their money was running out. It was a fact that Lissa could no longer deny. She sat at her beeswaxed dressing table and counted the coins they had left. Already they had used Aunt Sophie's last bequest. Now they were dipping into their savings, which over the years they had scraped together in order to move from Nodding Knoll.

Lissa always kept this money tucked in a violet-scented sachet. They dreamed of moving to some little town, in the Cotswolds perhaps, or renting a flat in London. They wanted to go anywhere that the Alcester scandal couldn't follow.

Now their dreams were dwindling as fast as their funds. Lissa quietly took another pound note from the sachet. It was unusual for her to long for her parents, especially since that was to long for something she never quite knew. But now, with her near-empty sachet before her, she wished they were still alive. She wished they were around if only to let her lean on them, to hold her up.

She released a heavy sigh and shook her head. Wishing for her parents wasn't the solution. As spoiled and self-indulgent as they had been, they probably wouldn't be any help. On the contrary, she'd have two more persons relying on her to carry them through this difficult time. That would be unbearable.

Disheartened, she put the sachet beneath her mattress. She was simply going to have to make Wilmott marry her, and soon. Her wistful dreams of falling in love and having a family would have to be pushed aside. As if reliving a bad dream, her thoughts drifted back to the night at the castle. Again she pictured Ivan Tramore's hard visage shadowed in the dim light of the billiard room and the scorn in his eyes as he took her in his arms. No, there could be no more wistful dreams for her. Even now the shadow of debtor's prison skulked in the foreground. According to her calculations, the Alcesters had about another month of fighting off poverty. After that, poverty would win.

"Lissa, come and see!" She heard George's voice calling from the outside. Strolling to her bedroom window, she looked out and saw him standing in the yard below with, of all things, Ivan's two mastiffs. She looked around anxiously for their master, but she didn't see Ivan anywhere. Shaking her head, she ran down the stairs.

"George Alexander Alcester! What are you doing with those two beasts! And on a Sunday too!" she exclaimed as she threw open the front door.

"Lissa, don't be mad. Ivan lets me take them if I promise to return the pups to the castle by evening." George patted one dog's head and looked to her for approval. He found none.

"Why do you call him Ivan? You should be addressing him as Lord Powerscourt," she said fretfully.

"He told me to call him that. That's his name. That's what he said," George answered.

"Dear Lord," she whispered.

He gave her a strange look. He appeared as if he wanted to ask her a question but wasn't sure if he should. He seemed to grapple with something before finally deciding to speak. "Lissa," he began, "Ivan—er—Lord Powerscourt says he used to work for us."

She was dismayed at the statement, yet hardly surprised. George wouldn't remember Ivan, for he'd been less than four years old when the last of the Alcesters left Alcester House. She answered his unspoken question as best she could. "It was a long time ago, love."

"When we lived at the big house?"

"Yes."

George thought on this a moment. It appeared as if the thought of his sister having more of a past with Lord Ivan of Powerscourt didn't rest well with him. He also looked as if he felt he should do something about it. Something to guard his sister. But from what, he couldn't possibly know.

He suddenly scowled. In his most manly voice he vowed, "I shall take them back, Lissa. You don't like the pups, because you don't like Ivan—er—Lord Powerscourt."

She gazed at her baby brother. Tenderness for him almost overwhelmed her. Yet that tenderness was laced with irritation. After all, children had a particularly wicked way of stating the obvious.

"It's not that I don't like Lord Powerscourt, George. I really don't know him." *Anymore,* she added truthfully to herself.

"I'll take the pups back," George stated, giving his sister a look that was much too knowing for his age.

She watched him turn and begin down the rutted little road that would lead to Powerscourt. The two mastiffs followed him quietly as if also admitting defeat.

She loathed herself then. She didn't want to end George's fun. She and Evvie had promised him a dog for years but had never quite gotten around to getting him one. Still, she knew she couldn't bear for George or anyone to believe that Ivan Tramore unsettled her, unsettled her enough for her to cast away two of her brother's playmates—beasts though they were. Suddenly she found herself calling out to him.

"George, why don't you bring the dogs to the kitchen. Perhaps we could find a treat for them." She opened the door further.

"Truly?" he asked with widening eyes.

"Of course," she said with an uneasy smile. She let

her brother pass, and then, with a mute sigh of regret, she allowed the dreaded curs to walk through her immaculate parlor.

The following Wednesday, Powerscourt was again lit for guests. There weren't many who came this night. Just a couple of fashionable swells from London named Hylton and Treadle, a wealthy bishop who'd crept away undetected from the neighboring parish, and, of course, Wilmott Billingsworth.

The men played whist in the library. After they cut, the bishop was the first to stand out. Already disgruntled by his luck, he procured a seat near the fireplace and impatiently waited for the first rubber to end.

After several rubbers, it was clear the betting was getting extravagant. Treadle was beginning to look relieved when it was his turn to stand out; soon Hylton was eager to join him. After another hour or so, even the bishop was looking a bit grim. He, however, played like the consummate gambler. Bishop Wright was sure his luck would turn with the next draw, even when Tramore, looking cool and detached, trumped again.

"I say, it's a long ride back to London, and Treadle and I . . . well, it looks to be time to leave." Hylton coughed and looked back at his young friend who sat near the fireplace.

"But gentlemen, I can provide you lodgings for the night. There's no need to return to London. Surely you don't mean to discontinue play?" Tramore countered.

"We must get back," Hylton stated sheepishly. He rose from the table and Treadle joined him.

"We shall make good those notes, Powerscourt. I shall send a man as soon as it is convenient," Treadle said, looking unspeakably relieved to be leaving at last.

"Of course, as soon as it is convenient." Tramore stood and rang for a footman.

"No need for an escort. We shall notify them in the Hall to get our carriage." Hylton opened the door for Treadle. They said their farewells, yet once they were gone, their voices carried in the passage.

"How much did we lose?" Treadle inquired worriedly.

"*Too* much," Hylton answered, his voice grim. "I say we take a long sojourn to Paris and hope Powerscourt forgets we were ever here."

As the two swells went farther down the passage, laughter broke out in the library.

Wilmott dabbed his eyes, teary from too much fun. "Good God! I've never played with anybody so incurably green! 'I say we take a long sojourn to Paris'!" he mimicked. Laughter broke out again.

When the men finally sobered, the bishop looked crestfallen. "But now what are we to do? There goes our fourth, and I was hoping to cut some of my losses before dawn."

Tramore looked at his nails. "We could always play *dummy.*"

"Dummy whist?" Wilmott interjected. "Why, that's a brilliant idea. But you'll have to play with me, Powerscourt. We'll give James here a run!"

"Powerscourt shall play with dummy. I'll not be given a run." The bishop gave Wilmott a withering look. There would be no praying for Billingsworth's soul this Sunday.

"Fine. Cut the cards." Tramore poured himself another brandy, then handed the cut-crystal decanter around the table. When everyone had refilled his glass, it was time to draw.

The play went on for another hour. The stakes rose even higher. The bishop began sweating, and he used his coat sleeve to wipe his brow like a common gravedigger. Wilmott grew pale and a vein in his temple began to throb. Tramore remained cool, as always, and this began to unnerve his company further. Yet the game continued. The bishop was sure the next trick would turn their luck, and Wilmott, by pride alone, was forced to see the rubber out. But when he had bet his last hundred pounds, the suspense was almost more than the elderly man could bear. Wilmott almost went into apoplexy while Tramore studied his every hand.

The last game of the rubber was brutal. Tramore raised the stakes to celestial heights and the bishop matched with every trick. Wilmott looked at his partner as if he were crazed, but the bishop's eyes had suddenly acquired a gleam, as if a sign had been sent to him from the heavens that he was to go back to St. Albans a far richer man. The circumstance of the game was pulling Wilmott along like a tidal wave, and it was all he could do not to stop the final trick. The bishop watched with anticipation as Tramore played his last card. Already he was rubbing his hands together in glee. Wilmott saw this as a bad sign indeed, and he dreaded the card to be played. Powerscourt looked like a stone statue, his face revealing nothing. As he turned the card exposing its face, Wilmott felt the blood rush from his face.

"Trump," Powerscourt stated.

The bishop's mouth dropped open. His faith faltered altogether when the devil across from him played the final card. He would never be able to pay Powerscourt. Never.

"Look here, we've got to play another—" The bishop was cut off with a nod from Tramore.

"You'll have to speak much louder if he's to hear you." Tramore glanced contemptuously at Wilmott. The bishop turned to his partner and shock loosened his jaw once more. Wilmott slumped over the card table.

"My God," he exclaimed, "he's fainted dead away."

CHAPTER SEVEN

✿

Tea was ready in the parlor. Having become more desperate with each passing day, Lissa had finally sent a note to Wilmott requesting that he come to Violet Croft for a visit. She could not have been any bolder in trying to wrestle a marriage proposal from the man, but they needed money. George was once more getting into scuffles at school. It was only a matter of time before he would start skipping again.

Thinking of George now, Lissa waited for the appointed hour with equal dread and desire. Marriage to Wilmott Billingsworth was sure to be filled with untold misery. Still, Wilmott could easily afford to send George to Eton. She knew she could not bear to see her brother with another black eye, nor could she bear to lie again to Evvie about George's appearance.

"Come along, Wilmott," she whispered to herself as she walked to the parlor window. Already anxious for the visit to be over, she nervously tied and retied her cap. A cap was a ridiculously matronly thing to wear and she well knew it. The one she wore had even been discarded by her fashionable mother, and Lissa had been forced to retrieve it from an old trunk in the attic. The ungainly thing had long lappets and hundreds of lilies of the valley embroidered over the back. Yet she thought nothing of donning it for her suitor. She remembered that once Wilmott had said he liked women in caps. He'd also followed that statement with a long diatribe about women who wore caps knowing their place.

Now, standing before the little parlor mirror, examining her silly reflection, she knew Wilmott would be pleased. She knew her place all right, she thought bitterly, but what Wilmott didn't know was—her place was at the bank.

The sound of horse hooves brought her out of her musings. Her eyes turned to her door and she tensed. The knock was a bit timid, and immediately she sensed something was wrong. Wilmott's knock always boomed.

Lissa flung open the door and met with the Billingsworth footman named Jim. Jim courteously removed his hat and profusely begged her pardon. He then jammed a note into her hand and was mounted and away before she could even speak.

"Have we company?" On cue, Evvie came from the kitchen with a tray full of scones and teacups. As if rehearsed, she had a smile painted on her lips.

"He's not coming. That was Wilmott's footman," Lissa stated numbly.

Immediately Evvie's smile fractured. Relief swept her brow. "Well, then, perhaps he's taken ill. I hate to be so mercenary, but he might mention you in his will and then you won't have to—"

"I don't think he's ill. I haven't heard that the physician has made any visits to the manor." Lissa looked at the message in her hand. She fumbled with the wax seal.

"He sent a note?" Evvie asked as she heard the shuffle of paper.

"Yes." She read the thin scrawl and blanched. Her lips began to tremble with fury. With blurred vision, she scanned it again.

> *My dearest Lissa,*
> *You must understand that I cannot see you any more. I had a bad turn of luck at cards the other night and now am hopelessly indebted to Powerscourt. Our union was ill-fated from the start. I shall always remember you fondly,*
>
> *Wilmott*

Lissa slowly dropped to the sofa.

"What is it?" Evvie fretted. "Has he died? Oh, now I feel terrible about what I said about his will."

"Don't worry, sister, old Wilmott is in blistering good health." Lissa suddenly jumped up. She grabbed her mantlet from the hook near the door.

"Where are you going?" Evvie exclaimed. "What does the note say?"

"The note says Wilmott cannot marry me. And do you know why?" she asked angrily as she tied the mantlet's bow.

"No, why?" Evvie answered in a timid voice.

"Because Ivan has told him not to, that's why!"

With that she ran out the door toward the castle road.

The fury in her breast could hardly be contained. It had all been planned. She should have warned Wilmott away from that card game, yet it had sounded so innocent. Ivan had fooled them all.

And now what was she to do? Her stride grew longer. First she was going to confront Ivan and make him give Wilmott's money back. Then she would have to start wooing Wilmott all over again, and pray that she didn't appear to be more trouble than she was worth. George was counting on her, and as much as Evvie complained about Wilmott, she was counting on her too. Perhaps with more money Evvie could be taught Braille. They'd heard that books were being printed in Paris for the blind. Evvie would adore that. She had loved to read.

Now Ivan was taking all that away. But she wouldn't let him, she told herself. She practically ran up the castle road and was pounding on the castle door before she knew it.

"Yes, miss?" A dour housekeeper answered the door. Her widow's weeds looked as if her husband had died several decades before.

"I wish to speak with Lord Powerscourt," she gasped.

"He's occupied."

She looked at the tight-lipped housekeeper. "Occupied where?" she asked abruptly.

"That is not my place to say, miss. Now if you will excuse me . . ." The housekeeper began shutting the heavy door. Lissa cried out and tried to stop her, but the door slammed shut.

She was livid. Impotently she looked around the courtyard to see if she could waylay a footman who might tell her where Lord Ivan was. But the courtyard was empty save a few ravens that were perched on the crenelations way above her head. Her ears suddenly pricked at the sound of laughter, and she followed the sound until she was at the back of the castle. The stables were back there. She thought it a long shot, but perhaps Ivan had gone riding. The stable hands would know where he had gone.

In the stables, she found a group of men gathered around one stall. They were all dressed the same. All wore boots, breeches, and shirts. Some wore waistcoats, but the well-built stables were quite warm from so many horses so none of them needed coats.

"I'm looking for Lord Powerscourt—" she began, then stopped in her tracks. One of the men turned around and she was face to face with her enemy. Ivan had obviously just been out riding, for his boots and breeches were mud-spattered. A fine sheen of sweat covered his chest where his shirt was unbuttoned. There was amusement in his eyes, yet wariness as well. He knew she was furious.

"Well, well, Miss Alcester, how nice to see you." His voice was deep and smooth.

Lissa didn't answer. She merely looked at the stable hands, as if silently asking them to leave. They took her cue, for one by one they disappeared.

"You have something on your mind, or are you just here to take tea?" Ivan lifted one dark, infuriating eyebrow.

"You know why I'm here," she whispered angrily. "I want you to repay Wilmott right now."

Ivan feigned surprise. "You cannot mean for me to pay him. He lost."

"Then you cheated, no doubt."

"If you were a man I could call you out for that, my sweet." He crossed his arms over his chest and studied her. He seemed to find her appearance comical, for a small smile showed on the corner of his lips. "What are you wearing, Miss Alcester? Were you thinking of becoming Billingsworth's wife or his mother?" He nodded to her cap.

Unwittingly her hand flew to her head. In her anger, she'd forgotten to take off the cap. Though she had thought it silly before, now she would defend it to the death.

"Caps are all the rage in Paris, I'm told. But then you couldn't possibly understand why it's never out of fashion to look innocent and chaste." She gave him a withering glance.

"To look or to be?" His eyes locked with hers.

His retort wounded her to the quick. *Lusty Lissa. Lusty Lissa.* Already she could hear the children calling out. She lowered her hurt gaze. "*To be,* you beast," she answered him, then summoned all her anger. "I should like Wilmott's money returned to him this instant."

"I won his money quite fairly, Lissa. I see no reason to return it." He stepped closer. "But if you insist I return it, what shall I receive in its stead?"

"You cheated him. You deserve nothing!"

"Not true. In fact, there was a man of God who not only witnessed but participated in the game. He had no cause to say I cheated." His arms rested on the top of a polished mahogany stall door. "And if he and Wilmott do not, I think you do not either."

"So you duped this poor cleric too," she admonished.

"He was no poor cleric, but rather a well-heeled

bishop who had no right to gamble away his parish's funds. Nonetheless, I did not dupe him, as you so eloquently put it. However, he did owe me a rather heavenly sum by the end of the evening."

"Have you no shame?"

"None at all." He stepped aside and closed the stall door. Now there was nothing between them.

Suddenly nervous, she watched him walk closer. All at once she remembered those days in the Alcester stables, and it seemed as if she were back there now. Ivan was hardly dressed better than the other stable help in his muddy boots and plain shirt. With dreadful clarity, she recalled the kiss, the kiss that had changed her forever. It had made her cross over the line to womanhood and after that, her entire life had been ripped apart. Instinctively she stepped back.

"I said I would like you to return Wilmott's money. Even if you didn't cheat, it was unfair of you to go against those who were clearly not your equals in the game."

"They didn't complain when they were winning."

"But they did not win. What are you doing to the bishop, may I ask? Are you taking the food out of his orphans' mouths in order to be repaid?"

"I daresay he's never given a quid for his parish's starving orphans." His hand went up to caress her cheek. She turned her head. Slowly he began, "You weren't going to marry him. Wilmott Billingsworth was not the man for you."

"What are you saying? That you are?" she asked, taken aback.

"Yes," he answered evenly.

She didn't know what to make of this. Her heart hammered in her chest. Confused, she shook her head. "I can't believe this. Are you proposing marriage?"

"No."

Her heart stopped with a thud. She could have laughed aloud for what a fool he'd made of her, but her laughter was too bitter to release. Instead she swallowed and said, "Then I suppose you are proposing something else altogether."

"I am the man for you, Lissa. I always have been."

"How can you say that when the only thing you offer is . . . ?"

"Is it better to be a man's faithful mistress . . . or a man's faithless wife?"

A heavy silence followed his words. With the blood rushing from her face, she stumbled back. "I won't listen to your lies!" she cried in outrage.

"No lies, Lissa. You marry Wilmott, I give you less than a month before your eye strays. But then, who would blame you?"

Suddenly she stopped. With her back now turned to him, she said stiffly, "I am not like my mother. Do you hear?"

"No, she was not nearly the temptress you are."

She spun to face him. "You black-hearted villain, I demand you repay Wilmott! You repay him this day so I can forget I ever set eyes upon you!"

He took her by the shoulders and shook her. "I have already paid Billingsworth back. I gave him the choice. His debts or you. Need I tell you which he chose?"

She looked up at him, shocked to the core. "Not true," she said.

"True," he countered.

"You set this up, didn't you?" she demanded angrily, trying to push away from him. "You planned to ruin my engagement. This entire move to Powerscourt is simply for revenge. Are you planning to ruin everyone in Nodding Knoll whom you have a grudge against? Or just me?"

"If people are ruined, then it is simply because they put themselves in harm's way." He touched her lips. "Of course, you were in harm's way the day you grew to womanhood."

Her shoulders tensed. She felt him pull the string on

her cap. Her hands flew up to try to stop him, but he ruthlessly brushed them aside. The pristine linen cap fell down her back and onto the dirt of the stable floor.

"Enough," she whispered before his fingers laced at her nape.

"Kiss me," he demanded.

"No," she said furiously, grinding her fists into his unyielding chest. She tried to pull away but he quickly forced her back against a stall door. He nearly covered her with his body. She couldn't get away no matter how hard she struggled.

"I came here to get you to repay Wilmott," she panted, her eyes nearly spitting fire. "These tactics won't bully me into accepting anything less!"

"But I've ruined all your plans." His lips twisted cruelly. "So without his suit, how will you satisfy your lust for money?"

Her voice lowered to a husky whisper. "I haven't a lust for money—only survival. If you force me, I shall marry the first gentleman who crosses my path. And mark my words well: *gentleman,* I say." She hoped the words angered him.

They did. His face darkened. The scar whitened. "You'd best watch your methods, Lissa. You know what they say about a girl who goes from man to man."

If she could have summoned the courage to slap him, she would have, full across that wretched cheek. Instead, she reined in her anger and hurt and stared at him defiantly. "It's not true, what gossip you've heard. And I dare you to prove it."

"I don't want to prove it. I don't want to know."

His fingers, which were clasped behind her neck, tightened. He pulled her forward in an instant. His lips moved down on hers, and though she vowed not to accept them, they caught her easily. Too easily. She released a small shudder, denying the sudden burst of emotion that now demanded satisfaction. Her hand went to his chest to stop him, but her lame refusal just drove him further. His arms dropped to her waist and he possessively lifted her off the dirt floor to fall hard against his body. She was so close to him she could feel his heart pounding against his chest, but it was not beating nearly so wildly as her own traitorous one. His kiss deepened and he thrust his tongue ferociously into her mouth. Desperate, she ached to shun him, to turn him away, but it was as if they were fighting a war. And with every angry caress of her waist and every brutal movement of his lips, she found she surrendered another bit of ground. When she felt the beard-roughened texture of his cheek against hers, she knew she had lost another battle. When his tongue finally seduced hers to respond in kind, she knew, most definitely, the war was over.

Now the Pandora's box that she had fooled herself into believing she had closed was open wide. She had controlled those restless, longing spirits for five years, and only at this very moment did she discover that they had been loose all the time. Waiting for the return of their master.

She tore her lips from his and grasped the tatters of her sanity. He was treating her as if he full well believed all the gossip about her—that she was just like her mother. He wanted her to surrender to his lovemaking like a wanton, and use her desire for him like a drug, a drug that she well knew could all too easily kill.

Without another thought, she struggled from his embrace and ran. He caught her at the door and forced her back to the harness-covered wall, and her rage at herself, at him, exploded.

"Still forcing yourself upon unwilling ladies?" Panting from the chase, she inflicted another wound. "You act the gentleman, but that's all it is, an act—don't you know that no amount of fine clothing and riches can make you otherwise?" She did everything but utter the word bastard and immediately she regretted her words.

Watching him, she saw Ivan's face take on the hardness of granite, yet if she looked closer, she could find what she dreaded most. In his eyes was the slightest glimmer of hurt, the smallest hint of vulnerability. It was the only evidence that he thought what she'd said might be true—that he wasn't good enough; that, in fact, the damnation his father had wished for him was his true and only path.

"Oh, God, stay away from me," she gasped.

He pushed her away.

"Ivan—" she began, but he quickly silenced her. His hand grabbed her jaw and he forced her to look at him.

With deadly precision he said, "We'll be finished when I've given the devil his due. Not before."

"And what will that take?" she cried out, on the edge of hysteria. "What do you want from me?"

But he didn't answer. Instead he walked to the stable door and opened it. Across from her a row of riding crops dangled in the invading breeze.

She closed her eyes and groaned. "I'm begging you, Ivan, stay away from me. Please stay out of my life. For if you don't neither one of us shall survive."

Then, as if the hounds of hell were at her back, she ran through the door, passing him without looking back.

CHAPTER EIGHT

❀

It was a brutally cold day, and the promise of snow was fulfilled with the flourish of white flakes that fell outside the kitchen window. Lissa was helping Evvie bake a cake for George's birthday. The atmosphere was warm and relaxed. The only tension arose when Lissa looked at the hearth and saw the two mastiffs napping as if they belonged there. One of them—Finn or Fenian, Lissa couldn't tell—released a long sigh of contentment. This irritated her beyond all reasoning.

"George, really, shouldn't the pups return to the castle? They won't make it if the snow continues to fall much longer. You don't want something to happen to them, do you?" She turned to her brother, who was sitting at the kitchen table making a fort out of their Mason's ironstone dishes.

"Ivan told me—"

"*Lord* Ivan," she corrected crankily.

"*Lord* Ivan told me to keep them today since it's my birthday. I promised him I would." George looked up from his play. "I thought you liked them now, Lissa. I saw you give them a bowl of stew only yesterday."

Lissa began dismantling the fort by putting the ironstone back on the pine hutch. She felt guilty for being so waspish, but it wouldn't do to have George referring to the marquis in such familiar terms. The Alcesters needed to put distance between themselves and Ivan. The sooner George accepted that, the better.

"Yes, yes, well the dogs have grown on me a bit," she began, "yet we mustn't get too attached to them. Finn and Fenian belong to the marquis, not us. He may decide not to let them roam so freely in the future." With that cryptic remark, she turned to the oven to check on the cake.

"It's not done yet," Evvie stated even before Lissa could open the iron door. Lissa put down the dishcloth she used as a potholder. It was unnerving the way her sister could tell time.

Restless, she went to the little window set high in the thick plaster wall. The cottage had been built hundreds of years earlier, before the necessity of keeping warm gave way to the necessity of light and ventilation. She wiped at the thick, wavy glass and, on her tiptoes, watched the snow fall on Nodding Knoll.

It was a beautiful sight. The church steeple rose in the

gray, snow-flecked sky like a sleek falcon on the verge of flight, and the thatched-roofed cottages seemed to nestle deeper into the ground as if they were fat brown wrens warming their young. She smiled. In her toasty little kitchen she felt safe and secure, but then her vision roamed to Powerscourt. Its ramparts towered over the whitework of the treeline. The castle looked even more magnificent beneath the silent lacy flakes of the first snow. Uneasily she turned from the window.

"No, I do think we should take the dogs back now, George." Lissa ruffled her brother's hair. "I know it's your birthday, but they can't stay here forever, and already I think it will be difficult getting them back to the castle. The roads are completely covered."

"I don't have to take them back." George's leg began to swing. Lissa wanted to shake him.

"Now why is that?" she asked calmly, but on the verge of anger. If Ivan had given him the dogs, why, she would—

"Ivan—*Lord* Ivan will be taking them home."

"He's coming here? Whatever for?" she asked, her voice cracking.

"Because it's my birthday." George looked at his sister's pale face. "I know I shouldn't have invited him. You don't really like him, do you, Lissa? He said you would find the idea disagreeable."

"But, George, why couldn't you have invited Alice Bishop or Miss Musgrave?" she reasoned.

"I'm sick of girls!" He slid off his chair. George Alcester looked at both his sisters, who were lovely, yet hopelessly feminine. He shoved his hands in his pockets and stomped out of the room.

In his wake, Lissa and Evvie merely stood for moment in silence. Neither knew what to say.

Lissa finally cleared her throat. "He's, no doubt, in

his room. I suppose I should apologize. I've put him in a terrible dilemma."

"Ivan has been kind to him," Evvie stated quietly. "And he does need companionship of those his own sex."

"Yes, but looking up to Ivan is hardly the way—"

"*Lord* Ivan," Evvie corrected.

Taken aback, Lissa looked at her sister. There was a twinkle in her sightless blue eyes. Suddenly Lissa burst out in laughter. "Have I been that witchy?" she asked.

"Well . . ." Evvie choked back her own laughter, then bit her lower lip.

"All right." Lissa sighed, hating to give in. "*Ivan* can come here and pick up his beasts. And if he happens to come when we are cutting George's cake, then I suppose it would only be hospitable to offer him a crumb or two." She dreaded seeing Ivan after what had happened between them in the stable two weeks ago, but for George she would concede.

"I suppose that's the Christian thing to do." Evvie moved to the oven, picked up the dishcloth, and took the cake out. "It's done," she announced.

The two girls spent the next hour readying their cottage for their guest. Evvie plumped the cushions while Lissa dusted the mantel. Later they went to their rooms to bathe and change into their best tea gowns. Lissa felt better as the day progressed. Whenever she found herself thinking about Ivan and how passionately he'd kissed her in the stables, she would simply redirect her thoughts to her new suitor.

His name was J. Albert Rooney. She wasn't sure what the *J* stood for, but it was probably for jellyfish, for, unfortunately, Albert was a mama's boy through and through. She'd been acquainted with him for at least three years, yet most recently, whenever she'd see him in town, she noticed him glancing at her whenever his mother looked away. She happened to see him on the way to church two

Sundays ago, and this time she'd made it quite clear that she'd be amenable to his suit. While she had to admit that Albert succumbed to his mother's wishes far too frequently, when she'd tossed him her first coy look, Albert had ignored his mother's admonitions and pursued her.

She'd had dinner at the Rooney estate that very next evening and had even made plans to ask Albert to tea the day following George's birthday. Albert was growing on her. Though he was awkward and painfully thin, he was also pliable, eager to please, and . . . wealthy. His father had passed on, leaving him three cotton mills in Manchester and a match factory in Leeds. Albert lacked a sense of humor of any kind, yet she found she forgave him this, especially when she found out that he also owned a small gold mine in Australia.

She thought of Albert as she pinned her mother's gold brooch beneath her collar. No, he was not the man she dreamed about, he could never be that. But he had enough riches to take care of them all. And Ivan Tramore could not touch him. In fact, when she'd first dined with Albert, Lissa had brought up the subject of gaming and was delighted to hear him launch into a diatribe about its perils to modern society. She'd taken his arm and listened with rapt attention. She couldn't have agreed more.

Happy that J. Albert Rooney was heading right for her snare, Lissa smoothed her chignon and prepared to go downstairs. It unnerved her to no end that Ivan had managed to stomp back into their lives. He'd gotten the upper hand in every encounter. But this time it would be different. She might be more afraid of him now than ever before, but she vowed she would never let it show. To Ivan she would be cool yet pleasant; quiet yet charming. She would endure his company for a snowy afternoon. And then he would go home. With that thought, she descended the stairs.

* * *

The running footman dashed through the white pines and down the path to the road. He skidded in the snow, but that did not deter him. On he went, to deliver his message to the Rooney estate.

When he reached the wide mahogany doors of the manse, he knocked briskly, then rubbed his arms for warmth. The doors were opened by a butler, and the footman briskly handed him the message he'd been sent to deliver. That task completed, he disappeared down the frosty lane, running as fast as he could.

"What is it, Brickens?" Mrs. J. Albert Rooney, Sr., looked up from her wheelchair as the butler entered the drawing room.

"A message for Mr. Rooney, madam." The butler went to the man of the house, Mrs. Rooney's son, and presented him with the vellum. On it, written in bold lettering, was the name Albert.

"Who brought it?" the matriarch demanded.

"A runner, madam. From what household, I could not tell. He was not wearing his livery." The butler waited to see if there was something more. When there wasn't, he left the room.

As Albert cracked the wax seal, his lips formed a thin line as he anticipated its message. In ecstatic disbelief, he read:

> *Albert,*
> *It is urgent that I speak with you and so I ask that you come to the cottage at precisely four o'clock this afternoon. Discretion is the key, however, so I ask that you share this with no one. Until then, I am,*
> > *Yours truly,*
> > *Lissa*

"Well, what is it, son? Not bad news, I hope?" The stern invalid widow put down her needlepoint and looked at her son expectantly. Albert quickly folded the note and placed it inside his frock coat.

"It's simply a reminder, Mother. I promised a friend I would come to tea."

"You will be back for dinner? I had Jamie stuff a partridge just for you." Mrs. Rooney looked more than a little annoyed that her son hadn't read the note to her.

"I shall make sure of it, Mother." Albert rose from his seat, looming over his mother in the wheelchair. He bent his long, thin frame down to kiss her on the head. "I shall return promptly."

"Use the carriage blanket. You know how susceptible you are to a chill."

"I shall, Mother." Albert checked his watch, then absentmindedly left the room.

The knock came at precisely three o'clock. The confident pounding startled Lissa, especially since her stomach was already tied in knots. With all her heart, she dreaded opening the door. But she took one look at George's expectant features and she knew she had to go through with it.

Straightening her spine, she checked herself in the mirror and was pleased with her reflection. The dark-green silk of her tea gown made her look severe indeed. With her plain white collar and her hair tightly coiled at her nape, she felt as staunch as a Puritan. It would take a lot to ruffle that reflection. Bravely she strode to the front door and opened it. As expected, the marquis stood there, yet he looked chilled and—if she could believe her own judgment —a little bit hesitant, as if he wasn't quite sure of his welcome. His black hair was sprinkled with snow and the broad shoulders of his coat were also covered with the huge, glistening flakes.

Lissa wanted her welcome to be as chilly as the weather. Slowly she nodded in greeting, then let him enter. Yet when her blue eyes met with his she couldn't will away the tingle that spread through her belly. Ivan's gaze seemed to take in all of her: the way her chignon was held in her snood, the way her lips turned ever so subtly in acknowledgment, the way her skirts swayed as she held them out of his path. His eyes burned with an appreciation that soon melted the ice of her veneer. Before she could will it away, a blush heated her cheeks.

"Why, Lord Ivan, how nice that you've come." Evvie walked toward the entrance and held out her hand. Ivan grasped it and held it as if it somehow gave him strength. In the kitchen, the dogs began to squeal with delight, just having discovered that their master was on the premises. George immediately opened the kitchen door, and both mastiffs bounded out. It struck Lissa as an oddly domestic scene. It was as if they at the cottage were the family, and Ivan, their long-missed patriarch. Everyone seemed positively joyous to see him. But she was not, she told herself as she warily offered to take Ivan's heavy overcoat.

"Evvie, I've just added more peat to the fire. Why don't you take our guest to the parlor." She hung the wet overcoat on a peg near the door. When she entered the parlor, a heart-warming picture met her eyes. The pups were sitting obediently at their master's knee. Evvie was perched on the sofa across from Ivan, her hands folded demurely in her lap, her lips smiling at some pleasantry the marquis had just made. George hunched on the floor near the mastiffs, watching Ivan with blatant hero worship. Suddenly Lissa felt like the interloper.

"I'll get the tea," she said hastily before disappearing through the kitchen door.

When she returned with the tray, Evvie, Ivan, and George seemed to be having a grand time trying to predict the snowfall. They finally agreed it would be less than six inches, but by then Lissa had already poured out. She passed Ivan his cup first since he was the guest, but when she did so, George suddenly quieted, then Evvie. Her nerves already on edge, Lissa practically sloshed the cup in Ivan's lap before she'd set it before him.

"Shall I get the cake?" Evvie offered in the ponderous silence.

"No, no! I'll get it!" Lissa insisted, grateful to escape again into the kitchen. She let Evvie finish serving the tea.

He can't do anything to you, she reassured herself again and again as she fetched plates from the hutch. Albert is out of his reach. With that notion giving her renewed bravery, she entered the parlor once more. To impress George with his treat, she set the cake on the edge of the table near the hearth where the birthday boy was sitting. She was pleased when George's eyes widened and he unconsciously licked his lips.

He wasn't the only one licking his lips, however. Finn—or Fenian, she was never to be sure—suddenly stood from his place near George. The dog sniffed for the direction of the cake, then promptly rose on his hind paws to take it. In horror, Lissa watched the mastiff artfully knock it from the edge of the table, only to be joined by his sibling in eating it in several large bites.

"Good God!" Ivan jumped up and tried to pull the beasts off George's cake. He was successful in disciplining them, for soon the pups were seated in the corner, their heads contritely bowed despite the fact that they still had whipped cream on their whiskers. But when Lissa watched Ivan return to the scene of the crime, all that was left of the cake was several large crumbs and a white glob where the icing clung to the carpet.

"This is inexcusable. Believe me, I shall make this up to you." When Ivan spoke his dogs looked up. He shot them a deadly glance and immediately the beasts' heads lowered again.

"Oh, dear. Was it the cake?" Evvie felt the tea table for the damage.

"Yes, I'm afraid it was," Lissa answered fatalistically. She bent to George, who seemed a little stunned. "I shall go to the market first thing tomorrow and buy some more sugar for another. I promise. And we'll be sure to keep the dogs in the kitchen the next time."

"It's all right. I'm a man. I don't need a birthday cake." George squirmed out from under her attention. Her mothering seemed to embarrass him in front of the marquis. Without seeming to give his cake another thought, he turned to Ivan and pleaded, "Please don't punish the pups, Lord Powerscourt. They didn't mean it. I know they didn't."

Ivan looked disconcerted. "I told you to call me Ivan, lad. Have you forgotten?"

"No, my lord, only . . ." George looked at Lissa. Ivan's gaze soon followed.

Lissa stood beneath this perusal as long as she could. Finally she shot Ivan a cool glance before gathering the dirty cake platter onto a tray. She gave George a wistful, apologetic smile and made for the kitchen once more, this time to fetch a dishcloth to take care of the carpet.

She was hardly in the kitchen a minute before she turned around and found Ivan blocking the door back into the parlor.

"Your sister and George are cleaning up the mess," he stated when she tried to pass him.

"The mess your beasts made, I might add," she countered testily.

"I shall make it up to George." He blocked the door further. She gave him a look that said *may I pass?* When he refused, a furrow appeared on her smooth forehead.

"Well, what is it, Ivan?" One of her dark gold eyebrows raised tauntingly. "I suggest you tell me before my brother comes in to defend my honor."

The shadow of a smile crossed his features. "He would. That I know only too well."

"So be out with it." She sauntered to the hutch to retrieve the wooden washbowl. She was not about to let him see her wash dishes, but for some reason she needed something to do. In the back of her mind, a worry nagged at her. It told her to beware—not to trust him, or herself.

"George is doing better in school, I understand." He walked to the kitchen table and grasped the back of a chair. Leaning on it, he faced her.

The contrast between Ivan's expensive attire and the homely surroundings was almost absurd. Looking at him, she wished the pine table was not so scarred and that the whitewash on the walls not so old. In Violet Croft's little utilitarian kitchen, Ivan's presence seemed to take up all the space there was. Suddenly she wished they could have this conversation in the parlor.

"Yes, there don't seem to be any more problems." She nonchalantly put the washbowl on the table across from Ivan. It was almost as if she were trying to erect a barrier between them.

"He hates that school."

"Yes." She couldn't meet his eyes now. "But that's all there is in Nodding Knoll."

"He could have better. He's capable of attending any school in England. Any school . . . even Eton."

Her gaze flew to his. Her voice dropped to a whisper. "Why concern yourself with us?"

Evading her question, he continued. "George is bright. He should go to the best school there is. I've heard Eton is the best."

"And George will go to Eton someday." She fingered the rim of the washbowl.

"How?"

The question jarred her. A splinter caught in her index finger and she looked at the drop of blood. "My husband shall pay for George's education, of course," she answered.

"Of course." He straightened. "That milktoast Albert Rooney should have no problems sending the boy anywhere he wants."

"How did you know?" She snatched up a dishtowel

and wiped her bloody finger. How had he found out she was setting her cap for Albert? Those town gossips! When would they cease interfering with her life?

"I'm just glad to see you've thought of Eton. That is where George should ultimately go." He began walking around the table. She squelched the urge to back away.

"I have thought of everything. Your concern is quite generous, however," she told him politely. Too politely.

"But you haven't thought of *everything,* Lissa. One cannot predict the unexpected." He stopped beside her. "Take this afternoon, for instance. How did anyone of us know your little cake would be shanghaied by the pups?"

"I wouldn't doubt it for a moment if I found out you had choreographed the entire display."

His eyes glistened with wry amusement. "I'll have you know Finn and Fenian were raised for more dignified pursuits than stealing cakes from babes and wearing sweet cream on their whiskers."

She could have kicked herself for the small smile that escaped her lips. But the ridiculous picture of the mastiffs eating George's cake as if it were manna from heaven suddenly overwhelmed her. She could hardly believe those comical canines could belong to a master as stern and disciplined as Ivan was. Could their master be as they were, fierce and aggressive in appearance only? She looked at him, then her eyes helplessly found the scar. The smile died on her lips.

He stared at her. "It's strange to see you so somber, love. You of all people should appreciate mischief."

"I don't know what you mean." She lowered her gaze.

"You do, don't deny it."

"Ivan, all that was a long time ago."

"Not so long ago. Was it only six years ago that your parents gave that little picnic which you made so notorious?"

"That's far in the past."

"Sometimes I think of it as yesterday." He moved an inch closer to her. "Evvie was not blind then, remember?"

She nodded her head.

"And you both grew so weary of all those pompous acquaintances of your parents who showed up that afternoon."

"It was difficult. Mother and Father always seemed to forget to invite young people." Her eyes clouded. She hated remembering her parents. Deep down, she truly believed they were good people, but something, usually parties, trips, or gaming, always prevented them from spending much time with her, Evvie, and George. She knew too, with the crystal vision of maturity, that her parents didn't quite know what to make of those little persons they had brought into the world. And so they treated them like ornaments to be dressed and placed strategically on display. Since ornaments didn't get bored or have need of friends to divert them from mischief, her parents had never considered them when making plans.

"It was a beautiful day, do you remember?" Ivan prodded her.

"Oh, yes. Warm and delightful. The crowd of guests spilled right down to the edge of Silverspray Pond." She remembered the sight of Alcester House, its grand corninthian columns standing sentinel in the background. In many ways that day had been the zenith of her existence. Her eyes sparkled with suppressed laughter. In many ways it had been the nadir also.

"You were so bored, you and Evvie visited all the horses in the stables, do you recall?"

"Yes, and in our party frocks no less!" She smiled.

"Yours was blue," he added solemnly.

"Yes, it was," she answered in a hushed voice. "It was to be my coming-out gown. I even wore it for my portrait that Father commissioned. But then Mother decided it wasn't quite right for my debut so she told me to wear it to the picnic."

Her lips twisted as she recalled the portrait. She hadn't thought of it in years. Where was it now? she wondered. It had been auctioned off in London with the rest of Alcester House's furnishings, and by now it could have changed hands a hundred times. Even if she ever had the money to buy it, she would probably be unable to trace it to its present owner. It might even have been destroyed. Imperceptibly she winced.

"And even in that pretty blue frock, you thought nothing of climbing that tree—the oak that grew by the pond." He pulled her out of her morbid thoughts.

"Evvie climbed it too."

"But Evvie was thirteen. You were sixteen."

"Not quite sixteen."

"Too old to be climbing trees."

Her eyes brightened. "Yes, that's true."

"Do you recall what happened next?"

She nodded. "The branch gave way. Not Evvie's, just mine."

"And you fell into the pond."

"And you retrieved me."

"In front of two hundred horrified guests. And I recall George—he must have been four then—clapped the entire time."

She giggled and her hand touched him on the arm. "Oh, I'd forgotten that," she said.

"Do you know what I wanted to do to you after I'd brought you to shore?"

Her hand tightened on his arm. Her fingers felt like they were wrapped around granite. Innocently she shook her head.

". . . as you lay wet and bewildered beneath me?"

Again she shook her head. Before she knew it, he tilted up her chin. Their eyes met, then he tenderly placed a kiss on her lips.

Frightened, she quickly recovered herself and turned away. But his voice at once soothed her and commanded her. "No, Lissa. Don't . . ." he said. With a sob, she turned her face back to his and again found his mouth on hers.

How a man as cold as he was could have such warm, enticing lips was beyond her imagination. Her eyes fluttered shut as his scent, his touch, his taste filled up her senses. But all too quickly the kiss ended. He pulled back and looked at her. Her hand grasped his arm until she surely thought she would mark him.

"More, Lissa?" he whispered.

She didn't move, and by simply not refusing his offer, she gave her consent better than had she cried it out for all the neighbors to hear. His lips came down on hers once more. He was still tender, yet this time demanding as well. He demanded a response and he received one. She released a small, throaty moan, then melted into his embrace.

In truth, she knew she wanted him. Her lips craved his like a beggar craved gold. But it was wrong to want him. It had to be. His lips felt too good, his touch, too right. He was seducing her into more than lovemaking. He wanted her to trust him, and the way she felt at this moment, with his lips bruising hers with his passion, she almost could. Anything to go farther.

His lips left hers and moved hotly to her throat. Instinctively she tossed her head back as if inviting more. He accepted with pleasure, trailing his tongue down the length of her vulnerable neck and nibbling softly on the sweet skin of her nape.

"Oh, Ivan." She moaned as his hands went to her face. He kissed her once more and this time he was not nearly so gentle, for his appetite had grown. He took her lips in a long, hungry kiss, then he coaxed her mouth open so she could further receive his onslaught. She tensed as she felt him enter, but the sensation he created was too seductive to refuse. She surrendered to it, clutching the lapels of his frock coat while his arms pulled her so close she felt their bodies surely would meld into one.

In the back of her mind, she thought she heard a knock at the cottage's front door. Yet to quit this heady trip into paradise on the small chance that there actually was a caller at her cottage was too dear a price to pay. Her mind was spinning out of control, but still she tried to think. She vaguely remembered the snow and cold, and she easily rationalized that Violet Croft would see no further visitors this afternoon.

As if sensing her hesitation, Ivan's kiss grew even hotter. His seduction was hard to resist, and already he was persuading her to do the most wanton things. Her hand willingly caressed the fine dark hairs on his nape, and soon, she knew, she would be caressing that wicked scar, that terrible reminder of the man he had been and the man he was now.

"What is this?" a voice intruded, and behind her, Lissa heard a pitiful gasp of disbelief. The moment shattered like a crystal ball. She broke from Ivan's embrace and stood face to face with all the troubles that had dogged her these many years: The Scandal, her reputation, Ivan. Albert stood in the kitchen doorway with Evvie and George beside him. It was obvious they had seen them kissing—all but Evvie, that was, and by the look on Evvie's face, she hadn't had to see them kissing; she knew anyway.

Lissa's fingers went to her traitorous lips. They still burned from Ivan's kiss and she knew they had to be red and slightly swollen. A sob caught in her throat and she tried to look away, but Ivan wouldn't let her. His arm went possessively around her waist and he forcibly turned her to face the door.

"What brings you out here, Rooney?" Ivan asked as he held her fast. She tensed and tried to move from the circle of his arms, but without fighting like a vixen, she knew he wouldn't let her go. She would have sold her soul to have been able to turn on him at that moment, for she knew without a doubt this entire episode was his doing, but she'd already shamed her family with one scene. There was no need for two.

"Lissa, you sent for me," Albert replied bitterly. He then reached inside his overcoat and threw a piece of vellum onto the kitchen table.

"I didn't send for you. I wouldn't . . ." she answered, her voice quivering. She didn't need to read the note on the table. She knew what it said. It summoned Albert to Violet Croft and was undoubtedly signed with her name. It could not have been written in her hand, yet Albert had no way of knowing that. So he had come, only to find her in a compromising embrace with Nodding Knoll's most notorious citizen.

She looked at Ivan, her eyes blazing with anger and grief. He had tricked her. The motivation for his kiss had not been desire or affection, rather it had been a heartless attempt to humiliate her. He hated her that much— enough to destroy her last chance to save her family, enough to see her crushed by the fist of debtor's prison. Suddenly the vision of her rotting in a putrid-smelling cell passed before her eyes. Would he laugh to see her so denigrated? Or would he merely look upon her with pity in his eyes, returning the look that so many had bestowed upon him as he grew up Powerscourt's unwanted bastard?

His treachery threatened to consume her. But instead of succumbing to it, she hardened, as she had hardened when her parents died. Her face turned into a perfect porcelain mask—beautiful and doll-like to the eyes, cold and unyielding to the touch. Then she turned to Ivan.

"Does this please you, my lord?" she asked him icily. "Or were you hoping there would be a larger audience than just Albert? Perhaps you would see me ruined before the whole of Nodding Knoll?"

"Rooney shall speak of this to no one, Lissa," he answered gently.

She wanted to slap his face. "Oh, but how can he not speak of it? He has every right."

Ivan turned to Albert. A smug smile crossed his lips. "Rooney, as a gentleman, you have no need to mention what went on here. I needn't ask you to—"

Albert shook with rage. Suddenly he couldn't contain his anger any more. "I shall speak of it! I shall! You both deserve punishment for this infamy and, besides, Mother will ask why I am not courting Miss Alcester, and I could never lie to Mother!" Albert crossed his arms in front of his chest.

"That will only start rumors," Ivan told him, annoyance tightening his features.

"Then so be it. You both should have thought of that before—"

Ivan cut him off. "Rumors can be viciously untrue, my man." He looked thoughtfully at his nails before continuing. "For example, what if someone should start the rumor that you've taken to visiting, say . . . old man Norton?"

Lissa gasped. It was unthinkable what Ivan was threatening. Old Mr. Norton lived on the other side of town in a small cottage, and every once in a while a rumor would pass through the village that he'd been caught again wearing corsets and gowns and dipping into the rouge pot. Everyone knew about old Mr. Norton, yet no one spoke of him openly. It was too . . . indelicate. She cringed and looked at Albert. He was cringing too.

"You wouldn't dare," he said to Ivan. "It would be a gross lie."

"Yes, it would be," Ivan admitted. "However, take heart, old chap, only one in three would believe it."

"Good *God*!" Albert nearly swooned at the thought.

Ivan walked to the kitchen door and held it for him. Albert gave no pause. As if running from a den of thieves, he clutched his top hat in his hands and took off.

Ivan shut the door. Silence fell in the kitchen. Lissa

looked around her, first at Evvie, who seemed pained indeed, then at George, who seemed hopelessly confused. Finally her eyes turned to Ivan. Glaring at him, she picked up the note from the table and held it to her breast.

"He was not for you, either, Lissa." Ivan reached for the note. She backed away.

"Oh, but he was. I suppose you shall see to it that I never have another suitor?"

He remained silent, his eyes dark and distrustful.

"Answer me," she demanded in a harsh whisper.

"You'll never find the right man, so why search for him?" he said finally.

"Perhaps you're right. So I shall do without any suitors. I shall do without a single one, yet I shall do all right anyway, just to spite you."

He ignored the sharpness of her words. Instead, he tried to soothe her by saying "Give me the note, Lissa. I shall burn it." He held out his hand.

"Never!" She backed farther away.

"Why not? What do you want it for?" he demanded.

"Evidence."

"And what do you plan to do with it? Throw me in jail for forgery?" He chuckled. "Give it over."

"Never!" she repeated. "I plan on keeping it by my bedstead. I shall look at it every night." Her voice grew husky with hurt and despair. "And I will pray that all the misfortune of this family be bestowed upon your head."

"Lissa!" Evvie gasped at her sister's vengefulness.

"You foolish girl, I saved you from a living hell with that witless fop, and yet here you are spouting curses at me." Ivan scowled and reached for the note once more. But stepping back, she would not give it up.

"You're just doing this because Father would have approved of *Albert,*" she reminded him brutally.

"Then damn his eyes, Lissa. Damn his eyes."

Ivan looked at her, his expression as hard as granite. Without reverence for the dead, Ivan cursed again. Lissa watched as he assumed a stance of rock-hard rebellion, rebellion bred by the whip. He dared her to react, to rebel also, but there was no point in fighting now. She'd lose. Shooting him one last glance of pure hatred, she ran up the stairs, feeling utterly disgraced.

CHAPTER NINE

❊

That evening was a dark one indeed. Lissa spent the entire time in her bedroom, weeping softly into her pillow. She indulged herself in crying only because she knew nothing could be done about her family's situation that night, and also because she knew tomorrow she would have to begin to fight back.

Oh, and she would, she promised herself, wiping her tearstained cheeks. Ivan had not bested her. She would wake tomorrow and find some way to keep the Alcester family going, even if it meant becoming a scullery wench.

Staring off into a corner, she didn't hear the door to her bedroom open. She barely heard Evvie's quiet footsteps as she walked to the bed. Lissa did recognize the touch, however, for her sister's touch was always warm and knowing.

"I brought you some hot milk and honey. It will help you sleep." Evvie skillfully placed the glass on the nightstand.

"We'll make it. I swear I shan't let you down." Lissa wiped one last tear from her eyes.

"Of course we shall." Evvie lay next to her and put her arms around Lissa's shoulders. "Albert wasn't right for you, anyway. Ivan was correct on that point."

"He wanted to ruin me. And now he has done so."

"He hasn't done so. Ivan made sure Albert won't speak a word. You heard him."

"Yes, I heard him. He wants to be the one to spread the news himself. He hates me so!" Soon she was shaking anew from her sobs. Her pain seemed to find no balm. In one short afternoon, Ivan had repaid in duplicate the pain she might have caused him years ago.

"Lissa, he cares for you. I know he does," Evvie whispered, stroking her hair.

"Please, Evvie, you misjudge him. He's a black-souled villain, and he proved that this afternoon."

"What he did was appalling, that's true. But he wants you, Lissa. He didn't want you to go to another."

"Good God, Evvie." Lissa sat up and looked at her sister. "He's not the stableboy any longer. Do you think he cannot find the words or the courage to ask me to marry him?"

"Old wounds go deep, sister."

"Yes," Lissa agreed with a sob, "and that's why he's doing what he's doing. Revenge."

"Revenge was not on his mind when he kissed you. And I know he kissed you, for George confirmed to me he did."

"He wants me, all right. I know that. But if you think that his wanting me will result in a marriage proposal, Evvie, you're sadly mistaken. He's already had the opportunity to propose, and I tell you, he proposed something quite different from marriage."

Evvie grew grim. "You mean he wanted you to . . . ?"

"Be his mistress." Lissa covered her face with her hands and cried hysterically, "And must I? Can we get along without him?" The thought of all the unpaid bills that already cluttered the parlor mantel upset her further. Would going to debtor's prison be better or worse than sneaking up to Powerscourt to appease her keeper? Infinitely better, she finally confirmed, for there at least, even in some dark cell, she would be able to hold onto a little of her pride. If she sacrificed herself to Ivan, she would have none at all.

"We shall never speak to him again," Evvie vowed, obviously shocked by her disclosure.

"No, and I daresay even if we wanted to we shall never get the opportunity. He's through with us. No one shall marry me after what happened this afternoon gets bandied about in the pubs."

"We shall tell them he forced himself upon you!"

Suddenly Lissa quieted. Huge, silent tears slipped from her blue eyes. She fell back onto the bed and clutched her pillow. She couldn't even look at her sister.

"He didn't force me, Evvie."

Lissa thought of Ivan's kiss and of all the emotion that had roiled inside of her during it. She had wanted him, and she couldn't deny it. She had wanted the kiss to go on and on, and she had wanted to press herself so closely into Ivan's embrace that they would join completely and forever. There was a need in her that had lain dormant for five years, waiting for just that kind of blossoming. Now that she'd experienced it, the thought of never having it again caused her unspeakable anguish. Yet the thought of continuing led her to the blackest of thoughts.

"I'm just like Mother, Evvie." She began to sob and even her sister's fierce hugs couldn't comfort her.

The next day Lissa went to seek employment. Dressed in wool serge gowns, bonnets, and shawls, she and Evvie set out for the Mercantile. There Evvie occupied Mrs. Bishop's attention by asking her to help her choose a new pair of gloves while Lissa covertly looked at the announcements board beneath the words "Positions Available."

The Gilworths needed a chimney sweep and the Miltons were looking for a gardener, neither of which suited her. She looked further and found that the Ericksons were seeking a governess and old Widow Tannahill desired a ladies' companion. Both of those positions seemed more appropriate, but Lissa's beautiful eyes clouded. Old Widow Tannahill would no doubt have her thrown from her parlor for even thinking herself suitable as a companion. And the Ericksons? The young couple's estate had neighbored Alcester House. In fact, Kenneth Erickson had been the one to make funeral arrangements for her parents. But Lissa had seen them so infrequently since then, she wasn't sure how they would react to her applying for the position of governess. They had been pleasant when they'd seen her, but wouldn't remembrances of The Scandal ultimately color their decision? After all, they were seeking a governess, someone who would have some impression upon their children . . .

Her worried gaze suddenly lit upon another notice. It stated:

> Parlormaid desired at Powerscourt. Pay generous, duties genteel. Apply with Mrs. Lofts at the servants' entrance.

Lissa bit her lower lip. How positively unfortunate that Powerscourt should be seeking help. Ironically it was the only place in Nodding Knoll that would hire her, regardless of her past. But there was no way she would go there. At once the Ericksons' position seemed a less remote possibility. She'd at least have to try there first before even considering working at Powerscourt.

She wandered back to her sister and grabbed her hand. "Find anything that suits, dear?"

Evvie gave a start. "Well . . . actually no . . ." She turned her head in Lissa's direction and a worried look passed over her features.

Lissa turned her gaze to the shopkeeper. "Would you excuse us, Mrs. Bishop? I want to have a word with Evvie; she hasn't been feeling well today."

"Oh, certainly, loves, you both have a chat and I'll be in the back feeding old Tom." Mrs. Bishop picked up her large gray tom and breezed to her rooms in the back of the shop.

"What did you find?" Evvie whispered when Mrs. Bishop's footsteps had faded away.

"Nothing much, but the Ericksons are looking for a governess. I shall go there at once. Shall I return you to the cottage, or would you like to stay here and keep Mrs. Bishop company for an hour or so?"

"I think I should like to stay here. I know I'll just be pacing in the cottage waiting for you to return. Oh, Lissa, I can't believe it has come to this. What if the Ericksons won't—"

"Never mind that! Don't think of it!" Lissa squeezed her hand in farewell. "I shall be back soon!"

It took less than fifteen minutes to reach the Erickson estate, but to Lissa it seemed the walk took hours. Every step was painful. The position as governess would be perfect, but there were so many things that could go wrong. It was ever so much more difficult considering that she already knew the Ericksons. It would put them in a most awkward situation, even more so if they had to refuse. Her cheeks burned with humiliation just thinking about the possibility of rejection. But she had to go forth. George and Evvie needed her, and if this was the only way, she would do it.

"Lissa! Lissa!" A voice rang out behind her. Lissa turned and watched a carriage pull up alongside her. A well-coiffed, russet-colored head popped out the window and Arabella Parks greeted her with a wave.

"Lissa! How glad I am to see you! I've been so bad about not visiting! And now here you are!"

"Hello, Arabella," Lissa answered, all the while fervently wishing the girl would just disappear. It wasn't that she didn't like Arabella Parks; on the contrary, Arabella was probably her best friend. She certainly had been while

Lissa was growing up at Alcester House, and even now Arabella still called on her. But since The Scandal there always seemed to be the implication that the young lady was performing some charitable duty doing such. A couple of times Lissa half expected her to come calling with bread and medicine, as if the rich Miss Parks were visiting the most broken and destitute of paupers. When Arabella left, Lissa always felt like an ungrateful chit for being so annoyed by her visit, but seeing her now was like having salt thrown into her wounds. She was feeling particularly discouraged, and she wondered blackly if it wouldn't be too soon before the Alcesters would need bread and medicine.

"Lissa, whatever are you doing out here on the road? Do come into the carriage and I'll take you wherever you are going." Arabella assumed her most piteous look and quickly opened the door for her.

Lissa could only stand on the road. What was she to do? Tell Arabella she wanted to be dropped off at the Ericksons because she hoped to find employment there? Or remain where she was and refuse the ride, making Arabella feel only that much more sorry for her?

"Come along, dear. The wind is cold." Arabella shivered and tucked the mink carriage blanket even more tightly around her lap.

"I . . . ah . . ." Lissa stumbled on her words.

Noting her hesitation, Arabella smiled sympathetically. "Please don't worry, Lissa. I don't care if anyone sees us together. In fact, you must know, many have said it is quite admirable that you and I have remained chums. So you see now? You needn't be so anxious."

Lissa was caught between wanting to strangle the girl and wanting to thank her. "How good of them," she finally sputtered, choking back her gall.

"Now please get in. The chill is absolutely brutal and I shouldn't like to stand here bickering with you all afternoon. So where were you off to?"

Resigned, Lissa ascended the carriage. There was no

way she could ask Arabella to drop her at the Ericksons. It would be the final humiliation. Besides, her plan to become a governess seemed ridiculous now. No family in Nodding Knoll would want a woman with her past supervising their children. Lissa almost couldn't blame them. The Scandal was bigger than Nodding Knoll itself, and while the Alcesters were still there, they would never get away from it.

"Would you mind taking me to Bishop's? I left Evvie there." She settled herself in the carriage. Arabella gave her a strange look, for it was obvious she had been headed in the opposite direction. Nonetheless, Arabella knocked on the panel behind her and shouted instructions to her driver. In moments they were on their way.

Lissa was soon back at Bishop's Mercantile, where she thanked Arabella graciously for the ride. When she entered the store she expected to find Evvie waiting for her, and she was perplexed indeed when her sister was nowhere to be seen. Her curiosity escalated when she heard Evvie giggle from behind the huge damask curtains that partitioned the Bishops' living quarters from the shop. Knowing she was welcome, Lissa pulled aside the curtains and went to retrieve her sister.

The surprise on her face must have been obvious, for when she entered the Bishops' parlor, everyone ceased all conversation. But she couldn't help looking shocked when a man, the same man whose amusing story appeared to have reduced her normally sober sister into a giggling schoolgirl, rose from the tea table. Lissa knew he was Ivan's man, Mr. Jones, and she was not sure she liked the situation, never mind the fact that it was obvious Mrs. Bishop had played chaperone in her absence.

"Oh, Lissa love, you've returned. Have some tea with us, will you?" Mrs. Bishop cooed.

"I really—" She was interrupted by Evvie.

"Do you see who is here, Lissa?" Evvie smiled in her

direction. "It's Holland . . . I mean . . . Mr. Jones. Do you remember? At the soirée?"

"Yes, I believe we have met, Mr. Jones." Lissa nodded. He bowed.

"You must call me Holland also," he offered.

Not knowing what to do, Lissa simply smiled at him.

"We've been having the most lovely time," Mrs. Bishop interceded. "Holland here has left us in tatters over his stories and I don't know who has laughed more, Evvie or me!"

"Oooh, the stories of you at Eton were simply charming! I never knew anyone other than my little brother George who could cause so much mischief!" Evvie stifled a giggle in her delicate white-gloved hand.

"How nice," Lissa murmured helplessly. It was a delight to see her sister so carefree, yet was this another one of Ivan's manipulations? Had he sent his man down here to . . . ?

She abruptly stopped her train of thought. No! Ivan wouldn't go so far as to hurt Evvie—not directly, at least. And as she watched Mr. Jones steal a glance at her sister, she knew even Ivan Tramore couldn't command his man to look at Evvie in such a way. Holland Jones appeared as if he were worshipping a goddess, and Evvie played the part beautifully with her pink cheeks and sable hair. Her blue eyes shone like an angel's, and though she could not see her male companion, her eyes were filled with as much awe as his.

"Have you finished your errands, Lissa love?" Mrs. Bishop stood and bounced to retrieve the cookie tray. "I suppose you couldn't stay for a cup of tea?"

"Errands!" Evvie stood as if she'd just been struck by a lightning bolt. Obviously she had just recalled where her sister had been. "Good heavens! We must leave! Oh, Lissa, I am so sorry!"

"We needn't leave, Evvie," Lissa said.

"But we must! Here I've been sitting having tea while

you've been out running those—those—errands!" She nervously gathered up her purse and shawl. Standing contritely, she waited for her sister's arm.

"I suppose we have lingered after all," Holland stated reluctantly.

"Perhaps we should get home for George . . ." Lissa looked at Holland. He had such a nice smile and was handsome and gentle, full of dignity and fine breeding. She would have to tell Evvie about him when they were alone.

Mrs. Bishop led Evvie out to the store while Holland held the curtain for Lissa. When her sister was a few steps ahead of her, Holland touched Lissa's arm.

"Yes, Mr. Jones?"

He looked thoughtful. "I should like to pay my respects to your sister, Miss Alcester. Would tomorrow afternoon be too forward of me?"

Lissa looked up at him. Her face was flushed with hope because at least one Alcester girl was to be blessed with a decent prospect. Perhaps their future wasn't so bleak after all. She gave him a brilliant smile. "Mr. Jones, you are welcome to call at Violet Croft anytime. Anytime."

CHAPTER TEN

❋

For the next few days Holland almost became a fixture at tea. Both girls quickly came to like having a man at Violet Croft. Evvie adored it for all the obvious reasons, and Lissa soon looked forward to it because the visits truly made her sister sparkle, and besides Holland Jones was rare indeed; he was a gentleman through and through.

But while prospects for the Alcesters' future were improving, the present was not. Every day the store of coins beneath Lissa's mattress dwindled further and she began to wonder how they would continue to put up a front of nonchalance in front of Holland. It wouldn't do to have Evvie's suitor see them so piteously without funds, for perhaps that would scare him off. And yet he would certainly see them in dire straits if Lissa didn't do something soon about their financial situation.

It was the absolute last resort to answer Powerscourt's advertisement, but she rationalized that once Holland asked Evvie to marry him, she would be able to quit her employment. She would work at Powerscourt only long enough to get through Evvie's betrothal, which she was positive would come eventually. She assured herself that Ivan was the typical master who would have nothing to do with the hiring and overseeing of servants. Once hired, she was sure she could stay clear of him within the labyrinth of servants' passages she knew to be hidden within the castle walls. Her only comfort was that she would be in the ironic position of having used Ivan as her final means of support. The man who had tried to ruin her would ultimately become the man who saved her.

However, she was wrong.

When she arrived at Powerscourt one morning after lying to Evvie about where she was headed, Lissa went directly to the servants' entrance and asked for the Mrs. Lofts mentioned in the advertisement. When the dour-faced housekeeper arrived at the door, Lissa had the distinct impression that the woman had been expecting her.

Her suspicion was confirmed when the housekeeper looked her up and down with disdain, then led her to a small, well-appointed withdrawing chamber. Alone, Lissa nervously took off her gloves and bonnet, then had to wait fifteen minutes before she was retrieved and led to the library. There the masculine scent of mahogany and leather made her beware.

"Ah good, you've finally come."

She turned her head and met Ivan's gaze. He sat fac-

ing her in the window seat looking absolutely devilish in a
waistcoat of wine-colored paisley. Behind him, a halo of
morning sunshine poured through the bays of mullioned
windows, each pane catching the light at a different angle
so that the entire sweep of window sparkled like pavé diamonds.

"Yes, I have," she answered coolly. "However, I can
see now it was a mistake, so if you will excuse me . . . ?"

"By all means." He rose and swept his hand in the
direction of the door.

She looked at him a moment, distrust blazing in her
eyes. Then she made to leave.

"The position pays one hundred pounds per annum."

His words stopped her. One hundred pounds! Even a
well-paid governess could expect no more than fifty! Her
brow furrowed. But she couldn't let him interfere with her
life any longer. He'd already caused her enough grief. She
took another determined step to the door.

"How much have you left, Lissa? I expect no more
than a few shillings."

"It is enough," she answered.

"Yet I say it is not enough or you would not be here."

She spun to face him. "How was I to know the master of the house would take such an *interest* in hiring servants?"

"You were bound to come. You've not had many alternatives," he said, his voice softening.

"I *had* alternatives," she accused.

"Hardly," he stated dryly as if remembering all too
clearly Wilmott and Albert. "Now come, be reasonable,
my love. You need income and I have a position—"

"No, thank you, my lord. The Alcesters have better
prospects—one of whom is coming to tea this afternoon.
So if you'll excuse me, I must run along."

"What perfumed parlor snake is calling now?"

"No one you need be concerned with." She was
hardly going to mention Holland's name. Besides, Mr.

Jones was courting her sister, but just let Ivan think it was she who had the prospect. She faced him, triumph, for once, shining in her eyes.

"Lissa, I'm through playing games," he said quietly.

"Who invited you to play them in the first place? Not I, I assure you."

"Ah, but it was you, my beautiful little ice princess." He walked around her, blocking her exit. "And looking at you now would dare any man to try melting you."

Feeling trapped with him standing between herself and the door, she moved past him. "I should like to continue this conversation. However, I'm afraid I'm late and I don't like to keep guests waiting." She gained a yard or so before he grabbed her arm.

"Always the frosty little paragon of good breeding, aren't you? Always looking down that slim nose at those beneath you." His eyes narrowed.

"I said excuse me." She wrenched her arm free. With anger reddening her cheeks, she headed once more for the door.

"One word of advice, Lissa." He released a cynical laugh, then bade her halt once more. She looked up at him, furious. "To secure marriage to a 'moneybags,' I suggest you not succumb to another man's lovemaking."

"I'll never again!" she whispered indignantly. She pulled herself out of his grasp then strode to the door. Suddenly he lunged for her. Terrorized, she ran from the room, his laughter following her all the way down the corridor. She left the castle not even bothering to collect her bonnet and gloves.

In the days that followed, Lissa surrendered her financial worries for the much more pleasant concern of playing chaperone. Holland had invited her and Evvie to his house for tea on Sunday, and Evvie was in a dither the entire week. When the day arrived, Lissa gladly dressed her sister's hair and gave her their mother's most precious earbobs to wear. Even though their financial situation was dire, Lissa hadn't been able to bring herself to sell them. Now she was glad she hadn't, for Evvie looked absolutely stunning with the emeralds sparkling through her mahogany curls.

At the appointed hour, a hired hack appeared at the door and they were taken in style to Holland's house, which sat on Powerscourt's grounds at the rear of the castle. As the driver helped them descend from the hack, Lissa had the oddest feeling that they were being watched. But when she looked at the castle, all was quiet. Her imagination led her to believe that perhaps she saw a man's silhouette through one of the windows, yet she had to tell herself it was nonsense. By now Ivan had to know it was his man Holland she had mentioned that day in his library, and he had to be just as well informed that it was Evvie, not herself, whom he was courting. So why did she still imagine she saw the lonely, dark figure in the window? And why did she suddenly feel this perverse longing to go to him and give him solace?

Holland met them on the lawn and quite chivalrously ushered them into the house. Once settled in Holland's parlor sipping a cup of Darjeeling, Lissa found herself wondering where the illustrious Marquis of Powerscourt spent his Sundays. Alone in his library or brooding over the billiards? And what were his thoughts? Was he longing for London? Or was he longing for her? Lissa's eyes clouded and she became a little more solemn. Evvie had to say her name twice before she even noticed.

They spent two pleasant hours receiving Holland's hospitality. When a note arrived informing Holland that he was needed at the castle, both girls were reluctant to say their farewells. Nonetheless, they reascended the hired carriage. With unspeakable relief, Lissa saw Holland slip the driver several coins, then they departed, leaving Holland alone to go to Powerscourt. Lissa was just grateful that she did not have to go with him.

Heading for Powerscourt, Holland was afforded no such luxury. He was already anxious about the message and knew Tramore had been in a foul mood the past several days. Having the Alcester girls at his house that afternoon had probably worsened Tramore's mood, and Holland didn't doubt that the marquis had been watching their every move until they had disappeared inside the bailiff's house.

"Yes, my lord. You wished to see me?" Holland bowed stiffly when he was finally in front of the marquis. Recently Tramore had taken to holing up in his billiard room, imbibing too heavily of the spirits.

"Sit down, old chap! Have a brandy." Ivan pushed a glass into Holland's hand. It was appallingly full.

"Really, my lord, I haven't the need . . ." Holland's words died on his lips. Instead of Tramore's looking like he would throttle him, the marquis looked as if a refusal would wound him to the quick. Holland resigned himself to taking a sip. The liquid slid like silk all the way down. He took another.

"Sit down, I insist." Tramore held out a plush leather chair that had mellowed to a perfect amber. Holland sat and the marquis took the chair across from him.

"Evelyn Grace. That's a beautiful name, is it not, Jones? So divine, so full of serenity." Suddenly Ivan looked morose. "So completely without guile."

"Yes, my lord." Damning them, Holland felt his hands shake.

"Are you going to marry her?"

The question hung in the air like a net ready to drop on its victim.

Holland coughed. "I . . . ah . . . well, perhaps in the future, my lord. When the moment is right." He tensed for the storm.

"Good. You'll make Evvie a fine husband."

Tramore stood up and patted Holland soundly on the back. The marquis beamed like a proud father, and suddenly Holland felt the need of another sip from his glass. He took a gulp instead. What the hell was going on?

"She's really beautiful, isn't she, Jones?"

Holland looked at him and thought the marquis seemed particularly tormented today. He asked gently, "Do you mean Evvie . . . or Lissa?"

"Evelyn," Tramore answered quickly. Too quickly. Suddenly he chuckled and walked to the table that held all the decanters. He picked one up and walked back to Holland. "Drink up, old man! We've never had a snort together, now why is that?"

Holland watched the marquis refill his glass. Already his head felt light; if he imbibed as the marquis thought he should he would be too drunk to leave for home.

"Is there something you requested, my lord?" Unable to stop, Holland downed more of the brandy. It was heady and smooth.

"Not at all!" Ivan placed his hands behind his back and looked upon Holland. "It's just that you've worked so hard. Is there anything wrong with a master repaying those who serve him with a little joviality?"

Holland felt like saying, From *you,* my lord, very much so, but he kept silent. Already he was feeling no pain.

"How do you find your quarters, Jones? Is the bailiff's house to your liking, or would you like it to be fixed up?"

"It's quite—" Holland couldn't finish for the marquis's interruption.

"As my estates man, it wouldn't look good to have you entertain guests in a shabby environment."

"No, my lord—" he tried to say.

"I'll give you five hundred pounds. That should do it. Then when the Alcester girls come to tea, you won't be able to say I don't provide well for my staff."

Already the flush of drink was appearing on Holland's

face. He was definitely having a hard time following the conversation. But damn, Tramore's brandy was fine! "Five hundred pounds seems a bit steep—"

"Of course, if you do have all that work done, I should like to look in from time to time." Tramore calmly looked at his knuckles. "When are they coming back?"

Holland shook his head. It was definitely hard to follow the marquis. "And who is that, my lord?"

"The Alcester girls."

Holland thought on this a moment. He then answered, "I thought I should have them back again . . . some future Sunday."

"I see. Well, I shouldn't like to look in at an inconvenient time . . ."

The marquis stared at him for the longest time. Holland didn't know what to make of it, until suddenly, through his liquor-fogged brain, he realized the marquis was fishing for an invitation. For some reason he wanted to come to tea when the Alcester girls were about. Holland wanted to laugh aloud, but even in his inebriated state he knew better.

"My lord, if you are thinking of refurbishing the bailiff's house, perhaps you might be about in a few weeks and I could repay you by having you to tea." Holland hid his smile behind his glass.

"Perhaps." The marquis once more donned his dispassionate veneer. "When do you have tea on Sundays?" he asked nonchalantly.

"Four o'clock," Holland answered, thinking to himself, As if you didn't know.

"I see. Billiards?" Tramore walked to the table and picked up a cue.

Holland rose a bit unsteadily. "Why not?" he answered.

By evening both men were rip-roaring drunk. Holland found out the marquis played a vicious game of billiards, but he was able to win a game or two anyway.

Finally unable to take much more indulgence, he made his excuses and staggered to the door. But before he could go, Tramore reminded him of his invitation.

"You say tea is at four?"

Holland couldn't believe how sober the marquis sounded. "Yes, my lord," he answered. Looking at Tramore who stood by the carved stone hearth, he noticed the scar glint in the firelight and was tempted to ask him once and for all how he had acquired it. But then, chastened, he remembered a story he'd heard when the marquis had suffered a wrench to his leg and a doctor had had to be summoned. The doctor had treated him, then in parting blithely asked Tramore how he had come to receive such a nasty scar on his face. Tramore nearly bit the doctor's head off, and Holland paled just imagining the fury that one question had unleashed.

"Perhaps someday I'll try to make it." The marquis leaned over the table and hit one of the white balls.

"Very good, my lord." Holland suddenly felt dismissed. He turned and stumbled through the passage to the great Hall, all the while thinking that Ivan Tramore, the eleventh Marquis of Powerscourt, was a very complex man.

CHAPTER ELEVEN

❀

Though it was late in the fall, Tuesday bloomed unseasonably clear and fair. Lissa had been about to do some marketing when Holland showed up with his phaeton and begged her and Evvie to go picnicking with him. Unable to refuse, they quickly gathered their shawls and bonnets and joined him. The horses trotted at a brisk pace and soon they were esconced on a plaid blanket, high upon a ridge overlooking the whole of Nodding Knoll.

"More wine?" Holland offered.

Evvie covered her glass and smiled sweetly at him. Lissa allowed Holland to refill hers, however, then she lifted her face to the sunshine. It was a day to be cherished, warm and delightful. She wanted to believe it was perfect, but she knew it lacked something, something she could not quite put her finger on. Yet when she watched Evvie smile so softly at Holland, she realized she wished she could also have someone special with whom she could enjoy the day.

"I'm going to climb the hill," Lissa said, getting to her feet. She refused Holland's offer to escort her, and alone, she wandered off, slowly climbing the hill that gave the town its name. When she got to the top, she looked at the valley below her that was inescapably dominated by Powerscourt. She gazed at the battlements and stood there for a long time, letting the wind blow her hair.

Having watched Lissa go, Holland commented to Evvie, "Your sister seems restless today. Is there a reason?"

"Unfortunately I think she is lonely." Evvie's brow furrowed. "Yet, I daresay Lissa would be the last to admit that."

"She ought to be married."

"Undoubtedly."

"Your sister could have gotten any man she wanted. She should have been wed long ago."

"Yes."

Holland looked at Evvie. She appeared a bit sad, so uninvited, he took her hand in his. His touch seemed to shock her.

"Has she never found a suitable man?" he asked gently.

"I'm afraid the only suitable man to come along has been you." Evvie tried to laugh, then she slowly pulled her hand from his.

"And is that what makes you so solemn now? You feel she should wed me?"

She self-consciously smoothed her skirt. "I don't know that she would have you, yet I . . ."

Holland chuckled and tweaked Evvie's cheek. "So, you think she would not want me, and yet, despite this, you feel some obligation to have me offer myself to her."

"Would it be such a chore?" Evvie laughed uncomfortably. "After all, Lissa is quite a beauty. Even I know that. She was beautiful at sixteen and she must be doubly so now."

"And so she is. But there are other things a man looks for in a wife besides beauty. Sweetness, for one. Gentleness. And Lissa Alcester with her passionate disposition is certainly not the girl for me." Holland took Evvie's hand once more. This time Evvie held on tight.

"Oh, but Holland, she is the oldest and for that reason alone should have a husband. But more than that, Lissa deserves some happiness. You wouldn't believe the sacrifices she has made for her family."

"On the contrary, I would believe it," he said, his expression turning grim.

Tearfully she exclaimed, "And I am the reason she is turning into a spinster. How can I stop it? What can I do?"

"Love, believe me, you are not the reason she's remained a spinster. Tramore is."

"Ivan? How I've longed wished—"

"Please don't be so optimistic," he interrupted. "The marquis is hardly a family man."

"He's shocking, I know. But I truly believe they were meant for each other. And he must carry some fondness for her. Tell me, Holland"—she pulled his hand closer—"what does Ivan look like when he looks at her? Describe him for me. I've pictured it a thousand times in my head, but you've actually seen it. What does his face look like? What is his expression?"

Holland drew back and thought about it for a moment. He seemed a bit reluctant to tell her. Haltingly he said, "He looks as if he could ravish her right where she stands."

Evvie inhaled sharply. She seemed to blush right down to her toes. Finally she managed to say "Well, he is certainly not the gentleman you are . . ."

Holland touched her cheek quite apologetically. "But, my love, how do you know I'm not looking at you that way this very moment?"

Evvie looked in his direction, shock in her eyes. But she had no time for another reply for Holland began kissing her tenderly on the lips.

Lissa returned from her walk a quarter of an hour later. When she arrived, she seemed to think Evvie looked a bit different. Her sister certainly seemed flustered. And Holland certainly seemed pleased. Lissa had her suspicions about what had gone on but she kept them to herself. It was none of her business, really. And with her as chaperone, she knew Evvie wouldn't get into trouble.

They packed up the wicker picnic basket and Holland took them home before George was due back from school. He kissed both ladies' hands, and Lissa found it amusing indeed to see how profusely Evvie blushed. Something had definitely gone on during her walk, and as it was much too early for a proposal, she guessed that Holland had kissed her sister.

When Holland left, Evvie settled down to do some knitting and Lissa fiddled with a needlework canvas. George appeared to be late from school and that always made her nervous.

She couldn't seem to concentrate on her handwork, so she picked up an old edition of *Les Modes Parisiennes*. As she flipped through the magazine, a breathtaking layout of a bridal trousseau caught her eye. It cost an astounding eight hundred pounds, but each delicate peignoir and pantalette was fashioned out of the sheerest Brussels point lace. Unable to stop herself, she reflected dreamily on what it would be like to own such a wardrobe. She pictured herself in each sheer garment and the thought almost made her blush. Then, unbidden, she pictured Ivan looking at her in them, and she did blush. Furiously. But next her eyes found the warning that came with the drawing: *Have these displays not their danger? Should a mother allow her daughter to see them?*

Dropping the magazine as if it were a hot poker, she fled upstairs and changed into an old cotton workdress. Then to get her mind off her wicked thoughts, she went to the kitchen to make their dinner. Of course, the first thing she did was drop a tin of flour. Doubling her task before she had begun it, she was forced to get the broom and sweep up the flour. Absorbed in her work, she didn't hear the loud knock at the front door. A moment later Evvie entered the kitchen, an unsure look on her face.

"We have a visitor."

Lissa looked up from the stone floor she'd been sweeping. "Who?" she asked.

Evvie laughed nervously. "I'll give you three guesses."

Lissa stood and wiped her cheek, leaving a smear of flour on one side of her nose. "Oh, please don't tell me it's the marquis."

"I'm afraid so. . . ."

Lissa looked at her threadbare gown. Yet why should her appearance matter? she silently berated herself. Ivan was nothing to her. Walking past Evvie toward the parlor, she realized that the sooner she confronted the beast, the quicker he would leave.

As usual, Ivan was impeccably dressed and scrupulously neat. Lissa was sure that she, on the other hand, looked like a hag, not worthy of a man's bow. With this thought burning in her breast, she practically snapped his head off when they were face to face.

"And to what do I owe the pleasure of this visit, my lord?" she said sarcastically all the while pushing back the loose strands of silvery-gold hair that escaped her chignon.

Ivan seemed taken aback by something, then he

stepped forward and brazenly ran his finger along her tiny nose. "Dust?" he inquired.

She slapped his hand down. "If you must know it's flour."

"Ah, I see." With an inscrutable expression on his face, he let his gaze wander down her figure. He seemed to enjoy her tattered state, and he particularly seemed to enjoy her bosom, which was heaving in repressed anger.

"If you've a liking for my gown I shall send it to the castle, my compliments," she told him tartly, daring him to continue staring.

His smile was lazy and irreverent. "Only if you come with it."

She wanted to scratch his eyes out. How positively infuriating he was! "Unfortunately I am not for sale."

"Really?" He raised one dark eyebrow mockingly. "I thought you were, as long as the gent offered marriage and could prove he was still breathing."

Anger reddened her cheeks. She ached to slap him but fought back the urge. Slowly she said, "I hate to be rude; however, I am terribly busy, so I'll come right to the point. Why have you come? You must know that a visit from you is hardly desirable in this household."

He looked at her a moment, his mouth twisted in wry amusement. "In your haste to flee the castle last week, you left a few of your belongings. I thought it my duty to return them."

She watched his gaze dart to the tea table. Lying there were her bonnet and gloves.

She hardly knew what to say. She thought he'd come to play some trick on her, to torment her using any flimsy excuse he could find. Yet here he'd come to return her bonnet, a bonnet that he knew all too well she couldn't afford to lose. As it was, she'd been making do with Evvie's old one, but the wretched thing was literally crumbling away it was so worn out. She'd known she would eventually have to go to Powerscourt and retrieve her own bonnet. Ivan could have easily used it to lure her to the castle, but he'd chivalrously brought them back to her, asking nothing in return.

Her gaze softened a bit. Perhaps she'd been too hard on him, perhaps she'd been too quick to think the worst of him. But then she recalled how *he* had been the one who had made her leave them there. Suddenly she turned angry all over again when she thought of their encounter in the castle. What had he said to her in parting? *Try not to succumb to another man's lovemaking?*

Suddenly he laughed as if he'd read her thoughts. "Don't be so mad at me, love. I would have given you time to retrieve your belongings. I didn't make you leave in such haste."

"You? You didn't make me!" She was too angry for words. She simply stood there and stared at him in mute dismay. The only interruption was the clank of the latch lifting on the cottage door. At first Lissa ignored it, knowing it was George finally returning from school. But she couldn't ignore it for long because Ivan's face turned grim and his eyes flashed with fury.

Lissa turned and practically swooned at Ivan's feet. George stood before her as quiet as a churchmouse, the entire side of his face covered with dried blood. Tears streamed silently down his cheeks and his lips seemed to be swollen beyond recognition. But this time he had obviously given as much as he got, for his knuckles were bloodied also.

"George!" she cried out, and ran to his side. She was relieved to see the blood on his face was only from a cut to his brow and not from his eye, but she was still horrified by his appearance.

George suddenly put his arms around her. He didn't even seem to mind that the marquis was in the room watching him. He was too young and obviously too hurt to put up a manly front now. Lissa comforted him, letting him cry into her apron. She took Ivan's proffered handkerchief and wiped away her brother's tears and, with it, some of the blood.

"What is it! What is it!" Frantic with worry, Evvie practically stumbled into the room. Ivan immediately went to her side and gave his hand for support.

"George has been in a fight. I think we need . . . ?" Lissa looked around wildly, unable to articulate what that was.

"Why don't you get the boy some tea, Evvie. I'll come with you and get some hot water and a compress."

Ivan spoke with calm authority, the same calm authority Lissa remembered he'd used whenever an Alcester Thoroughbred was cast in its stall or whenever a foal had cut up its legs on the paddock fencing. Evvie must have remembered it too for she looked up at him gratefully.

While they were in the kitchen, Lissa tried to calm George down, but his sobbing would not subside. Soon, however, she had a warm compress placed on his swollen eye, and that seemed to help a bit. She comforted him by wiping at his cuts and bruises and fingering the rents in his clothing, but she almost needed comforting herself. Never had she seen him in worse shape. The brawl must have been brutal. She couldn't fathom what could have started it this time. After a while George began to hiccough and she knew his tears would soon end. She smoothed his raggedy dark hair and led him to a seat so she could look at him.

"Now tell me what happened." Lissa sat next to him on the sofa. The spring in the cushion that had threatened to pop through for the past year suddenly did so right next to George, and for some reason he found it amusing. A slight, quivering smile came to his handsome little face, and Lissa could have hugged him at that moment. She refrained from doing so only because she knew if she did, they would have to pry him from her.

"So come now, tell me. The children will have to be

punished this time. You know it." She encouraged him
with a quivering smile of her own.

"It was Clayton and Johnny." George looked as if he
were bent on murder. She was surprised at his sudden
willingness to tell her who the culprits were, but it must
have been because he finally believed he had nothing to
lose. He felt hopeless, and now, knowing who had done
this to him, so did she.

Clayton and Johnny Baker were from one of the
wealthiest families of Nodding Knoll. The only reason
they even attended the town school was because they'd
both been kicked out of Eton one too many times. No
private teacher could be kept more than a week, so they
had finally been placed under the helpless hand of Miss
Musgrave and left to run wild whenever her back was
turned. Which was obviously much too often.

"Well, don't you give up, darling." She patted his
knee. "I shall have words with Sir Baker this evening. After
all, he's only a knight. And I daresay he must be account-
able for his offsprings' actions."

"No!" George suddenly became hysterical. "Don't
speak with them! Don't!"

"What is it?" She tried to assuage him, then looked at
Evvie for assistance, but Evvie was merely sitting next to
Ivan, shaking her head in helpless disbelief.

"Calm down, lad, and tell your sister why you don't
want her to talk to Sir Baker."

Lissa looked at Ivan as he spoke. For some reason it
comforted her to have him there. He seemed so strong,
especially when all around them havoc reigned. His presence seemed to comfort George as well for he stopped
ranting and hugged her close.

"Hush, my darling," she whispered as his sobs began
anew. She was having a difficult time not sobbing herself.
Her heart was breaking for her tormented little brother.
Feeling impotent to help him, tears welled up in her eyes.
She wiped them with the back of her hand.

"Don't go there, Lissa," George cried softly. "They're the ones who told Clayton about me. Sir Baker is the one who told him I was Mother's bastard."

Outrage jolted through her. She looked at George in shock, then her glance darted to Evvie's horrified visage, only to rest on Ivan's granite hard one.

As if the moment weren't painful enough, she couldn't remove her gaze from Ivan. Never had she seen his face so completely hard nor so completely vulnerable. Pain and rage swept over his features. Ivan was not the kind of man who ever showed emotion, and now when he did she found it difficult to look upon. Without a doubt, he was seeing George as if he were seeing himself at that tender age. Suddenly she felt as murderous as a caged lion.

She wiped her wet cheeks. "It's not true, do you hear me! *Do you hear me?*" She shook George to make him listen.

"Sir Baker says it is!"

"And I say it is not!"

"But how is anyone to prove it isn't?" George's surprisingly mature logic confounded her, but only for a moment.

"You don't have to prove it. You just tell them it's a lie. They're the ones who must prove this vicious rumor." She gave him one last hug and their tears mingled when she kissed him. "Besides, you won't be dealing with them again. You're going away to Eton. I won't allow my brother to look upon the Bakers ever again." She heard Evvie gasp, but Lissa would explain later. George would be going away to school; she saw that Ivan thoroughly agreed with her. She would have no problem getting him to pay; the only question was, what would he want in return?

"Truly?" George asked, wiping his cheeks.

Lissa felt unspeakably relieved to see how this comforted him. Suddenly she knew it would all be worth it.

"Truly," she whispered, then kissed his head. "Now,"

she said, taking a deep breath, "you must be hungry. Why don't you let Evvie make you something in the kitchen?"

"I suppose." He got up stiffly, and she knew it was going to take a week or so for all his cuts and bruises to heal. If only his emotional pain would heal so quickly. Bastard! she thought. The word alone made her burn. How could people be so cruel?

"Lissa, will you be all right?" Evvie asked pointedly when she had George in hand. With an anxious gesture, she tilted her head in the direction of Ivan. The marquis scowled as if somehow Evvie's sudden nervousness had irked him.

"I'll be fine, Evvie. However, I think the marquis and I need to discuss a few matters. You don't mind looking after George, do you?"

Evvie paused. Lissa knew exactly what she was thinking and her next words only confirmed it. "Lissa, perhaps we should discuss other alternatives?"

Like Holland Jones, Lissa silently finished for her. But that was out of the question. They couldn't scare Holland away with these burdens. It was one thing for a brother-in-law to pay for such weighty bills as an Eton education, it was another to ask a suitor. Once Holland married Evvie —if he married Evvie—then God save him. But until then, Lissa was determined not to put anything in his path that might chase him off.

"I think there are some scones left from dinner. Why don't you heat those up with some honey?" Lissa watched as Evvie frowned. She was evading her, but now was not the time to discuss it. Once she made her agreement with Ivan, then they could discuss it at length.

Sensing her sister's reasons, Evvie quietly led George from the parlor. Lissa stared after them as the two disappeared into the kitchen. Then she turned to Ivan. He was watching her, his hand stroking his chin as if he were deep in thought.

She wiped the tears from her face, then took another

deep breath. Quietly she began, "I remember that you once said George belonged at Eton."

"I did," he answered slowly.

"Then I shall do whatever is necessary to send him there. I shall cook for you or do your wash. I shall even make your bed if you like. But I beg you"—her voice lowered to a whisper—"don't make me earn it in your bed."

He stared at her for a long time. He seemed to be unable to tear his gaze away. He took in her homey, dusty, winsome appearance, and a longing briefly lit up his face. The look was certainly sparked by desire, but somehow his expression seemed to want something more, something deeper. But soon the fleeting look was gone and abruptly he got up from his seat.

Scowling, he said, "I have enough money to pay for one boy's schooling without forcing his sister into servitude. Good day, Miss Alcester. I shall arrange things and get back to you tomorrow." He walked to the pegs where his overcoat hung. Without hesitation, he donned it and made ready to leave.

"Ivan, wait." She touched his arm. He turned to face her, and she felt very small as she tipped her head back to look up at him. "I can't let you pay for George. You must know that. But I shall gladly take the position for which Powerscourt advertised. It hardly sounded like menial labor. Then, when Evvie is married, we shall be able to repay you completely. Please, can we make a bargain?"

"You bargain with me, love, you bargain with the devil."

She looked at him shocked. "But—but—can't you see? I won't let myself be indebted to you—"

He grabbed her arm. "You tempt me, Lissa. And I say leave it be. I have offered to pay for George without compensation. I suggest you leave it that way."

"But we can make a simple bargain."

"As if any bargain between you and me could be simple." Roughly he let go of her arm.

"It can be, if you'd just let it!"

He laughed. "All right. You pushed and I shall agree to take your offer. You shall have a position in my household—though nothing so low as housemaid. You may assist me with my letters and aid the housekeeper with her lists. For that, I shall keep to my promise of one hundred pounds per annum. So let me see . . . how many years will it take for you to pay all of George's bills? My God, I shudder to think."

"It shall not be more than half a year. Holland will pay you the rest when he marries Evvie."

"Holland's money be damned. It's all my money anyway and I won't accept it. Now, do we have a bargain?"

"Why must you be difficult?" she asked him in a panic. "You know I can't work at the castle indefinitely."

"And why can't you? Or do you look forward to your many years living as a fifth wheel with Evvie's family, and being known only as Mrs. Holland Jones's spinster sister?"

His cruelty brought tears to her eyes. "Of course not. And how kind of you to bring that up, she whispered."

"I'm being realistic. Now do we have a bargain?

"Yes, damn you, we have a bargain. But I shall not repay you working in your bed. Is that clear?"

"Perfectly."

A heated flush of relief rose to her cheeks. She hated to speak of such indelicate matters, but he'd forced her. At least now they were seeing eye to eye. "All right then, we have an agreement. Shall we shake hands on it? Do you give me your word as a gentleman?"

"I give you my word, yet because I'm not a gentleman, we will not seal this bargain with a handshake. Instead I should like a kiss."

"You are to act like a gentleman. It's part of the bargain."

"I shall act like a gentleman. To finalize this, *you* are to kiss *me*."

Apalled, she stared at him in disbelief.

"So now I ask you, do we still have an agreement?"

She took a moment before she answered him. "Yes," she said, "but what you ask is just what I told you I won't tolerate."

"One kiss. From you. Then I assure you, you may play the part of the consummate virgin, for I'm not in the habit of chasing the help around the furniture. Nor do I plan to be in the future."

"After this, no more?"

"I'll leave that up to you, love. So kiss me."

She paused and decided that what he asked was innocent enough. They were in her parlor, and Evvie was only a call away. He could never compromise her.

She stood on tiptoe and tried to kiss his lips, but he was utterly uncooperative. Without his bending his head, she couldn't reach his mouth, and so she was finally forced to put her arms around his neck and pull his head down to hers.

As close as he was, she could see the midnight color of his eyes, the way they sparkled with desire yet hid every other emotion brilliantly. The scar she hardly noticed, because it now seemed as much a part of him as his nose or his ears. She licked her lips before she kissed him, for her mouth had become unbearably dry. She was anxious to have this over with, and so she placed her mouth upon his and gave him a quick innocent kiss.

It was done in a second, yet still she was amazed at how disturbing his lips had felt. The inside of her belly seemed to melt, and her own lips tingled and quivered from a desire for more. But as unsettling as her reaction was, Ivan's was even more so. With her hands still wrapped around his neck, she thought she'd see passion on his face. Instead his expression was distant and cool. His eyes seemed to be daring her to go further, as if enticing her to break down his resistance. She didn't want to but the temptation was too much, and deep down she felt disappointed that he had not been affected by her kiss. If she was more truthful, she would have admitted that with his passion there was power. Now that it might no longer be hers, she was not about to let it go.

She pulled him to her for another kiss. Her lips moved across his in an artless seduction. Her fingers caressed the back of his neck. But still there was no response. Above her Ivan remained as cold and implacable as ever.

She kissed him again and instinctively she made this kiss wetter. Her lips hungrily sought his and her mouth grew more bold. Still there was nothing.

By the fourth kiss, she felt him stir. It was almost imperceptible, merely a light slackening of his jaw and a slight movement of his lips. So she kissed him a fifth time, hoping this one would bring forth a response.

It did. Unable to take any more of her teasing, his hands went to her face and he guided her lips ferociously to his. With his unleashing his desire, a fire lit inside her and she shuddered with delight. He was hers after all.

Her hand stroked the dark curls at the nape of his neck while their kiss grew deeper and more sensual. His tongue slid inside her but this time she wasn't shocked. Kissing Ivan this way seemed as natural as laughter and ever so much more pleasurable. She wanted it to go on forever.

Finally, as the bloom of their kiss faded away leaving them hot and breathless, Lissa closed her eyes and brought her cheek to rest upon his chest.

"It should always be like this," he whispered to her.

She looked up at him and he tenderly outlined her lips with his finger. Suddenly she felt like crying again, but for what reason, she didn't know. When he pulled from their embrace, heaved on his overcoat and walked out the door, she had to force herself not to stop him.

CHAPTER TWELVE

❦

Ivan had taken it upon himself to escort George to Eton College. When he returned from Buckinghamshire, Lissa was amazed at the deference given the assumed protegé of the Marquis of Powerscourt. In less than three days a post came from the Provost of Eton who wanted to personally assure them that George Alcester was not only well suited to be a colleger, but that he would most definitely be an asset to the intellectual, spiritual, and social community of the school. The Alcester girls were thrilled and, as if unable to believe their good fortune, Lissa read the letter aloud to Evvie every day for a week.

Meanwhile, an odd thing happened to Clayton and Johnny Baker. Their father, Sir Baker, had always been a flagrant spender, so it was no surprise that rumors soon had it he was becoming a candidate for debtor's prison. Yet surprisingly, Sir Baker's debts were paid off just in the nick of time. But then, instead of Sir Baker's resuming his previous lifestyle, he sold his estate to a mysterious buyer, put Clayton and Johnny in a wretchedly strict boarding school up north, and left town without a word. Needless to say, Lissa had been delighted to hear the Bakers had all left Nodding Knoll, but the entire episode smelled of the marquis. And he already had too much power.

Soon the cost of such luck came due and Lissa was summoned to Powerscourt by the housekeeper, Mrs. Lofts. Upon their second meeting the housekeeper's attitude toward her soared to the heights of unpleasantness, yet Lissa could not quite figure out why. Since there was no proper way to ask the tight-lipped woman about it, she could only keep her speculations to herself.

In the beginning Lissa found the work quite tolerable. She had been delighted when Mrs. Lofts informed her that the first rule of employment at Powerscourt was that she was never, ever to be seen by the master unless he specifically called for her presence. As she had guessed, within the castle walls there was an entire network of servants' passages and silent, baize-covered doors for use only by those who worked in the household. From the other servants, she had learned that Ivan was not so intolerable as some who would fire any servant unlucky enough to have been caught outside the tunnel when the master was about. However, Mrs. Lofts was. The housekeeper seemed pleased to inform Lissa in no uncertain terms that if the marquis saw even her skirts slide behind one of the baize doors and she was to find out about it, Lissa would be out on her heels that very same day.

Ironically it was hardly a week before Ivan caught her. Mrs. Lofts had asked her to bring to the scullery all the glass chimneys that needed cleaning in the drawing room. It was not the kind of task Lissa had thought she'd be performing, but she was not about to complain to Ivan, and most definitely not to the dour Mrs. Lofts. She had just lowered the gasolier when she looked up and found Ivan watching her from the conservatory. Nervously she searched the room for the servants' exit, but she couldn't recall where it was. So she took an uneasy step backward and made for the main passage.

"Where are you going?" Ivan's voice shot out from behind her.

Without turning, she said, "I must leave you alone."

"Come back here. Tell me about your duties with which I see Mrs. Lofts has you well encumbered."

"Ivan," she said, running up to him, "please don't tell her you saw me. If you did, she said she'd have me—"

"Yes, I know all about that. She's quite a witch, isn't she?" He sank into a nearby sofa.

"Well . . ." She looked at him, uncertain. She didn't want to appear ungrateful.

He only chuckled at her expression. "My sentiments exactly. What say we replace her?"

"We?"

"Of course. I shouldn't like to oust employees on my own account. Much better we both agree she's no good."

"But I couldn't have that on my conscience," she said. "Perhaps she has a family to support? Perhaps Mrs. Lofts has some sickly mother in need of care?"

"She is a spinster and at her age, I doubt sincerely she has any living parents. Besides, the woman hasn't posted a note in a century. How could she be sending her wages to anyone?"

"Then I suppose she isn't," she answered in a small voice. It unsettled her that a woman's entire livelihood depended on this man's whim. She had no love of Mrs. Lofts. On the contrary, that very morning she had seen the housekeeper viciously cuff one of the sculleries. The poor girl was so hurt, she'd left the kitchen in tears. Having watched the entire display, Lissa hadn't been able to contain her anger any more. She'd demanded to know what on earth could be so terrible that the housekeeper felt it necessary to strike young girls. It had been the wrong thing to say, indeed, for the imperious Mrs. Lofts exited without saying a word. Only later did Lissa find out from the butler that she'd been given the chore of polishing the silver. She'd been forced to do that all morning, and now her hands were blistered and raw.

But even so, she wanted to give the old woman the benefit of doubt. Perhaps Mrs. Lofts was simply having a bad time of it. That was no reason to dismiss a servant who'd obviously been doing good work for years.

"She adored my father, you know." Ivan's voice brought her out of her thoughts. She turned to him. With a slight smile, he said, "In fact, I think she was quite in love with him."

"Then you surely mustn't be so cruel as to throw her out on the streets."

"You mean you don't want me to? Is there a warm heart beneath all that ice and acrimony?" He looked at her in mock horror.

"She's been with your family a long time. I don't see any need for haste."

The speculation on his face deepened. "She hates me. So tell me, Lissa, how does one go about tolerating a servant so vile?"

"She seems nothing but dutiful to me. How can you say such things?"

"Because it's in her eyes. And because she spent so much time with my father."

Her eyes met his. There was something she wanted to say, but she had difficulty forming the words. "Your father —Ivan—you must forget him—he's like a poison."

She half expected a rage to follow, but none did. Ivan grew solemn, then gave her a dark, distrustful look. After that, he promptly changed the subject.

"Here, let me look at you in that silly frumpish garb." He motioned with his head. "Go ahead, turn around so I can see all of it."

Haltingly she turned for him. She felt foolish doing so, but anything was better than tempting his ire. When she faced him once more, she was blushing.

"Fetching, fetching indeed," he murmured as he looked at her black dress. She hated the silk twill gown, for its color made her dreadfully pale. The only relief to the uniform's severity was the pristine white collar and cuffs, and the little white cap of ribbons that fell down her back like a wedding veil, but it wasn't enough to put color in her cheeks nor a spark to her eyes. It seemed only he could do that, and he always did it brilliantly.

"Lissa, come sit here beside me and tell me of your duties."

She glanced at him uneasily. "I really cannot. Mrs. Lofts will not like it."

"What are we, two truant children hiding from their

nanny? Damn the woman! Come and sit beside me." Suddenly he grabbed her hand and pulled her down to the sofa, yet her hand was still blistered from all the polishing and she winced.

"What is this?" he asked as he pulled open her palm. He scrutinized its raw appearance, then, as if in apology, he kissed its center. The burn of his lips made her pull back, but her palm curled into itself anyway as if to hold the pleasure of his touch.

"No, Ivan, don't," she said as he tried to take it again. He turned angry, but for once his anger was not directed toward her.

"Where did you acquire such blisters?" he demanded. "My household or yours?"

"Mine," she lied.

"And how did you get them?"

"I—I was polishing some of my mother's silver." That was closer to the truth, and she at once felt much more comfortable.

"Your mother must have left you a fortune in silver then, considering the condition of your hands." He suddenly tried to grab one again, but this time she anticipated it and stood up. Before he could rise from the sofa she was halfway across the room. He seemed to think her a coquette for suddenly he laughed, but she only tensed. Behind her in the passage she could hear footsteps. The thought that they might belong to Mrs. Lofts sent a chill down her spine.

As if he'd read her thoughts, he said, "She's not your employer, I am. You need answer only to me."

Her worried azure gaze darted to the door. But how very miserable Mrs. Lofts could make her life in Ivan's absence. With that thought, she searched for the servants' exit. She found the baize-covered door and opened it silently. It closed just the same way.

At her swift departure, Ivan's expression darkened. A gleam lit his eyes when he caught a last fleeting glimpse of

her ankle surrounded by the confection of petticoat ruf-
fles. He was sufficiently tantalized to pursue her but just as
he stepped toward the door, Mrs. Lofts entered the drawing room.

"You have a visitor, my lord," she announced in her
perfunctory manner. Seeing the gasolier down, she duti-
fully went to raise it.

"Who is it?" he asked, an annoyed expression on his
face.

"She says her name is Mrs. Kovel. Mrs. Antonia
Kovel. She said you would know who she was."

Suddenly the annoyance left Ivan's face and it was
replaced with bemusement. "Send her in," he said, then as
an afterthought added, "And make us some luncheon, will
you? Just bring it in here."

"Will that be all, my lord?" Mrs. Lofts inquired, the
slightest hint of a smirk on her face as she used his title.

"Yes, that will be all." His eyes narrowed as if he'd
caught her disdain. "For now."

"Very good, my lord."

When Antonia Kovel entered the room, Ivan was gazing out the great expanse of windows that overlooked the
South Lawn. His hands were clasped behind his back and
his feet were apart; he looked like a captain viewing his
fleet. Seeing him, the beautiful black-haired woman smiled
softly. Her green eyes sparkled with emotion. They
seemed glazed by tears of sadness and delight. She picked
up the skirts of her black velvet riding habit and walked
into the room.

"Ivan. I'm here," she whispered.

Immediately he turned around. Antonia giggled like a
girl, though it was clear by the etching of lines on her
lovely face she hadn't seen girlhood in at least twenty
years. His arms went out and she rushed into them.

"How grand you've become, Ivan, I hardly recognize
you." She brushed a fallen tear from her cheek, then gig-

gled again. "Oh, old Powerscourt must be turning in his grave with you roaming these halls."

"He's beginning to accept it, I think. I haven't seen his specter here since two weeks past."

Antonia started, then softly slapped his chest. "You rogue, to trick an old woman." She looked up at him fully and for the first time noticed his scar. She raised her hand to stroke it, but then, for some reason, thought better of it. With her hand back at her side, she said, "So I see the past seven years have not been completely kind."

He ruefully touched the scar. "I'm beginning to think it's not the past I should be worried about."

"As well you should not," she agreed. She broke from him and sauntered around the drawing room. Her hand caressed the cream satin tufting on a ladies' chair, then she swept across to the conservatory entrance to give the jungle of glass and fragrant greenery an appreciative inspection. When she'd seen enough, she went back to his side and said, "Your Powerscourt is magnificent, Ivan. It's everything you could have wanted."

"Not everything," he stated enigmatically.

"Ah, of course." She smiled a secret smile. "There is a certain blonde, I understand, who, despite her hardships, has grown into an exquisite young woman. Am I close?"

"Perhaps." He seemed anxious to change the subject. "You look exquisite yourself, Antonia. You haven't changed a bit."

She threw back her shoulders proudly. "But I have! I've aged seven years and I don't mind telling you I look every bit of it!"

"Has it been that long?"

"Yes, indeed. You forget, my darling, it wasn't because of me you left town. Your interest in Nodding Knoll's reclusive Widow Antonia waned years before that."

He patted her velvet-clad bottom affectionately. "My interest in a beautiful woman never wanes."

She tried not to smile but she couldn't help herself.

"You shameless flatterer. But you must know, lover, some men are not so young and handsome as you, and when they tell me I'm beautiful, I believe it."

He chuckled. "Kovel?"

"After five years of marriage, he still thinks me quite a prize. Imagine."

"You are quite a prize." He caressed her cheek. "You know I would have married you."

"You never would have." She tweaked his cravat.

"You were my first, Antonia. I was completely besotted."

She smiled and her face took on a bittersweet expression. "I couldn't have been your first. You taught me more than I could have ever taught you."

"I was only seventeen. Quite callow."

"Pooh. You were born old, Ivan. You were never seventeen. And you were never callow. I vividly remember that day when I first saw you in the stableyard. You brought me that stallion I'd bought from Alcester. That very moment when I first glanced at you I thought you were a man. Later that evening in the stables when I went to check on how you were doing with the stallion, I can remember all too well how you proved to me you were."

Ivan's mouth twisted in a wry grin. "I still hold to the theory that it was you who corrupted me."

Antonia laughed. "Well, it must be true—because look at you! You're a confirmed rake and hellbent on staying that way I hear. What have I done?"

"You could have reformed me while there was still a chance."

"You know as well as I do we could have never married. People would have called you all sorts of nasty names, 'fortune hunter' to begin with. And you would have never been faithful. Not once Lissa Alcester shed her adolescence."

He didn't seem to know how to respond to that remark. The relief on his face seemed extraordinary when

Mrs. Lofts suddenly entered the drawing room with the tea cart.

"Refreshments?" Antonia shot Ivan a coquettish look, then she walked over to the cart, looking over the meats and cakes and scones.

"I take it it was a long ride from Cullenbury?" he stated dryly, dismissing the housekeeper with a nod.

Antonia looked up, a petit-four already in her mouth. Her eyes crinkled with laughter. She swallowed and said, "It was. Dreadfully long. But I just woke up this morning and said to Kovel, 'Ivan is back. I must ride out to Nodding Knoll today and see him.' "

"Kovel is a generous husband to let his wife ride across the countryside to see her old lover."

"Kovel is a dear who has nothing to be jealous of. He makes me laugh, Ivan, and that will see me into my dotage. I am happy at last."

"I know. I see it."

Antonia's eyes locked with his. There was a sadness between them and she seemed unable to bear it. Finally she said softly, "You must find your happiness too, Ivan. I couldn't find it in castles, and riches, and supple younger lovers, nor will you."

"I know that."

She filled his plate to overflowing. When she handed it to him she said, "Then you, my love, are a very wise man." She kissed him briefly on the lips and went back to pour out their tea.

They sat in the drawing room for hours, reminiscing about days long past. When Antonia was ready to leave it was near twilight, and Ivan insisted she take his coach back to Cullenbury. Their parting was bittersweet for though they were no longer lovers, they each seemed to find a deep satisfaction in their friendship. Ivan promised to call on her and her husband soon and, with that, he said his farewells. He watched the carriage wind down the castle road, then he returned to the drawing room deep in thought.

Lissa had just brought Mrs. Lofts her evening linens when she spied the carriage pull away from the castle. She was in the servants' north stairwell, and it was so cold in there that her breath came in little white puffs. But she stopped midflight, nonetheless, to look out the little window at the departing carriage.

Assuming Ivan had gone out for the evening, she was eager to get to the drawing room and finish cleaning the chimneys. She'd spent the entire day performing the worst kind of drudgery and longed for it to end. After she'd fled the drawing room, Mrs. Lofts instructed her to go to the pantry and finish her polishing. Thinking she'd had that task completed, Lissa had gone to the pantry only to find even more tarnished hollowware stacked on the table as if put there by a sorcerer's apprentice. She'd spent the rest of the day huddled in the pantry while all around her the house had buzzed with news of a visitor. Now, at dusk, Lissa had thought she was finally through, only to realize she hadn't finished in the drawing room.

Walking at a brisk pace, sure she'd be done in less than a half hour, she burst into the drawing room from the baize door and, in her haste, didn't see the two feet that were stretched out in her path. To her surprise, she tripped and fell right into the arms of the marquis, who was sitting in the chair next to the servants' door. She was so shocked to find him there, it took her a moment or two before she could even struggle to a sitting position.

"But—but I thought you'd gone out," she said incredulously, looking at Ivan as if he were a ghost. "I saw your carriage leave—"

"I lent my carriage to a friend." His hand swept the ribbons that ran down her back as if they were her tresses. All at once she remembered where she was. She looked down at his lap, then tried to get up. But he only pulled her back down and held her there. "What are you still doing here? Night has fallen."

"I never finished—" Her frustrated gaze flitted to the gasolier. She squirmed and tried again to get off his lap. But this only seemed to flame the desire she already saw sparking in his eyes.

"You are not to perform such tasks. I hired you for more gentle duties. Besides, you should be home. What is Evvie to do without you?" His knuckles lazily caressed her cheek. His touch startled her. He was looking at her strangely. There was tenderness in his eyes, which she had never seen before, and she was not sure she trusted it.

"Evvie knows how to make supper. But I'm not supposed to be in here while you are, so I should be off—" Again she tried to rise.

"That's ridiculous," he said testily, locking his arms around her. "As ridiculous as your playing servant . . . and me playing lord."

Sensing his mercurial mood, she trod carefully. "But you are lord here, Ivan. And I am a servant. So I beg you to quit treating me like a barmaid. We're not play-acting."

"No? I thought riches and fine clothing do not make a lord. Your words, if I recall."

He smiled and ran his thumb over her lower lip.

Uneasily she grasped his hand and placed it at his side. "Your sending George to Eton is a lordly thing to do. But—this—is—not."

He peered at her through heavy-lidded eyes. Abruptly he changed the subject. "You should be home. Why aren't you readying to leave?"

Released, she clambered off his lap and got to her feet. "I shall then, since you're so anxious to be rid of me." She had had a terrible day and she was in no mood to deal with Ivan's maddening temperament. If Mrs. Lofts reprimanded her in the morning for not getting her work done, then so be it.

"Get your mantle and bring it back here. Since it's dark, I shall see you home." He stood and held open the baize door for her.

"I don't think Mrs. Lofts would approve," she said, taken aback by his offer. He was definitely hard to predict this evening. She wondered who had come to visit this afternoon to put him in such a strange and introspective mood.

"Go get your things. Mrs. Lofts will be overjoyed. Believe me." He smiled at her then, and it was the old Ivan smile—wicked and brilliant. Mrs. Lofts was surely in for trouble now.

"I see" was all she said before leaving the drawing room. In the chilly passage, she looked back once. He was staring at her. He smiled again and she smiled back uncertainly.

There was something in his look that made her quiver inside. For some reason, walking home with him in the dark seemed terribly foolish. Right then, she decided to gather her mantle and purse and sneak home alone through the servants' door.

CHAPTER THIRTEEN

❦

The next day Lissa barely had time to hang up her printed Norwich shawl before Mrs. Lofts informed her the marquis would see her right away. As she was led to the Baronial Hall where, apparently, Ivan liked to have his breakfast, she overheard several servants whispering about the marquis's foul temper. No one seemed to know the reason for it, but nonetheless, Lissa had noticed when she'd first arrived at the castle that everyone hopped whenever the bells rang over the kitchen staircase. Today no one dared keep the master waiting.

So it was with some trepidation that she entered the Hall and found Ivan sitting before one of the enormous limestone hearths. Mrs. Lofts discreetly returned to the kitchens and, before she knew it, Lissa was left alone to face the lion in his den.

"My lord?" she began, and watched him raise his head from his breakfast. Though he never faced her, she could see he was angry. She didn't doubt that she was the cause of it.

He placed his elbows on the table and joined his fingertips. Still not looking at her, he demanded, "Why did you leave?"

"Leave?" She hesitated. "You mean last evening."

"Of course I mean last evening."

She stared at him. He still refused to look at her, but what could she say? That his unusual friendliness that evening had made her uneasy? That his smile had told her to beware? That she was more afraid of him like that than even now when he looked as ferocious as a lion? She frowned and tried to reason with him. "It's hardly your place to see the servants escorted home—"

He flung down his napkin and stood. Finally he faced her. "You will never do that again!"

"I can see myself home."

"Never after nightfall! What if something had happened to you! What if you'd come across some ruffians?"

She giggled despite the tension in the air—or perhaps because of it. "Ivan, this is Nodding Knoll. There are no ruffians here. And Violet Croft is hardly a half mile away from the castle."

"If you ever do that again I'll see your brother extracted from that school so fast your head will spin, do you understand me?"

Now this was serious business indeed. How dare he blackmail her by threatening to jeopardize George! Stiffly she said, "Some nights I must surely stay late and you cannot take it upon yourself to see me home. It's not proper."

The master of every situation, he calmly sat back down to his breakfast as if the conversation were over, at least her part of it. His every motion infuriated her—from the way he replaced his napkin on his lap to the way he gazed away from her. He took a bite of ham and stated imperiously, "From now on, no matter when you leave, you will be escorted home by my stablemaster, John Dover. He is an elderly man and I have great confidence that you will be safe in his company. I also must tell you that I've instructed him to escort you here in the mornings, so I'd advise you not to leave your little cottage until you hear his knock on the door." He took another bite of ham and summarily dismissed her. "That is all. You may leave."

She was so taken aback she could hardly summon a retort. His thinking that she needed an escort was ludicrous. There had to be twenty women who came and went alone from Powerscourt to Nodding Knoll on any given day. He was being utterly irrational, which made her want to behave in an equally irrational manner. It was completely unlike her, but suddenly she had the urge to stick out her tongue at his unyielding profile.

"I said that will be all." He didn't look up from his meal.

"Yes, your majesty," she said sarcastically before leaving.

Her duties that day were much lighter. For some reason Mrs. Lofts seemed to be avoiding her. The tasks the housekeeper gave her were easily accomplished, and at one point she was left in the servants' hall with nothing to do. It was then that Mrs. Lofts entered the hall and found her seated on one of the pine benches. Lissa was sure she would give her a lecture on the slothfulness of servants, or even try to box her ears as the severe elderly woman was wont to do with the kitchen wenches. But to the contrary, the housekeeper merely gave her a baleful glance and kept going. Lissa jumped to her feet, but by that time Mrs. Lofts was gone.

As evening came, Lissa was ready to leave. If anything, her new position was now turning into torture by boredom. Just when she had donned her mantle, however, a surprise came her way. An elegant older man appeared at the kitchen door and introduced himself as John Dover. The slim, white-haired gent promptly gave his arm to her, and he walked her back to Violet Croft, exchanging pleasantries the entire way. Lissa was so taken by the charming stablemaster that she found it hard to begrudge Ivan's overbearing protectiveness any longer. When she left Mr. Dover at the door of her cottage, she was actually looking forward to the morning walk, if not the morning duties.

She entered Violet Croft in a lighthearted mood. She tossed her paisley shawl upon the pegs and sauntered into the parlor. To her astonishment, Evvie sat in the middle of the floor, surrounded by gold-embossed boxes. Boxes were everywhere: on the blue sofa, scattered across the mantel, even piled on the little scratched rectory table. Practically dumbstruck, Lissa could only stutter, "W-what on earth?"

"I'm so glad you're home. I really don't know what to make of it!" Evvie stood shakily and cleared a path to her sister. She went to their lace-covered drum table and handed Lissa a note.

Lissa took the note and broke the seal. It was from London. She read aloud the only words written on the creamy vellum. They were: AUNT SOPHIE'S LAST BEQUEST.

"Is that what all this is?" Evvie questioned.

"I suppose so," Lissa mused, walking around a particularly large gilt box. Her name, *Elizabeth Victorine,* was handwritten on one corner. Heavily embossed on its top was another name: CHARLES FREDERICK WORTH.

"What's inside?"

"I guess we'll have to open it to find out." Lissa lifted

the heavy cardboard lid. Her eyes widened and a gasp involuntarily left her mouth.

"Oh, Lissa, I can't wait a moment more! Tell me!"

"It's a gown. The most beautiful gown I've ever seen." She lifted the heavy satin dress from the box.

Evvie reached out and caressed the costly fabric. "What color?"

Lissa pulled the gown to her chest and looked down. She could hardly believe her eyes. "It's the deepest rose—a most beautiful dusky hue. There's darker rose *passementerie* all over it, in a honeysuckle pattern." As she stroked the silken gown, her hand felt as if it were gliding over angel's wings. She fingered the low neckline that dipped *à la grecque* and the short sleeves that were adorned with tiny, flirtatious satin bows. The gown was exquisite. Surely the most beautiful she'd ever seen.

"Is there another one?" Evvie asked, perhaps a bit forlornly.

Lissa looked up and smiled. She said, "You goose! There must be! You can't believe all the boxes!" She laid the rose satin gown over the back of an armchair. She then attacked the other boxes with a vengeance.

In some were dozens of pairs of white silk hose, embroidered handkerchiefs, and kidskin gloves. In others, she found two well-molded Parisian corsets, several corset covers of Honiton lace, and six of the sheerest chemises made of dotted Swiss muslin. When there were still two boxes left, Lissa picked the largest—the one with *Evelyn Grace* written on the corner.

In it was Evvie's gown, and if could be so, it was equally exquisite as Lissa's. Made of a most lustrous midnight-blue silk velvet, the gown was corded around the hemline in a Greek key pattern, and Valenciennes lace teased at the low neckline. Her sister would look positively breathtaking, and already Lissa could picture Holland's expression when he first saw her in it.

"Is it beautiful?" Evvie whispered.

Lissa laughed, feeling like a fairy-tale princess. She tossed the unbelievably heavy gown to her sister. Evvie barely caught it, then, surrounded by the rich velvet, she began laughing too.

"It is true," she exclaimed in a hushed voice.

"It must be." Lissa reverently stroked the rose satin thrown over the chair. Her eyes then wandered to the waning hearth. She meant to get some more peat, but then her gaze found the last box, still unopened on the mantel.

"One more, Evvie. Is it for you or for me?"

"For you! I insist!" Evvie could hardly take her hands from the velvet to wave her on.

Lissa smiled and retrieved the heavy satin-covered box. The names *Bronwyn and Schloss* were gilded discreetly on the top. She eagerly opened it, thinking it to be a pair of slippers or perhaps a beaded purse.

She couldn't have been more wrong. Her gasp brought Evvie to her side.

"What is it? It must be something outstanding."

"Evvie, it's the most dazzling thing—" Lissa extracted a snood from its nest of black taffeta. Woven of silver satin cords, it was strewn all over with a thousand shining glass crystals. The hairpiece cascaded over her hand like falling ice; even the meager firelight couldn't dim its brilliance.

She could hardly describe it to Evvie, but when she did her best, Evvie giggled and said, "Oh, wouldn't it be wonderful if those crystals weren't crystals at all—but diamonds!"

Lissa looked at the magnificent snood as it sparkled, brilliant and fiery. She laughed too. "We'd be rich as pirates if these crystals were real!"

They laughed again at the absurd thought until Evvie finally sobered. "But how wonderful it would be, Lissa, to have all our troubles over. If the crystals were real we could pay back Ivan and then you wouldn't have to go to the castle any more, and we could move—to London, even!"

"And we could fly if we had wings, but what's the sense of these imaginings?" Lissa quietly put the snood back into its box.

"We'll have to sell the gowns, won't we?"

A heavy silence fell between them. It was a tragedy to think that they would have to part with either of the dresses, but the gowns had arrived at a most opportune time. Their savings were almost gone, and Lissa knew all too well that her salary from Powerscourt was far below the cost of George's schooling. Not a shilling of her income would find its way to Violet Croft. Yet as she thought all of this, Lissa watched Evvie turn back to her blue velvet ballgown and lovingly stroke its nap.

"Nonsense," she finally whispered. Seeing Evvie so happy, she was only more determined that her sister should keep her gown. If any dress should be sold it should be the rose one. She had no place to wear it anyway, not like Evvie, who, God willing, would soon have a husband to please. The blue velvet would be her only dowry.

She turned to the rose satin and began repacking it in the Worth-imprinted box. If any gown was expendable it was this one. After all, she told herself guiltily, meeting her sister's sightless gaze, how would Evvie ever know she didn't have it any more?

She would go to Cullenbury on Saturday, Lissa thought the next morning when she was in the Powerscourt kitchens. Cullenbury was the next largest town, and she was pretty certain that she could sell the rose ballgown there at a nice price. Besides, few people in Cullenbury knew her, and she would be far less conspicuous than if she went to Nodding Knoll's dressmaker.

With that on her mind, she hardly thought about the

task in front of her. As she stared ahead, musing on what price the gown would command, her pen fell idle. When she next looked down, her list was ruined by a huge ink puddle. She hastily crumpled the paper and started again.

Today all Mrs. Lofts had instructed her to do was recopy a list of things the footman was to get on his trip to London. There was nothing interesting on the list other than a casket of hatpins from Brandreth's Emporium which Alec, one of the stableboys, had requested. It was, no doubt, a gift to one of the housemaids. Lissa thought the girl's name was Edith, but it could have been Edna. Powerscourt did have over fifty servants, after all. She shrugged and turned her attention to the clean sheet of paper.

"The marquis has gone out for the day." Mrs. Lofts suddenly appeared in front of her, her hands clasped, her lips taut.

Lissa swept the white ribbons of her headpiece off her shoulder and looked up at her.

Mrs. Lofts continued. "You shall go to the Hall and dust."

"I see." Lissa stood.

"And when you're through there, I want you to dust in the morning room too."

"Of course."

With her reply, the housekeeper gave her a covert look, one to which Lissa was becoming accustomed. She wondered why Mrs. Lofts hated her so, yet somehow she thought it had something to do with the fact that her duties had been so light. Ivan had obviously spoken to the woman. Perhaps she ought to tell him she should not be treated deferentially at the castle. It obviously did not sit well with the other servants.

"I also want you to dust the drawing room, the chapel, the billiard room, the library, the dining room, the steward's room, and my room. And when you're through, I'm sure I can find some other things to keep

you occupied. That is, if you finish tonight," Mrs. Lofts
added with a vile look on her face.

The housekeeper seemed immensely pleased with Lissa's shocked expression, for she didn't even wait for the
younger woman to acknowledge her orders. Mrs. Lofts
handed her a stack of clean linens, then left the pantry.
Lissa watched her go, too stunned to comment.

The first three rooms took all of seven hours. Mrs.
Lofts came in to check on her every thirty minutes and was
quick to point out a vase or a chair left undone. If there
was nothing to criticize, Mrs. Lofts then took the position
that everything in the entire room needed another dust-
ing. It was cumbersome work and, Lissa found herself
growing weary quickly. It didn't hearten her that she still
had six more rooms to go.

But thoughts of quitting weren't even a consider-
ation. She wanted to get along with Mrs. Lofts, for surely
her work would only become more miserable if she didn't.
And she didn't want Ivan interfering on her behalf because
she had gotten into this position with her eyes open. The
servants at Alcester worked equally as hard. She would
endure the situation with as much dignity as they did.

And so the day progressed. John Dover came to escort her home at one point, and though he quite bedev-
iled her when he insisted he was to take her home at five,
he finally went away, promising to return every hour until
she was through.

She surmised that Ivan had still not returned to the
castle, and she was determined to finish everything before
he did. But when Mrs. Lofts reinspected the dining room
for the fourth time, Lissa grew impatient. She swore she
would outlast the stern housekeeper. Yet her resolve was
sorely tested when she was told to redust the mantel for
the fifth time.

Nonetheless, she vowed to endure. Grimly she made
for the mantel with the feather duster. There was a lot to
clean. Not only did she have to remove all the Stafford-

shire figurines, she also had to take off the mantel lambre-
quin and shake it. Yet she would do it again, if only to
prove to Mrs. Lofts that she was not going to fold. She
picked up the first piece, a tobacco jar in the shape of a
dog's head, and went to put it on the dining table. But
because she was growing tired, or simply because her mind
was not on her work, the jar slipped from her grasp and
shattered on the tile hearth.

As if she'd expected such a mishap, Mrs. Lofts was at
her side in a second. Lissa felt the vicious cuff on her cheek
before she saw it coming. After the attack, all she could do
was hold her damaged cheek and stare at the housekeeper
in disbelief.

But indignation and anger soon swelled in her breast.
How dare this woman strike her! She was Elizabeth
Victorine Alcester; she was a lady and she was not to be
slapped about like some street urchin. All her instincts
came into play at once. She raised her hand in retaliation,
but all at once the housekeeper froze. Mrs. Lofts wasn't
even looking at her; she was staring at something behind
Lissa's shoulder.

Horrified, Lissa dropped her hand and turned
around. Ivan was standing in the doorway to the dining
room, and it was obvious he had witnessed the entire episode because he looked furious. A hint of dark amusement
was also on his face, and Lissa wondered if it hadn't been
caused by the shameless slap she herself had been about to
dole out. Suddenly she hated herself as she had never done
before. Ivan had seen the entire, horrid display.

"My lord," Mrs. Lofts acknowledged, her face burning with suppressed anger and resentment.

Ivan didn't even respond to the woman. He merely
gave her a deadly stare and raised one of his jet eyebrows as
if in surprise that she still dared stand before him.

Mrs. Lofts didn't dare long, for quickly she disappeared behind the baize-covered door that led to the

kitchen passage. Lissa longed to do the same, yet Ivan stopped her with a word.

"Halt."

With that, she didn't move. Ivan walked around her, examining her as if she were something to be skinned and weighed at the butcher. She found it hard to meet his eyes.

"What are you still doing here?" he asked.

"I had duties to perform," she said defiantly. For some reason, his imperious tone raised her ire to new heights—at Mrs. Lofts for being so cruel and forcing her into unseemly behavior; at Ivan for being such an ungodly arrogant beast; and finally at her parents, for having died and left her to fend for the family in the first place.

Ivan touched her reddened cheek.

"Don't," she told him, and turned away.

"You're hurt," he said.

"I'm not," she refuted. Quietly she stooped to pick up the pieces of the shattered Staffordshire dog. She didn't want him to see her like this. She felt as shattered as the jar. Her hands shook deplorably.

"Lissa—"

"No, don't. Don't say a thing." She scowled. "I take the blame for all this."

Suddenly she was brought to her feet by two strong hands. Forcibly he made her release the shards. She heard the pieces of Staffordshire again fall on the hearth. "No one has the right to strike you."

"Except you, perhaps?" She laughed, but her laughter soon turned into a sob.

"You're overwrought. Let me take you home."

"No!" She pulled from his grasp. Again she tried to clean up the broken porcelain.

He looked at her, frustration darkening his eyes. "Quit being a pig-headed child, Lissa. Do you hear?"

"I hear," she answered. "But you more than anyone know what a pig-headed child I am, and I told you that I would pay for George's education. I'll not be indebted to you, and I meant it, every word. If Mrs. Lofts tells me to dust, then I shall dust." How could she have tried to slap Mrs. Lofts? The very thought made her shrink back in horror. Yet worse, how could she have let Ivan see that? She brushed a tear from her cheek. Then she swore to kill herself before she'd let him see her cry.

"You want to earn your pay, baggage?" He again pulled her to her feet. "Then I'll see that you do. From now on you'll report to me and only me. I'll keep you well occupied."

Her eyes opened wide. "No doubt you will. But we had an agreement."

"That you should get such delicate treatment from me!" He pulled her over to the dining table. He grabbed a klismos-shaped dining chair, sat, and stretched out his long legs. Without even looking at her, he said, "Remove my boots, wench."

She gasped, completely taken aback.

"I said, get down on your knees, Lissa, and remove my boots."

"*You,*" she spat, "are a monster."

He laughed and said mockingly, "No, not me! You jest, Your Highness!"

Now both her cheeks were equally red. Refusing to continue this inane conversation, she meant to turn and walk away. But this was hard to do when he held two fistfuls of her black silk skirt.

"Come back here, servant. You want to play peasant and king, so be it." A smile tipped one corner of his lips. "Take off my boots."

He had pulled her so close that she could feel his breath on her face. She gave him a most glittering stare and they stayed there for several moments, locked in a silent battle of wills.

Second by second, he seemed to move closer. She knew if she just closed her eyes, they would meet in a kiss

—a kiss that she secretly longed for, indeed bitterly ached for. Yet she couldn't let it happen. If she did, she might never be able to stop. She was truly Rebecca Alcester's daughter, for the path to wantonness seemed to beckon her at every turn. Her fear alone that she would reach the same end as her mother if she didn't keep this ravenous desire well leashed, was enough to make her pull back.

Anguish covered her face. She felt as if a bandage had just been ripped off a festering wound. Without a word, she knelt and silently pulled at one of his muddy boots. She felt Ivan's hand stroke her hair, but his touch only made her tense. His hand fell idle and she forced all her concentration on the task before her.

The boot was tight and it took several hard pulls to get it off. When she did get it off, she did it so forcibly that she ended up on her backside. She met Ivan's eyes; if stares could maim, he would most definitely never sire children.

She went for his other boot. As she knelt again their gazes locked; his desire and mirth met her cold disdain. She pulled on his boot and once more landed on her backside. It was all she could do not to squeal in fury when she saw his smile. And how she loathed him, especially when he picked up one of his muddied boots and promptly put it back on.

"What are you doing?" she asked.

"How can I escort you home in my stocking feet?" His very glance taunted her.

"You'll escort me to hell first!" Suddenly she couldn't take any more of his tyranny. He was worse than the despotic sixteenth-century Russian tsar who bore his same name. He was Ivan the Terrible incarnate. She stormed from the room, vowing not to look back. He followed behind her, tripping and laughing while he tried to put on his other boot.

CHAPTER FOURTEEN

❊

It took a long time for Lissa to sleep that night. After Ivan escorted her back to Violet Croft, she stumbled up to bed, exhausted. But soon she was tossing beneath her comforter, unable to forget the events of the evening. Her cheek still hurt, yet more painful was the reminder of how she had lost her temper. She'd acted like the spoiled daughter of the manor, and it was hard to forgive herself.

Rolling onto her back, she wondered what foul mood Mrs. Lofts would be in tomorrow. Things were bound to be bad when she arrived at Powerscourt in the morning. How she dreaded going there—yet what alternative did she have?

In the shadowy corner of her room, her gaze found the large box that held the magnificent rose satin gown. How much could she get for it? More than one hundred pounds? Perhaps with the snood, she might.

She settled once more beneath the quilts. That was the answer: to part with the dress. The thought relieved and saddened her at the same time. The dress and the snood were the most beautiful things she had ever owned, including the lovely attire she had had as a girl. Having been deprived of such finery, she longed for it even more. Aunt Sophie had been kind to give them the gowns. The dresses were hopelessly impractical, but perhaps in her old, eccentric mind, Sophie had thought they might bring her impoverished great-nieces husbands, or at least admirers.

Lissa smiled softly as she pictured herself and Evvie in London at some posh ball, surrounded by a dozen young men as they each begged to refill their glasses or sign their dance cards. Her daydream became a bit more detailed, and she found herself dancing the night away in the arms of one darkly handsome man. He was a head taller than she, and when he whispered some endearment, she was forced to tip her head back to look at him.

It was Ivan, of course, and she wanted to kick herself for allowing her imagination to roam so freely. He would never look at her with admiration and love in his eyes, and it had nothing to do with the fact that he was a bastard, or that she was now his servant. Their fates had been driven apart years ago, and there was nothing either of them could do to change that.

Her little room never seemed so cold and forlorn as the nights when she thought of Ivan. Now she recalled their walk home and how he had tried to play the gentleman. The night air had been frigid and remnants of the last snowfall still clung to the sides of the road, making a ghostly outline. She had shivered beneath her thin mantle and before she could protest, he had thrown his greatcoat over her shoulders. His *surtout* was incredibly heavy, but Ivan's warmth lingered in its folds and she immediately ceased her shivering. They walked at a brisk pace. To their left, the little hamlet of Nodding Knoll slept peacefully beneath a starry night.

When they arrived at the cottage, he bent and kissed her cold little hand. He opened her cottage door for her, then waited until she entered. He had to be chilled without his greatcoat and she knew a moment by the fire would do him good. But she wasn't about to invite him in. Warily she gave him back his coat. He nodded and left for Powerscourt.

He had been chivalrous in giving up his coat and, though she admitted it only grudgingly, also in seeing her home. Still, she feared him. Her thoughts went back to earlier in the evening and their near kiss. Even now she longed to recapture it. She ached to see it go further. Day by day she was beginning to understand what had driven her mother to madness. The more time she spent with Ivan, the more she longed to step over the line of propriety and satisfy her growing, inexplicable desire for him.

Her hand ran over her taut, burning stomach and she rolled to her side. But to be truthful, it wasn't only Ivan she feared. She feared herself perhaps even more.

The first thing Lissa found out the next morning was that Mrs. Lofts had been sent packing and a new woman, Mrs. Amabel Myers, had been summoned from London. John Dover had told her the news as they walked to the castle. Though she had no great love of the old housekeeper, Lissa still felt slightly guilty that she might have been the cause of the woman's dismissal. But John made it clear that Mrs. Lofts's position had always been precarious beneath the new master. All the other servants knew the marquis had taken an instant dislike to her and that he had made arrangements for a replacement immediately upon arriving at Powerscourt. London was a good two days away and Mrs. Myers was apparently already in her situation. Lissa could only surmise she had been sent for as early as last Monday.

This bit of news greatly lightened her heart, and she walked toward the castle much more briskly. The weather was fine and clear. The snow was all gone and only a crystalline layer of frost clung to the grass now. She breathed in the morning air and, for some odd reason, was actually looking forward to her day.

The first thing she did was meet Mrs. Myers. The new housekeeper was as motherly as Mrs. Lofts was cold and forbidding. When the woman walked there was a bounce to her step almost like Mrs. Bishop's, and her white, frilly cap was a pleasing sight, especially in contrast to the severe gray bun Mrs. Lofts had worn. Lissa liked Mrs. Myers immediately, and the new housekeeper seemed to be fond of her too. Yet Lissa experienced a moment of discomfort when she realized that Mrs. Myers seemed taken aback by her appearance.

Lissa didn't know that Mrs. Myers, being a gem of a

housekeeper, knew of everything that went on in her house from basement to attic. The woman was all too familiar with Elizabeth Victorine Alcester, at least all too familiar with her face.

The uncomfortable moment passed quickly, however, and soon Mrs. Myers and she were getting along famously. In fact, Lissa was hard-pressed to leave the butler's pantry when the marquis rang the bells over the stair at ten o'clock.

Lissa found the library in the maze of corridors in the East Tower. Ivan was adding more coal to the fire in the hearth when she entered, and she thought he looked a little annoyed that she had caught him performing a servant's task. The Marquis of Powerscourt certainly had enough servants to perform any task, no matter how trivial. Yet for some reason, the fact that he didn't bother a servant to climb the cold back staircases just to place more coal at his hearth endeared him to her. Despite the rancor that had gone on last night, she couldn't help but smile, which seemed to take him aback.

Uneasy, he brushed the coal dust from his hands. She appraised his appearance this morning and was pleased by his attire. He wore only a batiste shirt and gray trousers with black braid running down the side seams. His clothes suited him well; simple and masculine. She watched him go to the huge leather-topped partners desk and hand her a stack of papers. She looked down at them. They contained only names.

"May I ask what these are, my lord?"

He seemed to prickle at the use of his title. "A list of the guests I am inviting to the Powerscourt ball."

This surprised her. In her entire lifetime, she had never heard of a ball at Powerscourt. The former marquis was a man haunted by the fact that his first wife had died without issue. He hated people and lowered himself to follow only a few rules of polite society. He had teas but never dinners. He discreetly shed his lusts upon the wandering gypsies, never upon the more proper ladies of Nodding Knoll. Though he should have supported Powerscourt's town much more than he did, most people were glad he was a recluse.

Now Powerscourt, made magnificent again, was to have a ball. Perhaps it was time.

"You'll do the invitations. Of course, I expect it won't take you more than a week."

She looked at him. "A week?"

"There are over eight hundred invitations to be sent."

Lissa scanned the list. The ball would be an enormous affair. But the marquis never did anything halfway. Not even when he'd been a stableboy.

"I'll have them done in a week," she promised.

"Fine. You'll stay in here. I've sent for everything you'll need." He went back to the partners desk and held the chair for her. She sat by a stack of cards engraved with the Powerscourt crest. With ink and pen in hand, she began. Ivan settled in a chair to read. Every now and then she looked up because she thought he was watching her, but his head was always bent toward his tome. Strangely disappointed, she would go back to her task.

Saturday was the day she'd planned to go to Cullenbury to sell her gown, but instead she spent it continuing to write out the invitations. She worked every day in peaceful seclusion in the library with Ivan. Though they hardly spoke a word to each other, she looked forward to her work more and more as the days progressed. Mrs. Myers would bring them luncheon at noon and tea at precisely four-thirty. In many ways the week was idyllic. And like all sweet times, it ended much too soon.

When all of the invitations were written they were sent by post, mostly to London, for all of Nodding Knoll was to be invited by banner. Lissa had hardly thought of whether or not she and Evvie would attend, partly because she was so busy inviting others, and partly because she knew she would have nothing to wear to such a grand event. In three weeks' time the rose satin gown would be gone. Yet Evvie would have her blue velvet, and Lissa knew that the Bishops would be happy to chaperone her sister so that Evvie could have her waltz with Holland.

Ivan didn't mention the ball in any manner other than to inquire about her progress with the invites. By the end of the week, Lissa had made up her mind that she would not attend, until she got her semi-annual 'charity' visit from Arabella Parks.

Arabella came to visit bearing gifts for her destitute friends. She gave Evvie a huge jar of pickled tongues that her cook had just put up and presented to Lissa her old editions of *The Ladies' Cabinet* and *Les Modes Parisiennes*.

Lissa thanked Arabella, a bit stiffly perhaps, then led her to the parlor. Evvie merely stood by, holding the disgusting jar until Lissa could look at it no more. She took the tongues from Evvie's hand and put them in the kitchen. She came back bearing a pot of chocolate.

"It's so kind of you to call, Arabella. How's your mother?" Lissa put down the tray and looked at the clock. It was almost noon and she wanted to get to Cullenbury that day. Thankfully Arabella wouldn't linger, Lissa knew that all too well.

"Mother is ecstatic, Lissa. You've heard of the Powerscourt ball, of course?" Arabella asked, accepting the cup of chocolate Lissa offered her.

"Well, we've heard rumors. . . ." Lissa discreetly pinched Evvie who was seated next to her. Evvie had to cough to keep from giggling.

"Mother thinks I would be a fine marchioness. I believe I may finally set my cap."

Suddenly their fun was over. Evvie sat deathly still, and it was all Lissa could do not to let her jaw drop. It was absurd, but the thought of Ivan taking a wife had never occurred to her. Now, as she looked at pretty, red-headed Arabella, the possibility was all too clear. Arabella looked stunning in her changeable silk dress. The taffeta was all the rage; though the gown was burgundy, it was also woven with luminescent green silk threads and the deep shadows of her skirt were colored spruce. It suited Arabella perfectly. Yet Arabella wasn't just attractive, she was also kind. Her kindness was a bit superficial, perhaps, but no one could fault her for that, especially not Lissa. Arabella was the girl she might have become had circumstances not changed.

"So should I set my cap for the marquis, Lissa?"

Lissa took a sip of her chocolate. She tried to enjoy it for it was the last they had but it tasted bitter. "Of course you should, Arabella. You've already waited so long to be married. Does the marquis share your sentiments?"

Arabella hesitated before answering. "If not now then I am determined that he will."

"So you should be," Lissa answered, relief and dread swelling in her breast. Ivan was not for her, she knew it only too well. So why did this conversation put her in agony?

"Oh, Lissa, it's so wonderful to have a dear friend like you to talk to!" Arabella suddenly stood and gave her a kiss on the cheek. Then she took up her magnificent mantle of black curly lamb and walked to the door. "Of course, I shall see you both before Christmastide—at the ball!"

Lissa was just about to make their excuses when Arabella added as an afterthought, "You know, I have several of last season's ballgowns I can send down to you girls. Why don't I do that? I know both of you would just love them!"

Lissa wasn't sure whether to be grateful or insulted.

"Oh, no! You mustn't bother," she said. "Evvie and I already have our gowns for the ball." Lissa could hardly believe what she'd just said.

Arabella gave her a puzzled look, then shrugged. "Until the ball, then!"

"Until the ball!" Lissa answered, watching Arabella being helped back into her carriage by the footman.

After she'd gone, Evvie could hardly contain her excitement. "Lissa, you mean we're really going? I've wanted to, but I was sure you wouldn't."

Lissa sighed. Why had she been so impetuous? She should have simply made her excuses to Arabella and trotted off to Cullenbury. But her temper had gotten the best of her again. Last season's ballgowns indeed! Suddenly the picture of Ivan waltzing with Arabella was almost more than she could stand. Ivan was going to see her in that rose satin ballgown if it killed her.

Unfortunately, it probably would.

She turned to Evvie and said, "We're going to Ivan's wretched ball, all right. Just let anyone try to stop us."

CHAPTER FIFTEEN

❋

Though the ball was still a week away, Powerscourt practically shook from all the activity within its stone walls. Housemaids prepared guest apartments; two additional cooks were summoned from Paris; and lads hopeful of playing footman for even just one night came and were measured for livery.

As the preparations and confusion built to a crescendo, Lord Powerscourt was not to be found. Mrs. Myers mentioned that he had taken off for London, and while Lissa didn't want to seem at all interested in the marquis's comings and goings, it seemed the housekeeper could read her thoughts. She assured Lissa he would be back in plenty of time for his ball.

Apparently the marquis so desired to be back at his castle, he rode all through the night, and showed up at Powerscourt late the next morning. When Lissa arrived, Mrs. Myers told her that the cook had the marquis's breakfast waiting in the hot closet. With some trepidation in her voice, she added that Lissa was to bring it up to his apartments.

The request, though made in the innocent light of morning, seemed to make both women anxious. Mrs. Myers fluttered about the servants' hall like a bird guarding its nest while Lissa warily listened to her explanation of the route to the marquis's suite. She was then handed his breakfast tray, which was made of heavy coin silver. Her arms ached with the weight and she was anxious to have the task over with. Mrs. Myers seemed to be equally concerned, for just as Lissa was ready to leave she added ominously, "If you are delayed, love, I shall come find you."

The first bad omen occurred when Mrs. Myers's instructions on how to find the marquis's apartments went askew. Powerscourt was a huge castle, and Lissa knew she should have listened more attentively to the directions. More than once she found herself in a corridor that seemed to lead only to dark oblivion.

Finally she did find the massive double doors with the Powerscourt coat of arms emblazoned on it. She set the tray on the floor and tentatively knocked on the door.

The second omen occurred when there was no answer. She stood there for several moments contemplating what she should do next. She couldn't leave the tray where it was for he would never know it was there. Yet to enter Ivan's chambers unannounced most certainly gave her pause. He could be napping—or worse, bathing. He could be doing any number of private things.

She frowned. In indecision, she fingered the ancient splintering oak of the doors. When she could procrastinate no longer, she knocked loudly, then cracked open the door. She fetched the tray and pushed against the door to pass through, yet suddenly it flew open and she nearly dropped the tray at Ivan's feet.

"What are you doing out in the passage?"

Lissa barely heard the question for she was too busy trying to steady her tray. When the milk pitcher was no longer wobbling, she looked up at him and was again startled, this time by his appearance. He wore nothing but black trousers.

His feet were bare upon the huge Turkish Kelim rug. His upper half was bare also, and though she'd seen him shirtless many times when he'd worked in the stables, now her eyes seemed to find every supple muscle, every crisp hair, that covered his chest. When she finally dragged her gaze from the play of muscle at his torso, she looked up and saw he was still wiping the soap from his partially shaven jaw. She almost smiled. Of course, Ivan the Terrible, with his distrust of mankind, wouldn't have his valet shave him. God save the poor soul who dared take a razor to that throat, no matter how innocent the circumstances.

"Have you nothing better to do than gawk?" he demanded.

Taken completely aback, she stuttered, "I—I am not gawking, I assure you."

He laughed the moment her cheeks flamed. Then he rubbed his chest, taunting her to look further. His brazen attitude about his nakedness shocked her even more, and she wished only to make her excuses and be gone. She saw a Nonsuch chest against one wall so she quickly put the tray down on it.

"I've brought you your breakfast," she said.

"Why didn't you take the servants' stair?"

"Mrs. Myers suggested that I not use it for fear I might end up in the wrong room." She met his eye and could only surmise by his expression that he wouldn't have minded her ending up in the wrong room, especially if that room was his bedroom.

He began walking to a chamber beyond, and she was relieved that this encounter seemed to be over so soon. She was premature in her thinking, however, when he commanded, "Set up my meal on the table. I shall be back in a moment. *Do not leave.*"

She watched him go, suddenly feeling every bit like a lamb being led to the slaughter.

The only table in the anteroom was a huge marble tripod that appeared as if it had been taken from the ruins of Pompeii. Just out of spite, she found the most uncomfortable chair—one with a triangular seat and a back made entirely of spindles that looked like the quintessential medieval torture device—and dragged it to the table. She set out his linen and the prerequisite twelve pieces of silver flatware he would need in order to eat. When her tray was empty, she took it up like a shield and surveyed her surroundings.

In all the castle, these chambers seemed to be the only ones in their original condition. None of the furnishings looked to be newer than the sixteenth century. There were several trestle-form stools with Romayne medallions; a great oak settle with linen-fold panels; and a huge ambry that, no doubt, used to store the castle's weapons. Every coffer and desk was decorated with turnings, and Gothic tracery was carved into all the stone ceilings and walls. The place was like a museum, only more magnificent for its provenance. The passions of Ivan's ancestors lay buried there, and Lissa could well understand a reluctance to disturb them. But somehow, she doubted Ivan had left the rooms alone because of a reverence for his ancestors. He hated them. Most likely, he had kept the chambers intact for fear that change might rid them of their ghosts. And he wanted them there, so he could shake them up and make them wail. After all, the ghosts were all that was left of his family to torture.

Lissa clutched the tray in her delicate hands. Her eyes surveyed the dank, dark chamber once more. She wasn't looking for ghosts—ghosts didn't frighten her—but she was looking for reassurance. She soon found something familiar resting on an upholstered Farthingale chair. It was an ancient balalaika.

She put down the tray and went to it, her mind flooding with memories. As if it were yesterday, she could hear it being played in the night, softly from the stables. It seemed she had always fallen asleep in the summertime with "Meadowland" or some other Russian folk tune floating into her open window. The notes were the saddest sound in the world, doubly so because the ancient balalaika was the only remembrance Ivan had of his mother.

Drawn to the instrument, she picked it up and ran her hands over the Cyrillic script that covered the triangular body. She easily recalled what Ivan had told her it said:

Tears of sorrow touch these strings
Tears of joy shall I then bring

It was signed by someone named only Ivanovich, St. Petersburg 1702. The original owner had long since departed when Ivan's mother had come upon it, yet it had obviously been the gypsy girl's most prized possession, for she had named her only son Ivan and, as rumor had it, died with it in her arms.

In a moment of sadness, Lissa strummed the three strings. She wondered if she let a tear fall upon it, would her dreams really come true? She wished that Evvie would marry soon, and she wished Great-aunt Sophie's solicitor would suddenly discover some misplaced funds so that she could pay for George's education. But more than that, she wished she could return to the past—not forever, but just for one night. As she had for years, she again wished for the opportunity to do things differently. She wanted desperately to right all the wrongs—as desperately as she wanted to reverse those tragedies that kept her in spinsterhood.

She put the balalaika down. It was hard to admit to herself how brutally she had once wanted Ivan's love. When she'd been sixteen Ivan had been all she had daydreamed about. She had been so lonely back then; his gruff, insolent attention was all she had. But because it was all she had she craved it like a drug. For Ivan she would have lived over her own stables, defied her own father, or run from the only home she'd ever known. For Ivan she would have done anything.

But now that seemed a lifetime ago. She was still lonely, but she was no longer a child and she knew only too well how cruel people could be. She had once thought she had wanted his love, but now she wondered how she had ever dared to desire such a thing. Ivan was no longer her stableboy, but a dark, forbidding man who possessed a great deal of power, more than enough with which to be cruel. And he was a man who for all ostensible reasons had every right to exact revenge.

She would never win his love now, she knew that all too clearly. And the irony was that it hadn't been her wealth that had cast him off, nor had it been her father's disapproval. The horror of it was that it had been her own wretched, spoiled self that had forced him from her, and now she would never have him. Ever.

"Do you want me to play it, Lissa?" Ivan's voice came up behind her.

Her cheeks drained of color. All she could think of at that moment was how desperately she still wanted him and how completely he would ruin her if he knew it. Trembling, she turned and her gaze locked with his. "No," she answered.

"Then why did you pick it up?" He was so close to her she could see just how beautiful and blue his eyes were.

"I had forgotten about it."

"So let me remind you." He took the balalaika in his hands.

"Please, no," she implored him.

"Why not?" he asked, his eyes narrowing.

"Because it's too melancholy, don't you see?" A sob caught in her throat. Her eyes glistened.

He stared at her, studying every emotion that crossed her face. His voice grew husky and he gripped the balalaika in his hands. "Shall you cry on this, Lissa, and see all your wishes come true . . . ?"

She shook her head.

". . . or shall you shed your tears in vain and fall victim to its promises . . . as others have . . . as my mother did?"

"Neither."

He placed the balalaika on the chair. "Then what will fulfill your deepest wish?" His strong index finger slid beneath her chin and tipped her head up.

"My deepest wish can never be."

"How do you know that? Tell me what it is, and perhaps I can help."

She turned away from him. "You cannot."

"Why is that, Lissa? Is it because I am what you wish for?"

She started. He was hitting dangerously close to the truth. "If I were to wish for a man, I would wish for his love first above all else."

"Then is it my love you wish for? Do you love me?" He pulled her into his arms. Her hands pressed against his warm, muscular chest, but that didn't deter him. "Answer me, damn you."

"No," she whispered, refusing to meet his eye.

"Say it. Say you love me, Lissa." He shook her. "Say it!"

"Say it and be cursed forever? I think not!" she cried.

"Say it and have all the glory that's within my power to give." He cupped her chin. "Don't say it and have more depression put upon that little soul."

"*You* depress my soul! Now release me!" She struggled to pull her arms out of his grasp. Her breath was coming fast and furious as his arm went possessively around her waist. She almost moaned for despite her rebellion his touch felt so right.

"But I don't, do I, Lissa?" The soberness of his voice quieted her. She looked up at him, terrified. He took her wrists in a shacklelike grasp. "It's what you deny that depresses you, isn't it?"

"N-n-no," she stammered, but they both knew it was a lie. Her guilt choked her. Still, she wasn't about to martyr herself for him. She felt his fingers at her throat and the first jet button of her gown give way. She raised her hands to stop him, but he caught them.

"So don't deny any longer, Lissa." He undid another button. "Say that you love me," he whispered, "and come to my bed."

"I will not," she snapped. She felt another button come free and her anger exploded. He wasn't going to take her. Ever. She would never be that foolish. She twisted from his hold and covered her bodice with her hands. Backing away, she said, "My coming to your bed will not change the past, and I'll see myself forever damned before I'll seek your forgiveness there."

"Damnation is more penance than I want." He stepped toward her and his fingers caught the opening of her bodice. She violently ripped his hand away but several buttons went with it. She looked down in dismay and found her corset cover peeking out from the rent.

She was frantic to get away from him now. His candor and proximity scared her. When he came for her again, her eyes desperately sought escape. But there was none. She was pushed against the wall. Her hands made an effort to hold him back, yet his intentions were too strong. Her fingers tugged on his black locks to try to pull him away. Yet he ignored her protest. He parted her bodice, staring at the tops of her lush breasts, and then let his tongue burn into the silken hollows of her throat.

She kept telling herself that she was ice and that he could not melt her. But as his hand slipped beneath her bodice and caressed the swell of flesh that rose above her lace-edged corset cover, she knew she was wrong. Fatally wrong. She was fire and only Ivan could make her burn.

Inch by painful inch, she found him winning. He

caressed and kissed her merely to torture her, to humiliate her; she could find no other reasons for it. But though she desperately wanted to fight him, it was difficult when his lips took hers in a brutally possessive kiss. His mouth muffled her protest as it moved frantically over hers and his hands moved up to hold her face for the onslaught.

She wanted escape, and there were a million things she could think of to do to get him to stop. She could slap and scratch and kick, but deep down, a part of her wanted him to continue—the part of her that had once wanted his love; the part of her that was lonely and begging of forgiveness—so she did none of those things. Instead, when his tongue finally sought hers in a wickedly fierce manner, she moaned and let him in, hating herself but hating him more. He would never love her, yet while her mind told her she was playing the fool, his passion seemed to whisper something else altogether, something she wanted with all her heart.

Almost in a daze, she felt him pick her up and take her into the next room. Everything was moving too fast. She struggled to be free of his arms but he tossed her upon a heavy Genoa silk counterpane and pulled her beneath him. With him on top of her, she was completely restrained. A warning sounded in her head as she realized they were on his bed, but when he took her mouth in a long, hot kiss, she couldn't think clearly anymore.

His hands parted her bodice, and when he stopped kissing her she stared up at him. He looked like a man obsessed. The creamy skin of her throat seemed to fascinate him and he studied it for a long time, almost as if in wonder. He buried his face in the hollows of her neck and seemed to revel in the scent he found there, as if he had dreamed about it for a very long time, and now, at last, it was his. Next his strong white teeth nipped at her breasts above her corset, and her taste seemed to please him beyond reason. When her chignon fell, his hands stroked her tresses as if they were some sort of lost treasure now found. Then he kissed her so deeply his spirit seemed to meet with hers.

"Lissa, tell me you love me," he whispered. "Say the words and be mine completely."

Panting and bewildered, she met his gaze. Her eyes became a smoldering azure. All she had to do was nod and she would finally be his. He could touch her as he had just done and she could revel in it as eagerly he seemed to. She could melt beneath his hands and lose herself in his kiss. Her longing for him would then be satiated; her desperation quieted.

"Lissa," he said, his breath coming just as fast and heavy as hers, "you know it was to end up like this. Come, say the words."

"I won't," she said, struggling to sit up, trying to cover her open bodice with her hands.

"You want me. I know it." Again he forced her down upon the bed.

Pushing hard against his naked chest, she said, "Ivan, I know what kind of hurt you have planned for me."

His fingers stroked her cheek. "You shall have only pleasure."

"But there are other hurts besides physical ones. And I won't let you hurt me now." Her eyes, glittering with defiance, met his.

He suddenly turned grim. "Lissa, you're mine. You've always been mine. You'll always be mine."

"I'm your servant," she protested, "and that is all I'll ever be. Because I work for you doesn't mean you own me or will ever own me. In the eyes of the law I don't belong to anyone until I marry."

Her challenge seemed to anger him beyond reason. He rolled off of her and said, "The law be damned! Can the law make one person love another? Can the law bring back the dead?" He turned to her, black fury on his face. "Can the law truly take a man out of bastardy?"

"Ivan—" she began, but he interrupted her. His

hands went to her arms and he pulled her onto his lap. "Did you know I'm not a bastard any longer?"

He seemed to be speaking in circles, and she could hardly follow him. Slowly she shook her head. Her confusion made him laugh. It was a terrible sound.

"Hasn't anyone wondered how a man who is *nullius filius* can inherit such wealth? Because *my father,*" he spat the words out like a curse, "requested in his will that an act of Parliament make me legitimate. Powerscourt was to go to his only issue, even if that issue was despised above all others. Yet what has all that changed? Did he marry my mother? Can that even help me find her grave so that I may put her in the family vault?"

Lissa watched him, the pain on her face surely mirroring what he must feel. She felt a draft. Her gown was off her shoulders and she absentmindedly tried to pull it up. But he wouldn't let her.

"The law can't change much, *alainn.*"

She stiffened at his endearment. *Alainn* was Irish for beautiful. He'd told her once that it had been his mother's name, yet she doubted it. Somehow, it seemed more logical that the tenth marquis had used it as a pet name for his gypsy girl, and Ivan's mother, tragically, had kept using it, hoping against hope that someday she would again be the former marquis's *alainn.*

She looked down at the muscular arm possessively locked around her waist. Was that all she was to be? His darling? Another girl to go mad with grief over the Marquis of Powerscourt? Her fingers pried at his arm. It didn't budge. She felt his hand at her nape. He pulled her to his mouth for another kiss, but this time she could not be persuaded. She sat stiff and pale in his lap, refusing his touch.

Annoyance was darkening his eyes. "You were meant to come to me, Lissa, don't fight it."

"I won't listen to this." She pulled again at his steely arm. It was useless.

"You would have come to me no matter what. We were fated to be together."

"No! That's not true. I won't let you hurt me."

"There are things that can overshadow the pain."

"But only for a moment."

"We've all had our pain to bear. You of all people should know that."

"No!" she cried as she began struggling for release, but he anticipated her every move, refusing to relinquish his hold. Finally, exhausted, she let out a moan of frustration. "Why must you make it like this?"

"I don't make it like this, *alainn.*" He roughly nuzzled her throat. "You would have come to me eventually."

"I wouldn't have."

He let out a sarcastic laugh. "You could have married old Billingsworth, and still you would have come to me."

"No!" she refuted hotly.

"We were fated to be together. And even if it drove Billingsworth to your father's recourse, you would have found your way to my bed."

Unable to take any more, she raised her right hand and struck him across his cheek.

It took her a moment to realize what she had done. She had slapped him across his scarred cheek. Already she could see the scar changing color to an angry white. And in his eyes she found all that he thought of her reconfirmed.

"I'm not your whipping boy, *Miss Alcester,*" he said through clenched teeth. He snatched her guilty hand and forced it behind her back. "You'd do well to remember that."

"Perhaps if you didn't act like such a bastard then maybe I could." When all that met her was his cold, dispassionate gaze, she no longer even felt his iron hold. She was too numb and horrified at what she had done . . . again.

"If you think I'm a bastard now," he whispered cru-

elly, "let me show you what a bastard I can truly be."
Roughly he forced her down on the bed again and jerked
away her bodice. His palm reached for her breast and she
struggled to keep him from touching her, but he suppressed her rebellion by pulling her arms up over her head
and holding them there with one strong hand.

She thought that he would reach for her bosom
again, but this time his approach was more subtle. He
eased himself down upon her, his unyielding chest meeting with her full, half-bared breasts. She writhed beneath
him, trying desperately to make him stop, but it was useless.

His lips burned across the delicate veil of her eyelids,
then slowly moved downward. She moaned against him
and tried to shove him away with her body, but then his
tongue trailed down her smooth temple. He paused ever
so briefly at her cheek, then his diabolical lips took hers in
an unwilling kiss.

She told herself to be cold and unresponsive, but it
was difficult. Desire, hate, sweetness, and fury swirled in
her breast and she longed for peace. His lips seemed to
promise her just that, but they lied. She knew too well his
aching, burning kisses filled her, then left her hungering
for more. They terrified her and exhilarated her. They captured her; they set her free. But they never promised anything more than the moment. And they were not such
liars that they ever promised love.

"No more." She sobbed when he broke from her and
moved downward. His mouth trailed down her throat
while his free hand pushed up her petticoats. Shuddering,
she felt him grasp her thigh; his touch scorched her
through her pantalets. She knew exactly what he was going to do and she couldn't bear it. She struggled like a cat
to be free of him, but she only used up her remaining
strength. His was the worst sort of seduction, but now she
could no longer stop him. Crying tears of anguish and
frustration, she turned her head away and wept against his

arm as she felt him caress her through the slit in her lacy drawers.

Yet somehow her tears seemed to reach him whereas her struggle had not. He paused and looked down at her tearstained face. Then he closed his eyes and swore beneath his breath.

"Not like this—" she begged.

His expression hardened and slowly he released her.

When her sobbing subsided, she finally looked up at him, unable to hide the hurt and distrust deep in her eyes. But before she could speak another word, he was off the bed, taking a shirt that was laid out on a chair and walking out of the room. He shut the door to his apartments behind him with a heart-wrenching thud.

A black feeling of doom overwhelmed her. "What cruel God ever brought us together?" she whispered at the ancient door. But there was no one to hear her. Without the hope of a response, she fell to the counterpane and cried as if her entire world had come to an end. Now there seemed nothing left but tears and remembrance.

PART TWO

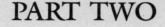

They say the angels mark
* each deed*
And exercise below,
And out of inward pleasure feed
On what they viewing know.

BEN JONSON,
"Musicall Strife:
in a Pastorall Dialogue"

CHAPTER SIXTEEN

❀

The spring of 1850 was remembered not only for the tragedies that occurred then but also for the perfect beauty that the season had provided.

The rains had come early and May debuted like a young girl at her first ball. Tall, supple stems of irises rose to the cloudless sky while trumpets of lilies heralded another brilliant day. Pearl-pink roses trailed over the arbor and even the hyacinths, long past their time, burst with new blooms. There was an irrepressible vitality to the air that spring, and no one was more susceptible to it than a sixteen-year-old girl.

The winter had been a long one for the Alcester children. Their parents had been absent since Christmas, and the servants whispered of their mother's scandalous behavior in London. But the servants always whispered about Rebecca Alcester, and Lissa, the eldest, was the first to ignore them. Besides, she had more important things on her mind this May than the gossip of addle-brained servants.

In the one precious letter Lissa had received from her mother all winter, Rebecca had mentioned returning to Alcester House sometime in June to bring her daughter out into society. Already the dresses had arrived from London—great trunkloads of them made from every fabric imaginable, from tarlatan to *gros de Naples*.

A part of Lissa was thrilled. She'd pictured her ball a thousand times. Her father would look dashing in a black cutaway. He would lead her to the dance floor for her first waltz and her beautiful mother would look on, pride shining in her azure eyes for her lovely daughter. Sometimes it was all so glorious, Lissa could hardly stand it.

But in the midst of all her excitement, she experienced moments of dread. If she were to have a debut, suitors were sure to follow. No doubt her parents would fill the Alcester ballroom with dozens of them, each one richer and more handsome than the other. Yet the one she most wanted to be there would never show. She would dance the night away in another man's arms, and with every step her world would move even farther away from Ivan's.

But the worst part wasn't that she would be swept away by suitors she had no desire for, nor was it the fact that the ball might spoil her for anything less. The worst part was that she would be courted by a dozen magnificent men and Ivan would never even notice.

Sitting outside on the great marble steps of Alcester House, Lissa stared morosely at the stables in the distance. She was attired in her best riding habit—a midnight-blue velvet with a coordinating white cashmere vest. Her cravat was black, as was her felt hat with the long net veil that swirled around her pale ringlets like a mist. One gloved hand sported a riding crop, which she occasionally tapped on the stone. The other hand was gloveless. She spent several painful moments staring at the stables and chewing on a nail.

He was never going to notice her. Short of brazenly confessing her feelings for him and making a complete fool of herself, he would never know she was alive.

Her sky-blue eyes clouded. But he had to notice her before her ball, before she was thrust into the world. She didn't really want society balls and satin dresses and wealthy young suitors. All she wanted was Ivan.

Of course, she knew what was said about him, that he was the bastard of the Marquis of Powerscourt. She also knew he possessed no last name. He was only Ivan, a man born on the wrong side of the covers, without kin of any kind.

Yet he was the reason she rose in the morning. To see his handsome face even fleetingly was the entire meaning of her day. To her, he was like the stars in a midnight sky, beautiful and elusive. He was the very portrait of male virtue, the exact model Michelangelo had been seeking for *David*.

And he was never going to notice her.

In disgust, she pulled on her other glove and swept the excess of her long velvet skirts onto her arm. The riding crop tapped even harder on the marble. She was going to have to do something very soon or her dreams of her stableboy would never come true.

"There you are! I've been looking all over!" Evvie came up behind her dressed in a similar habit, this one of burgundy velvet. Her slightly developed fourteen-year-old figure was quite fetching, and she looked gamine with her sparkling eyes and rosy cheeks.

"I suppose the ponies should be ready by now." Lissa looked furtively toward the stables.

"Of course. Come along. I shall race you!" Evvie took her hand and pulled her down the steps. Their skirts tripped them up and Lissa couldn't help but laugh. Evvie was not about to let her pause though. She took Lissa's hand and pulled her all the way down the brick road.

Their ponies, Dancing and Melody, were procured as soon as the two Alcester girls reached the first paddock. To Lissa's disappointment, the stablemaster, Mr. Merriweather, brought the ponies to the mounting block. She looked all around for Ivan but he was nowhere in sight. Disheartened, she mounted Dancing and took up the reins with little relish. Suddenly she had no desire to ride. She watched Evvie mount, then looked around for their groom, Jack, but he wasn't accompanying them today. She found the towering figure of her daydreams right behind her, mounted on the Alcester's most temperamental Thoroughbred.

Suddenly the day looked bright indeed. Syrian needed exercise and Ivan, as everyone knew, was the only one who could manage him. Her eyes sparkled beneath her veiling and she gave him a worshipful glance.

"Are you ready, Lissa?" Evvie asked, obviously eager to get to the fences.

"Completely," she answered, stealing another look at their stableboy.

"Then let's be off!" Evvie called out, already cantering ahead. Lissa soon caught up with her and their handsome groom followed, easing his high-strung mount into a trot.

Ivan seemed in a particularly black temper this day. Some days, especially ones like this when the weather was clear and pretty, he could be coaxed into some conversation. She or Evvie would do something girlish and amusing, and a slight smile might pull at his lips. Eventually they could begin to chat with him and if they were fortunate, he would answer their questions with more than his usual one-word replies.

But today he seemed particularly distant. A chill spring wind whipped at his back and he looked cold. He never seemed to have enough clothes to wear, and today was no exception. Besides leather breeches worn smooth between the thighs from exercising all the Alcester mounts, scuffed boots, and a patched linen shirt, his only covering was a thin linsey-woolsey waistcoat, hardly enough when compared to the warm, comfortable clothes the ladies of the manor sported.

"Lissa, let's take the east field. I found an old stone fence the last time I was there and it looked just the right height." Evvie pulled her pony to her side and brushed a wind-blown sable lock from her cheek.

"Dancing cast a shoe last week and he's still not going completely sound. He shouldn't be jumped," Ivan stated.

Lissa looked behind her and found he was obviously not inviting debate on the subject. She decided to be difficult anyway, for at least he would be forced to speak to her then.

"Dancing is fine, aren't you, my pet?" Lissa rubbed her pony's sleek black neck. "A few fences shouldn't affect him too badly."

"His leg shouldn't be strained. He might not get into the fence right and you'll be toppled."

"I've fallen before. It's not so terrible." She was testing him now, but when she looked back at him she was disappointed by his expression. Nothing seemed to crack him today. He peered at her as dispassionately as if she were an unruly kitten.

"No child will break her neck while in my care."

Hurt clouded her blue eyes and she immediately turned away. Hearing herself referred to as a child, especially by him, was beyond endurance. She was no child! And her only wish in the entire world was that he would one day wake to see that.

She urged Dancing into a canter, then into a gallop. She reached the east field long before Evvie and Ivan and she circled the violet-strewn meadow, while her face burned with anger and humiliation. She would show him. Her coming out would prove she was not the child he thought she was. She would flaunt her suitors at him and watch him writhe with jealousy.

Evvie and Ivan soon caught up with her and Evvie led the way to the fence. Melody neatly took the ancient stone wall and Evvie giggled with delight. Lissa stood by on Dancing, obedient for only the moment.

"You mustn't call me a child any longer. I'm not one, you know. I'm sixteen now," she told him petulantly when Evvie was cantering on the other side of the fence.

Ivan looked at her, his gaze brazenly skimming her velvet-clad figure. Annoyance and amusement warred in his dark eyes. His voice brooked no argument. "But you are a child, Miss Alcester, and for your own good, I think you had best pray to remain one for a very long time."

She shot him a sharp glance, not sure at all how to take his remark. The only thing she was sure of was that he'd insulted her. Her cheeks colored but she sought comfort thinking again of the grand suitors she would trail before him, and how she would force him to think of her as a woman. But again she was overcome with the terrible dread that he wouldn't care a whit how many suitors she had. Nor how rich they were, nor how handsome. He would pass her by without a glance, and she would be left standing alone, still nursing her terrible ache for him.

With a burst of fury, she gathered Dancing's reins and trotted away, unable to bear his loathsome company for another second. She cantered aimlessly through the field, but then she was ready for something more daring. She turned Dancing around and faced the crumbling stone wall. The horse backed nervously, but she still wanted to take the fence. She wouldn't let Ivan dictate to her. Dancing seemed as sound as ever, and she was too agitated to spend her afternoon cantering tamely around a field.

She took the fence at a well-collected canter, sure that her mount would have no problem. But Dancing's stride was a bit off and they took the wall short. Her pony's hooves scraped the stones and before they could land on the other side, she was unseated. She tumbled to the ground, falling painfully on her backside, while Dancing galloped away free.

She was not hurt, except for the side of her temple where it had grazed the fence. Raising herself on her elbow, she put her hand to her head to steady it. She meant to get to her feet, but before she could even move, Ivan leapt over the fence, looking furious. She thought he'd come to help her, yet he looked as if he could have as easily killed her instead.

She cringed back, yet to her utter shock, when he reached her, he caught her up in his arms and clasped her as if he would never let her go. Bewildered by his concern, she let him hold her, delighting in his closeness and the wonderful way he smelled. But all too soon he tore himself away to look her over for any damage. Feeling only the pain of his separation, she instinctively pulled on his shirt and brought him to her once more. As he bent over her, she was sure he had never looked more beautiful. His expression was as hard as stone, but in his eyes, she saw anything but indifference. She wanted to cry out her joy, but instead she reached up to him and gave him a sweet, hopelessly chaste kiss on his cheek.

When she pulled away, her hand found the place where her lips had been. But this seemed to unnerve him as nothing had before, and his dark-blue eyes blazed with something she had never seen—a fiery, restless need. As if he were trying to resist an impulse, he raised his hand slowly and caressed her scraped temple. Then he bent, as if to return her kiss, but before he could do so, his gaze shot up at Evvie who had just appeared on the other side of the fence.

Lissa met her sister's eyes. She could see Evvie was more concerned over what she and Ivan were doing than whether she had suffered any bodily harm from her fall. At once Lissa felt Ivan lift her to her feet. He gave her a stern, assessing glance that seemed to reassure him she was all right, then he abruptly mounted Syrian and cantered off to look for her missing mount. Without a word, Evvie handed her a hankie for her scraped temple and the girls waited by the stone fence until Ivan returned.

They rode back to Alcester in silence. Ivan scowled every time Lissa dared open her mouth, and Evvie, being the youngest and most impressionable, remained mute, every now and again bestowing a shocked, awestruck look at Ivan.

By the time they reached the stables, Ivan had become so cold and distant, Lissa was beginning to wonder if she had dreamed the entire episode that had taken place at the fence. When she was to dismount, he assisted Evvie and left her to Mr. Merriweather. Then without a backward glance, he coolly led Syrian into the stables where she could see him no more.

Vexed, Lissa stood in the stable yard, trying to control her temper. Yet when Evvie's sympathetic expression met her eye, she could take no more. She furiously gathered up her velvet skirts and ran back to the house, anxious to be alone.

Lissa spent the evening huddled by the fire in her chambers. Her room was grandly appointed in pink and cream, and there were tufted daybeds swathed in *moiré d'antique* that she could curl up on and cashmere throws with which to cuddle. But that night she was too miserable to enjoy such luxuries, and she found the warmth of the hearth too reassuring to move far from it. Now out of her riding habit, she was dressed in a simple gown of blue-green wool. A pristine white linen bertha collar made her look the picture of innocence, especially with her tresses falling free down her back in a shining cascade of silver-gold curls. The frown on her face was the only thing that spoiled the effect.

How could he have tried to kiss her, then afterward ignored her? The furrow in her forehead grew deeper. Was it true what she had seen in his eyes today, or had it only been the product of her wishful thinking? She stared into the flames, trying desperately to reassure herself either that what she wanted was so or that it had all been a figment of her imagination. But try as she might, she could come to no satisfactory conclusions.

She looked behind her at her bed, draped in cream shot silk. She would never sleep tonight with all the doubt and anger swirling in her breast. She wasn't at all sure what to do about it when her eyes spotted her pelerine tossed onto a pink satin couch.

Her gaze lowered as she pondered the scandalous idea that had just come to her. What harm could come from a quick visit to the stables? She knew it was after dark, and no doubt it *was* brazen of her to even think of venturing out at this time. But she had to know! She had to know what Ivan thought of her! And as soon as she got her answer, she would scurry back to her safe chambers with no one being the wiser.

She rose and donned the short green cape. The little wool garment would hardly keep her warm, but all she needed was her answer and then she would be back.

When no one was about she exited through the servants' door. The spring night air held a chill but the breeze had died, making it a bit more bearable. The stables loomed before her like a huge gabled inn. Candles shone through various windows where the help had its quarters, and she could hear men singing a bawdy tune from the tack room where the only stove in the stable was always kept fired. Suddenly nervous and shy, she stopped near the closed tack room door, unsure of what to do next. Yet the door abruptly opened and there was no turning back.

Five men were in the tack room, including the one who held the door. Lissa quickly found Ivan as he sat sharing a bottle of spirits with the man next to him. Mr. Merriweather was not among these fellows; all looked to be the younger grooms of the estate.

"Why, looky, lads, we've an angel in our midst!" The man at the door, a groom named Scarborough, let out a crude, deep laugh. Then all eyes turned to her as she stood not five yards from them in the darkness of the stalls. Seeing her, Ivan immediately stood.

Besotted with drink and forgetful of his place, Scarborough opened the door wide. "Come on in, my heavenly beauty. What sin have we committed that brings you out tonight?"

With frightened eyes, Lissa looked at Ivan. She was not used to drunken men and she was not at all sure how to handle them.

Scarborough pulled a flask from his jacket and held it out to her. "Would you have a snort, beautiful spirit?"

She was completely taken aback now, but this time Ivan was at her side. He gave a toss to his head, and for some reason Scarborough retreated to the tack room. Everyone watched them as Ivan gripped her arm and began dragging her out of the stables.

"Where are we going?" she asked quietly, still quite aware of the men in the tack room.

"Back to the house from where, after nightfall, you will never venture again." His grip grew even tighter.

"Are you angry at me?" She dug her delicately slippered heels into the dirt of the passage and tried to slow him down. "Please don't be angry at me. I wanted to talk to you. I wanted to know about this afternoon."

He paused, grabbing her up in his hands. "You just forget about what happened this afternoon, little girl."

His tone angered her. She tried to pull free. "I'm not a little girl. Doesn't today prove that? What I feel—"

"What you feel!" He tipped his dark head back and laughed. His mirth broke her heart.

"You felt something! I saw it in your eyes!"

He tensed. "It's your imagination." He again tried to pull her farther along the dark stalls toward the house.

"But, Ivan, I saw it." Her voice began to quiver. "I beg of you, answer me. It is true you feel nothing for me?"

"It's true." He pushed her against a stall door. "It's true."

He was so close she could smell the liquor on his breath. It was a disturbing smell, yet not unpleasant. At the dim end of the stables, she could barely make out his features, yet she could see that his eyes glittered unnaturally. She realized he'd probably taken his share of the bottle the men had been passing around, but when he spoke, his words were sober and deliberate.

"*Alainn,* your little pranks might have been tolerated a year ago, but now they won't be, do you understand?"

She looked at him, all her dreams dashed. He didn't care for her at all. He was just angry that she'd interrupted his drinking. He probably had some kitchen wench he was fond of. He most likely never thought of her. She was as close to tears as she could be without one splashing onto her cheeks.

"Have you heard anything I've said?" He shook her gently.

"Yes, I've heard it all." She fixed her gaze on his patched linen shirt and asked what she had come to ask, though she dreaded the answer. "Tell me, won't you, before we go back to the house—why don't you think I'm pretty? What's wrong with me that you shouldn't like to kiss me?"

He inhaled sharply then he tensed even further. Suddenly he seemed hell-bent on getting her out of the stables. Her feet barely touched the ground.

She tried desperately to stop. "I won't go in until you answer me, Ivan."

He refused.

"Tell me! Tell me what's wrong! Is it the color of my hair you don't like? Or is it my eyes?" Her voice trembled with pain. "Have you a fancy for someone else? Someone prettier? Tell me, what is it? Why didn't you kiss me this afternoon?"

All at once she was pushed against another stall door. As if he were a madman set free, he grabbed her and claimed her mouth in a brutal kiss.

This was nothing like she had imagined: a kiss that was sweet, tender, and yearning. To begin with, this kiss yearned for nothing—for whatever it desired, it took with great relish. His finely molded lips took hers as if she were an experienced woman, not an innocent girl. He moved over her mouth with an appalling amount of experience and he was so demanding, she wasn't sure whether to be frightened or overjoyed.

The only thing she was sure of was that she was shocked to her core. Her hands hung limp at her sides and her legs felt as if they would buckle at any moment. But somehow they held. She could feel him enticing her lips into giving him an entrance. Already their kiss was so deep she could taste the whiskey on his tongue, and she was hesitant to go further. Yet he was clearly too impatient to wait for her and he thrust his tongue into her mouth, jolting her into a panic.

She released a muffled sob, but he continued, now holding her face with his two hands. She wasn't sure what to do, but somehow she knew she wasn't ready for this. He had seemed to know it too, for now all his warnings seemed crystal clear. But she had refused to let it go, and now she was in over her head.

"Jesus man! What are you doing?"

She felt someone pull at Ivan's back, but the man didn't seem strong enough to pull him off of her. After another moment of panic, he was physically thrust away from her, and she was appalled that it had taken all four of the men who were in the tack room to do it.

"God in heaven, Ivan, what are you thinking of?" she vaguely heard Scarborough say. "You've been here since you were ten years old—have you a penchant now to be living on the streets?"

She was too shamed to meet any of the men's gazes. Sobbing silently into her fist, she could only look down where their lantern made a circle of gold in the straw-littered passage. Dimly she made out the frightened voice of another young groom, a lad named Willy.

"Ivan, look at her, she's terrified—she won't say a thing. But you won't do that again, will you? If you promise, we won't tell old Merriweather."

Ivan remained brutally silent. When she dared to look at him, he was breathing hard and still in the clutches of the other stable lads. Several black locks of hair had fallen onto his forehead and he seemed furious—as if he'd been a lion feasting on his kill and had been pulled away before he could get his second bite.

Horrified, all she could do was stumble along the stall door, numb to everything but the desire to get away.

"That's right, Miss Alcester, you go on to the house," she heard Willy say.

She needed no urging. She grabbed up her woolen skirts and ran out of the stables toward the estate house as if her life depended upon it.

CHAPTER SEVENTEEN

❊

Fascination had turned into obsession.

After her midnight visit to the stables, Lissa refused to leave her room for three days, pleading a headache. She refused to eat; she refused to dress. She simply moped about her chamber in her wrapper, occasionally staring into the fire, but mostly staring out the window toward the stable yard.

Now that she'd been kissed, she didn't know whether she loved Ivan even more or despised him. His indifference had been disproven but he had frightened her and, worse, disgraced her in front of other men. She could hardly keep from blushing every time she thought of Scarborough, Willy, and the other grooms who had watched Ivan kissing her.

This day was no different. With her hair unbound and unbrushed, and her blue satin wrapper wrinkled from so much wear, she was staring glumly into the flames of her hearth when she heard a huge commotion outside her window. Curious, she looked outside and her eyes opened wide with surprise. Coming down the tulip-lined lane was her parents' carriage, at least a month earlier than expected.

With a great burst of excitement, she ran to her lace-covered dressing table and picked up a comb. She had hardly gotten the thing through her tangled blond hair when her maid appeared at the jib door. Sally was obviously aware of the impending company, for she scurried to Lissa's wardrobe and quickly tossed an appropriate gown on the bedstead.

She was ready in a miraculous half hour and she burst from her chambers, eager to see her parents. It had been so long! It seemed she could hardly remember what they looked like. She hurried down the wide marble staircase that led to the hall and then practically ran to the drawing room, both hands full of her skirts.

". . . and we've all been quite good, Mother. Even George hasn't been into mischief—"

With her hasty entrance, Lissa interrupted her sister. All eyes turned to her and suddenly Lissa knew something was terribly wrong. She looked first at the settee where Evvie sat stiffly next to their mother. Obviously she had been filling Rebecca in on what had happened during her absence. Lissa's eyes slid to their mother.

Her lovely mother—the beauteous Rebecca—looked as if she hadn't slept for days. She also looked as if she'd been crying for just as long for her eyes were red and she held a twisted hankie in one hand. But Rebecca wasn't crying now, and when Lissa stepped toward her, obviously concerned, she brushed off her daughter's unspoken questions with a slight shake of her head and held out her arms. Lissa ran to her.

"There's my pretty girl!" Her mother reached up and kissed her forehead. "I was just going to ask Evvie where you've been. No doubt out in the stables with your pony?"

Lissa pulled back, trying to smile though it was difficult. "No, I just had to make myself presentable."

"You're always presentable to your mother, love." Rebecca's lips trembled in a melancholy smile. Lissa looked into her mother's eyes and the sadness there was so deep and troubled, she wondered if there were even words to explain it.

Disturbed, Lissa looked behind her and found her father gulping a brandy at the mantel. There were lines in his face she hadn't remembered. He was usually so jolly. He loved his girls, Evvie and herself, and it was usually he who spurred on any visits to Alcester. Now he looked old and unhappy, as if all his hope were gone.

"Father?" she said in a little voice.

All at once he put down his drink. He strode across the drawing room and silently, as if he were fighting back tears, he took her in his arms and hugged her within an inch of her life.

"Father . . . what is it?" she whispered, but to no avail. As quickly as he came up to her, he released her, going back to the mantel for his drink. There he seemed more interested in his brandy than in either of his daughters whom he hadn't seen for months.

"Shall you see George, Mother? Father?" Evvie asked from the settee. Lissa looked at her sister and saw the fear in her eyes. It was clear Evvie was as bewildered as she was.

"Oh, shall we?" Rebecca rose and took both her girls' hands. "Is he in the nursery?"

Painfully Lissa took in their mother's state. When Rebecca stood, no one could miss the rumpled dress and desperate edge to her manner. Unable to speak, Lissa looked to Evvie to answer.

"Probably," Evvie said. "I'm sure Nanna was planning on bringing him down any moment, but perhaps we should seek him out instead."

"Shall you come too, Father?" Lissa asked, finally finding her voice.

"Later, girls," Rebecca whispered.

Lissa looked at her mother and saw the tears welling in her beautiful blue eyes. It was more than Lissa could bear, but bear it she must. Her mother squeezed her hand as if to say "be strong for me." Lissa bit her trembling lip and the three Alcester women headed for the nursery.

Even as an infant, George had been handsome. Now that he was four, he was even more so. Rebecca seemed completely won over by her boy's dark locks and black eyes as he rode his gilded rocking horse, unaware of the company. When he did chance to look up, 'is mother took him in her arms. George seemed instinctively to like it there.

"George, what do you say to your mummy, eh, my lovekins?" Nanna prompted.

George smiled a wide cherubic grin and pointed to Lissa. "She's my mummy!" he proclaimed.

"No, no!" Nanna said, horrified.

"Mummy!" He pointed to his sister again.

Rebecca only kissed his pink cheek. Then he seemed restless and she was forced to release him. Apparently he had something important waiting for him in his playroom, and he stomped away, his "nanna" obediently following.

"George—" Lissa called, ready to retrieve him.

"No, love." Rebecca took her arm and stopped her. "That's all for now. Besides, I'm tired. I really think I should go to my room and rest. Will you both excuse me?"

Mutely Lissa and Evvie nodded. Desolate, they watched Rebecca descend the little wooden steps that led to the children's quarters.

Neither girl could fathom what was wrong. Evvie was sure someone had died, but Lissa quickly discounted the notion. If that were the case, then they would have been told. Whatever it was, it was something so terrible neither of their parents could even speak of it, and that was what worried Lissa the most.

The anxiety seemed to wear heavily upon Evvie. Lissa took note of how pale she was and promptly ordered her to go to her room and have some tea. She walked her sister there, ordered refreshments, and only when Evvie was lying on her daybed, wrapped in a blue alpaca lap shawl, did Lissa feel right in leaving.

She had to talk to her father.

She made her way quietly down the great marble stair. It was dusk now and through the dim hall she could see light from beneath the drawing room doors. Just as if this day were any other day, a maid had come around and lit the gasoliers. It was small comfort, but Lissa was grateful not to find her father brooding in darkness.

"Father?" she asked, timidly entering the room.

Hearing her voice, he raised his head from his hands. He was sitting on the sofa and before him the brandy snifter sat partially full. He'd obviously not drunk much, yet somehow that fact unsettled her. It was as if his problem was so great, it couldn't be assuaged by drink even for one evening.

"Come in, child. Close the door." He smiled at her and she suddenly wondered when he had aged. When she had last seen him, he was jovial and handsome. Now he seemed a shell of a man; too tired to live, too broken to care. Tears welled up again in her eyes.

"Father, Evvie and I are worried. You and Mother seem so—"

"What God hath joined together, let no man put asunder," he interrupted as if he'd never even heard her speak.

Her face became a mask of confusion. "I don't know what you mean," she whispered.

"I thank the Lord you don't, my Lissa." He put his hands together as if in prayer.

"What's happened?" She went up to him. "Please, tell me. I'm so frightened."

He stood and walked to the windows. Before him lay the now-dusky patchwork of Alcester fields, rippling with yellow flax and green wheat. It was a beautiful sight, lush and full of promise, but she could see her father found no solace in it. He turned and looked away.

"Lissa, child, come tell me what your life has been like these past months." It was obvious he didn't want to hear about her dull little days at Alcester. He was too full of his woes to listen, but somehow she gathered her wits and haltingly began.

"Evvie has learned to jump Melody and with quite respectable equitation—at least that's what Mr. Merriweather says."

She paused. He had his glass again and was taking an absentminded sip. He didn't seem to notice she'd stopped speaking.

"I've been using Dancing as my hack, but soon I hope to ride Syrian."

She looked at him, her mind whirling with dark speculations. What had gone so wrong? Were they to become paupers? Had her father been told he possessed some dread disease? Had her mother lost a child? What could it be?

Her father cut short her mental hysterics when he released a small smile and said, "Your life is simple, isn't it, Lissa? You've not a care in the world. I want you to remember I said this to you, child. I want you to remain carefree . . . no matter what happens."

"What is to happen then?" she asked, almost relieved she was finally going to know.

"Tell me what else goes on in your bucolic days. Have you liked the pretty dresses I sent from London?"

She looked at her father, frustrated that he wasn't telling her. But in his vulnerable state, she couldn't bear to be cross with him. Gently she answered, "They're beautiful. I adore them."

"I knew you would!" He seemed pleased with her response, then he sank back into despair. "But I should have sent you a doll! That was thoughtless of me. I don't know how I could have forgotten my little girl like that."

"A doll?" Lissa stared at him, beset by worry. Her father was talking like a madman. She hadn't played with dolls in six years.

"Father, you must be thinking of Evvie." She tried to smile. "But even Evvie is now too old to play with dolls."

He seemed not to hear her. He continued, acting as if she were still a little girl. "No, no, I was thinking of you,

Lissa love. You're my beautiful little girl—the exact image of your mother. And I've been thoughtless, child. I don't know how to make it up to you."

"Please listen, Father—"

"No, no. I shall send the butler out to get you a doll this very night. Even if it's the last thing I do." He went to the claret-colored silken bell pull that hung in the corner. She barely stopped him in time.

"No, Father!" A tingle of fear went down her spine. She grabbed his hand and squeezed it. "Please don't send Cheatham to London on this errand. You're tired. You must sit down."

"I've let you down. You wanted a doll!" He began to get distraught.

"But I'm too old for dolls, Father. Don't you see that?"

He quieted. "You mustn't act older than you are, child."

"But it's true," she said, trying to reason with him. "You and Mother were going to give me my debut this spring. I'm almost old enough to marry." She thought painfully of Ivan. "And old enough to be kissed."

"Kissed?" His face suddenly turned angry. "And have you been kissed?"

She didn't know whether to answer him or not. But he was her father and she couldn't lie to him. "Once," she whispered.

Without word or warning, he slapped her. Tears of pain and fear spilled down her face as she clutched her sore cheek. In horror, all she could do was look at him. He had never treated her like this before. Never.

He grabbed her, tears running down his face also. Suddenly he was contrite and he sobbed. "You must never accept another kiss, you promise me, my little girl?"

"What have I done?" she asked.

"You mustn't turn out like your mother! It's sin enough that you look like her!"

"What—what has she done?" she stuttered, now not at all sure she wanted to know.

"Rebecca—my lovely Rebecca!" He sobbed into his hands. "I never—I *never* wanted to believe what others said. I laughed, I tell you! When I heard such rumors! But it's true. It's all been true. My angel has fallen. Committed the most ugly of crimes! No denying it now. I found her myself in that man's bed . . ." His voice trailed off and he no longer seemed aware that there was another person in the room. His sobbing came in long, wretched gasps and he appeared to be in a world of his own, a world that was dark and inconsolable, as dark and inconsolable as Lissa's had suddenly become.

She touched his shoulder and thought of all the servants' gossip. She had always believed the stories were false, products of cruel and vicious tongues. But now they were true. And there was no running from them any longer.

She stood there, her expression a mixture of denial, fear, and shock. She ached to tell him he was wrong about Rebecca, that her mother hadn't hurt him, but she couldn't deny the wounds when her father stood bleeding before her. He was completely destroyed, and now, knowing why, she felt destroyed too.

"No, Father, don't cry any more," she said, wrapping her arms around him. "It will be all right. We'll all make it right again. Mother"—her voice caught in a sob— "Mother is sorry—I know."

As she hugged her father, a part of her began dying inside. Perhaps it was the last clinging remnants of her childhood, or perhaps it was simply her belief in angels. She didn't know, nor did she care. Her face turned pale and grave, and she ceased her crying for the tears seemed to freeze in her eyes. Helpless, she tried to get her father to at least look at her, but he was a thousand miles away, in a world of his own, full of darkness and despair. He pulled from her only to weep bitterly into his hands.

When it was clear that there was nothing she could do, she finally left him to his grieving and slipped out of the drawing room.

In the dark hall, with her father's sobs the only sound, Lissa wondered if she might go mad too. There seemed nowhere to turn. She couldn't bear Evvie's learning of this, nor the servants. And she couldn't go to her mother.

Rebecca. The very name made her feel sick. Her mother had done something evil indeed. Lissa remembered her father's slap. She touched her tender cheek. Perhaps even she was to come to the same end. In agony, she recalled Ivan's kiss. It had frightened her, true, but it had seduced her as well.

Looking around the dim hall, she felt the great marble walls closing in on her. Her whole life seemed to be tumbling into ruins.

She ran to the mahogany and glass front doors. Opening them wide, she let in great gusts of cold air. A wind had kicked up and there seemed the promise of rain in the air. Suddenly all she wanted was to leave. She wanted to gallop like a madwoman across Alcester's fields. And never come back.

Running, she made her way to the darkened stables. It was Saturday night and she knew most of the grooms had gone to the pub in Nodding Knoll. The stables were deserted when she arrived, and it only took her five minutes to light a lantern and tack up her mount. Dancing was in a rare temper with the wind beating at the stable's clapboards, but she was glad to see he bore no ill effects from their jump three days before. She mounted on the block, paying no mind that she had no shawl or mantle to keep her warm. Somehow keeping warm didn't seem to matter. Getting away seemed the only thing worth doing.

With crop in hand, she gathered up the reins. The wind banged the doors and Dancing seemed ready to bolt.

She was about to give him his head when an arm reached out and took hold of her pony's bridle.

"What are you doing, you little fool?"

Pale and frightened, she looked down and found Ivan reaching for her reins. He was furious.

"I'm going for a ride!" she cried out, backing Dancing into a corner.

"What is this madness? You dismount this second!" He held Dancing's head and reached for her waist. He was obviously hoping to pull her down, but she refused to let him. She was going to escape, if only for an hour, and he was not going to stand in her way.

"Ivan, let go of Dancing's bridle!" She whipped her pony's flanks and he reared. Enraged, Ivan held on.

"You spoiled brat, you do as I say!" he said as the pony tried knocking him aside.

"I shall not! Ivan, get out of the way!" Fury crackled in her eyes. She was no spoiled brat. Her world had just crumbled to dust and nothing made sense anymore. Nothing. She was so frightened that she wanted to run as far as she could go and never look back. And he was not going to stop her.

"You aren't to go out there tonight, girl! Has one kiss left you addled?"

A cry of frustration caught in her throat. In warning, she raised the viciously thin tip of her riding crop. If anything, he, and her feelings for him, contributed to her confusion as much as her mother's infidelity.

"How dare you tell me what to do!" she cried to him, jerking away the reins.

"You're too much of a child to know what's good for you! Now get down!"

"You're nothing but a servant, do you hear?" she sobbed. "Nothing but a lowly stableboy!"

"You haughty little miss!" he snapped furiously. "You think you're so above me! Well, I'll see you brought down a peg or two. Now give me those reins!"

"No! I said let go and let me be off!" she demanded.

"Get down!" He lunged for her once more and she raised the crop even higher. When he had her, she screamed. Then, instinctively, she slashed the crop right across his face.

He stumbled back, clutching his left cheek. A moan escaped her lips when she saw the blood oozing between his fingers.

"Ivan!" she cried out, beside herself that she had hurt him so.

"You bitch," he said though clenched teeth, his eyes closed in pain.

Free from any hold, Dancing was anxious to be off and she had a hard time controlling him. She backed him into the corner where he reared. She meant to try to help Ivan; she even had thoughts of dismounting, when Ivan made one last attempt to keep her in the stables. Though obviously hurt, he reached for the reins, his bloodied hand covering her own. But half crazed from all the traumas that had befallen her, she instantly rebelled. She tore free of his grasp and gave Dancing his freedom. The pony galloped from the stables, taking her into the inky, windswept night.

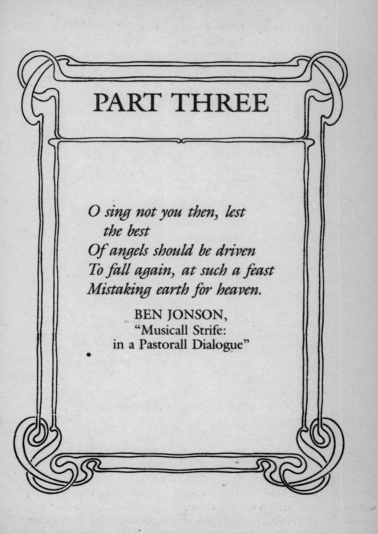

PART THREE

O sing not you then, lest
the best
Of angels should be driven
To fall again, at such a feast
Mistaking earth for heaven.

BEN JONSON,
"Musicall Strife:
in a Pastorall Dialogue"

CHAPTER EIGHTEEN

✤

Remembering the entire episode again was like tearing a bandage from a festering wound. Lissa's tears wet the Marquis's brocaded counterpane that she lay upon, and in her grief-stricken heart she wished she could drown in them. Vaguely she thought she heard Mrs. Myers come into the chamber, then discreetly leave, but Lissa hardly paid any attention. Her sobbing seemed never to end, especially when she thought again of how cruelly Ivan had just treated her; and the reason for it: the scar she had viciously inflicted upon him for the rest of his life.

When Dancing and she had left the stables that night, no one had found her until dawn. She was at Georgette's Leap overlooking the sound when Mr. Merriweather finally caught up with her. She was quiet and sorrowful as he told her of the grooms, including Ivan, who were scouring the countryside looking for her. Then, in grave silence, the stablemaster told her there had been a tragedy at Alcester. Without asking another question, as if she somehow already knew what it was, she followed him back to the estate without uttering a sound.

It was a brutal remembrance. She had not been allowed inside the drawing room to see the bodies, but over the years she had heard enough gossip about the incident to glean a picture of her parents' last moments on earth. Both were shot in the skull. Her father was in the armchair, the pistol beneath his outstretched hand. Rebecca had been found with her head on her husband's lap, as if her last gesture had been begging him for reason. In her grasp she held a note that Lissa now kept in her jewelry box. It was in her father's hand and it said simply:

I lived for you—I died for you.

They were buried two days later in the Alcester cemetery with those very words inscribed on their tombstone.

Lissa never saw Ivan. The other grooms told her he had taken off for parts unknown the moment he was told she'd been found. She'd been heartbroken by his absence, but her whole world was so wrenched apart that his leaving became just another hurt. Eventually she seemed to go numb. Yet the one thing she could not get rid of was the terrible guilt that stabbed her whenever she thought of the riding crop and that last night in the stables.

The first year after her parents' death was the worst. Lissa quickly found out what a tenuous existence they really led. Her father had left no will and there was no solicitor to look after the estate. Nor were there any relatives. Alcester House soon slipped from her grasp. She quickly found out when a death occurs the bill collectors come like crows to pick at the corpse. The collectors' cries refused to be silenced, and soon the remaining Alcesters were living at Violet Croft with only the funds left them after all their parents' debts were paid.

It was certainly a step down from their previous lifestyle, but Lissa would have traded all the wealth in Britain if she could have just saved her parents, if she could have just prevented the illness that had later left her sister blind; if she could have kept her brother away from the cruelties of the children at school. But she hadn't been able to prevent any of the tragedies that had befallen her family.

And then there was Ivan to grieve over. Her thoughts of him hardly diminished at all in the five years she spent at Violet Croft. She devoured every bit of gossip about him as a beggar devours crumbs. When she'd heard Powerscourt had finally recognized Ivan as his own, she'd been secretly thrilled. Ivan was finally getting justice for a mean life. She heard about his decadent life in London after he received his inheritance, and his wildness saddened her.

But her only truly unhappy moment came when she'd heard he was to return to Powerscourt. She knew he was coming to open old wounds. And to show how absolutely their fortunes had been reversed.

Now, as she clutched the Genoa silk counterpane, she wondered how she would carry on. It was brutally obvious that Ivan felt no tender emotion for her. Though it broke her heart all over again, she knew there was no way to make him love her.

She sat up and numbly picked up her cap. She pulled her fingers through her knotted tresses. Chagrined, she wondered what Mrs. Myers thought of this whole episode. Surely the housekeeper knew something was afoot. Undoubtedly her reputation was diminished, but there seemed nothing she could do about it. Her hand trembled while she repinned her hair. Clutching together her bodice, she headed for the door.

All she had to do was hold on until Evvie was married, she told herself as she made her way through the passage. Then Holland would take care of George and she would be free. She would go to London, she decided. There no one would know of her reputation. With her education, she could certainly become a governess, or a ladies' companion. She would fend for herself and try desperately to forget Ivan.

As she wandered the passage, unsure of the way out of the castle, she ended up in one of the loggias overlooking the Baronial Hall. There was quite a bit of activity going on; scaffolding had been erected all over one wall and, high above the tapestries, a painter was working on the Powerscourt crest.

Loosely blazoned, the Powerscourt arms consisted of a black "gutte de sang" shield surmounted by a sword. Two reguardant wyverns, collared in blue and chained in gold, supported it. The motto of the Powerscourts was appropriately chilling: *A ma puissance,* "According to my power."

She knew the Powerscourt arms well, as did every citizen of Nodding Knoll. It was a shock to see them being changed, but not nearly a shock like the one she had when she realized exactly what the painter had been commissioned to do. He was adding a bend-sinister, a thick band across the shield that went from the top left of the shield all the way down to the bottom right—the sign of bastardy. If "gutte de sang" meant drops of blood, then it was appropriate that the bend-sinister was being done in "gutte de larmes," drops of tears.

Looking at it, Lissa felt Ivan's fury as she would a fierce, howling wind. She gripped the balustrade for support. Legally he was no longer a bastard, yet he was not going to let anyone forget his beginnings. The people of Nodding Knoll would have quite a surprise at the ball when they arrived and saw the new Powerscourt arms. Already she could see Ivan enjoying himself at their expense, reveling in their shocked silence.

"*A ma puissance,* Lissa."

From below she heard Ivan's voice. She looked down and found him watching her from the Hall. He seemed more grim than usual, especially when he took in her pale features and red eyes. Yet he looked triumphant too, as if everything he had ever wanted was almost within reach.

Their gazes clashed. He was a beast to have done such a thing to his coat of arms. It would shock everyone in Nodding Knoll, but she alone was destined to pay the price for his twisted vengeance.

For she was the one who had fallen in love with him.

CHAPTER NINETEEN

✤

Mrs. Myers carried the decanter-filled tray through the maze of cold passages that led to the marquis's antechamber. The ball was to begin in only two hours; still, the marquis had not yet dressed. His valet hadn't even been summoned—Mrs. Myers had left the old fellow down in the servants' hall while she brought the spirits upstairs.

He was still looking melancholy. Ever since that day when Elizabeth Alcester had brought him his breakfast, he'd been brooding about the castle. Lissa had also looked quite inconsolable during the past few days, and the kindly housekeeper desperately wished something could be done about both of them.

"I've brought your brandy," she said, a look of mild disapproval on her face. "Are you ready to dress, my lord? Shall I send for Sedwick?"

"No, he can come up later." The marquis reached for the decanter and poured himself a healthy three fingers.

The housekeeper watched him, the disapproval on her face deepening. Yet Ivan Tramore was no child to be scolded for his tardiness; all she could do was stand before him, waiting to see if he needed anything else.

He didn't so she turned to leave. But before she disappeared through the servants' jib door, she realized she had forgotten something. She reached into the pocket of her white linen apron and took out a letter.

"My lord, Mr. Jones sent this note. I've been remiss in not getting it to you earlier. With all the preparations today, I forgot about it."

"It's all right." Tramore walked up to her and took the note. He seemed to already know what it said. "You've done an excellent job—as always. I could never find fault with you."

"Thank you, my lord." The housekeeper looked at him. Her eyes filled with sadness that such a good man was so unhappy and alone. She nodded and made her way back to the kitchens.

When Mrs. Myers left, Tramore glanced at the note and its wax seal from the bailiff's office. He quickly opened it and read its contents:

> *My lord,*
> *I will be having tea next Sunday at four o'clock with the Misses Alcester. It would be my great pleasure to have you join us. Until then, I am,*
>   *Your humble servant,*
>   *Holland Jones*

Unconsciously Tramore's hand lifted to his face. His finger followed the scar as he reread the note. He seemed thoughtful for a moment, then as if he was suddenly reminded why he had the scar in the first place, he crumpled the vellum in his fist and angrily threw it into the fire.

"Lissa, what if this snow ruins the ball?" In her lustrous blue velvet gown, Evvie sat by the front window, waiting to hear Holland's carriage. It was already the hour of the Powerscourt ball and her eyes were filled with anxiety as she turned to her sister for reassurance. "I still don't hear him. How deep is the snow now?"

Lissa looked at her lovely dark-haired sister and tickled her with her gilt paper fan. "It's still about six inches, silly, the same as it was a minute ago. It's falling swiftly, I admit, but surely not that swiftly."

"But I don't want anything to keep us from going tonight. Perhaps his carriage is stuck—"

Lissa cut short her worrying. "I'm sure it will taper off any moment now. Never you worry, love. Holland will be here. He'll take his sleigh tonight, and, besides, you know the castle is not very far."

"I'm being a grand ninny, aren't I? But I'm so excited! Imagine, we're to go to a ball, a real ball, just as if we'd never left Alcester House. But how do we look, Lissa? Are we truly beautiful in our gowns? Or is my imagination gilding the picture?"

"I promise everyone in Nodding Knoll shall be green with envy."

"Oh, do you think so?" Evvie giggled.

"I'm sure of it," Lissa answered, and breezed to the sofa to get her mantle.

Of course, she couldn't have been less sure of it, but she wasn't about to let Evvie's fun be spoiled. If the truth were known, she had never dreaded an occasion more in her entire life. Ivan's ball seemed to loom before her like some interminable wake. Yet here she was, dressed in the most magnificent of gowns, with her hair glittering sinfully from the crystals on her snood, ready for the soirée of the century.

She had meant to sell the rose satin gown by now. Furious at Ivan, she'd planned to go to Cullenbury at the very first opportunity. Her grand plan was to approach him in the Baronial Hall and fling the coins at his feet. "According to my power" indeed. She would show him she wouldn't succumb after all.

She'd endured the past few days only because she'd had this reverie to cling to. Yet somehow it had never come to pass. Mrs. Myers was frantic that nothing should go wrong with the ball, and Lissa hadn't the heart to tell her she was quitting. Besides, the housekeeper had been so generous in not having spoken a word of her being found crying in Ivan's chambers that Lissa found herself indebted to her. Mrs. Myers could have sorely damaged her reputation, yet the motherly woman had only looked upon her with a kinder eye and warmer heart. So instead of immediately quitting her position at Powerscourt and going to

Cullenbury, Lissa had spent all her time making lists for the house staff, arranging Chinese peonies in heavy baroque vases, and running after the cook to make sure he'd been informed of the delivery date of his partridges.

But now that the ball was here, she had finally told Mrs. Myers about her plans to leave. When she'd heard the news, the housekeeper had looked pained, as if she somehow blamed herself, but Lissa had impulsively given her a hug and her reassurance that she would be all right.

She was still determined to sell the gown, but on impulse, she had decided to wait a couple of days. Wearing it now, she was terrified of soiling it and decreasing its value. The rose satin would have been far safer in her little room, tucked in its big gold box, than out waltzing at Powerscourt. But somehow she hadn't been able to bear the thought of donning the slate-colored taffeta gown that she had worn the last time to the castle. And she wanted Ivan to see her in the gown. That was probably her sole reason for enduring the night. She wanted him to stare hard, and then she wanted to waltz by in another man's arms. *A ma puissance* might be his motto, but it still couldn't make her throw away her pride.

"I hear a sleigh! And sleigh bells! He's here! Oh, Lissa, we're going to a ball!" Evvie got up from her seat and paced the room like a nervous sparrow. Lissa could only laugh, a bit painfully perhaps, for she was not at all anxious to be off.

"Come here, silly. Take your mantle. Do you want to catch your death?" She handed Evvie her gray woolen cape and donned her own, all the while thinking it was a shame they both had to cover up their grand gowns with such homely apparel.

"Lissa, are you wearing Mother's pearls?" Without warning, Evvie reached up and tried to touch her throat.

Lissa tensed. She'd lied to Evvie for a long time about their mother's pearls. She'd sold the necklace years ago, and they had lived on the proceeds for the better part of a year. Just when Lissa had felt they would have to forfeit their mother's emerald earrings too, Aunt Sophie's first letter had appeared like a gift from God. She felt a stab of guilt over the lovely pearls, but she quickly stepped from her sister's reach. "I have them on, love. Now let's not keep Holland waiting." She took Evvie's arm and briskly went to the front door.

The Powerscourt ball proved to be a dazzling affair. When she, Evvie, and Holland arrived, tucked warmly in Holland's red sleigh, most of the other guests were already there. There was a slight hush to the crowd as they assembled in the Hall, for everyone was all too aware of the new bend-sinister that loomed over them in the Powerscourt crest. Every now and then someone would actually send a startled glance upward to look at it, but that was rare. Most seemed to want only to forget it was there, as if it were something too terrible to look upon. Besides, Nodding Knoll was not a town full of souls who desired to tempt the wrath of their betters, therefore most concentrated simply on their mead and the company. Not a difficult task when the Hall looked so magnificent. High above the loggias, garlands of pine boughs were hung with fat red velvet bows and hundreds of scarlet belladonna lilies filled every corner. But the most pagan oddity was at the end of the Hall.

Surrounded by a hundred guests was a German Christmas tree. It was aglow with tiny candles that were wired to its branches. Hanging from its boughs were dolls and toy soldiers, chessmen and half eggshells gilded and filled with comfits. Glass birds perched on every branch and garlands of bright red holly berries gaily festooned the entire tree. A footman stood nearby with a sponge tied to a stick, on the chance one of the doll's petticoats might catch fire. But thankfully no such accidents had occurred so far. The decorated evergreen was quite popular, especially with the children, who were already eager to see the evening end so that they could take home a treat from its boughs.

Lissa knew Christmas trees were becoming quite the thing. Several years ago she had even seen the picture in the *Illustrated London News* of Queen Victoria sitting by her family's evergreen. Yet the last time she had ever heard of one near Nodding Knoll, it was in Cullenbury and its owner was charging an entire shilling to see it. She'd heard from Arabella that it was quite spectacular, but somehow she knew that one would have never measured up to the one before her.

She suddenly wished George had been able to come home early from Eton for his holiday so that he could see it. She missed her little brother terribly and his letters, though frequent, couldn't make up for his absence. But it was all worth it, no matter what troubles she had had, to be able to give George a brighter future. She only hoped their good fortune would continue. Unwittingly her glance slid to Holland and Evvie.

Their mantles were taken by some supercilious elderly footmen and immediately Lissa felt conspicuous. With her hood gone, her crystal-strewn hair seemed to draw an inordinate amount of attention, especially from the male guests. Her and Evvie's gowns found their admirers too, for theirs were among the most spectacular—not an easy feat, considering the loftiness of the guests in from London. From everywhere, Lissa felt eyes upon them. Yet nowhere did she see Ivan.

She looked through the crowd of crinolines and cutaways but no one seemed to stand as tall as Ivan did. Nor was any gent as handsome. For some strange reason she was suddenly filled with disappointment.

"I do believe I'm with the two loveliest ladies here." Holland smiled at the both of them.

"I can just feel that there must be a thousand people at this ball. Ah, musicians! I hear them warming up!" Evvie clung excitedly to Holland's arm.

"Why don't you take Evvie to the Christmas tree and describe it to her, Holland?" Lissa suggested.

Holland gave her a concerned look.

She laughed. "Oh, you can't mean to have me tailing along. I think it would be terribly difficult for the three of us to waltz." She motioned to a velvet bench pushed along one wall. "I'll be right there when you come back."

"But—" Holland began.

"No one will compromise me, I assure you, dear Holland." She tossed him a brilliant smile and quickly glided away to claim the bench.

She took great pains not to wrinkle her voluminous skirts. Then when she was finally settled, she suddenly felt forlorn. There was a great crush of people in the Hall and the music from the orchestra seemed only to draw in more, yet there seemed no one for her. The ball was turning out just as depressing as she expected, only more so, for just as she looked up, she caught the eye of Albert Rooney. He was dancing with Arabella, though neither of them seemed involved in what they were doing. Each seemed to have their attention elsewhere.

"Would my lady accept a glass of punch?"

Startled, Lissa looked to her left and found a man standing next to her. He seemed a bit young, but he had dazzling leaf-green eyes and a perfect Roman nose. He was a difficult youth to refuse.

"How kind of you," she finally said, accepting the glass.

"Allow me to introduce myself—" the youth began, yet was never allowed to finish for another voice sounded behind him.

"Miss Alcester, it's certainly a pleasure finding you here!" Albert suddenly cut in with his own glass of punch. He acted as if nothing had ever happened between them, though if she looked closely, there did seem to be a hardness about his eyes that she had never seen before.

"Albert" was all she could say before, unexpectedly,

another "beau" cut in. It was Harry McBain dressed in his cleanest shirt and frock coat. Even he sported a glass of punch, and she suddenly began laughing at the absurdity of her situation. And here she was thinking this ball would be dull!

She had just finished refusing Albert's offer of a waltz when she glanced up to one of the loggias that overlooked the Hall. Ivan stood there, dressed splendidly in a black cutaway and trousers, a brilliantly white starched shirt set off by a black satin bow tie, and a sinfully expensive black satin waistcoat. He was glaring down at her, as if he dared her to have a good time at *his* ball. She was caught off guard by his intense scrutiny, then her cheeks burned with anger. He had no right to look at her like that—as if he somehow owned her, as if he had the right to claim her like chattel.

Suddenly the idea of dancing seemed irresistibly appealing. She was going to waltz off in another man's arms, and she wildly hoped that this would infuriate Ivan to new heights. She stood and, to Albert's surprise, accepted his arm.

Albert was a well-schooled dancer, and Lissa found herself easily led around the floor. Her skills sharpened with every step and soon she was almost enjoying herself. She looked about the room so that she could be sure Ivan saw her, yet he was no longer in the loggia and she couldn't find him in the crowd.

Their dance was soon over and Albert led her back to her bench. Holland and Evvie were there by now, though Holland looked a bit shocked that Albert had been her waltzing partner. Lissa didn't make much of that, however, for Harry promptly asked her for the next dance.

He led her in a crude country waltz that was more like a polka. It wasn't the kind to make lovers jealous as Albert's had been, yet she couldn't help but feel flattered by the look of utter awe Harry bestowed upon her. When the dance was over, she found herself actually laughing again, and she became even more determined to enjoy herself and forget about the pain Ivan had caused.

She waltzed for hours, it seemed. The nameless youth turned out to be a knight, Sir Gilbert, and he was also a superb dancer. If she'd actually been a debutante, she was sure she'd have wanted him to fill every space on her dance card.

She danced with Albert again, though it seemed every time she did, he became more and more somber. When the orchestra sounded the last dance before dinner, Albert had abruptly taken her arm and led her to the floor, completely without invitation. She was almost irate enough to call Holland, but he and Evvie were having such a good time waltzing that she couldn't bear to interrupt them. Besides, she was sure she could handle Albert herself.

That was before she found herself waltzed into one of the Hall's oriels. The nook was out of sight from the rest of the guests, for it was behind the great limestone staircase and surrounded by heavy velvet drapery. Immediately Albert stepped from her arms and closed the curtains. She was suddenly thrown into darkness; the only light was that which spilled beneath the velvet partition. In consternation, she made to open the drapery and leave, but Albert blocked her exit with his body. Unable to quit the place, she moved against the huge bay window. She was already feeling chilled. The drafty panes at her back didn't help warm her either.

"Whatever are you doing, Albert? Are you hoping to cause a scene?"

He stepped toward her, a brilliant gleam to his eye. "I've never been so humiliated in my life. Never." He grabbed her arms and pulled her to him. She looked up at him in surprise. She didn't know Albert could be this forceful.

"Tramore is no gentleman," he continued. "I wouldn't have even honored him by attending this blasted ball if it weren't for the slim chance to see you again."

He was holding her arms so tightly she was sure he was bruising her. With some hesitation, she tried to answer him. "It was unthinkably cruel what he did to you, Albert. But you must put it out of your mind. No one knows about it. And I promise, no one ever will."

"He ruined my chance to marry you!"

She lowered her eyes. "You may still have the chance." She couldn't believe she had said that, for she didn't love him. Yet somehow she still clung to the belief that marriage was the answer to her problems. If Albert felt so strongly about her, then perhaps they could make a good marriage. And Albert would relieve her of her debts to Ivan.

Albert turned from her, disconsolate. "No, no. He's compromised you. I saw it. Mother would never approve."

Anger seethed in her breast. Her last shreds of respect for this man fell from her shoulders. She turned to go, but she found his hand on her waist, holding her back.

"Don't you touch me," she hissed. She pulled off his fingers and made for the drapery once more.

"Lissa, stop. I must have you. And if we can't marry, then I want to set you up, perhaps in London. Far away from Mother."

The fury inside her exploded. She turned and vented it upon him. "I am *not* that kind of woman, you—you milktoast! Nor shall I ever be! So unhand me before I scream and fetch your mother to take you home for the night!"

"Lissa, my lovely, that's him speaking, not you! Don't you see? Tramore has got you in his clutches and I'm here to set you free!" Without warning, he pulled her to him and his thin, wet lips sought hers. She was overcome by revulsion, yet also by the desire to laugh. The man's kiss was impossibly inept; his offer pitifully absurd.

Albert was a poor example of manhood, it was true, but he was still stronger than she was. She made several struggling attempts to leave his embrace, but she was held firm by his wiry arms. His lips caught hers again and this time she shook from rage. Her hand found his face and she clawed at his cheek, but to no avail. He seemed bent on having her, no matter how she felt about it. As secluded as the oriel was, she wondered how far he would dare go.

A light shined in her eyes and she heard the drapery being opened, then closed. Behind them in the darkness, she heard Ivan's voice. She could have sobbed in relief.

"Have you a death wish, Rooney?"

Albert's head shot up and, in his surprise, he dropped his hold. Lissa sank to a nearby bench, panting from her struggles.

Albert stammered, but he stood his ground. "We—we want to be together, Tramore. And—and you've not got the power to stop us, no matter your trickery."

"I see." Ivan looked as if he were going to chuckle, but suddenly his fist went out and it met squarely with Albert's jaw. Albert crumpled on the bench right next to Lissa, unconscious.

Horrified, she looked down at the poor man. "Ivan, you've killed him."

Ivan grasped her hand and pulled her to her feet. In the dimness of the oriel, her eyes had to strain to see his face.

"Rooney's fine," he answered. "Though now that you've given me the idea, I should probably finish him altogether by getting a footman and having him dropped in the moat."

"Don't even think such evil things," she admonished in a hushed voice.

"I *think* of far worse, Lissa."

In the tiny nook, they were so close together, her satin skirts were crushed against him. Just the sound of his voice was a painful reminder of their previous encounter in his apartments. All at once she wanted to be away from him.

"Ivan, I must get back. Someone will wonder—"

"First you tell me, is this how you repay me?" He suddenly turned angry. "You put on your pretty frock and fall into the arms of the first man who wants to kiss you?"

"Rooney forced me in here. I didn't want him to kiss me—" Her brow suddenly furrowed. "And repay you for what?" He was being particularly infuriating tonight.

She felt his fingers touch one of the rose satin bows on her shoulder. Her belly tightened. Suddenly she felt as if she were on a steeplechase, instead of being at a sedate ball detained by the host.

"You owe me a great deal, Lissa. More than you know," he said pensively. His voice grew husky. "Have I told you how exquisite you are tonight, *alainn*? My God, even that gown doesn't do you justice."

She stiffened. At the name *alainn*, her heart constricted once more. Painfully she forced it back inside its bindings. "I must go," she said.

"Then let's both abandon this wretched ball."

"I hardly think that would be proper." She pulled back her skirts so that she could pass. Before she could, he took her arm.

"Why is it you're so cold with me, love? Why is it I find Rooney extracting more passion out of those frigid little lips than I can? And why do I keep hearing the rumors that say you fully earned that lusty little nickname, *Lissa*, when I don't see it at all?"

"Those rumors are lies, I tell you—all of them—" she whispered bitterly.

"I wish they weren't. For my eyes only, at least."

"But not for Albert's? Or what about that delicious youth with the green eyes?" Her eyes narrowed. "He's a knight, you know."

He gripped her arm brutally. "As if a mere knight could compare to my station."

"Yes, but look, his beginnings were not as humble as yours."

She knew she had hurt him, but somehow the words had driven by themselves, spurred on by her broken heart. All that she'd ever hoped for she had laid at his feet, and though she might have deserved it, he had trampled her dreams with unnecessary relish.

"Did you know, in times past, my love, the lord of the castle could have a wench flogged to death for making such comments?" He shoved her away and she knew if the light was better, she would have seen his handsome face taut with anger.

"And, no doubt, you'd think that wasn't enough punishment."

"Not the *correct* punishment. Indeed, especially not for you."

She let out a tormented laugh. "Then thank heaven for these modern times." Her hand went to the drapery and she discreetly opened it. She shot her last comment at him. "Now if you'll excuse me. I must return to my beaux."

She felt his eyes upon her until the drapery fell back once more. In the light she hoped he hadn't seen how shaken she was from their encounter, but as she left him, Albert was coming to and, furious, Ivan had turned his attention on him. The delirious man had the misfortunate to utter her name, and this enraged Ivan all over again. With a look of disgust on his face, Ivan took a holly wreath that had been hanging on the window and pulled it over Albert's thin shoulders. Then he too left the oriel.

CHAPTER TWENTY

❦

Lissa only wanted the evening to end, but it loomed long and interminable before her. Dinner was a grand affair and no delicacy was too costly to be served, much to the delight of the townsfolk. But Lissa found her appetite gone, and even Sir Gilbert's witticisms couldn't bring it back.

They sat at Ivan's long table in the midst of a hundred strangers. Evvie and Holland sat near them, and the Bishops, but after that it seemed everyone the marquis wanted to honor at his table was from somewhere else, not Nodding Knoll. An unfamiliar black-haired woman sat on Ivan's right, and she and Ivan seemed to get along famously. The beauty seemed all too familiar with the marquis, and though her husband was not seated two seats from her, she once even dared pat the marquis's unblemished cheek. Watching her, Lissa could hardly get down her wine. Her stomach felt as if it were coiled into a knot and when the last cordial had been served, she wanted to fall to her knees and give thanks that the meal was finally over.

Ivan stood and helped the beauty to her feet. As Sir Gilbert did likewise to Lissa, she overheard snatches of the host's conversation.

"Antonia, I'm heartened to see you're as difficult as always," she overheard Ivan say good-naturedly.

"On the contrary, my lord, I'm as biddable as I always was—as biddable as an unspoiled country lass." The woman smiled into her fan and her bewitching emerald eyes turned to an elderly man next to her. "Aren't I, Kovel?" she asked, and the man promptly began to laugh.

"You see?" Ivan interjected. "Even when I tell you you're difficult, you contest me." He turned to the gent who was obviously Antonia's husband. "How do you endure her?" he asked in jest. "You tell her the sun rises at dawn, she says dusk. You inform her the trees are green, she tells you yellow!"

Laughing, Kovel slapped Ivan on the back. "It's true! It's true! I tell you, Ivan, if she wasn't so dazzlingly rich, I'd have tossed her out long ago!" The gent wiped his eyes and tried to stop chuckling. When he had calmed a bit, he said, "You know what I need, Tramore. I need that awful black stare of yours to keep her in her place. I need those black eyes!"

Antonia smugly put her arm through her husband's. "Blue, my love. Ivan's eyes are blue."

At that contrary statement, Kovel once more broke into laughter. Antonia smiled at Ivan and Lissa found herself wanting to drop back into her seat from the shock of it all. There weren't many who had gotten so close to Ivan that they were able to discern that the true color of his eyes was blue, not black. Lissa had thought that perhaps she was the only one. Now this woman, this sophisticated, breathtaking beauty, knew it too. Stricken, all Lissa could do was watch her, a blush of jealousy staining her cheeks. Yet as if Antonia Kovel sensed Lissa's distress, she turned and met the younger woman's eye. Antonia's whole being seemed to radiate warmth and approval. Then, at a moment when her husband and Ivan weren't looking, she did the most unusual thing. Antonia winked.

The astounding moment was gone in a flash, and quickly Lissa found herself in the crush to leave the dining hall. Ivan and the Kovels had disappeared and she was left alone to figure out the meaning of the extraordinary gesture.

For the rest of the evening, Lissa did her best to avoid Ivan, but it seemed wherever she looked, he was there, appearing to have a magnificent time. After they had dined, the guests returned to the Hall and the orchestra began another set of waltzes. As her eyes once more searched for Ivan in the crowd, Lissa again found him surrounded by a swarm of ladies. Women seemed as attracted to him as bees to nectar, and, later, whenever she chanced a look into the waltzers, she found Ivan's tall form every time holding a different beauty. He had just returned Arabella Parks to her chair when he approached the beauteous Antonia Kovel for a third dance. With that, Lissa found she could take no more. Somehow, someway, she had to leave.

Her immediate solution was to retire to the ladies' quarters and plead headache. She was just searching it out when she ran into the Bishops who were in the passage donning their cloaks.

"Lissa love! You look so grand, why then the pale face?" Mrs. Bishop gave her a concerned look.

"No doubt she's been waltzing too much!" Mr. Bishop interjected pleasantly. "Mathilde, you know such a lovely creature as our own Lissa must be worn out just from refusing the offers to dance." He shot Lissa a proud, fatherly look. Lissa was sure she had never loved him more.

Releasing a tired little laugh, she said, "I'm afraid to disappoint you but the truth is I'm not feeling well. I was just going to the ladies' chamber to rest—"

"Love, what it it? The headache? Oh, no, and on such a glorious night." Mrs. Bishop hovered about her like a mother hen. "Then you should come home with us. We're leaving early because of the snow, you see. I'd love to make you some tea. And we've plenty of room. Plenty of room."

"I couldn't put you out," Lissa answered not too convincingly. The idea of spending the evening at the hearth with the dear Bishops seemed like a balm for what ailed her. She could escape this ball and not think about Ivan for the rest of the night, if that could ever be possible.

"Let's get your mantle and be off." Mrs. Bishop linked her arm with Lissa's. "Herman will bring you back first thing in the morning."

"But wait! I forgot about Evvie—"

"Evelyn is here too?" Mrs. Bishop paused. "Why, we haven't seen her. How wonderful that she could accompany you. But wherever is she?"

Lissa thought for a moment. She knew Evvie was with Holland somewhere in the Hall. It was absolutely scandalous for her to even think of leaving Evvie at the castle unchaperoned. But she ached to be away from Powerscourt. Just the thought of spending another moment here made her head truly throb. Yet Evvie was in good company. She couldn't relinquish her care to a better person than Holland.

"I hate to ruin Evvie's fun, and besides, I know she's in good hands. She'll get back to Violet Croft safely, I'm sure," Lissa mused. "But do let me write her a note, will you?"

"Of course, love." Mrs. Bishop patted her hand. Mr. Bishop went to get a footman.

Lissa penned a quick note explaining that she would be at the Bishops' for the night and that no one was to worry. After signing off that she would see her in the morning, Lissa handed it to the footman and, taking him aside, asked that it be given discreetly to Mr. Jones.

With that task accomplished, she gathered her skirts and hurried down the passage to retrieve her mantle. The Bishops, meanwhile, headed for the door to claim their carriage. Lissa was not gone for five minutes before, mantle in hand, she was again rushing down the passage. To her right and left the parlors were filled with guests, but she moved past them, deaf to their gaiety, intent on only one thing—departure. She was so anxious to be gone, she hardly saw the hand that reached for her from one door. Before she knew it, she was grabbed and pulled into Ivan's billiard room.

"Where do you think you're off to?" Ivan asked her, his voice filled with annoyance.

"I'm leaving. Evvie is in good company. She'll do

without my chaperonage for tonight," she practically hissed at him.

"I suppose she's with Holland. No doubt, you think he's less a man than I? Return to your sister's side, Lissa. Don't give Holland the temptation."

Her cheeks heated with suppressed anger. "You, of all people, dare to defame his character? You sink to new levels, my lord."

"I'm only stating fact. Evvie is quite beautiful."

"Oh, but surely not as beautiful as Antonia Kovel?"

The moment after her words were out, she could have horsewhipped herself. She hadn't meant to blurt that out, but somehow once more he'd gotten the better of her.

Suddenly Ivan's interest was piqued. His eyes narrowed thoughtfully. "So you've noticed Lady Antonia." He released an ironic laugh. "But then, you would. You're both alike in so many ways. Come, I shall introduce you." He made to take her arm but she pulled it from him.

"I cannot meet *Lady* Antonia because the Bishops are waiting for me in the bailey." She moved to the door. He was right behind her.

Once they were out in the passage, Ivan called to a nearby footman. She ignored him but was only a few steps on her way when she heard Ivan say, "Tell the Bishops that Miss Alcester won't be coming with them, that she's decided to do the correct thing and chaperone her sister. That will be all."

She spun in the passage and glared at him. The footman immediately left, and she spent a moment or two debating whether or not she could beat the youth to the bailey. But in her crinoline and satins, she knew she couldn't. So she picked up her skirts and mantle and, with a vengeance, made her way back to the Hall. If Ivan wanted her to chaperone Evvie, she would, to the exclusion of everything and everyone else.

"I'd like a waltz, Lissa."

"It'll be a cold day in—"

Before she could even finish her oath, he had taken her mantle from her and flung it onto a bench in one of the Hall's inglenooks. He then took her by the waist and, in moments, they were dancing among the guests.

Lissa's movements were stiff and angry, but she didn't dare pull from Ivan's embrace. He was, after all, the host, and to reject him in front of his guests would be the height of impropriety. That was something neither she nor her reputation needed.

"You are an arrogant, self-serving, licentious, dissolute . . . rakehell!" she whispered harshly, all the while smiling to the guests.

"Try bastard, sweet. That word always works well." Ivan glided her across the polished stone floor.

"Only because you work so hard at being one," she hissed.

Ivan chanced a look at his guests—a studied mixture of London nobility and Nodding Knoll townsfolk. His gaze was almost contemptuous when he answered, "Believe me, it takes no effort at all."

His hand tightened at her waist and he swept her past a long line of windows that led out to a snow-covered balcony. They both fell silent. The music was tender and dreamy, and though her cheeks still burned with anger, her nerves were soothed by the beautiful waltz. With Ivan's possessive lead, her movements grew lighter and soon they waltzed in glorious unison, like the hero and the heroine of a fairy tale.

While they glided past the crowds Lissa chanced a look at Ivan. She was struck by the intent expression on his face. He was watching her as if she were as unearthly and beautiful as an angel fallen from the clouds. The moment stood still as their gazes locked, their eyes all too clearly expressing their unspoken thoughts. It was unbearably intimate, and she found herself wanting to look away. But Ivan wouldn't let her. He held her tightly and close, and if they had been alone, and not in a crowded ballroom, she was sure he would have kissed her. And this time, whether because of the music or simply the dark, needful gleam in his eyes, she just might have let him.

"It's me you love, isn't it, Lissa?"

Hearing the question she dreaded most from him, she stumbled. Although he caught her, she couldn't continue. Without word or warning, she broke from his arms and ran to the adjoining inglenook. Then, because the hearth couldn't cool her raging emotions, she flung on her mantle, forced open the French doors, and stepped onto the snowy balcony.

Along its length, some of the Hall's doors were cracked to allow air to circulate. The music had stopped but she could hear the tinkling of punch glasses and merry conversations. The snow was sure to stain the hem of her gown, but suddenly she didn't care. Her heart was warring with her mind and she didn't know where to turn. Ivan's question had taken her off guard. She had stood on the precipice of disaster and she had almost fallen in. If she didn't get away from him once and for all, she would be lost altogether and grow as mad from grief as her father had.

"Lissa." She turned to find her nemesis right behind her, his black attire in stark contrast to the snow. He was so close she could see the great, lacy flakes caught on his hair and shoulders. She backed toward the carved stone balustrade.

"Ivan, don't. Go back to your guests," she whispered.

"What are you afraid of?"

"I'm not well. I need to go home. You should have let me go with the Bishops." She put her hand to her temple and looked away.

"Then let me take you upstairs—"

"No!" She thrust his hand from her elbow. "Ivan, just leave me alone. I beg of you—"

Just then a peal of feminine laughter rang out to the

balcony. Lissa looked up and saw that Arabella and several other girls she remembered from her childhood had gathered in the Hall right by one of the open doors.

"Letitia, you're such a goose! You tell me the marquis's scar frightens you, but then you've pouted all evening because he hasn't asked you to waltz," Arabella said.

"Lettie's just jealous," another girl chimed in, one whom Lissa had seen dancing with Ivan only a half hour before.

"I am most certainly not! Besides it's Arabella who's set her cap for him, not I!" Letitia nervously fanned herself. A pleased look appeared on Arabella's visage, yet she let another girlfriend respond.

"Well, I know one thing, my mother says no one will get him, not with Lissa Alcester still in Nodding Knoll—"

"Oh, pooh!" Letitia interrupted. "Your mother knows better! Even a man with the marquis's wicked reputation wouldn't marry Lusty Lissa Alcester! Why, everyone knows that!" They all broke into laughter again, as if Letitia had said the most hilarious joke. Lissa watched Arabella and though she didn't seem to find the comment particularly funny, Arabella didn't defend her either. She merely watched her chums with a placid expression on her face, as if she were blind to their cruelty.

Lissa moved away from the window. The pain seemed to choke her. She couldn't even look at Ivan. He had wanted her hurt. Now he hadn't even had to lift a finger to do it.

She felt Ivan's hand touch her arm. Softly he said, "Lissa, you're not one of them anymore. So don't let yourself be judged by their morals."

Tears threatened to spill upon her cheeks at any moment. His comment only made things worse. He seemed to be throwing her poverty in her face. She glared at him and stated sarcastically, "But you couldn't be more wrong, my lord. I *am* still one of them. I was born into their station and my morals remain just as high."

"*Alainn,* you misunderstand."

The first tear fell to her cheek. She was lost now. She reclaimed her arm, then released a bitter laugh. "No, it is you who misunderstands. They might think it's you who wouldn't marry me, but they're mistaken. Arabella may have you, you ignoble gypsy, for you fall far short of my equal, . . . and always have!"

With that, she ran to the balcony stairs that led down to the bailey. She was determined to leave the ball now, even if it meant she had to walk home. The stones beneath her slippered feet were slick with snow, but miraculously she didn't fall. Behind her Ivan called her name, but she refused to listen. She was leaving and no one was going to stop her.

She descended the snowy steps just as she heard Ivan slip. He cursed heartily, but she didn't pause. His colorful oaths alone told her he was all right, and now she was ahead. She meant to make the most of it.

The snow was high in the bailey and the only path was cut from the sleighs leaving the front doors. Looking around, she noticed a pony cart by the kitchen door, no doubt left by one of the townsfolk who was now probably in the kitchens tippling gin with the help.

She would return it in the morning, she vowed, trudging through the snow, unmindful of her wet, ruined hem. Her slippers were also ruined, but she made it to the cart and took the reins of the little snowy Shetland. With her palm, she wiped the tears off her cheek, wishing fervently that they would just freeze there. There was no time for further indulgence, however, for Ivan was again right behind her. So she flicked the reins and forced the pony forward. When the little Shetland found the sleigh path, it broke into a trot.

"Damn it, Lissa! I said stop!" she heard Ivan call out, but she paid him no heed. She urged the pony on and soon she was beyond the gatehouse. The only thing that followed her after that was Ivan's curses.

Beyond Powerscourt, the snow fell swift and silent. Her pony's breath came in silvery puffs as it left the sleigh path to town and turned toward Violet Croft. A merciless opaque sky left them in darkness and they struggled to stay on the road, which was now blanketed in virgin white. The Shetland went a respectable distance, but quickly the snow grew too deep. Soon the cart became hopelessly bogged down in the drifts, and, in her disappointment, her tears began anew.

She cried for a moment, then descended the cart and went to the pony. Her mantle slipped from her shoulders when she pulled on the Shetland's bridle, but she was unmindful of the cold. All she wanted was to get home and forget the entire evening. To her joy, the pony took another step or two with her help, and she climbed into the cart, relieved to continue. But again the sensible pony refused to go farther.

She felt she would go mad from frustration when a tall, shadowy horseman appeared behind her. She feared the rider was Ivan and she expected him to bear down on her, yet the dark figure paused, as if, somehow, he found her a fetching sight: a girl in a pony cart, her hair and gown iced with snow, the flakes glittering like the crystals in her hair, the night a velvety backdrop to her portrait. The rider seemed almost enchanted by her, but soon the spell was broken and he purposefully urged his steed closer until the falling snow no longer blurred his image.

She frowned and eyed the horseman with unveiled dislike. It was Ivan after all, and her anger only increased when she realized she was trembling before him.

"It's the height of impropriety for the host to leave his ball, my lord. Or hasn't your posh London lifestyle taught you that yet?" She flicked the pony's reins in a futile attempt to get it to move.

Without a word, he dismounted. His silence was ominous as he walked to where her mantle lay in the snow. He picked it up and tossed it to her. It fell wet and heavy into her lap.

"What are you doing?" she asked nervously when he began unharnessing the pony.

"We're going back."

Her eyes flashed with annoyance. "Indeed *we* are not. I'm going to Violet Croft."

He didn't even bother to debate the issue. His anger was all too clear as he tied the Shetland to the back of his Thoroughbred. Acting as if she were a child, he walked up to the cart and held out his hand, waiting for her to comply.

She refused.

"I'm returning to Violet Croft, Ivan. So take the pony back with you. I shall walk the rest of the way, if I have to."

He laughed, dashing all her bravado. "I believe you would, *alainn,* but you've not just the snow to contend with now. You've got me. So get down from that cart before I drag you from it." He held out his hand again.

But again she refused it. He was just about to climb onto the cart when she knew she had to do something. She clambered down the other side, barely pausing to don her mantle, and ran toward her cottage. Yet as she waded through the snow, with her ungainly satin skirts tripping her up more than the drifts did, Ivan had little trouble reaching her.

"I won't go back with you, Ivan! I won't!" she cried when he lifted her into his arms. She was thrown against his chest and though she wanted to fight him, the warmth of his body was almost welcome in the frigid night air. Still she knew this was madness, so she pushed against his chest with all her strength.

He merely laughed, seeming to enjoy the fight. Only when she had quieted did she know how much.

His desire was all too apparent when she was crushed against him in an intimate embrace. His arms were locked around her and he had lifted her completely clear of the snow. Though there were many layers of silk and wool between them, she could feel his hard, muscular body pressing against hers. The familiarity made her face flame. "Ivan, let me down," she demanded.

"Shall you come with me back to the castle then?"

"I want to go home—"

She felt his hand move to her bottom. He squeezed her fondly. Her eyes opened wide in shock.

"Back to the castle?" he asked, lifting one of his jet eyebrows.

"Yes!" she blurted out hastily, willing to say anything so that he would release her. But even so he took his time letting her go.

Once released, however, she was not quite ready to admit defeat. This time, she gathered her cumbersome skirts in her hands and plunged through the snow toward Violet Croft. With every step, she was sure she could make out her cottage's outline in the snowy night. But Violet Croft never quite appeared before Ivan seized her and they plummeted into the snow.

She gasped as he fell on top of her. His tall, well-conditioned frame seemed like a prison, and though she knew she should try to get away, now it was impossible. She'd let herself become hopelessly vulnerable. She should have never gone to the ball; she should have never run away. She should have remained by Evvie's side and refused any waltzes. Then Ivan wouldn't have been able to torment her; then she never would have been hurt by Letitia's cruel comment.

Yet even that hurt dimmed beside the pain that Ivan had caused. She pushed on his implacable chest. Her desire for him was becoming a torture she could no longer endure.

Warily she met his gaze, then promptly lost another battle. In his eyes, she glimpsed something she had never seen before—something that was sacred yet dangerous. It was as dark and beautiful as the midnight sky, and just as unreachable. It promised both heaven and hell; and she knew that in order to get one, she would have to chance the other.

"Come back to the castle, love. Don't fight me any more," he whispered to her.

She shook her head and smiled bitterly. "Ivan, we'll destroy each other."

He reached for her cold little hand and brought it to his mouth. He placed a burning kiss into her palm, then achingly brought her hand to his scar.

"So let's destroy each other," he answered in a husky voice.

A soft moan escaped her lips and his mouth came down on hers in a soul-stealing kiss. His lips grew impossibly demanding until he would accept nothing less than her full participation. He forced her to kiss him with equal ferocity and when she did, there was nothing in the universe but Ivan and her passion for him, which she had held in check for so long.

She prayed that as the phoenix could rise from its ashes, so could they, but when he brought her to her feet, her fears overwhelmed her. They were both covered with snow but neither of them seemed to notice. Without a word, without a glance, he took her hand and tried to lead her to his steed. But she pulled back, frightened.

"I can't, Ivan. I won't," she told him.

He turned and faced her. His hand gently brushed the snow from her hair. "I've thought about this night for five years, Lissa. Don't deny me it now."

"You've thought about it for revenge and only revenge. I'm not so foolish—"

"Foolish! Foolish!" he snapped. "It's I who has played the fool! I've been through this torment so many times, I can't see straight any more. Let's be done with it, Lissa. Tonight I'll rid you from my soul and you can do likewise!" With that, he lifted her into his arms and onto his saddle. She gasped her protests and tried to dismount, but he stopped her. He mounted also and soon they were heading back to the castle.

The snow was falling more heavily now, but somehow Ivan seemed to know just where to go. They arrived in Powerscourt's bailey within minutes. The steed and the pony were promptly taken to the stables by the grooms, and though Lissa pleaded with him to take her back to the ball, he refused.

He pulled her across the snowy bailey and ducked them into a covered servants' door just as another crowd was leaving in their sleighs. Unseen by the guests, Ivan pulled her to his chest and cupped her face with his hands. His palms were callused, yet their rough texture was almost pleasing. When she next looked up, his expression took her breath away. Intense and impatient, he then kissed her, devouring her with his mouth, and she knew without a doubt there was no turning back. He was not to be denied now. From the look on his face, an army of men couldn't stop him.

Before she could catch her breath they'd gone through the servants' door and were in the keep. There wasn't a soul around as he took her by the hand and forced her through the back maze of passages that led to the lord's apartments. She tried to comprehend what they were about to do but her emotions clouded her ability to think. She was afraid yet exhilarated. Deep down inside, she knew she wanted him, but what would tomorrow bring? Nothing but heartache. He would once more begin his notorious pursuit of other women and she would be left behind, forgotten like an old toy.

Terrified, she stood still on the stone floor of the passage. She had to stop him. If she didn't, then what Letitia had said about her might become all too true.

"Ivan, no—" she began, but he was in no mood for words. Seeing her reluctance, he lifted her up like a bag of horse feed and carried her to his apartments. When they were finally in his bedchamber, he laid her trembling body down before the great fire that burned in the hearth. Before her stood Ivan's stately Elizabethan bed, massively carved in oak, heavily draped in Bargello needlework. Above her the pinnacled ceiling and ogee arches glimmered in the firelight. The room was dark and masculine, redolent with Romanticism and medieval Gothic. Though it had been Ivan's father's room and his father's before that, it was only another irony that it suited the present lord perfectly.

She started when she felt his hands upon her. He slid her wet mantle off her shoulders and it landed heavily behind her. She was cold. Whatever hair wasn't in her snood now hung in damp tendrils about her face and neck, and her hem was frigid with clinging, melting snow. But she shivered even more as she watched Ivan move about the room, a wicked expression on his face. He went to a massive bog oak chest and poured something amber from a decanter. He brought a glass to her and put it in her chilled hand.

"Drink this, *alainn.*"

Alainn, she thought, and took the liquor in one fiery gulp. The name reminded her of all that was terrible in their relationship.

"More?"

She shook her head. Mutely she allowed him to take the glass from her hand.

He eased himself down on the hearth next to her. She looked at the unnatural light in his eyes, and suddenly she knew without a doubt that the only way to stop him now was to kill him. He had her and he was not about to let her go. She trembled. He was so close she could smell his breath laced with the essence of brandy. His jaw bore the shadow of a beard, and when he bent to kiss her cheek, her nose, her throat, she felt his rough skin. She inhaled and he filled her to bursting. If colors were fragrance, his scent would be a dark, sparkling burgundy, warm and rich. Soon a shiver ran down her spine as she felt his fingers on the back of her bodice. Instinctively she drew away, but there was nowhere to go. It was another exquisite torture, but one by one the silk lacings holding her gown together were undone.

His gaze never wavered from her own. He stared at her for a long time, taking in all of her appearance. The gown, or rather how she looked in it, seemed to captivate him. The way the gleaming rose satin hung from her shoulders, barely on, yet barely off, lit a possessive spark in his eyes. The snood pleased him also, but, unexpectedly, it was the next thing to go. He tore it off her hair and the crystals dropped to the stone floor like hail. Her tresses fell free in a silver-gilt cascade, and that seemed to be what pleased him most of all. He picked up a silky curl from her shoulder and rubbed it between his fingers. The color seemed to fascinate him beyond reason. Finally he murmured, "I'll never be rid of you, Lissa. You'll haunt me forever."

His words offered her no solace. The scar on his face, that cruel, white scar, was cast in the firelight. Suddenly his statement seemed absurd. Of course, Ivan would never be rid of her. Not as long as he could look into a mirror.

He wrapped his hand in her hair and pulled her to him for another kiss. He wouldn't accept any holding back, and all too quickly her tongue met traitorously, deliciously with his. She felt him work at the ribbons on her corset cover and she was jerked by the force of his pull. Still his lips wouldn't release her.

The task was done in an astoundingly short amount of time and she was dragged to his bed. There, he left her holding her loosened dress and corset to her bosom while he walked to the fire. His cutaway came off first, then his waistcoat. He dispensed with his collar and bowtie. Finally he ripped off his shirt, revealing a magnificent, well-muscled chest.

She trembled for she knew it well. Hardly a summer

day had gone by when she hadn't watched him from her room while he toiled shirtless in the Alcester stable yard. Now as she looked at him though, she felt a great jolt of emotion that had barely stirred within her years before. Desire coursed through her veins like an opiate. It made her belly tighten and her legs grow weak. Her palms curled around the heavy Genoa silk of the counterpane as she watched him walk to the bed.

"Take off your gown," he told her in a rich, low voice.

Hesitating, she grasped the gown even tighter to her chest. All her instincts told her that she was doing something dangerous. Anything she wanted this badly had to be.

"Ivan, you must listen—"

"Lissa, give me the pleasure of watching you undress."

She put her hand out in a futile effort to stop him. "No, you must listen. Those names I've been called. They're not true. You must know that I've never . . ." She was so pitifully naive she didn't even know how to delicately explain what she had never done.

His mouth curved in a strange little smile. He walked to her and trailed his finger down her bare shoulder.

"Are you telling me that, contrary to what I've heard, you've never lain with a man?"

She couldn't look at him. Uneasily she nodded, and a grim smile came to her lips. "I hate to disappoint you, but I'm not the hardened character everyone believes me to be. And I'm not the girl for you now."

She tried to rise from the bed. His hand stopped her. He tipped her head up and he stared at her as if he could look into her soul.

Finally he whispered, "Lissa, you take my breath away. You're an angel fallen from heaven and I want you so, I'll go mad if I can't have you."

A shadow passed over her eyes. Bitterly she reached

her hand out and traced his scar. "I'm no angel," she whispered.

He grabbed her hand and stopped her movement.

"Perhaps you are. Perhaps it's you who might save me." With that, he bent his head and his lips trailed down her neck until he met with the hollow of her throat. He left a scorching kiss in its sensitive recess, then his hands impatiently pushed her gown down from her bosom. His teeth grazed the swell of her breasts and he desperately tore at the buttons of her chemise. Her petticoats were expertly untied; her garters unclasped. Soon her dress joined the ornate pile of discarded garments, along with her ruined slippers and her drawers edged with Brussels lace. She was left with only her strapless corset and chemise to retain her modesty, and that was fleeting, for without warning, he grabbed her laces and wickedly ripped her corset in two.

She gasped, shocked by the violence of his actions. But he wasn't through with his onslaught. As if she were naked, his hand slid over her full breast, making the fire in her belly only burn brighter. She was still in her chemise, yet the fine dotted muslin was like a transparent sheath. Ivan seemed to find her quite tantalizing in it, and her nipples soon ached from the savagery of his caress.

Too quickly, he wanted more. Again she was shocked by his methods; he dispensed with her chemise in the same manner with which he had her corset. With her last garment in tatters at her feet, she was suddenly overcome by terror. Naked, she tried to pull back from him, tried to put her hands over her breasts, but he wouldn't let her. He forced her arms to her sides, then cupped her chin so that she would look at him. When her frightened gaze locked with his, he inexplicably confessed, "My beauty, you take my breath away. So don't pull back now."

His words were too ferocious for her to tell him nay. She moaned in protest, but before she knew what was happening to her, his mouth had covered one dusky pink nipple and she shook from the pleasure he gave her. Time seemed to stand still as his warm palm slid between her legs. He caressed the inner satin of her thighs, and when he finally felt her response, he groaned, unable to wait any longer. He stepped from the bed and removed the last of his clothing.

She watched him in the firelight, her eyelids heavy with desire. He was so beautiful, more beautiful than she had ever imagined in her simple girlish dreams. Now she would dream of him as a woman should—picturing him in minute detail. She would remember the broad chest well covered with crisp, black hair; his long, powerful legs perfectly formed to handle the most willful Thoroughbred; the buttocks hewn of pure, rock-hard muscle. He was ardently well endowed with manhood, and a tremor of excitement and fear ran through her as he came back to the bed. Her arms again wrapped protectively across her chest and she tensed when his weight came down on the mattress.

But soon she was enveloped in such warmth she wondered if she could ever feel cold again. He rolled on top of her and kissed her as if he had never kissed her before. When he seemed as if he couldn't hold back any longer, he filled his hands completely with her ample breasts, and he whispered against her pale hair, "I've waited so long for this. An eternity. But no more."

But no more. The words made her eyes fill with bittersweet tears. He had wanted to have her. Tomorrow, when his lust was satiated, his interest in her would surely wane. He'd made it all too clear that she was a demon he wanted to exorcise from his soul. When he had done that, perhaps he would even move back to London. And leave her behind in horrid little Nodding Knoll, never to be thought of again.

A tear escaped her eye. This night was probably destined to be and its outcome was perhaps also as preordained. It was her terrible secret that she loved this distant, despicable man, and her pride was ultimately the price she would pay for it. She stared up at him and studied his hard, handsome features in the firelight. She had every reason in the world to avoid him, but somehow he had caught her—with his heated touch, his passionate words. Suddenly she knew she couldn't fight him any more. Her only choice now was to grab her happiness with both hands, because tomorrow it would all be gone.

Impulsively she pulled his dark head to hers and kissed him with all the fire in her soul. Understanding as no other could, he returned her kiss, then eased between her supple thighs.

She had never felt so complete as that first moment when he entered her. His thrust was strong and sure. Though there should have been pain, the pain in her heart dimmed any other she might have felt. Her hands clung to his muscular arms and she lost herself in the power of the moment.

Ivan took her with ferocious glory, and beneath him, Lissa began to understand her mother's insatiable desires. Yet now she almost wanted to laugh. To think she had ever feared that she would turn into Rebecca, when it was far worse than that. Her mother's affliction had been to want too many men, but now Lissa knew the truest hell was to want only one man, the one she could never really have.

Her fingers dug into the muscle of Ivan's forearms. He groaned her name and she almost wept. His rhythm was hard and unbreakable; she soon began to quiver from excitement. Her pleasure was building until she wanted to beg him to stop. But she didn't beg him, and he didn't stop. His breath came quick and furious as if he were holding back. The scar on his face was as white as she had ever seen it, and she couldn't stop herself from touching it. But then she could bear no more. She moaned his name and in her delirium, her nails raked down his cheek. She flung her head back, taking her fulfillment in long, exquisite waves. Above her, she heard him gasp "Lissa . . . *my* Lissa" before he groaned and found a pleasure as long and exquisite as her own.

If ever there was a night as black as this one, she had yet to live through it. In the flickering, dying light of the hearth, Lissa watched Ivan sleep. His knee rode intimately between her thighs and his arm rested possessively at her waist. Her hair was spread over his chest like a mass of sunlit threads, in startling contrast to the coal black curls behind it. As she lay near him, she felt his breath coming even and deep. Unable to stop herself, she rested her hand lightly against his chest. Beneath her palm lay warm skin and hard muscle; deeper still, his heart beat strong and sure. She looked at him and her eyes filled with tears of grief and love. In slumber, Ivan Tramore looked more like the angel Gabriel than the notorious bastard eleventh marquis.

And now she would have to leave him.

She closed her eyes and fought back her tears. She tried to summon the courage to go, but her courage failed her once more and her mind drifted to more pleasant hours. He had made love to her three more times, and with each moment, his need for her only grew more desperate. The sheets bore testament to her truthfulness, and the fact she'd been a virgin had seemed to please him immensely. He had kissed her so deeply then she wondered if it were possible for them to meld into one.

Yet now she would have to leave him.

Numbly she sat up. It was time to go. If she lingered in his warm bed, he might awaken. He would surely take her again, and though a part of her heated at the thought, another part of her wept. It was all too clear that they had no future. She had found no forgiveness or love in his bed. There was no more between them now to build a future on than there had ever been before. The only thing she left behind were the remnants of a torrid, hateful past —a past he would never let go. Even Letitia's mother knew that; Arabella knew it too; and most of Nodding Knoll. And when he opened his eyes in the light of dawn, she would see he knew it too. The rejection would be there, unmistakable, undeniable. It would shred her heart into a thousand bits and leave her incapable of going on. He had wanted retribution for their past, and now that he'd got it, there was nothing left for her, except to leave, so she wouldn't see what was in his eyes.

Carefully she disentangled herself from his embrace. Not making a sound, she slid to the other side of the bed and in dismay looked around for her clothes. They were scattered throughout the great chamber. In the waning firelight, the crystals in her snood still shot a fiery sparkle, but she realized the beautiful headpiece was no more. Ivan had ripped it and now the crystals lay scattered about the floor like snowflakes.

She was just about to rise from the bed in search of her chemise when a hand reached out and caught her arm.

"Where are you going?" Ivan asked testily.

Her whole body stiffened.

"Answer me," he demanded.

Don't look at his eyes, she told herself. Unwillingly a tear escaped and slid down her cheek.

"Lissa—"

"It's late," she finally choked out. "And I must go."

"Turn around and face me."

She refused. Clutching the sheet to her bare bosom, she tried desperately to maintain her composure. Her eyes searched for her chemise and she finally found it on the stone floor, torn to shreds.

"You're not leaving," he stated evenly, his hand tightening on her arm. "So come back to bed."

"Holland and Evvie will come looking for me if I don't."

"Let them come, *alainn*. They have no power to make you leave."

She twisted her arm from his grasp. Discreetly she wiped her fallen tears. She then scooped her ragged chemise from the floor and used it to hide her nakedness. Without even glancing at him, she gathered her clothes and dressed in haste, desperately needing their protection.

She tensed when she heard the bedstead creak. Before she could pull on her tattered slippers, Ivan embraced her around her waist and her back was thrust against his chest.

"We're not through," he said angrily. "How dare you leave when we're not through."

Another tear streamed down her face, but she dropped her head, vowing he'd never see it. "We are through. This should never have never happened. I was not raised to share the bed of my stableboy," she lashed out.

Her words were met with a cold rage. "You've shared the bed of a wealthy marquis. Don't you ever forget that, Lissa. Don't you ever forget who I am now."

"How could I?" she whispered vengefully. "But as I recall, sharing the bed of a marquis didn't comfort your mother, nor has it offered you solace in bearing your ignoble birth."

He thrust her away from him. A terrible silence descended upon them. Finally he said, "My birth might have been ignoble, but if you hadn't noticed, our stations have been reversed, *Miss Alcester,* and I now see no basis at all for your particularities. Stableboys or marquises, what difference should that make to the likes of you?"

Her head snapped up and she met his furious gaze. All the rage in her heart spewed forth. "I hate you, Ivan, do you hear? Tonight shall be the curse of my existence and I'll hate you forever for forcing it upon me. Forever!"

He took a threatening step toward her. The crystals of her snood rolled underfoot and she was surprise they were not crushed into sand beneath his weight. He paused and looked down. Just seeing the glass beads seemed to cause him agony. Violently he scooped some up and forced them into her palm. He held her hand closed in a brutal grasp while he said, "Then take these with you when you go, Lissa, as payment for a job well done."

She did truly hate him at that moment. His words cut her like a knife, and if she'd had the strength she would have fought back. But she didn't. All she could think of was getting back to Violet Croft and getting away from him and his hatefulness.

"Let me go," she cried, his grasp on her hand hurting her. "You've gotten what you wanted, you wretched gypsy."

He shoved her away and she lingered no further. With a sob, she dropped the crystals in her palm and swept up her mantle. Barefoot and corsetless, she ran from his chamber in a rush of tears. The last sound she left him was the thud of the great emblazoned doors as they shut.

A harsh, black silence filled the room once she was gone. As if contemplating murder, Ivan leaned naked against a bureau, crossing his arms over his chest. He stared morosely at the floor. The crystals seemed at once to infuriate him and titillate him with their brilliance.

He bent and held one in his hand. He turned to a small inlaid mirror behind him and cut Lissa's name into the glass with the stone. He looked at it for a moment, but then he lost control, venting all his fury by smashing the little mirror with his fist. The glass shards fell to the floor, red with his blood, but he seemed to feel nothing. His only oath was "*A ma puissance,* Lissa!"

CHAPTER TWENTY-ONE

❀

In tears, Lissa ran down the cold passage and ducked into the servants' stair. The candles sputtered in their last pools of wax as she wound her way down the frigid stone stairs. There was only one place she could turn, so she avoided the servants' hall, still bustling with activity, and slipped through the game larder. The help's bedrooms were just beyond the gun room, and she soon found the door she sought. She knocked swiftly yet quietly. Her heart was in her throat until the door was answered.

"Why, what on earth, child?"

As John Dover's aged eyes opened in shock, Lissa became all too aware of her wretched appearance. Her hand went to the dried tears that covered her cheeks. It was obvious beneath her mantle that her dress no longer held petticoats. Her hair fell in a long tangled mass down her back, and her feet were shamefully bare.

At once she regreted her decision and wanted to flee. But before she could, the kindly stablemaster asked in a concerned voice, "Are you hurt, lass?"

Mutely she looked at him and shook her head. She was hurt, but not in a way she could ever explain to him. Suddenly she blurted out, "Would you please help me get home? I must get home and the snow—" Emotion caught in her throat and she lost her voice, but John Dover seemed to need no further explanation. He promptly went back into his shadowed room. She watched as his bent silhouette pulled on breeches and boots over his night-gown. He threw on his greatcoat and they departed for the stables without delay. The elderly gent was sensitive to her need not to be seen, so he left her in the bailey and brought the sleigh around to her. Quickly they were on their way to Violet Croft, and Lissa never knew that Ivan watched her go as he stood in the oriel of his chambers.

When her cottage lights shone through the flurries, she prayed that time had not passed as quickly as she thought it had. She suspected it was near dawn, but seeing the lights, it was obvious Evvie was still readying for bed. Holland must have just brought her home and she was probably now in the parlor, reliving her glorious night at the ball with a cup of tea.

As the sleigh stopped at her door, she hardly knew how to thank John Dover. She gave him a kiss on his leathery cheek.

"You're a true gentleman, John Dover," she whispered.

"Get inside, child, before you freeze," he answered gruffly. As if something weighed on his mind, he added enigmatically, "And you come to me if you get into . . . 'trouble,' all right, lass?"

She nodded, suddenly horrified, for she knew exactly the kind of "trouble" that he was speaking of. As he drove off, she was infinitely grateful to him. Without a doubt, John Dover would carry the knowledge of this secret sleigh ride to his grave.

It had been a painful and emotional night, and now at long last, she was home.

As she opened the cottage door she was about to call Evvie's name, but when she walked into the parlor, her words died on her lips.

Obviously not expecting her, Holland stood shirtless in front of their blazing hearth. In a self-satisfied manner, he leaned back on the mantel. His arms were crossed over a well-conditioned chest, liberally sprinkled with dark-gold hair. He still sported his black evening trousers, but when he had last put them on he hadn't used care and the top button or two had yet to be done. His hair was tousled; his face, mellow and relaxed. Though he was wearing his spectacles, he wore no shoes; no waistcoat; no frock coat.

In his state of undress, he most likely should have been chilled. Yet with a dread Lissa had never felt before, she knew exactly what had been keeping him warm.

Without a word they looked at each other. Holland tensed at her unexpected appearance, but then he seemed to find her dishevelment just as shocking as she found his. While they stood there, accusing each other with their eyes, Evvie sauntered in from the kitchen. Lissa's gaze darted to her and her worst fears were confirmed. Evvie's hair was unbound and she was clad only in her thin silk wrapper. Her lips were red as though from much kissing and her sightless eyes had taken on a brilliance that spoke of only one thing: consummated love. Unable to accept it, Lissa could only mutely stare at her as Evvie held out a plate of stale scones.

"Holland, my love, I fear all I could find in our bare cupboards—"

"Evvie," Holland interrupted. "Your sister has come home."

The plate of scones slipped from Evvie's hand and shattered on the floor. As if she didn't even realize what she had done, Evvie took a step forward, but Holland quickly grabbed her up in his arms and kept her bare feet from being lacerated by the shards. He then forced her back to the stairs and placed a sweet kiss on her lips.

"My love, go upstairs and fret not," he said. "I must speak with Lissa." He stroked her smooth cheek with his thumb.

Distraught, Evvie nodded, then looked wildly about, as if she still had her sight and could search for her sister. "Lissa?" she finally uttered as if to confirm that what Holland told her was true.

"I'm here," Lissa said, her words full of grief.

Evvie choked back a sob. Her beautiful blue eyes welled with tears. As if she felt she had betrayed her sister beyond redemption, she covered her face with her hands and fled up the stairs.

When she was gone, Holland turned back to Lissa and grimly assessed her bedraggled state. For some reason her bare feet seemed to anger him the most.

"Your note said you were going to stay with the Bishops," he said pointedly.

"I meant to." She stared at him while he found his shirt. When he was buttoning the last button, her fury burst its bounds.

"Holland, I'll kill you if you don't marry her. Do you understand me? I'll kill you. I'll see you dead," she uttered in a low voice.

"I've planned to marry her all along."

"This week—Boxing Day if you have to."

"Boxing Day, then."

The night was wearing on her. She felt herself growing hysterical. To calm herself, she walked to him and gripped the back of a chair for support. "It shall be done, Holland, because I swear upon my parents' grave to see this righted. And if I could, I'd lock you in this cottage until it was time to go to the church."

"Lissa, it's not your sister you need to worry about."

Her hysteria rose further. "Evvie is the only one who matters here. After this, she must be married!"

Holland's words were toneless. "Is that you talking or the girl you left behind in Tramore's bed?"

Suddenly her temper snapped. She flew to him and beat him with her fists. He easily got control of her, but still she persisted. Finally, to quiet her, he pinned her to his chest and forced her to look at him. When she did, she practically spewed venom.

"I should kill you for that comment alone," she panted.

"Perhaps you should." Abruptly he let her go and walked to the couch where he'd left the rest of his attire. When he had on his shoes and greatcoat, he made ready to leave. But before he departed, he said, "I may look the villain tonight, Lissa, but hear me well. Your sister and I shared this evening because we love each other. Perhaps things got a bit out of line, but tonight changed nothing, for I've intended to marry Evvie all along. However, upon my marriage to her comes the responsibility of this family. So mark my words: When I'm the head of this household, not only will the marquis have no more access to you, but I shall seek restitution for his leading you astray. The same restitution you seek from me."

"You're sadly mistaken, Holland," she told him defiantly. "The marquis has done nothing wrong."

Her denial took Holland aback. "Lissa, you wear Tramore's conquest as clearly as you wear your tattered hem. Why do you protect him?"

She stared at him, bristling at his tone of authority. He spoke as if he, not she, headed the Alcester family. But it would do no good for Holland to leave his post and endure hardship just to seek revenge on Ivan—even in the name of family. Besides, Ivan was not the kind of man to be strong-armed into marriage, especially to her. And even if he did offer, she would never marry him. Not after what had just happened between them. She now hated him as passionately as she had thought she once loved him.

"Lissa, answer me."

Her voice quivered. "Leave him alone. He'll just make you look like a fool. I will never attest to his seduction."

"You're the fool, Lissa. Don't let him do this to you. Fight back!"

"I shall fight back!" she vowed with misplaced anger. "For I will see you tomorrow, Holland, when we go to the church to make arrangements for your wedding to Evvie."

He looked at her one last time, then he shook his head in disgust. When he shut the door behind him, the night seemed to collapse in on her. Unable to stop herself, she dropped her head in her hands and sobbed.

* * *

Boxing Day was long in coming. Though less than a week away, Lissa felt it would never arrive. Somehow she couldn't shake the irrational fear that Holland wouldn't show and Evvie would be left at the altar a ruined woman. It was absurd, especially when Evvie had no such worries, and Holland, ever the gallant, even drove them to Cullenbury Christmas Eve to meet George at the train station.

The minute George had stepped down from the locomotive, he was bursting with tales about his new chums. The son of a duke had even asked him to spend part of his holiday in Scotland at the duchal retreat so that the boys could ice skate. Of course, Lissa had been delighted to comply, and at that moment, all the sacrifice seemed worthwhile when she saw George so happy and accepted, even among the peerage.

Christmas passed all but unnoticed in the flurry of wedding plans. With no time to order a gown, Lissa cleaned, pressed, and mended Evvie's white wool gown, the one striped in violet satin—the one Evvie had worn that first evening at Powerscourt.

On the morning of Evvie's wedding, Lissa laid the prepared gown on her sister's bed, all the while thinking how quiet they had both been since the night of the ball. Because of her own fall from grace, she herself had been loath to bring any subject up except the impending wedding, and Evvie was understandably reluctant to offer any explanations for that night. Lissa was sure Evvie had no idea that she and Ivan had consummated their relationship that night, so the silence between them was a blessing. Besides, it was clear by Evvie's behavior that she expected her older sister to stand in judgment of her, yet Lissa was all too painfully aware that it was up to those without sin to cast the first stone.

Thinking of Ivan was still excruciating. Their night together was not yet hazed by time, and it remained all too clear in her mind. If there had been some mercy for her, that one night with him would have driven him from her soul. Instead there was no mercy. She tried her best not to think of Ivan, but he commanded her every waking minute; at night, in her dreams, she succumbed to him even more. There were times when she wondered if she would ever find a cure for her agonizing thoughts of him.

Lissa tried to cast off her dark mood and emulate Evvie's disposition, but it was impossible. The bloom on Evvie's cheeks could not be matched and the sparkle in her eyes was just as unattainable. Today Evvie looked every bit the blushing bride, and her happiness could be seen in every gesture and expression.

Lissa, on the other hand, had suddenly realized how lonely she was going to be with George on holiday in Scotland and Evvie in Venice on her honeymoon. The days loomed long and empty before her. With nothing to distract her, Ivan seemed inescapable, but she knew that nothing, not even intense loneliness, could make her return to Powerscourt. She planned to fill her days as much as possible with busywork and take them one at a time.

"Lissa?"

Lissa turned from the window and found Evvie standing in the doorway. "Over here," she answered. Her brow furrowed slightly as she pondered one of her ideas. "Evvie, you know I've been thinking. You'll be gone for quite a while in Italy—at least a month, I should think. Perhaps I should ask Holland if it's all right to purchase some fabric. In that amount of time I could make you a whole wardrobe of new gowns—and you'll need them as wife to Powerscourt's bailiff."

Evvie looked chagrined. "Oh, Lissa, that is so dear of you. Yet Holland told me on our way home, we're to stop in Paris and have gowns made for me there. He mentioned something about Ivan's wanting to pay for my trousseau as part of our wedding present."

Stiffly Lissa turned back to the window. "I see." Even in his charity, Ivan seemed destined to crush her. But he wouldn't. She would have to send him a gracious note of thanks on behalf of her sister. That would show him. And then she would have to find another project to keep her busy. She would needlepoint. That was it. She would needlepoint an entire carpet if that would keep her mind off Ivan.

"Are you angry with me, Lissa?"

"Of course not, love," she quickly assured her. "It's simply grand that you'll be going to Paris. But you must promise on your return to make Holland give me your Baedeker—on Venice too. I want to read about all the places you visit."

"I promise," Evvie answered in a small voice.

Lissa turned to her and for the first time saw the paper box in her hands. It must have just been delivered.

"What have you got there?"

"Holland had it delivered. I hoped you would open it for me." Evvie held it out to her.

"Of course."

When they were both seated at the edge of the bedstead, Lissa broke the wax seal and opened the box. Nestled in tissue was a wreath of fresh roses. The tiny, delicate buds were tied to a veil of satin streamers. It was simple yet exquisite; the perfect bridal veil for Evvie.

Lissa took it out of the box and placed it on Evvie's crown. Her sister examined it with her fingers, then she asked, "What color?"

"White . . . as it should be," Lissa whispered. Suddenly they both hugged each other and she felt tears come to her eyes. The silence of the past days was forgotten.

"Oh, Lissa," Evvie said, wiping her eyes with a hankie, "I can't stand the thought of being away from you an entire month. Won't you please reconsider and come to Venice with us?"

"No. Never." She stood and put the freshly pressed white wool gown in Evvie's hands. "You are going on your honeymoon. Even as solicitous as Holland is, I know he would much prefer I not be there. He loves you very deeply. He wants his time with you alone. It's his right." Lissa touched Evvie's hand. "It's your right."

"Perhaps, but neither one of us wants you to be here all by yourself. I just wish there was someone you could stay with."

"I'll make my own plans—so don't spend another moment worrying about me."

"Plans? With Ivan, Lissa?"

A pained look passed over Lissa's face. She was heartily glad Evvie couldn't see it.

"No, you goose. Why would you think that?" She then quickly changed the subject. "But now you must get dressed. Holland is obviously a man who does not like to wait."

Evvie blushed, not at all missing her sister's first reference to the night of the ball. Without another word, she began to disrobe.

As soon as Evvie was dressed and waiting in the parlor with George, Lissa went to change into another gown. She wore a simple dress of gray worsted adorned at the bodice and hem with black braiding. She knew her attire was a bit melancholy, but her best dresses, including her slate-blue taffeta and her rosebud printed tartan, were packed in Evvie's valise for her honeymoon.

Evvie had no idea she had done this, but Lissa was sure her sister would need them during her month abroad and that she herself would not. She had also slipped in their mother's emerald earrings. Rebecca's pearls were notably absent, and Lissa had felt quite a pang when she thought how beautiful Evvie would have looked in them as she walked down the aisle. From that moment onward, however, she suddenly knew what to get Evvie for a wedding present. She would buy Evvie some pearls just like her mother's, even if it took her years to earn enough money.

In her simple attire, Lissa was soon ready to go. She

went to the hook where she kept her mantle, but she paused when something caught her eye. A small sparkle shot from the bottom of her cloak. In amazement, she bent down and found one of the crystals from her snood caught in the fray at her hem. She had worn her cloak every day for almost a week and it seemed impossible that the crystal hadn't fallen off. Yet there it was, its silver setting clinging tenaciously to the frayed threads as if waiting for her to find it.

She picked it out and held it in her palm. Staring at it, all kinds of memories flashed through her mind, terrible and exquisite. As if the little glittering bead were a great treasure, she pressed it to her breast. Had she not been driven by her emotions, she would have tossed it out her window and never given it another thought. Instead, she took a pin off her dresser, unbuttoned her bodice, and pinned it next to her breast. Her hands shook as she refastened her bodice and she knew she was being a fool. But still, it was her secret and no one else's. She would wear the crystal bead next to her heart, right where it beat the strongest. And the knowledge of its past would be solely her own, one that she would carry to her grave. No one would ever know how strong her weakness had been.

CHAPTER TWENTY-TWO

❧

The wedding of Evelyn Grace Alcester and Holland Thomas Jones took place at four o'clock the day after Christmas. They were married in Nodding Knoll's little chapel before a grumpy minister who had squeezed them between services. There weren't many people in attendance for no banns were posted. Yet Lissa had been pleased to see the Bishops arrive and a handful of other townsfolk who had stayed friendly to the Alcesters. Holland's family remained in London. His mother was elderly and it was difficult for her to travel. So Holland had promised to introduce his bride to her and his brother's family as soon as they returned from Venice.

There was no pomp and circumstance, yet it was a lovely ceremony, full of grace and simplicity. Evvie made a beautiful, wistful bride, and seeing her, Holland seemed unable to believe his good fortune. She was finally his and he stood proudly beside her, handsome in a gray frock coat and black striped trousers. As Lissa watched them say their vows, she couldn't help but believe their future was bright, sure to be blessed with love and children. At long last, Evvie would be taken care of properly, and from the manner in which Holland looked at his bride, Lissa could have fallen to her knees in thanks that he had come their way. Already his transgressions were forgiven and forgotten.

When the ceremony was over a tear of happiness escaped Evvie's eye as she met her husband's lips for their first matrimonial kiss. No one could remain unmoved by the joyful picture the couple made, especially Lissa, who frequently dabbed her eyes with a hankie. Even the grouchy minister seemed touched by their embrace. As he ushered them into the parsonage to sign the wedding certificate, he released a rare smile and even gave Holland a congratulatory slap on the back.

"Shall we never see Evvie again?" George suddenly asked in a distressed voice as he watched Evvie and Holland disappear into the parsonage.

Lissa looked down at him and slid her hand through those black locks she loved so much. "Of course we will. She'll go on her honeymoon and then she'll be back."

"But not at Violet Croft," he stated dismally. His lower lip began to quiver.

"But you'll see her at Holland's house. And if you like, I'm sure you may stay there during your holidays from Eton."

"But where will you be then?"

She tipped his face up and made him look at her. A playful smile touched her lips. "Well, I've given it a bit of thought, love. And I've decided to come live with you at Eton. Your chums won't mind, will they, if I come and keep you company in your garret?"

"But—but—Lissa!" he sputtered, looking absolutely horrified. "You cannot! Eton is only for men!"

As if this were somehow a great revelation, she opened her eyes wide. "Are you sure?"

"Quite," he answered hastily.

"Well, then, I suppose the only thing left for you is to have faith that you shall see me on your holidays and leave it at that."

Looking as if he'd just escaped the hangman, George nodded reverently. With that, Lissa couldn't keep herself from laughing. Bemusing her little brother to no end, she tweaked a lock of his hair, then kissed him well on his cheek. She was still smiling when she turned to walk down the aisle, but all at once her heart froze in her chest.

Standing next to the church's carved double doors was the marquis. His black *surtout* was still covered with snow, but it was apparent that he had witnessed the entire ceremony. He leaned casually against the back wall with his arms crossed over his chest and she noticed that his hand was bandaged. She wondered what had happened to him, but his wound seemed not to distress him at all; he looked completely at ease. The only chink in his armor, however, was his eyes. They shone dark and brilliant, an exact mix of anger and desire. His stare seemed to burn right through to her soul and the intensity made her gasp. It pinned her feet to the aisle and forced her to fall beneath its spell. Without even realizing it, her hand moved to her bodice where her crystal was pinned. As if to protect herself, she pressed the stone into the soft flesh of her bosom. But still his hold continued. Only when she heard Evvie and Holland returning from the parsonage did the magic ever falter. She glanced back at the rectory. The next time she looked back, her demon lover was gone.

Holland and Evvie left for Cullenbury right after the ceremony. They were to bring George to the train station so that he could catch the 3:12 train to Perth, and they'd already made arrangements to spend their wedding night at the Cullenbury Inn. From there they would travel to London, where they would board ship for Italy.

Lissa refused to make it a teary good-bye. She knew if she even let a quiver of emotion escape her, Evvie would be beside herself and refuse to go. So she had remained cheerful to the bitter end, giving her brother and sister a fond farewell and seeing them up into the carriage.

But oddly enough, it was when she said good-bye to Holland that she almost lost control. As she looked up at him, their eyes met with a bitter understanding, an understanding that had everything to do with Ivan. She was suddenly aware of how angry Holland was that there was nothing he could do for her. With that new knowledge, a tenderness for her brother-in-law overwhelmed her. Impulsively she stood up on tiptoe and placed a light kiss on his mouth.

"Welcome to the Alcester family, Holland," she said, wry amusement in her voice, "and may God have mercy on your soul."

He looked down at her, his eyes filled with joy mixed with frustration. With a gentle caress, he touched her cheek in farewell. "And why do I fear you'll be the one I'll need it for?"

"I? Never," she vowed, a brilliant smile on her lips. "I shall behave like an angel during your absence."

At once his face turned grim. Powerscourt loomed in the distance behind the carriage and he shot the castle a worried glance. Whispering for her ears only, he said, "But not a fallen one, promise me?"

His words shocked her, but his concern was so real she couldn't be angry. All at once she realized just how lucky she was that he wanted to look after her.

"I promise," she whispered, tears springing to her eyes. When at last her vision cleared, he, Evvie, and George were on their way to Cullenbury.

Alone, the walk back to Violet Croft was long and difficult. Mrs. Bishop had asked her to dinner, but Lissa knew she wouldn't be good company so she refused the kind offer.

When she arrived home, her movements seemed to echo throughout the cottage. She spent the rest of the afternoon working on her needlepoint, but by evening she was heartily depressed. Ivan wouldn't stay out of her thoughts. In an effort to cheer herself up, she made a huge fire in the hearth and put the kettle on. But then she was at a loss. The entire evening stretched before her like a great yawning cavern.

Sitting on the faded blue sofa, she let her thoughts return to the wedding. But all too soon she was again remembering Ivan—how he'd looked, staring at her from the back of the church. Unbidden a tingle went down her spine. Her eyes darkened and she let her imagination roam where it may. Ivan would know how to ease her loneliness.

For the moment.

A frustrated frown appeared on her brow. She turned her head to the fire and watched the sparks shoot up the flue. How was she going to get through this month without losing her mind? Somehow she knew her needlework wasn't going to be the answer. As the minutes ticked by she fought the urge to think of Ivan, but it seemed a greater task than she could accomplish. All too soon her reveries took over and she began imagining Ivan in her parlor. She pictured every detail—his coat, his hair, his scar. He stood over her as she sat on the sofa, his eyes glittering with suppressed desire. She wanted him to kiss her and quickly he was, pulling her up from the sofa and into his arms. His hands found her bare skin and she burned from his rough caress.

Presently they were upstairs, their clothing shed and scattered on the floor. He made love to her as a lover should: tenderly, yet impossibly demanding. She reveled in his touch, his kiss, and the very weight of his body upon hers. She wanted him all and immediately, so she took her pleasure as violently as he took his. When at last there was no more pain or rage or unfulfilled desire between them, he lay quietly between her legs, and she watched him, praying she would never have to let him go.

But then her fantasy changed. Unwillingly, her mind pictured him leaving her bed. Even in her dreams she couldn't stop him. At her window, she heard the harnesses jingle from his waiting carriage. She shivered. Suddenly everything was cold: the sheets, the room, him. She clutched the blankets to her and called his name, but he didn't respond. He didn't even look back. Quickly dressed, he made for the stairs. She begged him not to abandon her, but again her cries fell on deaf ears. Sobbing, she went to her window. Below, he ascended his carriage and drove off, whether heading for Powerscourt or another woman's bed, she was never to know.

Releasing a gasp, she snapped out of the reverie. Her hands were shaking so she pressed them to her cheeks to keep them still. Her mind had played a dastardly trick on her, yet the worst part was that her daydream was all too true. She had visualized exactly what she feared. Ivan would take everything she could give, then make her a beggar for his love. Perhaps she was halfway there already.

Suddenly a knock sounded at her door. Startled by the intrusion, her gaze flew to the entry. It was late for visitors and as she moved to the door, she was overcome by the fear that her visitor might be Ivan. She almost didn't answer the knock, but instinctively she knew it wasn't Ivan. His knock was commanding; this one was feminine.

"Lissa." Arabella Parks stood in her doorway. Her face looked pinched as if she were rather angry. Lissa was so surprised to see her, it took her a moment to invite her in.

"Arabella, it's so late. Is something wrong?" Lissa stepped away and allowed her to enter.

"I had to see you." Arabella looked back at her carriage. With an abrupt nod, the driver tipped his hat and drove away.

Lissa closed the door. Frowning, she commented, "Shouldn't your carriage wait for you?"

"Wilson will take Mother home. Then come back for me."

"I see. So you've been out—"

"Yes, we've been out. To have dinner with the marquis. We've been to Powerscourt." Arabella flung her mink-lined cloak across the blue sofa, then she sat on it as if the worn upholstery was not fit to cushion her bottom.

Lissa stared at her, her mind whirling with possibilities. But she couldn't think of any reason why Arabella had come. Mostly all she could think of was that Arabella had been with Ivan. And she herself hadn't.

"Have I grown warts, Lissa?" Arabella snapped.

Quickly Lissa looked away. At a loss, she fiddled with the tea set, then put the kettle on the hearth. Arabella waited patiently until she was done.

"Refreshments shall be ready soon," Lissa said as she sat opposite her. For some terrible reason her hands began shaking and she was forced to clasp them in her lap.

"Lissa, I must be blunt," Arabella finally began. "I've been your friend now for some years, despite . . . well, despite *everything*. And I've tried to look out for you—tried to help in any way that I could."

While Lissa listened to her dread seeped into her

breast. Somehow this had to do with Ivan. Somehow she
knew the news would hurt her.

Arabella continued, but this time, her anger seemed
to surface. "We were invited to dinner tonight but the
marquis—Ivan—was quite preoccupied, quite moody.
And do you know why?"

Lissa could barely whisper an answer. "No. Why?"

Arabella paused as if what she had to say was quite
painful. But finally she said, "Because there is an ugly rumor that you seduced him the night of the ball and are
now trying to entrap him in marriage."

All at once she felt as if a dagger had just been thrust
through her heart. Why on earth would anyone start such
a vicious rumor—unless Ivan were the one behind it? Her
shock grew worse.

Arabella stood and began pacing the room. "It's horrible, I know, but I had to tell you. As if you could be
capable of that!"

Once again Arabella was being infuriating. Upon that
last comment, Lissa wasn't sure if her friend had just de-
fended her honor or exclaimed at the absurdity of her
being able to get Ivan to the altar. Yet at the moment,
Lissa didn't really care.

"Ivan—*Lord* Ivan told you this?" she asked.

Arabella seemed as if she were somehow torn. Finally
she answered, "No, Ivan didn't." Then too quickly she
added, "But from his mood tonight, it was clear something dreadful was on his mind. It had to be the rumors."

"I see." Lissa stared at her knuckles, now white from
tension. She didn't know what to think. Had Ivan started
those rumors? Everyone knew he was an angry, unforgiv-
ing man. He wanted her ruined. This was a brilliant way to
do it.

"It's all a dreadful lie." Arabella gave her a pointed
look. "Don't you agree?"

"Yes! Yes!" she said vehemently. It *was* a dreadful lie.
However the gossip had got started and whether founded

in truth or mere speculation, it was all wrong. Ivan had seduced *her* that night. And she was by no means entrapping him to do anything. On the contrary, all she had asked from him was that he leave her alone.

"Well, what are we going to do about it, then?" Arabella knelt down before her. She took Lissa's hands in her own and clasped them warmly.

"I don't know. I don't know what to do," Lissa murmured, unable to think. She was too angry; she was too hurt.

Very quietly Arabella suggested, "You could leave, you know, Lissa. Evvie was married today, wasn't she?"

Lissa pondered the idea. It was what she had wanted for so long. To simply leave Nodding Knoll and start a life elsewhere, where no one knew anything of her, good or bad.

"Where should I go?" she asked suddenly, as if somehow Arabella could give her direction.

Surprisingly, Arabella could. "Why don't you go to London? With your education, you could surely obtain some kind of genteel position—governess perhaps or the like."

"London?" Lissa mused. Perhaps that was the place. London seemed so dreamlike, so far away. And she would be nearer to George. She could look in on him now and again.

"I'll be happy to give you the loan of our carriage. And some money, if you like."

Lissa looked up, a furrow marring her brow. "I have money, Arabella," she said coolly. And she did. Holland had left her some funds for the household. That would certainly be enough.

"But do take the carriage, Lissa. That way you can go tonight if you like. Why wait? What is here for you? What's ever been here for you, Lissa?"

Nothing! Lissa practically screamed to herself. It seemed she had shed more tears in the past week than she had in an entire lifetime, and now she felt as if she could cry buckets all over again.

"I should go to London, shouldn't I?" Lissa stated quietly. She looked at Arabella. She knew the girl's motives were not based solely on friendship, but still Arabella's solution was the best. It was the answer to all her problems. There she might be able to put Ivan out of her mind once and for all. A shiver ran down her spine as she thought of the reverie she'd been having when Arabella had knocked on the door. She had to get away from him. She had to get away from everything. "So I'll go," she finished tonelessly.

"I'll have the coach sent back in an hour to pick you up. Will that be enough time?"

Numbly she nodded. "Thank you, Arabella. I'll never forget you for this."

"It's the least I could do, Lissa."

Impulsively Lissa gave her a hug. She then murmured as if to herself, "I suppose I should get my things together."

"It's best," Arabella answered in a strangely sad voice.

When Lissa disappeared up the steps, Arabella bit her lower lip, as if in indecision—as if she had just done something wretched and couldn't quite reconcile it within herself. But then she heard her coach returning and she went to Violet Croft's door. She told her coachman she would only be a moment, next she looked toward the lights of Powerscourt in the distance. Her eyes filled with hope. Glorious, everlasting hope.

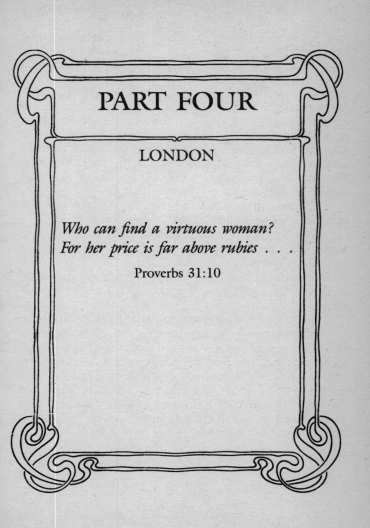

PART FOUR

LONDON

Who can find a virtuous woman?
For her price is far above rubies . . .

Proverbs 31:10

CHAPTER TWENTY-THREE

❋

Arabella's coach took Lissa as far as Grenham, where she caught the North-Western Railway to London. Though some cars had rich mahogany wainscoting and ruby-colored plush seats, with her fare, Lissa's cab sported only cushionless oak benches and whitewashed walls. The train left Grenham at 5:23 A.M., so she wasn't afforded many views of the countryside. However, by midday she was actually enjoying the rush of landscape, whenever she could catch a glimpse between passengers in the crowded car.

She was going to forget Ivan.

She told herself that all during the long coach ride to Grenham. She told herself that now. Of course, she knew it to be a hearty lie, but it was her only solace. Her anger at Ivan increased by the mile. There were moments she felt she wouldn't be able to contain the rage and pain within her breast; they were too deep even for tears. So she spent the train ride sitting grim and silent, unable to comprehend that Ivan was so cruel as to start those horrid rumors about her seducing him for marriage. Those words were so viciously untrue, the gall choked her whenever she thought about them.

But now, thanks ironically to Arabella, she had saved herself from him, and the thought gave her strength. Perhaps she was saving herself only physically—for her mind was still consumed by dark thoughts of him, and her desire for him still tormented her—but she would never again be at his mercy. In one impulsive act, she had thwarted his plans to ruin her. She was running to London where no one would know or care what was being said about her in tiny Nodding Knoll. And she was running far away from those terrible, desperate passions, those same uncontrollable passions that had brought her own parents to such a tragic end.

Someday the pain in her heart would diminish.

She smiled a grim, bittersweet smile. Another lie, but it was her only hope. Her only reason for going on.

They stopped in Kilburn Wells and, as some of the passengers disembarked, she took the window seat. They were now less than three miles from London and her nerves were wearing thin. She had spent the night sitting in the car and her whole body was stiff and sore. She longed for a bed, but she knew it would take her awhile to find the ladies' hotel Mrs. Parks had told her about. In her mind, she went through all Mrs. Parks's instructions. She was to get a hansom and go to the boardinghouse. The next day she was to make several polite inquiries about governessing at the homes for which Mrs. Parks had provided references. Mrs. Parks had been all too kind. Uncharacteristically kind. But Lissa forced herself not to question her fortune. She was offered a grand escape; she could not afford to spurn any help.

The first whistles blew, signaling their approach to Euston Station, and for a moment she felt almost optimistic. She had finally escaped Nodding Knoll.

Euston Station was crowded as their train pulled up to the station building. In nervous anticipation, Lissa gathered her purse and black leather satchel and tied her bonnet. Then she disembarked. She had never seen such a sight. Hundreds of people milled about, either waiting for departure or having just arrived. Women dressed in bombazine hustled along, pulling their children behind them. Men in top hats and checked trousers lounged by the station buildings smoking. Having only known the quiet sameness of a small-town existence, she found the frenzied pace thrilling. Everyone seemed to have something important to do, somewhere important to go. And now she, Lissa Alcester, did too.

When she entered the Graeco-Roman Hall of the station building, again she was taken aback by the confusion and noise. Somewhere nearby she heard a child crying and a gentleman arguing with a railway clerk. Above her light came from enormous windows set near the coffered ceiling. She looked around for the exit but couldn't find it.

"Excuse me—" she began, turning to an elderly, pleasant-looking gent, yet before she could utter another word, the gent moved on, ignoring her completely.

She was not used to such rudeness. In Nodding Knoll, people had gossiped about her, but no one except Old Widow Tannahill had ever been so blunt as to refuse to speak to her.

"I say, excuse me," she next called to a pretty woman who was sauntering by with her entourage of trunk-bearing servants. However, the haughty young miss only raised her eyebrow and moved on, leaving Lissa completely bemused.

"You need something, mum?" A soberly dressed young girl, obviously one of lady's maidservants, stopped.

"Thank heavens! Yes, could you tell me where I might get a hansom?" In relief, Lissa clutched her purse to her chest.

"Up the stairs, mum. It's quite simple. The cabbies are parked before the gateway."

"Oh, thank you ever so much!" Lissa smiled and watched the girl catch up to her mistress. Then she mounted the stairs.

The hansoms were lined up beneath the long portico that led out to Euston Square. However, before she could summon one, she needed to be able to tell the driver where to go, so she unknotted her long silk purse and reached inside it for Mrs. Parks's directions. As was fashionable, her purse was sewn with steel beads, which jangled while she dug for the paper. She soon discovered she was drawing attention, so she moved out of the path of traffic toward a wall.

A man whom she thought was a cabbie swaggered by.

He was young and seemed rather shabbily dressed for a hansom driver. He leaned against the wall next to her. Frightened, she moved away from the man, but he only began to stare at her quite rudely. She clutched her purse in her hand and was about to move farther away when the man grabbed her purse. She wanted to scream but she was so terrified, her voice caught in her throat. Instinctively she pulled her purse toward her. But to no avail. He was much stronger; in one swift tug he had it. Then the cocky purse-snatcher grinned crookedly, his eyes sweeping appreciatively down her face and figure. "You're quite a morsel, mum," he said before he took off down the lane to Euston Square.

She could hardly comprehend what had just happened. Putting a trembling hand to her mouth, she thought of crying out for help, but her voice failed her once more. All around, people bustled past, unaware that her purse had just been stolen. She wanted to cry out for a bobby, but she saw none in sight. She felt she must tell someone of the robbery that had just occurred, but then she thought of the rude gent and the lady she had encountered in the hall. Staring at the hurrying figures before her now, she suddenly wondered if any of them would even pause long enough for her to spill out her tragedy, let alone to help her.

Numbly she moved from the wall and looked around, wild-eyed. She didn't know what to do. Clutching her satchel to her bosom as if for her life, she took a few steps toward the cabs, but then a voice startled her. She spun to face it.

"Have ye a halfpence to spare, miss?" A wizened hag held out her palm.

Lissa's gaze darted to the cabs. Inching back from the woman, she explained, "I haven't. I'm sorry. My purse was just stolen from me."

The hag frowned in sympathy. "Oeeeii, ain't that a shame!" She moved forward, her hand still out. "But surely you've got a little bit tucked away somewhere else, miss. I just want a halfpence . . ."

Lissa stumbled back into a hansom. She did have a few coins tucked in her satchel, but now those few pennies were very precious to her. She most definitely couldn't afford to give any to this woman. As it was she wondered how she would get along on the meager funds she had left.

The hag pressed forward again and then Lissa didn't know what to do. She'd never dealt with beggars. Nodding Knoll hadn't any beggars. She didn't know what would put this woman off.

"Move along, Deara, you're hurtin' the business." A man's annoyed voice sounded from on top of the hansom Lissa was pressed against. Lissa turned her head and the driver was scowling at the woman. He wore a black frock coat and a full gray beard, but even his somber appearance couldn't diminish the Irish sparkle of his clear periwinkle eyes.

"Jack! You son of a cur! And you're hurtin' mine!" Deara spat into the tall wheels of the cab.

The driver ignored Deara's foul gesture. He got down from his seat, then tipped his top hat to Lissa. He opened the door for her and held out his hand for her satchel. "Get in, miss, and we'll be off. That's the only way ta get rid o' the likes of her!" He nodded his head distastefully in Deara's direction.

Lissa looked at the driver. She desperately wanted to get into the cab, but with her purse gone, along with Mrs. Parks's directions, she now didn't have the least idea where the hansom should take her.

"O'Hurley's the name, miss. Where ya be goin' today?" the driver asked.

"I'm—I'm not sure."

"Was someone ta meet you then?" O'Hurley already looked disappointed over the loss of his fare.

"No, it's just that my purse was stolen. Right over

there." Lissa pointed to the wall of the station. "Now I haven't the name of the hotel that was recommended to me."

"Nor the coins for a cab, I think." Disappointed, O'Hurley remounted his hansom. Even Deara wandered off to beg from another passenger.

"Mr. O'Hurley, I don't know anyone in London."

Lissa reached into her satchel and dug out the last few coins she had left. "Would you please tell me where I could find a room?"

O'Hurley looked down at her. Though his face remained irritated, he suddenly seemed touched by her plight. His faded blue eyes softened when he analyzed her meager funds. They softened even more when his gaze rested on her beautiful, frightened face.

"Where ya·come from, miss?" he finally asked her.

"Nodding Knoll, sir."

"Well, I want ta give you a bit o' advice. Take those pennies you have left and buy a ticket back ta Noddin' Knoll. London is no place for the likes o' you."

Lissa cast her gaze downward. Nodding Knoll had never looked so good. She was almost tempted to do just what he suggested.

But then she thought of Ivan.

"I can't go back, Mr. O'Hurley. I just can't." She raised her eyes again and said, "Please won't you tell me where I might stay?"

O'Hurley, now thoroughly disgruntled, visually counted up her funds. He then shook his head. "The only room you could get with those coins, miss, is a room in St. Giles-in-the-Fields."

"St. Giles? Where is that?"

"Ya *can't* stay there, miss. Do ya know what goes on in St. Giles-in-the-Fields? Now take those coins and get yarself back ta Noddin' Knoll." O'Hurley began studying the hansom in front of him as if, by taking his eyes off her, she might just go away.

Obviously she wasn't going to get any more help from him. Lissa put her coins back into her satchel and murmured, "Thank you very much for your assistance, Mr. O'Hurley. I'm sorry I took so much of your time. I'll inquire about a place to stay with someone else." She began to walk away, but for some reason whatever she said seemed to stir O'Hurley into action. He called to her and she walked back to his cab.

"Listen, miss," he began, "if yar goin' ta be so stubborn as ta stay here in London, the Bell and Garter ain't so awful. In fact, I go there meself every now and then for a mug o' stout."

"Oh, thank you!" Her eyes turned brilliant with newfound hope. "Will I find this place in that St. Giles you were speaking of? Is it within walking distance?"

O'Hurley looked uncomfortable, as if he wasn't at all used to being charitable. "Well, ya head down Tottenham Court Road—of course, leaving the station ya take New Road—St. Giles is at the east end of Oxford Street—" He looked down and read the utter confusion on her face. He then scowled. "Oh, get in. I'll take ya."

Lissa looked hesitant. "I'd like to, but I'm afraid you were right. I really can't afford to take a cab."

O'Hurley's scowl deepened. "Go on, get in. I wouldn't have made a fare no matter, for I was just about ta head out for the day. And don't it confound all but I've a sudden thirst for some stout from the Bell and Garter."

She looked up at him, a smile of gratitude on her lips. But knowing that her thanks would only irritate him further, she mutely climbed into the open carriage. When he heard the door shut, O'Hurley cursed heartily at himself and headed out of Euston through the great Doric Gateway.

The Bell and Garter was not what Lissa had expected. It was a ramshackle half-timbered structure almost three hundred years old with a huge yard to the rear for carriages. The inn sat on the east side of Charlotte Street, and much to Lissa's embarrassment, its sign was a painting of a rusty iron bell, artfully wrapped with a multitude of ladies' silk garters.

O'Hurley seemed to know a fair number of the inn's patrons, for when they pulled up several men leaving the yard called in greeting. By the time he had dismounted and opened the door, a small crowd had gathered around.

For some reason Lissa, even in her drab little costume, appeared to be an oddity. It was as if they had never seen a lady before or, at least, not in a very long while. A tingle of apprehension went down her spine as she felt the men's eyes on her like a pack of winter-starved wolves. As if instinctively knowing it would only offer encouragement, she refused to even look at the men, and she stepped nearer O'Hurley's side.

"Jack! Haven't seen you since you lost your arse on Stir-Up Sunday! Come to win it back in a game of craps, have you?" She watched as a tall, thin, aging man who appeared to be the ostler stepped from the gathering. He wore a dingy apron. His trousers looked almost like leggings for they buttoned down each side from waist to ankle.

"Sly! Ya old dog!" O'Hurley smiled wryly at the innkeeper. "Ya won't get me again! The last time I threw the dice I almost found meself in Newgate for me troubles."

"Well, you're welcome anytime, Jack!"

O'Hurley rolled his eyes.

Suddenly the ostler seemed to notice Lissa. For some reason he appeared affronted. He turned to O'Hurley and said, "What have you got here, Jack? You bring your own tart when my girls are—?"

O'Hurley cut him off by waving his hands. He shot Lissa an apologetic glance, then he lowered his voice. "Not so, Sly. This is Miss—ah, Miss—?"

"Alcester," Lissa volunteered, her face pink from embarrassment. She knew what a tart was, all right. She'd been called one often enough. Still, she wasn't sure what the innkeeper had meant by "his girls."

"You see, Sly," O'Hurley continued, "I picked Miss Alcester up at Euston. Her purse was stolen. She just came down from Noddin' Knoll and doesn't have too many friends here ta put her up, so I knew ya'd be able ta accommodate her on what funds she has left."

The ostler gave her an appreciative glance. It was so shockingly thorough, she found herself stepping back.

He opened his mouth to respond but O'Hurley wouldn't let him. He said, "I know what ya're thinkin', Sly, so just scrub out that mind o' yours. Miss Alcester's a good girl, and she won't be working for the likes of you. All she wants is a cheap room."

"And since when have you been the one to help foundlings who come in at the station?" Sly asked.

"I don't." O'Hurley scowled. "But seein' as how she's here, I think ya can give her a room. After all, for the coins I've lost ta ya in craps, I ought to own one o' them rooms by now."

The ostler laughed and slapped Jack on the back. "And wouldn't you like that fine!"

O'Hurley's whiskered mouth twitched in embarrassment, but he picked up her satchel and walked toward the black battened door that was the entrance to the inn.

Lissa followed, utterly confused.

"What's the girl's room ta be, Sly?" O'Hurley asked when they entered the common room. It smelled of stale hops and even staler cigar smoke, but the bar was well polished and the floor swept clean. She reassured herself that that was a good sign. What was not a good sign was the fact that at this time of the morning only a few patrons were about, and oddly enough, most of them were women who either sat boredly shuffling dog-eared cards or joking with the handsome barkeep. Suddenly all her worries congealed into a dread, unspeakable thought. With it, everything was beginning to make sense.

"Number Three, Jack." From a counter beneath the wainscotted stairs, Sly threw O'Hurley a rusty iron key. Lissa followed her benefactor up the stairs to her room.

Number Three's only charm was the fact that it was clean. The floorboards were waxed and the linens fresh and white. However, the whitewash was gone along with the plaster in several places and the only chair in the room looked as if a sparrow could knock it to the floor. There were two pegs above the bed where she could hang her clothes.

O'Hurley dropped her satchel next to the bed. He watched her as she peered out the only window, a grim set to her mouth.

"That's Leviticus Cemetery. Jews are buried there, just like in Whitechapel," O'Hurley told her.

She studied the huge, crumbling mausoleums and shivered, then immediately turned from the mullions. "No ghosts, I hope," she said, the whisper of a smile on her lips.

"No ghosts." O'Hurley laughed. "At least none that I've heard o'."

Lissa walked up to him. "Thank you. You've really been too kind."

Immediately O'Hurley looked uncomfortable. He stepped back into the hall and, for the first time, removed his top hat. "Get a good job, miss, and don't let Sylvester suck ya inta doing his kind o' work."

She now understood perfectly what he was telling her. Sly's girls were unrepentant Magdalenes. And here she was right in the midst of them with nowhere else to go. But nonetheless, she was going to make the best of it. With the last pennies from her satchel, she had paid for her room for a week. When that week was out, she'd be on to greener pastures.

She nodded her head, assuring him. "I'll be looking

for a governess position tomorrow." Ruefully she thought of the references Mrs. Parks had given her. Those that were in her purse.

"See that ya do." O'Hurley nodded. With nothing more to say, he stomped down the stairs.

She closed the door behind him. Instinctively she went to the key lying next to her satchel and locked the door.

Unpacking her bag took almost no time at all for she hadn't brought much. She had another wool gown, some underclothing, her hairbrush. And the Worth gown.

Gently she unpacked it from the bottom of her bag. She shook it out and, in dismay, she surveyed the damage. It was hopelessly wrinkled, but the wrinkles could be ironed. The tatters at the hemline were another matter altogether. Though the rips were physical proof of her attempt to save herself from Ivan's clutches, that proof would do her no good now. More than ever she needed to sell the gown.

After hanging it on a peg, she ran her hands lovingly over the rose-colored satin. She knew she should go out right away and try to sell it. But somehow now she was too disheartened to do it. She knew she would have to part with it eventually, and she would, when the time came. But not now. Not today.

Drained, she moved to the bed and curled up on it, not even bothering to remove her shoes or crinoline. Feeling incredibly lonely, she hugged the pillow to her breast. She tried to make plans for tomorrow, but soon her solitude led her down paths she didn't want to follow. She didn't want to return to Nodding Knoll; she didn't want to return to Ivan. Now suddenly she could think of nothing else.

In disgust, she tossed on her bed and stared morosely through the soot-covered window. Beyond she saw the crumbling mausoleums, and soon she almost wished that ghosts did inhabit the graveyard, for surely even they would be better company than her terrible thoughts of Ivan.

CHAPTER TWENTY-FOUR

❦

By the end of her week at the Bell and Garter, Lissa was not even close to finding a position as a governess. She'd found many families in need of one, but they always wanted references in Nodding Knoll. While she was able to offer Mrs. Parks and the Bishops as references, she was always a little afraid that somehow the gossip about her would find its way to London and destroy her chances for a position. Worse than that, however, was the wait. Most told her they would check on her and she would have word in a fortnight or so, which seemed an interminable amount of time.

By the end of the second week, she still had no position. She was paying the innkeeper, Sylvester, for her room and board by bartering off her belongings. Already she had given him her black leather satchel, but she suspected quite soon he would ask for something more, and the only thing she had left of any value was the Worth gown. For some reason, the thought of her satin gown on one of Sylvester's "girls" sickened her. She knew she would do almost anything to avoid giving it to him, so she kept inquiring about positions, and she continued to call on those families that were writing for references. It seemed they would never make up their minds.

The Bell and Garter was almost beginning to be home by now. She had not become friendly with the "girls," partly because whenever she saw any of them, she found she was met with a most hostile stare. They didn't like her, nor her quiet clothes, and they made that quite clear. The girls weren't the kind of company Lissa desired anyway, but still, in the mornings, when she came down to eat her porridge, she did long for company.

More times than she wanted to admit her thoughts wandered back to Nodding Knoll. Never in her wildest dreams did she ever think she would miss it, but she did, more desperately with each passing day. Sometimes it was all she could do not to run back to Euston, but every time she wanted to, she only had to think of Ivan. If she returned to Violet Croft, she would never break her obsession with him. He would use her as the old marquis had used his gypsy girl, and her life would become a living hell.

But in her dreams she returned there again and again. She would find herself once more at Evvie's wedding. She would recall Holland's expression as he had gazed down upon Evvie, completely bedazzled by the jewel that was soon to be his. When she awoke, she always knew why she had dreamed the dream. Her sole wish in life was that Ivan would have just once looked at her the way Holland had looked at Evvie. And because he hadn't, when she awoke, her heart shattered all over again.

Now, at the beginning of her third week in London, she walked the damp, drizzly streets, and the wind cut at her like a knife. She had answered four advertisements by noon, but no offers were forthcoming.

She had just left Grosvenor Square and was walking up New Bond Street when she began to feel light-headed. Despite the dreary day, New Bond Street was busy with wealthy shoppers. Stopping at one side of the walkway, she grasped an iron fence railing trying to steady herself. The wind had picked up, but it seemed to have no effect now. She was warm. Too warm. Daintily she patted the perspiration off her forehead with her handkerchief. As much as she wanted to deny it she wondered if she were on the verge of getting ill. The walk back to St. Giles today seemed about as easy as a trek to the Hebrides. She didn't know how she was going to make it.

"Miss Alcester? Lissa Alcester of Nodding Knoll?"

Lissa looked up and saw that a dark-blue japanned carriage had stopped beside her. The door was open and a beautiful woman dressed in green peered out. The woman looked familiar but Lissa couldn't think of her name.

"Miss Alcester?"

"Yes," Lissa finally admitted. "But I'm afraid I don't—"

"Of course you don't remember me. But I remember you quite clearly. And if I may say so, you are the catch of the day. *Everyone* is looking for you. Everyone, that is, who has anything to do with the Marquis of Powerscourt."

All at once wary recognition dawned on Lissa. The woman before her was Lady Antonia Kovel. And now Ivan was looking for her. The thought alarmed her. She didn't want him to find her. He wanted her as he would a favorite pet that had had the temerity to run away. He wanted her back to teach her another lesson, to humiliate her once more. But she'd taken had all the lessons she was ever going to take from him.

"Miss Alcester, you don't look quite well. Will you come to the house for tea? My husband's family home sits only a few blocks away on Hanover Square."

Lissa wanted to refuse. She wanted nothing to do with a friend of Ivan's, but the thought of some rest and a warm cup of tea was difficult to resist.

"Come along," Antonia instructed, and she moved over on the cushioned seat. Before Lissa knew it, the driver had descended and was at her side, helping her into the conveyance.

"We'll be there in a moment," Antonia said, handing Lissa the carriage blanket. Mutely Lissa accepted it, then she took out her handkerchief and again patted her flushed face.

Antonia's house sat on the northeast corner of Hanover Square. Done in the old-fashioned Adam style, its

Ionic pilasters and stone balustrade edging the roof still
gave it a stark, regal appearance. Once inside, the original
Chippendale furnishings made it seem even more out of
date. In fact, Lissa felt sure the house had not been used in
years.

"Our tea will be ready soon," Antonia stated as she
moved across the gilt and pastel drawing room. She pulled
a ribbon-back chair to the hearth and motioned for Lissa
to sit in it. Antonia smiled and said, "I must apologize for
the shabbiness of my home, but Harewood belonged to
my husband's family and I haven't had the inclination to
come to London in a decade. Not even to see it."

"Harewood is beautiful. Please don't apologize for it.
You're being terribly kind as it is," Lissa said, accepting the
chair. There was an uneasy edge to her voice but she
hoped Lady Antonia hadn't heard it. The woman was being quite gracious, for she hardly knew her. Still, Lissa
didn't quite trust her. Perhaps because she was in London
now where trust was becoming a precious artifact. But
most likely it was because Lady Antonia was a friend of
Ivan's. A dreadfully intimate friend. Antonia knew the
color of Ivan's eyes and though Lissa hated herself for it,
she found it almost impossible to override the stab of jealousy she felt whenever she remembered the ball.

"Everyone has been wondering where you ran off to,
Miss Alcester," Antonia began. "Where are you staying in
London?"

Lissa hesitated and gave Antonia a wary glance. She
didn't want to tell her where she was staying, for if she did
that, there was the terrible possibility that Ivan might
come for her.

"Miss Alcester?"

Lissa cleared her throat. "I'm presently in St. Giles."

Lady Antonia stared at her, horrified. "You don't
mean St. Giles-in-the-Fields?"

"Yes, I do," Lissa said stiffly.

Antonia shook her head, then sat opposite her. "Ivan is worried about you. Why did you run away?"

Taken off guard, Lissa didn't know how to respond. A pained expression crossed her delicate features and she stated quietly, "Ivan needn't worry about me."

"Ivan worries about a lot of things that perhaps he shouldn't."

"I expect to find a position as governess quite soon. I was out this morning, in fact, interviewing with a household."

"I'm sure you'll succeed." Antonia studied her. Lissa's unnaturally pale visage didn't pass by her scrutiny, nor her feverish brow. She added, "However, in the meantime, I insist you stay here at Harewood. St. Giles is no place for a lovely girl like you, Miss Alcester."

Lissa was just about to refuse her offer politely when the tea arrived. She sat in silence while Antonia poured out.

When her hostess had handed her a cup, Lissa couldn't contain herself any longer. "I hope you won't think me ungrateful, but I wonder why you're doing this. I'm a stranger to you, yet, off the street, you invite me to your home. Now you ask me to stay as your guest until I find a position as governess. Please forgive my curiosity, but—"

Antonia interrupted her with a laugh. "Yes, you probably think me quite batty." She sipped her tea and turned thoughtful. "Miss Alcester, you must know, I've known Ivan a long time. Well over ten years. He was not even twenty years old when he . . . well, when we . . ."

Lissa tensed. Antonia didn't even have to finish.

"What does my being here have to do with Ivan?" Lissa asked nervously.

"Everything." Antonia put down her cup and stood. "I see you're upset. And you have a right to be. Ivan can be quite a pill at times." A glimmer of a smile crossed her face. "Of course, he does have other attributes that make him easier to tolerate, but that can't make up for everything, now can it?"

"No," Lissa said, putting down her cup also. She was feeling worse by the minute and it had nothing to do with her feverish state.

Antonia walked to the window of the drawing room. She pulled up the Austrian shade of robin's egg blue and looked out. Even in the gray light, Lissa could see the lines on her beautiful face, lines she'd missed the evening of the ball. For the first time she realized Antonia was probably quite a bit older than Ivan.

"I'm glad I found you, Lissa—may I call you Lissa?" She nodded and Antonia continued. "As you must have guessed, I'm a great friend of the marquis. In fact, Ivan and I were lovers."

Lissa's voice dropped to a whisper. "Are you still?"

"No," Antonia answered. She then turned and looked right into her eyes. "Truly I am a contented married woman once more. You see, I knew Ivan when I was newly widowed. As you might have already guessed, I've no fondness for town life. I stayed in Cullenbury after Bradley died and thus became quite lonely. Until I met Ivan. . . ."

"I see," Lissa said, on the verge of tears. Though she believed Antonia when she had said she and Ivan were no longer lovers, somehow the conversation upset her anyway. Perhaps the reason was still as simple as jealousy. Even at the ball Lissa had sensed a closeness between this woman and Ivan, a closeness she knew she would never have.

"I'm telling you this, Lissa, because I want to help you. I know all about your family—The Scandal and all. And I know how hard you've struggled to keep your family together. You deserve happiness now—you both do. And I know things that can help you."

"Help me do what?" she asked, brushing a silent tear from her cheek.

"To forgive him."

She looked up. With all the bitterness in her soul, she said, "How can I forgive him when he'll never forgive me?"

Antonia kneeled before her and took her hand in hers. "Is it the scar? He hasn't told me about it, but I knew it had something to do with you."

"Yes—and no," Lissa whispered. "The scar I didn't mean to do, but everything was so different then. I was so different then. The situation got out of hand."

She didn't want to continue; she didn't want to trust this beautiful woman, but once she had begun, all her dammed-up emotions came surging out. "Now, of course, it's more than that. When Ivan returned to Nodding Knoll I had hoped he might forget the past. Yet that first moment he looked at me, I knew he never would. In me he saw everyone in Nodding Knoll who had ever cast him a disparaging look. He wanted to get even with us all, but that was impossible. So he chose to get even with me instead. And he did. But still he isn't satisfied. He'll never be satisfied!" She began to cry in earnest now, and Antonia handed her a linen hankie that she'd kept tucked in her wrist. "So that's why I left," she said, weeping. "That's why I had to go."

"Ivan is a misguided fool!" Indignant now, Antonia rose to her feet and began pacing the carpet. "If he were to exact revenge upon every person who ever hurt him, then he should have begun with me!"

With that unexpected statement, Lissa looked up. Her lips trembling, she said, "He adores you. Anyone can see that. What could you have possibly done to have hurt him?"

"There are ways of hurting people simply by neglect." Seeing Lissa's puzzled expression, Antonia continued. "Ivan and I began our 'relationship' when he was barely a man. I was almost fifteen years older than he and brilliantly wealthy. And he was just a stableboy, and a bastard at that. He would show up at my door sometimes as late as midnight, smelling of the stables where he worked. But I'd let him in every time. And do you know why?"

Woefully Lissa shook her head.

"Because I wanted the sun and the stars and the moon. I wanted all those things, and Ivan seemed completely capable of giving them to me. He took my breath away and then promised me even more until I wanted so much from him that I thought I'd die waiting for him to show up at my door night after night.

"And do you know what he wanted from me?" Antonia laughed mirthlessly. "He wanted me to teach him to read! I can still picture him waiting for me in my husband's library, caressing the spines of my husband's books as if they held the key to the universe. And it was so out of reach. Not a soul in his entire life had ever taken the time even to show him the alphabet, much less to see that he attended school. Somehow, when he met me, I suppose he thought that I might take the time."

"Did you?" Lissa whispered.

The lines deepened on Antonia's face. "I had the means. My God, I could have seen to it that he was the most educated man in all of England. That little effort would have barely been alms for the poor in light of what he had given me. And that little bit I didn't do because I couldn't be bothered."

A heavy silence followed as Antonia wiped her eyes.

"He can read now, of course," Lissa said.

"Yes. In the end he taught himself, I suppose. I found out he had learned years later, after he was no longer coming to see me."

"Is that why he quit coming? Because you didn't teach him?"

Antonia smiled warmly and gave her a strange, knowing look. "No, Lissa. Ivan left me for all the reasons a handsome young man leaves his mistress. Because he found another who pleased him more. One who was younger and far more lovely than I, I'm afraid."

Lissa dropped her eyes and stared into her knotted hankie. Of course. Ivan had moved on. He had left Antonia, as he had probably left a hundred women; as he would have left her if she had given him the chance.

But she would never give him the chance. Never.

Seemingly without cause, Antonia brightened. As she studied Lissa approvingly, her brilliant emerald eyes sparkled with hope. "You love him, don't you?" she said quietly. "You just don't know if he loves you, isn't that right?"

Lissa refused to meet her eye. She took a deep breath and said vengefully, "Ivan is incapable of being loved. Any fool can see that."

Antonia surprisingly seemed to approve of her answer. A smile curved her pretty lips. "When I think of Ivan I only think of one word. Do you know what that word is?"

Lissa shook her head.

" 'Unattainable.' " Antonia again knelt before her and took her hand. "Ivan was something I knew I could never have. Not forever. From the moment I first saw him, that word, 'unattainable,' kept coming to my mind. But with you, Lissa, it's different."

"How is it different?" she asked morosely. "In truth I see no difference at all."

"Because you and Ivan were meant to be together. You looked at him at the ball and in your eyes I saw your soul crying out for him. And he wants you. His heart breaks with rage every time he sees you because you're not his."

"He does not want me!" Lissa abruptly turned away. Her hands went to cool her cheeks, whether warm from fever or impending tears, she wasn't sure.

"He does want you," Antonia said emphatically. "You're the only thing he does want."

"Well, he cannot have me!" she cried out. "I'm not chattel that he can use and abuse as he wishes!"

Antonia softened. "He is a difficult man, I know. But think what has made him that way, Lissa. He's never had one thing in his life he ever wanted. He wanted to read and all he got was a woman trying desperately to relive her youth; he wanted a father and all he received was a decrepit castle and a hollow title. And now he wants you and—"

"Do my desires play no part in this?" Lissa stood unsteadily.

"You want him, I know you do. *You love him.*"

She stopped. She did love him. But even in her feverish state she knew that if she brought that love into the light of day it would destroy her. "I must go," she said, gathering up her mantle. Her head felt unbelievably light and she could no longer tolerate the room's heat. She had to get some air.

"Lissa, no, please stay!"

"I cannot." She'd almost reached the door when the room began to tilt. Before she fell, she grabbed the nearest chair and eased herself down into it.

Antonia rushed to her side. "Lissa, Lissa, you're ill."

"No . . ."

"Let me take you to a bedchamber and get the physician."

"And let you summon Ivan to come and torture me further? I think not!" she sobbed. She didn't trust Antonia. The woman was too much on Ivan's side and no matter her kindnesses, she was dangerous. She tried to rise again but found she couldn't quite make it.

"You're not well. You look feverish. I'll bring you some water. Stay there!" Antonia ordered.

Lissa looked up and wiped her tears. Antonia had barely departed before she dizzily headed for the hall and the front doors. In moments she was out the door, blending into the traffic on Oxford Street.

CHAPTER TWENTY-FIVE

❋

By the time Lissa reached the Bell and Garter, darkness had fallen. The inn was gearing up for its nightly business, and even from the yard, she could hear men brawling and cheering in the common room.

With great trepidation she opened the inn's door and discreetly entered. She was shivering and her mantle and gown were damp from the rain. She hoped her poor appearance would keep her from being noticed; still, she kept the brim of her bonnet down and clung to the far wall.

The common room was packed to the rafters. The rain had driven many inside, and the lure of the trade had brought in as many more. From the trestles, a girl with a customer squealed in laughter; from a corner men were rolling dice. The stout drinkers were three deep at the bar and Sly could hardly keep them supplied, let alone happy. She barely got to the wainscoted stair before someone had her by the waist.

"Ah, Sly! I may be 'avin' a go yet with one o' yer 'ladies'! Where did ye get this little angel? Did she fall out o' the sky?"

Startled, Lissa looked up and found herself in the arms of a brawny young man.

"No, please, I'm not what you think" was all she could say before the man began untying her bonnet. He had it off before she could stop him and soon his hands raked through the fine-spun gold of her hair.

"Ye are a rare beauty," he admitted in a hushed voice.

"Unhand me, I say. Unhand me this instant," she demanded, but her protest sounded weak even to her ears. She couldn't fight this man off. Especially not now, when she couldn't even stop shivering. She made a futile attempt to extract his hands from her waist, but that only deepened the gleam in the gent's warm brown eyes. She gazed around her and saw a crowd was gathering.

"'ow much fer this one, Sly!" the man suddenly yelled across the room.

"You'll have to work that out with the chit herself," Sly shouted back. "I warn you though, she's a hoity-toity one. Thinks she's off to be a governess in one of them fine homes on Park Lane."

Everyone in the common room snickered. But her assailant seemed to find it particularly hilarious. His hand tightened more possessively at her waist. "Ye mean the wench don't know it that she's got a job just waitin' . . . 'tween 'er legs!" The man laughed even harder.

Soon, however, his face was etched in fear. From the crowd, a tall, shadowy man had pushed his way to the front. Before Lissa could even register that she knew that mask of deadly rage, a fist went out and smashed the brawny young man's face. His blood spattered on the wall behind him and, in terror, the man shrank back, holding his bloodied sleeve to his broken nose.

"I ought to kill you," Ivan hissed between clenched teeth as he shoved the man to the wall.

"Wha's it to ye? Wha's it to ye?" the man whined, hysterical.

Sick from the sight of the blood, sicker still that Ivan had somehow found her, Lissa leaned against the wainscoting and tried to keep from fainting.

"No more, man!" All at once Sly fought his way to the front of the crowd. He pulled on Ivan's arms like a pit bull. "Let him go, I tell you! The poor bloke did nothing! Are you a madman?"

Sly's words somehow seemed to jolt sanity back into Ivan. As if he were aware for the first time where he was, he abruptly let the man go. Absentmindedly he looked at his blood-covered knuckles, then it seemed to dawn on him just why he was there. With horror, Lissa watched as he stared right at her.

"Come here" was all he said to her, but it was all he needed to say. In that one utterance, passion and hatred were wed beautifully.

"No," she answered, her eyes glittering with defiance.

He took a step toward her and she fled up the stairs. No matter that she heard his footsteps behind her, she picked up her skirts and ran down the passage. Fumbling for her key, she unlocked the door just as he was upon her. She pushed to close it just as his hand reached through and grasped the edge. With his far superior strength he was in her room in seconds.

"Get out I say! Before they come up here and drag you out!" she panted as she backed toward her bed.

Ivan laughed sarcastically. "Yes, I forget how chivalrous the men are in St. Giles-in-the-Fields."

It was true. No one downstairs was going to stick his neck out to help her.

Behind her, she heard him close the door. The only light in her room came from the gaslights outside on the cemetery gates.

"Lissa," she heard him say with a hard edge to his voice, "are you . . . all right?"

She closed her eyes. She knew exactly in what way he meant. "Yes," she cursed.

"Thank God."

"How did you find me?"

He stepped closer to her. "I put a notice in all the London newspapers. I offered a reward, and people were lined up all the way down Piccadilly to give me news of you. But finally it was a bloke named O'Hurley who led me here. He came to the town house this morning and was actually sorry to have told on you. But he said you were better off back in Nodding Knoll and that he could certainly use the thousand pounds."

Lissa started. Ivan had offered a thousand pounds to find her? It was a huge amount of money.

"I still don't understand how you knew I was in London," she finally muttered.

"Harry McBain saw the Parks's coach stopped by Violet Croft the night you left. I demanded that Arabella tell me where you went. When she finally broke down, she told me how she and her mother had helped you leave. She made quite a display of it too," he added distastefully.

"She wants to be your wife." She almost choked on the words.

"Is that why she made you leave Nodding Knoll?"

Angrily she spun around. "No! I was going anyway! I wasn't going to stay and listen to those filthy rumors! And Arabella helped me! She is a dear friend!" Though she didn't believe the latter part for a moment, defending Arabella seemed to infuriate him all the more.

He crossed the room and took her by the shoulders, shaking her. "No friend would send a young woman to London to be eaten alive!"

"Stop!" she cried out. When he did, she broke free and stumbled to the window. Feeling unsteady, she grasped the sill. Then she faced him.

She should never have done that. She stared at him in the dim gaslight of her mean little room, and she suddenly knew her weakness for him was back with all the force of a thunderbolt. Unable to stop herself, she devoured every detail of him that she had missed: his glittering eyes, his taut lips, his angry white scar. She saw that he was still in his greatcoat and that his hair was damp from the rain; it was slicked back as if his hand had agitatedly run through it many times. With sudden brutal clarity she remembered running her own hands through it, and crying out his name. That night should have been long ago, but suddenly, it seemed like only yesterday.

"Lissa, I'm taking you out of here. Get your things. We'll discuss everything later."

He was speaking to her, but she could hardly hear him. The pain she felt by tearing her gaze away was terrible, yet she couldn't let him keep his hold on her. Already she felt as if she were growing mad from it. The room began to swim and she grasped the sill as if for dear life.

She felt as if she were watching from outside herself when she saw him grab her. He steadied her, then he swept one callused palm over her brow.

"My God, you're burning with fever."

"No," she denied staunchly.

"My coach is outside. I'm taking you now."

"No." She tried to pull from him.

"Lissa," he began angrily. Taking her chin, he forced her to look up to him. "You're not spending another minute in this rat hole, so don't fight me on this, you cannot win."

"And how will you make me leave? Shall you throw me over your shoulder and carry me out like so much baggage?"

"If I must," he answered quietly, too quietly.

Ignoring his warning, she struggled out of his embrace. She felt a giddy pleasure as she angered him further. She threw off her mantle. Her bonnet was by now long lost in the common room, so instead she removed whatever stray pins remained in her hair. She then began combing her tresses leisurely. Maddeningly.

"Lissa," he growled, his fury peaking. "You're going. Now."

"My, my, Ivan the Terrible has uttered his command, so everyone, jump to obey!" She turned back to her combing. She wasn't acting like herself. She was feeling far braver than she should have. Perhaps she truly did have some kind of fever. Certainly she burned every time she looked at him.

"Don't make me force you, Lissa. Not while you're ill."

"I am not ill!" she practically shouted at him.

Out of the corner of her eye she watched him pick up her sodden mantle. Purposefully he moved toward her, his face taut with anger. He would brook no disobedience now. Could she fight him? She doubted it, so she stumbled back, knocking into her bed. She lost her balance and landed on the edge of the mattress.

"Come," he said as if he were now talking to a child. He bent down and wrapped her in the mantle.

She closed her eyes and, for the moment, gave into her exhaustion.

With her eyes closed and him so near, his scent teased her. In his damp *surtout,* he smelled like a forest right after a rain. But she smelled underscents too, scents that she couldn't quite name. They were dark and heavy, yet they promised pleasure beyond her wildest imaginings. Just breathing in made her pulse quicken and her belly tense. Her nerves suddenly felt raw from denial.

She opened her eyes and looked at him. As if he had her well in hand, he fastened the silk frogs on her mantle. His fingers brushed her throat, and that one tiny caress shot a bolt of sensation right through her. Unwillingly, her eyes met his. As usual, he looked like the consummate conqueror.

As if sensing her mood, he rubbed the back of his hand against her cheek. Taunting her, he said, "You know, love, you must have been mad to have come to this wretched place. Whatever made you run here?"

You! she wanted to scream; but burning with resentment and, worse, passion, she refused to answer. She tried to turn from him, but he wouldn't let her. He held her head with both hands and demanded she look at him. When she did, he chuckled. Without remorse, she lifted her hand to slap him.

"Come now, Lissa," he whispered nastily. He caught her hand in midair. "You ought to know by now you can't win that way."

"Then how can I win?" she spat at him.

"This way," he told her, and pressed his lips to her own.

It was clear he had intended the kiss to be quick and punishing, but somehow it spun out of control. Her entire body stiffened when his lips first touched hers, but all too quickly she found herself growing hotter. Soon she was kissing him back, deeply, desperately. She could feel his reluctance as she opened her mouth to him, but she needed him too much to stop. She was no longer a child in the throes of an adolescent infatuation. She was a woman, and he alone had made her one. So he alone was the only one who could satiate her. Her body, soul, and mind had been existing in a desert the past few weeks without him, but now, as he kissed her, she was in Eden. She never wanted to leave again.

"Damn you." He abruptly tore her from him. His eyes blazed. "You're ill—what do you think you're doing?"

Hurt by his rejection, she turned away. Her fingers touched her kiss-swollen lips, but that only enraged her more. Defiantly she tossed off her mantle. Angrily he pulled it to her once more.

Again she closed her eyes. Suddenly she felt too weak to fight him any more. The realization of how much she had longed for him in the past wretched weeks left her with no defenses.

"Have you not missed me at all?" she whispered to him when at last their furious gazes met.

"Do you expect me to take you here—with you like this?" His hand cupped her cheek. Her warmth seemed to disturb him.

As if in a trance, her finger reached out and touched his lips. She traced them lovingly, then moved to his jaw, scratchy with his evening beard. Before she could stop herself, she boldly pressed forward and ran the tip of her tongue down his throat.

That made him groan. His hands grasped her shoulders and they tightened almost painfully.

"You're a wicked man, Ivan Tramore," she admitted huskily. "My curse is that I want you at all."

His eyes narrowed and he became speculative. He looked down at one of his hands. His knuckles were covered with tiny scars, and she surmised that must have been the hand bandaged when she saw him in the church. He seemed most reluctant, yet somehow, by looking at his hand, he came to a decision. With unspeakable relief, she felt him sliding her mantle off her shoulders.

"After this, *alainn,* you're coming with me," he said huskily.

She released a sigh of relief. "Perhaps" was all she said before he began unbuttoning the front of her gown.

Her body felt like it was on fire and she couldn't shed her clothes fast enough. Though it was cold in her room, a thin film of perspiration glistened on her bosom as he opened her bodice. His mouth grazed one swell of her lush bosom and she wondered how she tasted to him. She seemed to taste good, for his tongue trailed down her breast until he almost found her nipple hidden beneath her corset.

He stood and, with his glittering gaze pinning her to the mattress, shed his greatcoat. He pulled off his cravat, shirt, and trousers until he stood naked before her. In the dim flickering light cast up from the street, she could see the muscles flex in his thighs as he walked to her. She remembered running her palm down their hard, muscled length while she had lain next to him. Watching now, her fingers curled into her palms as if she again felt such a wickedly pleasurable caress.

Without a word, he eased himself down onto the edge of her bed and pulled her to stand between his legs. As if starved, he pushed back her tresses with both hands, then brought her face to him for another kiss. His tongue roughly entered her and a charge shot down her spine. She was so unbearably hot, she didn't want him to be gentle, she wanted him to be as impatient as she was.

With a moan, she felt his hand slide beneath her skirts. He easily found the split in her pantalets and though she gasped in protest, his hand claimed her anyway. His expert caress shocked her as desire darkened her eyes. He drove her mad with his touch, more crazed than she surely was already, but she didn't care. There had been nights when the thought of death seemed preferable to never having Ivan again. Now, as he brought her to a peak, she knew she'd been right. Having Ivan was all that mattered.

As if torturing her, he abruptly let her fall. She cried out as he removed his hand. She knew she couldn't wait for him any longer so she pulled him to her for another kiss. Gratefully he cooperated. Again his hand slid beneath her bodice for a caress, but suddenly something caught his attention. He broke free and roughly parted her bodice.

"What is this?" he asked as he pointed to the crystal pinned to the inside of her dress.

Her mind seemed too drugged with passion to answer, but soon she whispered, "It's nothing, I tell you." She tried to close up her dress, but he wouldn't let her.

He unpinned the crystal and held it in his hand. It seemed to hold an unaccountable fascination for him. "Why did you keep this?"

"Give it back, Ivan. I tell you it's nothing." Becoming more agitated by the second, she tried to get off the bed.

But he would have none of it. He smiled and pushed her to the mattress. Her hair fanned out beneath her and he caressed her locks with one hand; with the other he dangled the crystal tauntingly over her.

"Do you know how beautiful you were that night at the ball?"

She shook her head and looked up at him.

"You shall be dressed like that always," he mused, "or wear nothing at all." Disparagingly he looked at her somber gray woolen dress.

His attention elsewhere, she tried to grab her crystal,

but just as she did he closed his fist. He laughed as she tried again to get it, but to no avail. When she was worn out, she whispered, "You're a wretch to take that from me, Ivan."

He kissed her, letting his tongue go where it may, then he dropped the crystal maddeningly into the mass of her hair. When her hands reached to find it, he pulled them down and shackled them with his grip. Ignoring her protests, he went to work on her corset. After he'd freed her of all her garments, he eased her beneath his long form and took her mouth again, this time more wildly, more hotly. He seemed impatient now and she could feel his excitement grow. His hand forced open her thighs, then sought out the curve of her tiny waist, next the swell of her generous breasts. His hard mouth captured one nipple and a gasp caught in her throat as she experienced anew the familiar sweet ache she felt only for him.

"*Alainn,* you're like fire beneath me," he gasped. On massive arms, he pulled his body up off her as if she burned him. The slightest glimmer of guilt shone in his eyes. Then, without warning, he cast it away and drove deeply into her.

A grateful moan escaped her lips as she finally felt him inside her. Her need for him was soon to be banished. Forever, she hoped. Yet secretly in her soul she wondered if she was fooling herself, even as she welcomed his thrusts as if they were his love.

When their passion was spent, they lay naked on the little bed, entwined in each other's embrace. Her tangled hair fanned out on the mattress and he easily had her trapped by his shoulder, which lay upon it. He studied her, though she seemed hardly aware of it.

Exhaustion had made her weak. Her face, delicate and heartbreakingly beautiful, seemed too pale. Her eyes appeared glazed. Her body next to his burned unnaturally warm. It would not do to linger.

"Come, I've got to take you home."

Ivan rose from the bed. He picked up his greatcoat and wrapped it gently around her body.

"Ivan, you must leave me alone now. You must," she pleaded softly.

Pulling on his trousers, he moved to the edge of the bed and kissed her mussed hair.

"Do you hear me?" she asked while he shrugged on his shirt and found his shoes.

Ignoring her, he finished dressing. Next he took the Worth satin dress from the peg and stepped back to the bed.

"Your gown is too damp. Come, let me put this on you."

"I'm not going with you." Weakly she tried to sit up. The coat slipped down, exposing her breasts to his view.

He bent down and lovingly grazed one nipple with his knuckles. Then he covered her once more. "Lissa, you've got a fever. You're practically delirious. Shall I drag you downstairs naked or in this dress?"

"Please, Ivan, I beg of you, don't—"

Before she could finish, he was pulling the dress over her head. Mindless of her need for undergarments, he tightened the laces at the back. He again wrapped her in his coat, yet his hand swept down her hair as if to comfort her.

"Are you ready?" he asked, but she shook her head. A tear of exhaustion and frustration slipped down her cheek. He wiped it with his thumb, then something in her hair caught his eye. It was the crystal. He disentangled it and searched the floor for the pin. Gently he opened his greatcoat and pinned it to the inside of her bodice.

"I like where you keep this, *alainn*." With that he

placed a tender kiss on her lips and picked her up into his arms. He then carried her down to the yard to his waiting carriage.

CHAPTER TWENTY-SIX

❁

Lissa opened her eyes to a strange, unfamiliar place. She'd been dreaming of Ivan and in the last part of her dream, she was riding in his carriage as the rain pummeled the japanned doors. She had been tired, so tired that she had had difficulty just keeping her head up. Finally when she had let it fall back, her cheek hadn't met with the lush silk velvet upholstery of the carriage. Instead, she had unwittingly found herself against Ivan's chest. She had tried to sit up then, but she was induced to stay there when his arms went around her and held her fast. She had fallen asleep listening to the rain and the strong, sure beat of his heart.

Now she was awake and for the life of her she couldn't place her surroundings. As she raised herself on her elbows, she noted she was in a mahogany sleigh bed festooned with pale-lavender taffeta and matching silk tassels. A delicate papier-mâché table painted with roses sat next to her; below her, a lavender Brussels carpet woven with green trailing vines covered the floor from wall to wall. The only means of illumination was from the Argand lamp on her bedside table. In the dimness, her gaze trailed to the pier where she found a huge wardrobe painted with a scene from Chaucer's "Prioress's Tale." The two windows, well shielded from drafts with green moiré drapery, confirmed it was night.

"I see Sleeping Beauty is awake."

Startled, she looked to the other side of the bed. A white-haired man looked down on her, watching her.

"Where am I?" she asked in an unsteady voice. The man only smiled and tried to put his hand on her forehead. Frightened, she turned away. She tried to raise herself fully and when she did, she noticed she was wearing a night rail she'd never seen before. It was of the sheerest Swiss dotted batiste and hardly gave her any modesty at all. Nervously she clutched the covers to her bosom.

She still couldn't remember where she was, and the elderly man before her was a total stranger. As he sat familiarly at the edge of her bed, she could no longer contain her alarm. She desperately tried to move back, but at once a voice commanded, "Lissa, be still."

Looking down at the foot of the bed, she saw Ivan standing there, legs apart, arms crossed over his chest. He wore only a rumpled shirt and trousers. His eyes bore lines of fatigue and a dark fringe of beard shadowed his face. Nonetheless, he looked as implacable as before.

"Ivan," she pleaded, "where am I? I was dreaming and then I woke up here."

A comforting hand touched her shoulder. Her head jerked around and she looked up at the white-haired gent.

"You've been ill, Lady Powerscourt. Your memory will return."

"Lady . . . Powerscourt?" She turned back to Ivan. He seemed thoroughly annoyed.

"Lissa." He nodded in the direction of the gent. "Let me introduce you to the best physician in London. This is Dr. Knepp. He's attended you for the past three days."

"Three days!" She gasped. She thought she had been dreaming, but it had not been a dream at all. Ivan must have truly taken her away from the Bell and Garter. The room she was in was probably in his town house. And if that was all true, then the dream of his lovemaking and her own wantonness must be true too. Unable to stop herself, she colored all the way down to her barely covered chest.

"Your fever is gone, Lady Powerscourt. A little more rest and some of Mrs. Myers's mutton stew should bring

you back to your former health." She looked up and found
Dr. Knepp packing his black doctor's satchel. He now appeared much less ominous.

Ready to depart, he nodded to Ivan, who nodded
back. "I'll look in on your wife tomorrow morning, my
lord. Right now *I* could use some sleep. And, if I may
suggest, my lord, it wouldn't do you any harm to have
some too." With twinkling blue eyes, Dr. Knepp gave his
patient one last assessing look before he went to the door
and quitted the bedchamber.

"Your wife?" Lissa whispered when he was gone.
Somehow everything was turned upside down. She had
lost three days and had no memory of arriving wherever
she was now. Had she forgotten something else too? Had
Ivan somehow married her?

"I shall call Mrs. Myers up now that you're awake."

Ivan's voice interrupted her thoughts. Unable to wait
another moment, she asked, "Why did he call me your
wife?"

His face grew taut and she was almost afraid he
wouldn't answer her. Haltingly he said, "Would you have
rather I told him otherwise?"

She paled at the innuendo. Suddenly she felt like a
fool for even having hoped that what the physician had
said might be true. She again remembered that last night
at the Bell and Garter and fury sparked in her eyes.

"You took advantage of me," she suddenly accused.

"I see it differently."

"And how do you see it? My God, what kind of villain are you?"

Angrily he strode to the edge of the bed. He leaned
down and said, "If I'm a villain, surely you're a villainess.
You ingrate! If I hadn't come when I did you'd probably
be lying in that room of yours, too weak to keep the rats
from gnawing at your flesh. You owe me your life."

Wretchedly she looked away and said, "If I recall correctly, I paid you for my salvation in advance."

He took her chin and forced her to meet his dark, brooding stare. "Two payments do not erase a mountain of debt."

"I owe you nothing more!"

He released her chin and straightened. Ignoring her glittering looks, he asked smugly, "Shall I send Mrs. Myers up to bathe you, or would you have me do the honors?"

"I hate you, Ivan. Do you hear?" she whispered.

"I hear," he answered. "But then, if I recall, your sentiments were altogether different the night I found you at that inn."

"Oooooh," she cried out. Her hand met with the first object on the little papier-mâché table—a pearlware figure of a cat. She flung it at him with all her might, but he neatly stepped aside and it smashed impotently against the doorjamb.

In a cool voice, he stated, "I shall send Mrs. Myers up. I suggest you control your temper in her company." With that he left her alone to simmer in her own anger.

While Lissa was still fuming, Mrs. Myers popped her frilly-capped head through the door.

"Awake at last, I see! My, my, you gave us all quite a scare!" the housekeeper exclaimed.

Despite her mood, Lissa trembled a smile. "It's good to see you again, Mrs. Myers, but I can't believe you're here in London. I thought you were needed at Powerscourt."

"Oh, no, love, the marquis summoned me here the night he found you. And when I arrived, I'd never seen such a grim face on him—and grim faces are certainly his specialty!" The housekeeper chuckled.

Lissa watched her go to the armoire. She could hardly believe that Ivan had spent a moment's grief worrying about her, especially just after he so chivalrously threw her chastity—or rather, lack of it—in her face. She turned her frustrated gaze back to Mrs. Myers.

It was a comforting sight watching the housekeeper set up her bath. From the armoire, she took out several linen towels, a silver-backed hairbrush, and a fragrant bar of lily-of-the-valley scented soap. She placed these on a tufted bench and moved to the corner of the huge bedchamber. From behind an arabesque-painted leather screen, she pulled out a claw-footed tub. In minutes, several scullery girls appeared from the jib door and filled the porcelain tub from steaming kettles. When they had gone and Mrs. Myers had adjusted the water temperature with a pail of cold water, her bath was ready.

Lissa threw back the covers and made to stand, but she'd miscalculated her strength and almost fell.

"Child! Child! You've been abed for quite a while. You cannot expect to leap up your first time out." The housekeeper clucked her tongue and put her arm around Lissa's small waist. Slowly she led her charge to the tub and helped her out of the filmy night rail. Again helping her, Mrs. Myers saw her into the tub, then she bustled about the room, changing her sheets and setting out fresh bedclothes.

When the housekeeper was through with her tasks, she sat on the edge of the bench and studied Lissa's faraway expression.

"What are you thinking of, child?" she asked quietly. "Or should I say, whom are you thinking of?"

Lissa dropped her eyes. Trying to remain nonchalant, she took the soap in her hand and lathered up her thigh. "I suppose I was wondering where I should go. I mean, I can't stay here. After all, it's terribly improper that I've been here three days already."

"You're too weak to go anywhere else now. Besides," the housekeeper assured her, "your sister and Mr. Jones should be back from the Continent soon. They'll see to it that you're taken care of."

"But my staying here until then is not proper—"

Mrs. Myers shook her head. "I should think it obvious by now that Lord Powerscourt was not bred to pay homage to propriety."

"But I was," she replied. Quietly she sunk lower in the tub. Despair was etched all over her lovely face. "And even if Ivan was not," she uttered, "does that mean he'll never change?"

"You must always hope." Mrs. Myers smiled a rather secretive smile. "I do," she finished, before holding out a towel for her.

Four days later Lissa watched from the bed as Mrs. Myers laid out her clothes.

"Lord Powerscourt has gone out again?" she asked tentatively.

When the housekeeper nodded, Lissa was crestfallen. She hadn't seen Ivan since that morning they had fought. From then on she had stayed in bed, and he had stayed away from her room.

"I expect the marquis won't be back until after midnight," Mrs. Myers commented, "as he's done these past few days." Beneath her cap, the housekeeper studied her. Lissa's poorly-hidden disappointment seemed to please her immensely.

"What does he do all that time?" Lissa asked, trying not to sound too interested.

"Do? Good heavens! That is certainly none of my business!" Mrs. Myers exclaimed, and Lissa had the grace to look chastened. But then the housekeeper slyly added, "However, I do expect he does the usual kinds of things for a man of his station."

Though Lissa wanted to stop herself, she couldn't help but prompt, "The 'usual' things?"

The housekeeper gave her a twinkling covert glance. She then paused as if all of the marquis's entertainments were too numerous to recall. "Well, the marquis does frequent the Reform Club, but then there's always supper to be had at Claridge's. After that, perhaps there's Covent Garden for some theater or the Tavistock for a hand of cards. You know, those sort of activities."

"I see." Lissa cleared her throat. "I imagine all that activity is pretty tedious when one must do it alone—"

"Alone?" Mrs. Myers laughed. "The marquis alone? Why, what a quaint idea! Biddles can hardly answer all the invites that flow through this house!"

Lissa's disappointment at hearing this news only seemed to make Mrs. Myers more cheerful. "Come along, love, it's time you were up out of that bed! Why don't we dress you in this?" The housekeeper held up a stunning dress of powder-blue velvet with a sheer chemisette of Honiton at the collar. It was simple, innocent, and elegant, and couldn't have been less in accordance with Lissa's mood.

She looked at the gown, getting even more depressed. The dresses had arrived just that morning from a maker on Bond Street. She hadn't wanted to accept them, but then, she had no choice when all her things had been left at the Bell and Garter. It was wear the new gowns, or stay forever in her borrowed night rail. And she ached to go downstairs, just once, for a change of scenery.

"Oh, it really doesn't matter which one, Mrs. Myers. Any one will do," she said glumly.

"You look as though I'm holding up widow's weeds." The housekeeper ran her hand down the shimmering pale blue silk velvet. "Aren't you happy with it?"

"Yes, of course. They're all quite beautiful. It was too kind of the marquis to send them. You must tell him so."

"Why don't we get you out of this bed—and then you can tell him yourself. All right, love?" Mrs. Myers tossed the exquisite gown onto the tufted bench. She threw back the covers and began helping Lissa get dressed.

"Now, aren't you lovely?" Mrs. Myers said after she finished tying a ribbon of claret-colored satin around Lissa's neck for the finishing touch. "Let's be off, and I shall make you a hot cup of tea to enjoy in the morning room."

They went downstairs, and Lissa couldn't help but marvel over the wealth of the town house. The entrance hall alone was the twice the size of Violet Croft and possessed a stunning black-and-white marble floor. Reynoldses and Gainsboroughs graced the walls while a cheerful fire sputtered beneath a marble mantelpiece that appeared right out of a Piranesi etching.

The morning room was no less glorious. A huge oriel overlooked the gardens to the back. Though the flora was in the midst of a dreary winter, today the sun shone and flooded the room with warm yellow light. The furniture was entirely wrought out of cast iron in a trompe l'oeil pattern of silken cords and tassels. Plump feather cushions of gold jacquard completed the furnishings, giving the cheerful, summery room an air of comfort and wealth.

"Now, I'll be back with your tea in a moment, love. You just sit here and let the sunshine put some roses in your cheeks." Without another word, Mrs. Myers settled her in a chair, then hurried off to the pantry.

Lissa was still admiring the room when she heard a bustle in the entrance hall. An antagonistic male voice was speaking to Biddles. Startled, she looked up and found Ivan in the doorway.

"So you're out of bed," he commented.

Coolly she nodded. "I thought you were out."

"I came back to change clothing for the afternoon."

"Yes, I suppose frequent changes of clothing are necessary with your hectic social schedule." She frowned and thought of her conversation with Mrs. Myers.

"If I heard the right words, my plans could be changed," he said wickedly.

He came and sat down next to her. His large frame seemed to take up the entire settee, but she refused to pull back, even when his leg pressed intimately along the length of her own.

He rubbed the nap of her velvet sleeve. His gaze swept down her figure, lingering appreciatively where the velvet tightened at her bosom. "You look beautiful in your new gown, *alainn*. I hope they all do you this much justice."

"You were quite generous to lend them to me," she said stiffly.

"They're not a loan. In fact, when you're feeling better, I want you to be fitted for more."

Agitated, she stood and walked to the oriel. Outside, his gardens spread all the way back to the next street, and if she looked hard enough she could almost see the roofs of the flats on Bolton Row.

"Lissa, what is it now?" He came and stood behind her.

"I cannot accept any more gowns. That is the privilege of your wife . . . or your mistress, neither of which I am."

She began to move away, but he caught her hand. He seemed just about to say something when a cacophony of voices interrupted them from the hall. There was the sound of footsteps, then Antonia Kovel appeared at the morning-room doors with what seemed to be an army of servants.

"Lissa! Darling! I am so glad you're all right!" Antonia swept into the room and threw her arms around Lissa, artfully disengaging Ivan's hold. Bewildered, Lissa could barely stutter a greeting before Ivan demanded an explanation.

"Damned, if you aren't calling at an inopportune time, Antonia. What is it?" He scowled at the beauty.

"An *inopportune* time?" Antonia smiled and Ivan grew wary. "If anything, my dear, I am inexcusably late." She turned to Lissa. "Please forgive my tardiness, Miss Alcester. I came as soon as I knew you were here."

Ivan crossed his arms over his massive chest. "What are you babbling about?"

Antonia squeezed Lissa's hands. Lissa didn't know what to make of any of this. She didn't quite trust Antonia, but for some reason, probably because Antonia was so skillfully driving Ivan mad, she wanted to go along with her.

"I have come, Ivan dear, to take Miss Alcester into my nest and protect her from snakes in the grass such as yourself." Antonia calmly looked behind her to the servants who stood in the doorway. "I've brought all my personal servants, and we can have Miss Alcester's effects moved to Harewood this very afternoon."

"She isn't going to Harewood or anywhere!" Ivan boomed. "She's ill, can't you see that?"

Mutely Lissa stood by, watching Ivan and Antonia as if she were watching a lawn tennis match.

Antonia gave Ivan another coy smile. "All the more reason why she should be at Harewood with me. What are you trying to do to the poor girl's reputation? The minute you found her you should have called me and you know it! Staying here with you alone! For shame, you wicked rogue!"

Ivan ran his hand through his hair. He looked as if he were about to throttle Antonia. He was so thoroughly irritated, Lissa found she was actually enjoying herself.

"Miss Alcester," Antonia said, turning to her, "you do want to come and stay with me at Harewood? *You do want to make Ivan do the proper thing?*"

Lissa's gaze met with Antonia's. Suddenly she realized what the woman was about. Antonia was actually trying to help her. She was trying to remove her from Ivan's clutches and, hopefully, drive him either mad or to his knees for a proposal. Now, seeing Ivan so completely annoyed, Lissa wondered if Antonia's plan just might work.

"I accept your generous offer, Lady Antonia." Lissa smiled gratefully, refusing to look at Ivan. "You're truly a saint to help me like this."

Antonia clapped her hands, then pulled her arm

through Lissa's. They were just about to leave the morning room when Ivan said, *"Wait."*

Innocently they both turned around.

"Yes?" Antonia inquired.

Ivan hesitated and rubbed his jaw. "I want to speak with Lissa."

"Fine," Antonia answered, "I'll just sit here—"

"You'll just sit in the drawing room." His face grew stern.

Antonia studied him, then decided she had tested him enough for one day. Reluctantly she left, saying "I'll be upstairs helping to pack Miss Alcester's things."

Ivan nodded. When Antonia left, he turned his scowl on Lissa.

"You're not well enough to go to Harewood, Lissa."

Casually Lissa studied the lace at her wrists. "I can recuperate there as well as here." She then looked at him and prompted, "Of course, I needn't stay there long. As you said yourself, with the right words, plans can be changed."

Trying desperately to hide his fury, Ivan sat on one of the cast-iron settees. Again he ran his hand through his cropped hair.

"Well, if that is all, my lord, I should—"

"No that is not all!" he snapped. Agitated, he dug into the pocket of his frock coat. He thrust a black satin box into her hands.

" 'Bronwyn and Schloss'?" she read, the name sounding familiar.

"Yes. Go ahead, open it. I thought it would please you. As if anything could please you."

She ignored his caustic comments and opened the catch. Her crystal snood fell into her hands.

"I hope you don't mind my taking the liberty of getting it repaired for you?" He looked at her belligerantly.

"Of course not. How kind," she whispered, the snood bringing back all sorts of memories. She now remembered why she knew the name on the case. What a coincidence that Ivan had chosen to repair the piece at the same London jewelers that Great-aunt Sophie had bought it from.

She studied the snood, turning it over in her hands. The crystals were dazzling in the brilliant sunlight of the morning room. As if by enchantment, they caught her gaze and refused to let her go. She was held so spellbound by its glitter, she barely heard Ivan's voice.

"Tell me before you go, Lissa. When you look at this, what do you think of?"

She frowned slightly, hesitant to answer. "I used to think of diamonds."

"And now?"

She fingered one cold, hard, brilliant crystal. The memories of their night together at the castle, bitter and achingly sweet, came back to her. "Now I suppose all I think of are tears."

For the briefest of seconds, anguish seemed to cross his face, but then the emotion was gone. When she looked up, his features were as cold and hard as the crystals.

CHAPTER TWENTY-SEVEN

❀

Biddles moved imperiously through the marble entrance hall holding a small silver tray. He knocked at the library door. Tersely Ivan summoned him into the room.

"Yes, what is it?" the marquis growled as he stood by the dying fire in the hearth, an empty glass of brandy in his hand.

As Biddles could easily sense, the marquis was in no mood to be bothered. It had been over a week since Miss Alcester had left with Lady Kovel, and the marquis had spent most of his time either drinking at his club or drinking in the library. Though it was hardly evening, Mrs. Myers had already brought him his second decanter of spirits.

Biddles bowed and said, "This was just delivered from Harewood, my lord."

The marquis's head snapped up. He picked up the vellum perched on Biddles's silver tray and immediately broke the wax seal. He then read:

> *My dearest Ivan,*
> *I was delighted to discover that you've remained in town and have not returned to Powerscourt. If you would be so gracious as to accept my invitation to dinner, next Friday, eight o'clock, not withstanding, I would be most honored. Kovel and I are planning a small party for Lissa, with no more than fifty guests. Since it's my great privilege to introduce Miss Alcester to London society, I do hope you'll attend and assist me in this delightful task. Until I hear from you next, I am always,*
>
> > *Affectionately yours,*
> > *Antonia*

Ivan stared at the vellum for a long time. Finally Biddles cleared his throat. When the marquis looked up, he asked, "Will that be all, my lord?"

The marquis gripped the note in his hand until his knuckles turned white. "No, that will not be all," he said. "Summon my coach. I'm going out."

"Very good, my lord." Biddles bowed and went to carry out the marquis's wish.

"Antonia, what is the meaning of this?" Ivan stormed into Harewood's drawing room without even a greeting. Surprised by the intrusion, Lady Antonia and Lord Kovel looked up from their cribbage game.

"Why, Ivan, how deliciously furious you are! Whatever is the matter?" Antonia smiled and rose to greet him. Behind her, Kovel leaned back on his elbow chair and leisurely lit his pipe.

"You know what's the matter! What is the meaning of the note you just sent to my house?" Ivan demanded.

"Ah, I see." Antonia turned to her husband and winked. "I win the bet, Kovel. I told you he'd be right over."

"Yes, you did," Kovel answered, amusement in his voice. "And I concede that you were correct, dearest."

"What are you both talking about?" Ivan asked ominously.

With unveiled delight, Antonia stood and walked over to her guest, all the while studying his face. "I know why you're angry, my cold, dispassionate lord—I'm bringing Lissa out into society so that she can see all that she's been missing, *particularly* with you, and you are beside yourself with jealousy. In fact, isn't that brandy I smell on your breath? Have you perchance been feeling the need to drink, Ivan?"

"Don't be ridiculous," he snapped.

"Oh?" Antonia raised one perfectly arched eyebrow. "Kovel and I had a bet how you'd behave after you received our invitation. My husband said you'd ignore it, but I said most emphatically that you'd be here in a flash trying to convince me to call the entire dinner off. And, if I'm not mistaken, I've won."

Ivan crossed his arms over his chest. His eyes glittered with fury. "I didn't come over here because I'm a jealous . . ."

"Lover?" Antonia prompted.

Ivan shot her an ignoble look. "As I said, I've not come because I'm jealous. It's just that I see no reason for you to launch Lissa into society. She's got no use for such a life. And if I recall correctly, she's not impressed by such displays any more. She's changed. In fact, she wanted nothing to do with those gowns I gave her. Nothing at all."

"But, nonetheless, those lovely gowns will come in handy." Antonia smiled and touched his arm. "I agree with you, Ivan, Lissa's certainly no girl entranced with artifice, but she deserves to be brought out into society. She wants a husband and a family and, as I see it, this is the only way for her to meet someone who can give her those things."

"I should have never let you take her. I should have known you'd resort to this foolishness." Frustrated beyond expression, he ran a hand through his black locks. He looked as if he wanted to break something, and if Harewood had been his own house, he probably would have.

"Ivan, you misunderstand! I thought you'd be happy to see Lissa so well entertained!"

"You're scheming. And don't think I don't see that," he snapped. "You're trying to induce me to marry Lissa Alcester by making me jealous. But I won't be so manipulated."

"But haven't you been already?" Antonia smiled wryly.

Furious, Ivan looked as if he could throttle her. "We'll see about that. Good night, Lord Kovel, Lady Antonia." He turned to leave.

"Oh, Ivan, before you go," Antonia cooed, "I do hope you'll bring a lady friend to Lissa's dinner. I don't want you to get lonely."

Ivan didn't turn around. "I shall consider the possibility. Good night."

"Because, you see," she continued, "Kovel's just invited all his nephews to Harewood and with nine unattached men at the dinner, I'm afraid you may get quite bored watching Miss Alcester waltz."

Ivan's back stiffened.

Antonia smiled. "Good night, Ivan."

"Good night!" he roared, then left the house.

For Lissa, Antonia's soirée promised to be a delight. She couldn't believe what a friend she had found in Lady Kovel. Though she feared Antonia's scheming might not make a whit of difference in her relationship to Ivan, she still enjoyed Antonia's warmth and genuine regard.

She also enjoyed how utterly impossible Ivan had become in the days preceding the party. Antonia had told her how he had stomped into Harewood in the most foul of moods the day he'd received his invitation, how he had growled at all the servants who dared cross his path, and, when he had finally confronted them, how he had fixed her and Kovel both with a stare of glittering resentment and outrage.

It was heavenly.

By the night of the ball, Harewood blossomed like an English rose, its beauty mature and refreshingly subtle. Gone were the dust covers and cobwebs Lissa remembered when she had first taken tea there. In their stead, candle-light shimmered in every corner and the voluptuous chords of a Strauss waltz echoed through every passage.

The entire night took on a dreamlike quality. The dinner was delightful, made more so by the charm and wit of their hostess. Afterward, Lissa danced every waltz, each time in the arms of a different young man. And while she did so, she was all too aware of the eyes that watched her as she swept around the ballroom—eyes that were blue, as blue as the sky at midnight.

By the last waltz, Ivan still had not asked her to dance, choosing instead to remain standing against the wall, nursing a brandy. She was exhausted from all the activity, not still completely recovered from her fever, and when she saw Lord Charles, one of Kovel's handsome nephews, coming toward her anticipating the last dance, she almost dreaded being so put upon. But suddenly a hand appeared at her elbow and Ivan was leading her to the floor. Before she even realized it, they were waltzing. Miraculously, when his hand touched her waist, she found she was no longer weary.

"Lady Antonia is a grand hostess, don't you agree, my lord?" she said animatedly.

Ivan grunted an answer, then circled her around the room once more. She peeked at his face and was delighted by his scowl.

"I can certainly see why you were out so much while I was recovering," she mentioned, looking gaily around the ballroom. "In fact, if I were to lead this kind of life, I think I should never go home."

"Well, you don't lead this kind of life. So remember that." His hand gripped her waist even tighter.

"Now whatever does that mean?" She hid a smile. She should have been hurt by his comment, but with him behaving like such a malcontent, she found she just couldn't be. He was jealous. Thoroughly, unabashedly jealous. Whether that would bring him to the altar was an entirely different matter. But for once, it did her heart good to see him so unhappy.

"Lord Bradley's mother insists that I come to tea at the mansion on Berkley Street. And Lord Charles has invited me to a ball next Thursday. What do you think?" Her eyes twinkled with laughter. "Should I wear that silver satin ballgown of yours or the periwinkle blue one?" She lifted her eyes as if she truly sought his opinion.

He looked ready to explode, but as usual he mastered his emotions with an iron hand. "Why bother your head with such details, Lissa?" he answered coolly. "When that sniveling pup Charles looks at you, I can guarantee he isn't noticing your gown."

"What a wicked thing to say, Ivan. Are you implying that Charles is something other than a gentleman? You wouldn't think so if *you* had walked with him out on the balcony in the moonlight." She sighed dreamily. "You know, my lord, I think I shall wear the silver satin to Lord Charles's ball. It's a discreet color, to be sure, but that neckline . . . however did you find one so fascinatingly low?"

With that, he quit waltzing altogether. Angrily, he took her by the hand and led her to a little bench hidden in a drapery-covered apse.

"You're not wearing that gown. It's my gown, do you hear? And you will wear it when I ask you to," he rasped.

"Oh, what a foolish piece of baggage I am, Ivan. I forgot. It is your gown. So you must take it back. Holland will buy me one of my own." She raised one eyebrow. "I just hope I can copy that neckline . . ."

His hands grasped her shoulders and he said, "Lissa, I will not have you—"

"Will not have her what, Ivan?"

They both looked up and found Antonia standing by the drapery. While she surveyed the situation, a self-satisfied smile played on her lips.

As if Lissa were a poison, Ivan released her and stepped back. His face quickly turned dispassionate. "Miss Alcester and I were having a discussion, Antonia. I needn't tell you it was private."

"Private or not, Kovel wants to introduce Lissa to the Duke of Rankston. Everyone is looking for our guest of honor, and I cannot allow you to monopolize her time." She held out her hand. "Come, Miss Alcester. Let me take you to the drawing room."

Lissa rose from the bench. She gave Ivan one hesitant glance, but he only stood by, angrily rubbing his jaw. A look passed between him and Antonia. Resentment clashed with duty, but duty won. Antonia got hold of Lissa's hand and she promptly took her away. With nothing more to keep him at Harewood, Ivan abruptly left the soirée to seek out the warmth in his decanters of brandy.

CHAPTER TWENTY-EIGHT

❉

A week later, it was almost midnight when a loud, demanding knock stirred the marquis's household. A sleepy Biddles answered the door and to his surprise, Holland Jones stood angrily at the entrance. As if he were almost used to the bailiff's brusqueness, Biddles stepped aside and watched helplessly as Holland sought out the library.

"Good God, I should have forced her to come with us! Where is she?" Holland accused Ivan when he entered the room.

Unperturbed, Ivan sat listlessly in his leather chair, stroking Fenian's back with his booted foot. Blandly he said, "Ah, it's my brilliant estate manager back from his honeymoon. How was Venice, Jones?"

"Do you have her here?" Holland said ominously.

Ivan almost smiled. "It's not what you think, Jones. Lissa left for London on her own. I and my evil seductions didn't spirit her away."

"I know she left on her own. Her note at the cottage said as much. But then I heard you'd left for London too, and now I want to know where she is!"

"Well, she's not here."

Holland almost looked taken aback. "Then where is she?" he asked.

"She's staying, quite properly chaperoned, with Lord and Lady Kovel. She came to London—alone, I assure you—to see about getting a position. I found her at an old inn in St. Giles."

"St. Giles?" Holland gasped.

"Yes," the marquis answered, looking down into his half-empty glass. "So save your righteous indignation, will you? If I hadn't come to London looking for her, your lovely sister-in-law would have ended up in far worse hands than my own."

"I can hardly believe it," Holland stated flatly.

"Well, you must believe it, Jones, or ruin Lissa's reputation. Which will it be?" He gave Holland a scathing look. There was no mistaking the hostility between the men, it fairly crackled in the air.

Hesitating, Holland said, "If Lissa's all right then, I'll telegraph Evvie through the Bishops' this very night. She was sick with worry when I left her at Violet Croft."

"You may tell your wife that her sister is bursting with good health and vitality."

After this sarcastic statement, the marquis rose and poured them both a stiff brandy. Without ceremony, he handed Holland a glass, then motioned for him to take a seat. The marquis went to his desk and found a well-stuffed envelope. Soon they both sat before the hearth in the leather club chairs as they had done so many months ago.

"Now that you're here, Jones, there's a matter that I've longed to discuss ever since you went to Italy." The marquis tossed the fat envelope into Holland's lap. "Somehow there's been some misunderstanding that you owed this to me."

Holland looked in the envelope. It was crammed with ten-pound notes. Slowly he put it down. "I think my letter explained this money. It's to repay you for George's education."

"George's education has been paid for already."

"Yes, but that never was, nor shall it ever be, your responsibility. Since I am responsible for George now, I must repay you."

Ivan stared into the fire. "You cannot repay me for that, Holland. The debt was between me and Lissa. Your money cannot settle it."

"Consider this her money then." Holland tossed the packet back to the marquis.

"But we both know it's not her money. So shall you take it back, or shall I burn it?" Ivan leaned toward the hearth. He held the envelope precariously close to the flames. The heat alone blackened the edges.

"Good God," Holland gasped, "that is a heavenly sum of money!"

"Then take it back." When Holland no longer protested, Ivan laughed and threw him the notes.

Angrily Holland looked down at the envelope in his lap. He seemed as if he wanted to hold his tongue, yet suddenly it was impossible. "You must know, my lord, that I will no longer tolerate your cat-and-mouse games with Lissa."

Ivan looked as if he expected that statement. "My relationship with Lissa is of no account to you, Jones. Don't make it one."

"She's my wife's sister. Most of your dealings with her I've overlooked, partly out of duty to the Powerscourts, partly because I saw no real benefit to revealing them. But now it is all different."

"It is the same."

"No." Holland shook his head. "I'd have agreed with you before the night of your ball. But that night changed everything." He gave Ivan an accusing stare. "I know that you've compromised Lissa."

"And how is that?" Ivan asked, his eyes glittering dangerously. "As I recall, *you* were most definitely not there."

"I saw her state of dishabille when she arrived back at Violet Croft. It didn't take much to arrive at that conclusion."

"Aren't you a bit late, then, with your accusations?"

Holland gripped his glass. "The accusations would have come far earlier if my hands hadn't been tied. I don't know what hold you have over her, but Lissa adamantly refuses to admit that you took advantage of her."

"So what has untied your hands now?"

"When I thought Lissa was going to have to remain

in Nodding Knoll, I saw no point in adding to her misery by revealing your sordid obsession. But now I suddenly see a future for her. A future without you there to darken her door. Lady Antonia can realize all sorts of possibilities for Lissa. My sister-in-law needn't remain a spinster. She can do whatever she desires, and I plan to see that she does that. No matter what the cost."

Ivan heard him out, all the while letting his knuckles run agitatedly down his scar. When Holland was through he said forebodingly, "Those costs could be high, Jones. To everyone."

Holland stood and put down his glass. "Regardless, I will no longer let you hurt my wife's sister. Even if it means the Joneses finally break with the Powerscourts. Even if it means I tell Lissa *everything*."

For the first time, Holland thought he saw a flicker of apprehension in the marquis's eyes, but quickly Tramore mastered it.

"What are you saying, Jones? Are you blackmailing me into leaving her alone?" The marquis's voice was even and low, not revealing a whisper of his true feelings.

"Precisely," Holland admitted. "For some reason, Lissa doesn't quite hate you. But as you well know, I can see to it that she does."

Ivan thought on this a moment, wrestling with all the different courses laid out before him. His hand lifted to finger the scar on his cheek again, and this seemed to force him to a decision. Grimly he looked up at Holland. The picture of self-control, he said, "Get out."

Lissa sat at the lace-covered dressing table in her room at Harewood. Tonight was yet another soirée, and the thought of dressing, smiling, and waltzing was enough to make her feel wretched. That week alone she had been escorted to the Great Exhibition at Sydenham, attended a play at Covent Garden, a play at Drury Lane, and an opera at Haymarket, and endured a chariot ride through Regent's Park. In addition, she had appeared at three routs, two dinners, and a ball. The previous week had held just as many social engagements, but none of them had brought her much pleasure.

Though Ivan had attended many of the functions, he either stood by like an icicle while other men came to court her, or stood somberly in the corner drinking brandy and staring dispassionately at her false displays of enjoyment.

Already the Duke of Rankston had invited her out for a weekend at his house in Westbourne, and she was almost afraid that, without much prompting, the smitten duke might ask for her hand in marriage. Then what would she do?

Wild-eyed, she looked at her reflection in the mirror. She would either have to refuse poor Rankston and humiliate herself by proclaiming her unrequited love for Ivan, or she would have to marry the duke, forever chaining herself to a man she did not love.

In defeat, she put her head in her hands. She could never marry Rankston. That would be more cruel than anything she had ever done to Ivan. So what was left? Only the sure knowledge that when Rankston proposed—if he proposed—she would crumble. Ivan would have his merriment and she would be known as the madwoman of Violet Croft.

She moaned.

"Such a display! Are you going to a wake this evening or the Earl of Claymore's soirée?"

Lissa looked up and saw Antonia enter her room. Lady Kovel looked absolutely breathtaking in a gown of emerald satin. Though Lissa was as richly dressed, her pale, drawn features hardly complemented her elegant glittering costume.

"Lissa! Let me look at you! Annabel did a lovely job with your hair! Why are you so glum?"

Lissa stared at her reflection in the mirror. Antonia's lady's maid had done an exceptional job with her tresses. She had piled them high on her head and circled them with a wreath of tiny rosebuds, fresh from Lord Kovel's greenhouse. Her gown of mint velvet set off the unusual hue of the flowers perfectly. She had every device to look as stunning as Antonia, yet there was no hiding her crestfallen features.

Wearily Lissa laid her head on the dressing table. She couldn't even look at Antonia. "I don't want to go out tonight," she whispered.

Antonia came up to her and placed a tender hand on her head. Quietly she said, "Then we shall stay home. Is that what you want?"

"No. I want Ivan to love me," she confessed, her voice ragged with emotion. By now she was beyond tears. All she could do was lay her cheek against the fine lace and silently beg for comfort.

"What if I told you he does love you, Lissa?" Antonia soothed.

"With all my heart, I would want to believe it were true. But," she whispered unhappily, "he's never told me he loves me."

"How can he know how to say words he's never heard himself?"

Slowly Lissa sat up. "What—whatever do you mean?"

Antonia gave her a sad little smile. "Who has ever told the marquis 'I love you'? Not his father, I imagine. If his mother ever said those words, that's now most assuredly beyond his ability to remember."

"But you—what about you?" she blurted out.

Antonia remained silent. Lissa paused. Antonia had always made it clear that she and Ivan had never been in love. Their relationship had been driven by lust and need, and now by friendship.

Lissa's eyes darkened. "But still, Ivan must have had

many other women, I know it. Why did none of them speak the words?"

"Because they were all a poor substitute for the woman he really wanted. And they all knew it."

"Oh, if only I could believe you!" Lissa whispered longingly.

"You know what I think?" Antonia looked at her in her dressing mirror. "I think in the end the solution is yours if you will but take the challenge. Why don't you go to Ivan tonight? Teach him those simple words. Speak them once and I'll wager you'll hear them back for the rest of your life."

Lissa's tormented gaze met Antonia's. "In your own way, though you never did speak the words, you love him too, don't you?"

Antonia smiled softly. "Ivan's a difficult man, but I understand him. I see how desperately he aches for your love."

"Is it true? Could he really love *me*?"

Antonia laughed and turned Lissa's head toward the mirror. When Lissa looked at her own reflection, Antonia said in a voice that was as clear as a bell, "It's true."

When Antonia had gone, Lissa knew she would never attend the soirée. She meant to summon a hack that very hour and go to the house on Piccadilly, but a visit from Holland delayed her.

After he had checked on her that first morning almost a fortnight ago, Lissa hadn't seen Holland again. He had had matters to attend to for the Powerscourt estate, but he'd told her he'd look in on her before he went back to Nodding Knoll. Upon his first arrival, Lissa had profusely apologized for giving her sister and brother-in-law such a scare. She had then cabled Evvie to assure her herself that she was all right. She'd written her sister a letter or two since, and though she ached to see her again, Lissa vowed, especially now, not to return to Violet Croft until all was settled with the marquis.

"Holland, do tell Evvie how much I miss her, will you?" Lissa said while they sat in Harewood's drawing room. "And tell her I'm planning to return to Nodding Knoll soon."

"Are you sure you don't want to come with me in the morning?" Holland asked as if sensing her rather melancholy mood.

"No, thank you. I shall come back on my own—when I'm ready."

"Well . . . if you forgive me, I must be off." He rose. "I certainly understand your reluctance to leave London. Lady Kovel has been too generous. We'll always be indebted to her for taking you under her wing."

"Yes, she is truly wonderful." Lissa smiled. Antonia was the truest friend she had ever known. No matter what happened with Ivan, she would treasure her and the Kovels' acquaintance forever.

"I hope you continue to have a grand time. You deserve it, Lissa."

She looked up at Holland as she walked him to the drawing room doors. "Tell Evvie I'm making brilliant social conquests, will you?" She laughed. "Even if you are stretching the truth, I want her to think so."

He stopped by the doors. "I'm sure it's no lie, Lissa. You look lovely tonight. I'll describe every detail to Evvie." He studied her a moment, then motioned to the wreath of flowers in her hair. "I've never seen such roses—they appear almost lavender."

"Kovel grows them," she said lightly. "He's quite a horticulturist, I've come to find. He's got an entire greenhouse full of unusual specimens. These little beauties"—she touched the wreath—"grow only at Harewood."

"Fascinating." Holland smiled. "Perhaps Evvie shall come to London and be invited to tour Kovel's greenhouse. I'm sure the scents would please her immensely."

"That would be wonderful. When she's settled at the bailiff's house, we must do it."

"Good-bye, then, Lissa." Holland kissed her lightly on the forehead. "I leave you in Lady Kovel's capable hands. Write soon and tell us of your triumphs."

"I will," she said wryly, wondering if any triumphs would ever await her.

Anxiously she watched Holland quit the drawing room. When he had gone, her thoughts turned once more upon Ivan. It was a bold move to go galloping off to his house. Did she dare? Did she have the courage? She desperately wanted to speak with him, yet now her bravery seemed to be failing her.

Vexed she paced the room. He loved her! *He loved her!* Antonia swore he did. So could it be true? Was fate really being so kind as to grant her her only wish? If she would only say the words?

And if he didn't tell her he loved her back? She paused, then began pacing again as the answers came to her. She would be patient. His reaction to her words was all that really mattered. That, more than anything else, would tell her he loved her. His words would come later. She just had to have faith and believe it.

"James," she called out to the hallway where Harewood's butler stood sentry, "have Lord and Lady Kovel left for the evening?"

"Yes, miss. Almost an hour ago."

"Then could you please summon me one of their carriages?" She prayed she was doing the right thing.

The ride to Piccadilly was quick, despite the light rain that hampered traffic. The coach brought her right to the marquis's door. The driver helped her from the carriage and assisted her to the front entrance. A small, tremulous smile appeared on her lips as she looked back at the man. He was waiting for her to knock. Now for the first time in her life she had hope, yet suddenly she was afraid. All she

had to do was enter the house and say three little words;
now she wasn't sure she could do it.

But she had to. Her entire future rested on having
faith in what Antonia had told her. For her to hear Ivan
just once whisper "I love you," the risk would be well
worth it. Without further ado, she softly pounded the
brass knocker.

Biddles answered the door. Though he obviously
took great pride in his implacable façade, this night, it
slipped. His surprise at seeing her was obvious.

Trying desperately to smile, she said, "Hello, Biddles.
May I come in?"

She wasn't sure what her reception would be, but
quickly the majordomo remembered himself. He ushered
her in and took her ruby-colored cloak, now damp from
the rain.

"Is he in?" she asked.

"He's in the library, Miss Alcester." Biddles nodded
to a pair of closed doors off the entrance hall. He then
gave her what almost looked to be a smile. "I'm glad
you've come, miss. He's been in a fine temper. Cook's
ready to take one of her knives to him if he doesn't start
eating."

"Good heavens." Her eyes turned to the mahogany
doors.

Biddles sadly shook his head. "It's the worst I've ever
seen him."

"Oh, dear."

"Then I'll leave you, miss. But if you need anything,
anything at all, just use the bell pull."

Taking a deep breath, Lissa walked to the closed mahogany doors. Quietly she grasped the handle and let herself into the library.

She loved the room. Even the smell delighted her. As
her fingers touched the dusty tomes behind the door, she
felt overwhelmed by Ivan's presence. His library was as
dark, handsome, and moody as he was.

She found him sitting in one of the club chairs, frowning and staring into the fire. His hand clenched a glass of spirits. In the dark of the library, he appeared to be the loneliest man she had ever seen. Suddenly her very soul wept for him, for the cruel circumstances that had hardened him into such a morose figure. Her eyes softened with love as she studied that dear frown. She vowed, then and there, that if it were within her power, she would erase it from his face forever.

"Lord Powerscourt," she whispered.

His head snapped up. His gaze pierced her. "What are you doing here?" he asked gruffly. "I thought tonight was Claymore's little ball."

"Antonia and Kovel went to it. I was not in the mood."

"Not in the mood?" He released a cynical laugh. "What young woman is not in the mood to be fawned at until her admirers' spittle must be wiped off their chins?"

"Has it been that bad?" A smile of her own touched her lips.

"That bad!" He snorted. "I've never seen such a mockery of manhood."

"Were you never smitten then? Not even once?"

The question took him aback. He tore his gaze away from hers and stared into his near-empty glass. "I never behaved like those dandies—why, that Rankston practically trips over himself when you enter a room, and that Claymore! He stutters like a babbling fool whenever he speaks of you!"

"You're speaking of a duke and an earl, you know. Surely they possess more dignity than that."

"Dignity!" he scoffed. "Those two jackasses wouldn't know how to spell the word, let alone exemplify it."

"But you approve of Lady Antonia's nephew, what is his name . . . ?" She furrowed her brow and made a display of trying to recall.

"I haven't the foggiest," he stated dryly. "There are, after all, nine of them, if I recall."

"Bother their names then. Yet you do approve of Kovel's nephews? They behave in the most exemplary way. And are handsome and rich as well."

Suddenly he became furious. He rose from his chair and strode over to where she stood. He slammed the heavy, book-laden door behind her and put his hands on the case on either side of her head.

"You listen to me, Lissa. None of them is right for you, do you hear? And until that right man comes along, you'd best heed my advice."

She looked up at him, delighting in his dark, angry features. "My lord," she whispered breathlessly, "methinks you protest too much."

"I haven't protested enough! I've left you in Antonia's care and she, by God, is leading you astray. I hear Rankston is close to proposing—tell him no, Lissa, or I shall have to intervene."

"And how do you plan to do that?" she asked. "The same way you got rid of Albert and Wilmott? Do you plan to buy off every suitor I have? Every eligible man in London?" Suddenly she laughed, taunting him deliberately. "Even *you* haven't enough *money* for all of *that*."

Violently he gripped her arms and pulled her to him. His voice cracked. "I'll kill them then, if I have too."

She looked up at him, her eyes sparkling with emotion. "You won't have to, my lord. I don't want any of them," she said quietly.

"You don't want them?" His touch grew gentler.

"None of them."

"Whom do you want then?" he asked in disbelief.

Without speaking, she stood on tiptoe and pulled his dark head down to hers. He almost flinched when she tenderly rested her own unblemished cheek upon his scarred one. She held him against her until it was almost more than he could bear. His cold exterior cracked. He closed his eyes and his hand swept her hair.

"You, Ivan. I want you. *I love you,*" she finally whispered in his ear. She looked at him then, desperate for a sign, for even the possibility that he might one day love her too. Awe appeared in his eyes and she suddenly knew she'd found it. He seemed almost afraid of what she'd said, as if already he despaired of never hearing the words again. But his fear, like her own, did not stop him. When she pulled him to her, he kissed her as he'd never kissed her before. His mouth was hungry yet tender, and though he never said the words, his lips seemed to promise that the words would come. He held her so tightly within his arms, she felt she almost couldn't breathe. Nonetheless, she delighted in his embrace, wanting only to be closer to him. Tonight there was no past, only a future. When he kissed her again, a tear slipped down her cheek. Her heart wanted to burst with joy.

There were no words that could express their emotions. So instead they used their hands and their lips to tell each other how they felt. Anxious to feel him next to her, she brazenly began unbuttoning his shirt while he pulled at the laces fastening the back of her dress. Soon their clothes were strewn along a path to the fireplace; scattered last among them were the lavender-tinted roses that had adorned Lissa's hair.

When they both lay warm and naked by the hearth, Ivan pulled her on top of him and combed his fingers through her glorious hair. She looked down at his intent expression and knew she would never cease to love this man. Unable to stop herself, she touched his cheek, but this time she caressed his smooth one—the one unmarked by hatred and sin—the side of him that could love her. He looked at her then, and as if confirming what she thought, he placed a hot kiss on her palm. Then he took her mouth in a tender, soul-wrenching kiss and made love to her as if there would never be another time.

As they lay spent and exhausted in each other's arms, Lissa put her head on Ivan's chest. He pensively stroked the silken back and they each grew quiet, letting the stolen peace settle around them.

"Say those words to me again," he finally whispered, breaking the silence.

"Which words?" she teased.

"Those words," he said seriously, his eyes dark with emotion.

She studied his face as if she could not get enough of him.

"I love you," she said. "It's been my fate to love you. And if you left me tomorrow, I would still love you, for I cannot do otherwise."

Her words seemed to comfort him yet at the same time make him flinch. He grew thoughtful, then enigmatically he whispered, "Never forget you said those words, *alainn.* You must never forget you said them."

CHAPTER TWENTY-NINE

❧

It had been hard to part from Ivan, but still, in the early hours of the morning, she had had to insist that she return to Harewood, explaining what a scandal her absence might cause the Kovels. Reluctantly he watched her dress. It took almost a half hour for her to find her widely scattered apparel, and she was still missing a garter and several gold hairpins. In the meantime, he had pulled on his pantaloons and shirt, and instructed her to wait by the fire while he fetched their cloaks. When he returned, he lovingly wrapped her in her ruby-colored cloak and together they made the short carriage ride to Harewood through the silent, misty London streets. Before he left her in Harewood's drawing room, however, he gave her a thor-

ough kissing and told her he would call on her tomorrow
to discuss the "future" in fuller detail.

With the effects of his lovemaking still lingering on
her, she sleepily watched him go. Then she forced herself
to go up to her own little bed. But in remembering their
night, her sleep was sure to be as sound and trouble-free as
it had been in months. Her true love was going to marry
her, she was sure of it. And though he had not yet told
her he loved her, he had so desperately wanted to hear the
words from her, she knew in time that she would hear
them on his lips as surely as Antonia had foreseen. Releasing a soft sigh, she had stretched and dreamed of Ivan.

It was past nine in the morning when Holland arrived
at the marquis's house. This time he graciously announced
himself to Biddles, who politely informed him that the
marquis was still performing his toilet. Holland seemed
surprised at this statement for he knew the marquis to be
an early riser. Nonetheless, he thought none of it. He told
Biddles to inform his master that he was leaving for Nodding Knoll on the 11 A.M. train and that he had forgotten
to take his report on the marquis's holdings in Cardiff.
Holland stated that he would await the marquis in the
library, and before Biddles could protest that the hearth in
there had not yet been banked, Holland had already disappeared.

In the library, Holland meant to review some other
important papers in his possession concerning the marquis's holdings, but he quickly noticed that the room had
not yet been visited by the staff that morning. The leather
club chairs were out of place and something was strewn
across the hearth like confetti. Holland wouldn't have
made much of it, except his gaze suddenly registered what
the confetti was. Rose petals, tinged lavender, were scattered everywhere. He stepped to the hearth and a piece of
blue caught his eye. He bent down behind one of the club

chairs and extracted a lady's blue satin garter from beneath the rear leg. He then gathered some of the petals and studied them. When he could come to no other conclusion, he crushed them in his fist.

Without a word, he looked up and came face to face with the marquis.

"When is the wedding to be, my lord?" he stated, an unmistakable edge to his voice.

"What are you doing here, Jones?"

"I *said,* my lord, when is the wedding?" Holland took a threatening step forward.

The marquis's eyes narrowed. Anger made his face grow taut. "I see no reason to consult my estate manager on such a personal matter."

"But you will consult me!" He opened his palm and showed him the crushed rose petals. "You took her right under my nose! I'll see that wrong righted!"

"How do you know any of this? Lissa didn't tell you —of that I'm sure."

"She hasn't confessed, but then she doesn't need to now. I saw her wearing these flowers last night. They grow only at Harewood, I'm told, so there is no mistake. Lissa was here last night." Holland took off his glasses and prepared for battle. "Now that I have my proof of your nefarious deeds, I ask you again, when are you going to marry her?"

"In good time, my man. In good time" was all the marquis would say.

Infuriated, Holland moved forward. "That's not good enough. You've more than proven your desire to manipulate and humiliate Lissa. Now that your revenge is complete, it's my turn for revenge. You will marry her and I will not tolerate procrastination!"

"I won't be brought to the altar with you dragging me by the ear," the marquis said in a growl. "So I see no point in discussing this further."

"You see no point? See *this* point then!" With that

Holland's fist shot out, squarely meeting with the marquis's jaw.

From instincts borne of many brawls, Tramore didn't even pause to sort out what had happened. Instead he retaliated. He punched Holland twice across the face, then slammed him against the bookcases.

But Holland, too, was swift. He artfully sidestepped the marquis, then shot in and out, avoiding Tramore's punches like a Roman athlete.

"Your bloody crude methods won't save you from the beating you deserve!" he cursed.

"Jones, your pretty moves are no match for experience! You'd best quit now while you have the chance!" the marquis threatened.

"I was a master at boxing at the university. Let's see if I can recall . . ." Suddenly Holland's fist went out and he landed a punch in Tramore's gut. The marquis doubled over, but only for a second. His fury peaking, Tramore lunged for Holland and slammed him to the floor. Chairs scattered and floorboards groaned as the men rolled back and forth. Holland got in another two cracks to the marquis's jaw before Ivan tried to put his head through the paneling.

Fighting as if for his very life, Holland broke free and scrambled to his feet. Then he promptly forgot his sense of sportsmanship and the gentlemanly art of boxing. With a fury he didn't know he possessed, he kicked Tramore in the kidneys, then landed a punch to his side.

"You braying ass! I should have done that long ago!" he panted.

"What brotherly concern, Jones!" the marquis rasped, wiping the blood from his mouth. Obviously hurting, he stiffly got to his feet. "If I didn't know better, I'd say you fight more like a jealous lover—"

With that, Tramore did his worst. He lunged at Holland like a wolf and slammed punches into his head. When Holland could take no more, the marquis finished him off with a jab to the gut. Holland slid down the wall, nearly unconscious.

"I'll see that Lissa never marries you!" Holland said, slurring his words. "How could I have ever thought to lower her to such circumstances! It's bad enough I've had to work for such a bloody bastard! But to sentence a poor girl to marry you, there could be no worse hell!"

Ivan couldn't help himself. He knocked Holland cleanly across his face, almost breaking his fine English nose. Then he eased himself to the floor, and fell back against his desk, catching his breath.

His hand went to his fob pocket. He dug in it and finally produced a ring—an engagement ring—which he held reverently in his hand. But then his temper flared.

Crushing the ring in his grasp, he gave Holland's unconscious form a disparaging glance. "Bloody *bastard*!" he hissed. Yet it was unclear whether those words he'd uttered were for Holland, or for himself.

When Holland came to, he stiffly rose from the floor and looked about for the marquis. Tramore was nowhere in sight. Holding his battered head, he scooped up some of the lavender rose petals, then stumbled out of the house. When he arrived at Harewood, he found Lissa and Antonia finishing their breakfast in the eating room. Without a word, he appeared at the door and let Lissa's gasp signal his entrance.

"My God, Holland, what happened to you? There's blood all over your face," Lissa cried.

"Mr. Jones!" Antonia stood. She frowned at Holland's battered face and promptly called for some assistance.

"Holland, did someone attack you?" Lissa whispered.

"On the contrary, I was the attacker." Holland studied her grimly. "Go collect your things, we're leaving for Nodding Knoll this instant."

"W-what? Why?" she stuttered, a dread filling her breast.

"I shall fill you in when we're at the train station. Suffice it to say I am now no longer Powerscourt's estate manager."

Lissa stared at him fearfully. "What happened, Holland, between you and the marquis?" She wasn't sure what was going on, but it was clear Holland had been in a fight and she had the horrible feeling the fight had been over her.

"Lissa," Holland stated fiercely, "I am the head of the Alcester family now. You'll do as I say. No more questions. Get your things."

Her cheeks colored with anger. She had been glad that Holland had come into the family and taken the family's burdens from her. Now, however, his authority rankled her. She had helped the Alcesters survive for five long years after their parents had died, and now she was not about to be ordered about by anyone.

"Holland, I shall go when you explain—"

Holland did nothing but open his palm. Inside were several crushed rose petals—the exact same color she had worn last night. Suddenly her legs felt as if they were going to give out. Holland had been to Ivan's house and somehow found the petals in the library. When he next retrieved a blue satin garter from his pocket, she had to clutch the edge of the dining table just to remain standing.

"I—I can explain," she began.

"Then go on," he said, wiping the blood from his chin with a linen handkerchief.

"You think Ivan's done something terrible. But it's simply not true. He's going to marry me. He told me so last night."

Holland broke from the door and stood before Lissa. A pained, wrathful expression crossed his features. "If he were going to marry you, Lissa, would I look like this?"

She stared at him, unsure of what he was trying to say. Then suddenly she began to tremble.

"It's not true. He will marry me. Everything has changed, do you understand? Ivan wouldn't deny it now. Not now!" she practically screamed at him.

"Lissa, go get your things. We're leaving here. If he wants to marry you, he can find you easily enough in Nodding Knoll."

Wretchedly she turned away. She felt as if the very ground she stood on was falling away from her feet. Holland was about to speak again, but she couldn't bear to hear another one of his accusations. She covered her ears and ran upstairs to pack.

CHAPTER THIRTY

❁

Somehow she had to think. Somehow she had to stop all the madness that was exploding around her. The entire situation had to be a terrible misunderstanding. But as Lissa watched Antonia's maid gravely pack her dresses, she was at a loss as what to do. Holland was on a rampage and Ivan had yet to show at Harewood. A hack was already waiting in front to take them to Euston. Even as she thought all this, the maid was folding her last gown.

"Why isn't he here?" she fretted, and ran to the window. Down below, Holland was seeing that there was room atop the hack for her last trunk. All he was waiting for now was her.

"When Ivan arrives, I know things will be set right again. But that Mr. Jones has absolutely no patience!" Antonia rose from a small settee and began pacing the floor.

Inconsolable, Lissa looked out the window.

"Are you ready?"

She spun around and found Holland already in her doorway. A pained expression crossed her features when she noted the puffiness and swelling on his face. He would soon be black and blue. She only wondered how Ivan had fared in this skirmish.

"Holland, you must be reasonable. Please let us wait until he arrives—"

"I've left my post, Lissa, and I must move from the bailiff's house. I cannot delay. If the marquis wishes a word with you, he can make an appointment at Violet Croft." Holland watched the footman pick up her last trunk. When he was gone, he held out his arm. "Evvie is waiting," he told her.

Wondering if she would ever see Antonia again, Lissa gave her a last desperate hug. She then took Holland's arm and they went down to the carriage.

The train ride to Cullenbury was interminable. Holland said scarcely three words the entire way. When they finally arrived back in Nodding Knoll, Lissa had never been so grateful to see Violet Croft. Holland saw her settled in, then he immediately went to Powerscourt to begin his move. Lissa spent the rest of the afternoon sobbing into Evvie's shoulder and trying miserably to explain the situation to her.

Hardly a day had passed before there was word the marquis had returned to the castle. Lissa was anxious to hear from him, to try and settle the rift that seemed to be tearing her apart, but no word came down from Powerscourt. Another day passed and the silence grew ominous. Holland expressly told her to beware of the marquis should he try to see her while he was not around to chaperone.

By the third day she was beside herself. She miserably wandered the little rooms of Violet Croft, every now and again going to the window to stare at the towers of Powerscourt. When she felt she would go mad if she spent another day brooding at the walls around her, she grabbed up her bonnet and cloak and went to wander the estate grounds instead.

She had just found the path that had once been Alcester House's carriage drive when she heard the music. In wonder, she walked closer to the estate and began to discern the delicate sound of a balalaika being played. It was a sad, mournful tune, and it brought back a flood of memories, both painful and tender. As if the ghostly notes were beckoning her, she moved toward the stable. She should have been afraid, but she wasn't. She entered the decrepit stable building and found Ivan sitting on the stoop of the tack room, the balalaika in his arms. It was as if the past five years had never been. He was again the Alcester stable-boy and she was a young girl, full of hopes and dreams for the future. Entranced, she stood near the door and watched him. He was too intent upon his playing to look up, and for a moment she allowed herself to be captured by the dark, dreamily reflective melody.

But the moment vanished in an instant. For no apparent reason, he became disgusted with his playing and abruptly stopped. He pushed the balalaika away and cursed. The pups, whom she now noticed had been lying at his feet, sensed his foul mood and quietly skulked away. Then, without warning, he looked up. His gaze met violently with her own.

"My lord," she stated, sounding far more cool than she felt. Suddenly Holland's fears seemed to eat away at her boldness and she clasped her hands over her mantle to keep them from shaking.

He stood. There was something in his eyes that welcomed her—warmth, relief. But there was something in his eyes that made him hold back. It was wariness.

"What are you doing here?" he asked quietly.

"I was out for a walk. I heard you playing." A wry smile tipped her lips. "For a moment I thought you might be a ghost."

He stood. "I'm no ghost. I came here to think."

She paused; her entire body began to tremble. Everything she wanted seemed to be slipping through her fingers. Now she must grab it back, or let it go. "To think about what, my lord?"

He looked down at the balalaika in his hands. Then his eyes swept the scenery around him—the stables, the Great House in the distance, the fields, everything but her. "I've decided to buy Alcester House. Should I do it, Lissa?"

She was taken aback. There was so much they needed to say to each other, yet this was not any of it.

"Why would you want to buy this place, Ivan?" she whispered.

"I no longer find any pleasure seeing it so downtrodden." He looked at her.

"You would never live here. Your place is at Powerscourt."

"But you would like to live here again, wouldn't you?"

She put her trembling hands to her cheeks. What was he saying? He would buy her Alcester House? And she would live there and he would live at the castle? They would live apart? Holland's accusation rang in her ears. *If he were going to marry you, Lissa, would I look like this?*

She stumbled back. Tears welled up in her eyes and she vowed to run all the way back to Violet Croft before he could see them.

"Lissa."

He stopped her. She wiped her cheeks with the back of her gloved hand. Still she didn't face him.

"Do you no longer want to live at Alcester House?" he asked gently.

"I want to live with my husband. At his home," she blurted out.

"At Powerscourt?"

She could hardly whisper her answer. "Yes," she told him wretchedly.

With a strong, unwavering hold, he turned her to face him. As if in disbelief, he asked, "How can you love me? How can you possibly love *me*?"

She again wiped her tears. Her voice shook when she answered him. "I love you simply because no matter what I do, I cannot stop feeling this way."

Her words seemed to cause him pain. He didn't move to her. Instead he turned away completely. His head lowered and he rasped, "Despite all attempts to make it otherwise, I am a bastard, Lissa. I was born a bastard. I am still treated like a bastard. I've spent most of my life shoveling dung and wearing rags." His voice faltered. "What, in that, could possibly be worth your love?"

She looked at his forbidding back and she felt completely helpless to make him turn around.

Finally she whispered, "I loved you when you wore rags and I love you now. You've helped me protect my brother, you've been generous to my sister." Despite herself, she began to cry again. "All for a girl who scarred you for life. Oh, my lord, how could I not love you? I weep every day that I ever caused you such harm."

When she finished, she felt him pull her into his arms. Unable to stop the flood of emotion, she began crying against his chest. He held her and stroked her hair. She heard his harsh voice trying to soothe her, but she could not be quieted. For five long years she had carried her guilt. Now it was time for it to end.

At last, when her emotion was spent, she lifted her head. Their eyes met for a long soulful moment, and before she could stop herself, she reached up and touched his scar.

"Oh, Ivan." She sighed. "I must know. Did it hurt terribly?"

Slowly he shook his head. "I didn't feel a thing," he whispered.

"How shamelessly you lie then."

"But this is not a lie." He caressed her cheek and

turned grave. "I need you, Lissa. I'm empty inside without you. If you ever leave me again, I shall truly grow mad. I . . . love . . . you."

Astounded, she looked at him. "What did you say?" she gasped.

"I love you," he said, his voice filled with emotion. He then tipped her face and kissed away her anguish forever.

When at last they parted, he still kept his arms possessively wrapped around her. *I love you.* In her mind she again heard his words, and her heart swelled with joy. Looking up at him in awe and disbelief, she knew then she had never known such utter bliss. He had finally told her how he felt and he had said just the words she had prayed she would hear. Antonia had been right and now she thanked God that she had listened to her.

Gazing up at him, she studied every dear feature of his face. But suddenly, because her heart had never felt so light or because her spirit had never flown so high, she began to giggle.

"What are you laughing at, baggage?" he demanded.

"Oh, Ivan. Your face. You look positively dreadful. You look almost as battered as Holland."

He didn't seem to find the amusement in this. Instead he scowled. "Jones is lucky to be alive."

"I'm sure he is," she said, touching one particularly mean bruise on his temple. "In fact, I'm sure you both are!"

"Holland got what he deserved, no more, no less."

"Yes, he's become quite insufferable. In fact, he would be quite upset to find out I have seen you."

"And do you find his actions justified?"

She paused. "Holland is trying to protect me. He found the flowers I wore in my hair. He feels you have taken advantage of me." She finished slowly, "But as we both know, you have not."

"Snatching you away like that was unforgivable."

"He thinks you a villain."

"He's right. I am a villain."

She stared up at him. All at once, she turned cold with fear that he was somehow not going to ask her to marry him. But then his finger lifted to touch her lips. As he did, she kissed his palm.

"My beautiful girl," he whispered. His hand dropped to his waistcoat. From a tiny pocket, he produced a ring. He slipped it on her finger. The ring was made up of tiny stones—lapis lazuli, opal, verde antique, epidote, moonstone, and emerald—which, as was custom, taking the gems' first letters, spelled out a message. Ivan's ring said "love me." She was so stunned, for a moment she could hardly breathe.

"I shall speak to Holland this afternoon about a wedding. Would that please you?"

Almost drugged by her happiness, she nodded.

"Is a week too long to wait?"

Releasing a cry, her arms went around his neck. Joyously she whispered, "Yes, yes! Anytime is too long to wait!"

"I can't arrange it sooner, *alainn,* I have people to notify. It's not every day the Marquis of Powerscourt takes a wife. So many will want to witness this."

"Yes, yes, I understand!" She kissed him tenderly, full on the lips. When they parted he seemed loathe to let her go from his arms.

"*Alainn,* I want to make you happy." He stumbled on his words. "Yet, I'm afraid—that—perhaps—you could do better."

"No better," she told him. "There are no better men than you, my lord."

He held her against him as if needing the warmth of her body. "Then may God in His mercy keep you believing that forever," he whispered.

* * *

Lissa rushed back to Violet Croft to tell Evvie the wonderful news. As she burst into the cottage, she found Holland there too and she couldn't have been more glad to see him. Immediately she rushed into his arms and gave him a warm, sisterly kiss.

"I'm to be wed! I'm to be wed!" she cried out, dancing around the parlor.

Disconcerted, Holland watched her while Evvie laughed and clapped her hands.

"Oh, sister, is it true? Ivan really asked you? When did you see him?"

"Yes, yes! I saw him at the Great House. We were both walking there." Lissa fell back onto the sofa. She immediately took off the ring and put it in Evvie's palm. "He gave me this ring, then told me we must be wed in a week! He is to speak with Holland this very afternoon. Right before he leaves for London to make all the arrangements."

"Oh, Holland!" Evvie exclaimed. "Everything is to be all right now! Our darling Lissa is to become a marchioness. Ivan's marchioness!"

"Yes," Holland said rather flatly. A worried frown furrowed his forehead, but Lissa didn't notice it at all. She was too busy explaining which stones were in her ring and what it was set in.

"Oh, dear!" she suddenly exclaimed. "Now I suppose I do have to go to town! I must tell Mrs. Bishop! She's been so kind to us, it's only right she be the next to know!"

In a flurry, Lissa gathered up her cloak and gloves. Excitedly she checked her bonnet in the little hall mirror. She was pleased to see her cheeks had blossomed with color. Happiness did indeed suit her. She would never let it go again. With that thought in mind, she bid her farewells and flew out the door, unmindful of Holland's worried stare.

After spending a delightful teatime with the Bishops, Lissa returned home with excitement still beating in her breast. But her heart constricted a bit when she heard Evvie and Holland having a heated argument upstairs. In dismay, she paused in the parlor, not even taking off her cloak. She was completely unsure of what to do. Her instincts were to leave them alone, and yet, worried, she couldn't shake the terrible dread that somehow, their quarrel concerned her. Feeling like a thief, she nervously ascended the stairs. Holland's words to Evvie stopped her before she even got to the top.

"My God, quit defending him! Tramore's been 'Aunt Sophie' all along and he's been manipulating your lives as if you were all pawns on a chessboard—just to keep his grasp on your sister!"

Lissa's jaw dropped and a frown appeared on her brow. Every limb of her body seemed to go numb from shock. She was so astounded by Holland's words, she could hardly comprehend their meaning. What had he said? That their mysterious Great-aunt Sophie was really . . . ? She suddenly found herself choking on the name. Her hand went to her throat and she felt uncontrollably ill.

"It's a horrible revelation, Holland," she heard Evvie interject, "but if Ivan did really invent our Great-aunt Sophie, the charade has done us more good than harm. I don't know how we would have gotten along without his aid."

"He cut you off, remember? He did it just as he was coming to Powerscourt so that he could get Lissa completely in his grasp!"

"His deception is reprehensible. But I can't hate him. Surely he must be a good man deep inside, or why else would he have ever concerned himself with our destitute state?"

"There's more."

Hearing Holland's words, Lissa suddenly felt faint.

She closed her eyes and clutched the banister for support. She couldn't believe what was going on. She couldn't believe Ivan was Aunt Sophie. But, she thought as pain darkened her eyes, they had been cut off just before Ivan returned to town. And they had never met Aunt Sophie, never knew she'd existed, really, until they'd gotten that note from her London solicitors—Ivan's solicitors.

Horrified, she turned away from the stair. The deception *was* reprehensible. And though she screamed to herself not to start, she suddenly began to doubt so many things Ivan had done and said. She even began to wonder if she'd known him at all. Now Holland had said there was more. And from the tone of his voice, it was terrible indeed. She didn't know how she would endure hearing it. With a silent, heart-wrenching moan, she turned back to the stair and listened.

Worried, Evvie soothed her husband. "My love, you feel so tense. How bad can it be? Already it seems the worst has been told—"

"No," Holland said, cutting her off. "No, the worst has not been told. What I fear is far worse."

"What—what do you fear?" Evvie whispered.

Lissa grasped the banister until her knuckles were white.

"I fear Tramore may be waiting with a *coup de grâce*. He's lusted after revenge for more years than I know. Every day that scar has to remind him of his quest. I'm afraid that for him to forgive Lissa, he'd have to forgive everyone in this entire town who treated him callously. Could he do that? I just don't know. When I saw that engagement ring, the terrible idea suddenly struck me that perhaps there was method in his madness. I mean, that ring could be his path to complete retribution. What if he's asked Lissa to marry him . . . only to abandon her at the altar?"

"It's not true! It's not true! I beg of you to tell me it's not true!" Lissa suddenly cried out in anguish. She burst into the room and looked wildly around. Though she'd never felt closer to fainting in her whole life, she forced her legs to hold. Holland was speaking terrible lies and somehow she had to stop them. Ivan wouldn't abandon her at the altar. He loved her! He had said it! Shaking with fear and fury, she confronted her brother-in-law. "Holland, this is a lie! You must take it all back! It's a lie!" She stared into his face and found the anguish she had dreaded. All of a suddenly, she felt weak and drained. She could hardly look at him. "Tell me this is a lie," she begged, her voice lowering to a whisper. "Tell me he's not capable of such treachery!"

Evvie found her way to her side and bade her sit down. Numbly Lissa did as she instructed. But suddenly the burden of this revelation became too much for her. She buried her head in her hands, but no tears would come. Now there was not even that as a release for her grief. Ivan and his despotic love had even taken that away.

"Lissa."

She felt Holland pull down her hands.

"As God is my witness, I didn't want you to hear this."

She looked at him with beautiful, haunted eyes. "But now I have heard it. And damn you, I had a right to know. Why didn't you tell me this before? Before you left for Italy?"

"I wanted to, but there was no time. And . . . I thought you'd stay away from him."

"Oh, God, I wish I had." She closed her eyes and began shaking. Already she could hear Ivan's last few words. Their marriage preparations would take a week, because "so many will want to witness this." All of Holland's fears seemed about to come true. Ivan probably had no intention of marrying her, had never had any intention of marrying her. Knowing what she knew now, it made much more sense that he was still out for revenge. Her heart shattered into a thousand pieces just thinking that their whole relationship had been drummed up as an execution, not a marriage. He'd even told her he'd loved her. Had that too been another grand manipulation? Another lie?

"God, what shall I do?" she whispered, feeling herself growing more mad by the second. She wished Ivan had thrust a knife into her heart instead of this. That would have been far less pain. And ever so much more private. Already she'd told Mrs. Bishop, and by now surely half the town knew that Ivan had asked her to be his wife. Already her humiliation had begun.

"Lissa, you must be brave," she heard Holland tell her.

Suddenly she crumbled. She thought of how sweet her last meeting with Ivan had been and how utterly she had believed him.

"But I can't be! I can't be any more!" She rose from the bench and ran, stumbling, to her room. She still did not cry.

CHAPTER THIRTY-ONE

❀

Fifteen thousand pounds, Lissa thought morosely as she turned the snood over and over in her hands. The wedding was that afternoon. Even though Ivan had spent the week in London, somehow banns had been posted and guests of the marquis had been arriving for days. But she did not think of that. There was no point when she would not be at the wedding. Instead, she thought of her snood and the heavenly sum of money it had cost the Marquis of Powerscourt.

She found out from Holland that it was made of diamonds and silver cord. The jeweler, Bronwyn and Schloss, was apparently the finest in all of London. Holland had even seen the ticket when the piece had been delivered. Ivan had paid fifteen thousand pounds to have it made.

Fifteen thousand pounds.

The unbelievable figure kept coursing through her mind. To achieve Ivan's wicked goals, even fifteen thousands pounds had not stood in his way. It had probably amused him to no end to see her struggle with her poverty, while the means to its end were at her very fingertips. She remembered the night they had first made love, and how he had gathered up the diamonds and crushed them into her hand. He must have laughed heartily when she'd left her treasure behind, unaware of its worth. He'd probably had it repaired only so that he could torment her again.

She clutched the snood in her hands. But she would no longer be tormented. He could not torment a soul that had long since died.

She looked at the snood and again thought of its worth. Fifteen thousand pounds would secure her for life. Though she'd entertained thoughts of returning it to Ivan, of throwing the diamonds at his feet like so many worthless rocks, she now most definitely decided against it.

Because she'd earned those diamonds, she thought coldly. She'd paid for them with her mind, body, and soul. And now that he had taken all three, she had nothing else left but this glittering piece of jewelry in her hands. She would never give it back.

She put the piece in its black satin case and thought of Ivan's other treacheries. In the days previous Holland had told her all that he knew. The revelations were painful. Even hearing that the marquis had bought her portrait from a London gallery and then kept it in the attic, because, as Holland had put it, "he could not bear to see it properly displayed," broke her heart all over again. She was sickened by all the manipulations and lies, sickened beyond redemption. She had hardly left her room all week. Though Evvie tried to get her to eat or even cry, she couldn't. Her pain was too great to even allow herself the luxury of feeling it. Sometimes she wondered if she would ever feel again.

A knock came at the bedroom door. Her gaze lifted and she found Evvie in the doorway. Her arms were filled with the gold boxes sent from Powerscourt days ago. Her sister briskly brought them into the room.

"Why are you bringing those in here?" Lissa asked rather flatly.

"Because it's your wedding gown." Evvie ignored her sister's apathy and presented her with a white silk box.

"What is this?"

"Ivan returned from London this morning. His note was quite explicit that you were to get this this morning. To be sure, Holland read it to me twice."

Taking a deep ragged breath, Lissa opened the box. She was rather startled by the contents. Though the jewels were no more than pearls, the clasp bore the Alcester coat of arms. It was Rebecca's necklace.

"What is it, sister?" Evvie asked softly.

"Mother's pearls," Lissa confessed. "I lied to you that I did not sell them. Now Ivan has found them again and given them back to us."

"To *you*," Evvie reminded her.

"No," Lissa refused, putting on a most brittle façade. "These are meant for you. I want you to have them as your wedding gift. I felt quite awful not being able to give them to you then."

"Lissa, I cannot accept Ivan's gift to you."

"But the pearls were ours and I wanted you to have them."

"But now they are Ivan's. And he wants his bride to wear them on her wedding day."

"No wedding day!" Lissa cried out and leaped from the bed. She stared out her mullioned window, the crush of passing carriages only reminding her further of her anguish.

Her sister's hand touched her shoulder.

"I know how much he's hurt you with his lies," Evvie whispered. "You have a right to hate him. To hate him with all your being."

Lissa remained silent, not moving, not crying.

Evvie continued gently, "But that doesn't change the problem, does it? For you don't hate him. And that's what's tearing you up inside."

"I do hate him," Lissa countered furiously.

"You don't. You love him. You always have."

"And now look how I must pay for it!" At the breaking point, she wiped one tear from her cheek. She vowed there would be no more. "Because I dared love him, I'm being betrayed in the most cruel of manners. And there is nothing I can do about it."

"There is something you can do." Evvie clasped her hand. She paused and then said what seemed to be foremost on her mind. "My dear Lissa, I love you as I will never love another. You've done so much for me and though you've wanted me to believe that it's been easy, I know it has not been. It doesn't take eyes sight to see what is going on around you. In fact, I knew you'd sold Mother's pearls long ago."

"I didn't want to lie about them, it's just—" Lissa began, but Evvie stopped her.

"It's just that you wanted me protected. And that has made me love you more." She tightened her grasp. "Lissa, you must know I would rather God take away my hearing, my taste, and my touch too than ever want to see you hurt. My heart is breaking alongside of yours in this treachery. And it would break completely if I could just believe that Holland is right. But you see, though my mind says Holland is right, my heart says something different. My heart sees Ivan as half a man—a man who needs love to be made whole; a man whose only happiness can be found at your side. And in my heart," Evvie pleaded, "I believe that man will indeed show up at the church this afternoon."

"How I want to believe you," Lissa said desperately, "but as we've found out, Ivan is the master of deceit!"

"But you've seen this man I've spoken of! This horribly neglected and unloved figure!" Evvie cried out. She grabbed her sister's arms and forced Lissa to look at her. "You know him better than I! You've loved him! What does your heart say?"

Lissa broke down with heart-wrenching sobs. In defeat, she cried, "My heart says he will be there, but my heart is wrong!"

Evvie went to the bed and from one of the gold boxes produced an exquisite bridal gown the color of candlelight. She pressed it into her sister's arms and said, "You have no choice then, my dearest sister. You must follow your heart."

Never was there a more reluctant bride.

When Lissa ceased her weeping, she mechanically began to dress, even though she still was not sure she could go through with it. She knew Evvie was right, that in her heart she believed Ivan's words and that he did truly love her. They both had done things to each other that needed forgiving. Yet still her mind screamed that he wouldn't show. If he'd planned revenge, he had conceived it brilliantly.

Once in her wedding attire, she had never looked more beautiful, nor felt more wretched. The cost of the dress alone had to have equaled a lifetime of pay for most English citizens. Her bridal gown was made of creamy silk velvet with a detachable velvet train that rode from her shoulders. Honiton lace made up the veil and poufs of the same lace decorated the skirt. The bodice ended in a deep point in back and front and the shoulders were decorated with satin ribbons and fresh pink rosebuds that Evvie, though sightless, still skillfully pinned on. As was the custom, festoons of the same rosebuds were pinned to the front of her skirt and a rosebud wreath circled the top of her head. She, of course, carried no bouquet of posies, for traditionally that was for Ivan to give her after they were married. Now, as she looked down at her empty hands, she practically wept again. Chances were they would never hold his flowers.

Just as she wiped away a stray tear Holland appeared at her doorway. His face was quite grim, but he warmed at the hauntingly poignant picture she made in her bridal gown. She could see in his eyes that he was afraid for her, but it seemed he was more resigned now. She wondered how Evvie had managed to convince him.

"George is at the church," he finally said.

"Did—did he have a good trip up from Eton?" Lissa asked, feeling awkward in her attire, and worse, horribly afraid.

"He seemed excited . . ."

"I see." Depressed, Lissa sat gingerly at the window seat. Tearily she mused out loud, "Perhaps we shouldn't have summoned him. This may prove to be a terrible mistake. I mean, what a terrible thing for an impressionable boy to experience—"

"Evvie was adamant that George not miss his sister's wedding. For some reason, she is utterly convinced Ivan will show. So we don't have much choice now, except to have faith in her intuition."

"Yes," she whispered disconsolately.

"Are you ready?"

She looked up. Again her crystalline blue eyes clouded with tears. "I'll never be ready." She then gathered her train and allowed Holland to take her to the waiting carriage.

For miles, it seemed, carriages were lined along the Nodding Knoll Road all the way to the church that sat in the middle of town. The day was brilliantly sunny, but the sunshine seemed like a mockery, especially as it cast through the windows and onto the silent, grim faces in the carriage.

It was all Lissa could do not to bolt. Though she wished and prayed during the short ride to the church that Ivan would show, she was utterly sure he would not. There was a part of Ivan that was tender and good, a part of him she was sure she had reached more than once. But there was another part of him that was hard and terrifyingly cold, and that was the part of him she was sure would win out. He would not be there. In all probability, he now was most likely sitting anonymously in a pub in Cullenbury, waiting with glee for the first gossip that the Marquis of Powerscourt had stood up his bride.

With that thought, the panic began to rise to her throat and she shot a glance at the door. If she got out now, she thought, no one might ever know she had taken the marquis's proposal seriously. There would be gossip, surely, but if she never showed, no one would ever know how badly she was hurt, nor how much she had loved him.

Not even considering the consequences, she reached for the door handle. She meant to leap out and run back to Violet Croft, even if she left her train in the road. But suddenly she was stopped. Holland's hand reached out and pulled her back. Wild-eyed, she pleaded with him to let her go, but he shook his head. "It's too late to run. We're almost at the church," he told her flatly.

"No! *No!* Turn this carriage around! I can't go through with it! I can't!" She again tried for the handle but before she could reach it the carriage lurched to a stop. In horror, she looked up and found they were at the church. Everyone was inside except the minister and his acolytes. Upon the bride's arrival, they too disappeared into the church, leaving only the Powerscourt footmen there to usher in the bridal party.

"I cannot do this," she whispered, hearing the organ music begin. When the first notes to Bach's 'Jesu, Joy of Man's Desiring' drifted out the doors, an overwhelming panic seized her. In her bridal attire, she felt like a white dove trapped in a cage. All she wanted was out.

"Turn around! Go!" She looked straight at Holland. "He's not here! Do you see his carriage?"

"That doesn't necessarily mean he isn't here. He could have ordered the carriage out of the way until after the ceremony."

Gently Evvie leaned toward her sister. Shaking, Lissa clutched at her and said, "Please, Evvie, he's not here. We must return home!"

Evvie extracted herself from her sister's grasp. "I have to go in first. So I'm going now." Evvie somehow found Lissa's face and gave her a warm kiss on her cheek. "I love you, Lissa, and though I haven't the sight to see you, I know you are a lovely bride. If Ivan does not show, he should be taken out and executed."

Then Evvie allowed Holland to help her from the carriage. A liveried footman attended to her and, in seconds, she disappeared into the church.

"Holland, oh, Holland, please don't make me do this! He isn't there, I know it. I know it!" Suddenly she began to cry. She couldn't go through with this. She would never be the same if she went into that church and found an empty altar. It would destroy her. She would have nothing to live for ever again. Her days would become as dark and bleak as the moors in the winter. She would rather God take her life now than force her inside that wretched church.

Moved, Holland pulled her to his chest and comforted her as best he could without harming all her finery. He whispered, "Hush, hush," until she finally quieted. When they parted, he handed her his handkerchief and she wiped her tear-reddened eyes.

"He doesn't deserve you, Lissa. But you want him. So

if there's a God in heaven, he is standing in that church right now."

"I'm very much afraid he's not." Through her tears, she gave a bitter laugh. "Oh, but this is utterly wicked revenge, don't you agree? I do think Ivan's quite a genius. It's almost hard not to admire him."

He smiled softly. "Evvie has not come back. Perhaps that is a good sign."

"Yes," she said, trying to forget her sister was blind and could not see whether Ivan was there or not. Defeated, she took Holland's arm. "Perhaps that does mean he's here."

He helped her from the carriage and the footman spread her train out behind her. Almost blind with anguish, she took her first few steps up the marble stairs. They reached the church vestibule while the music swelled, and there a sea of faces met her. In the crowd she saw the Bishops and Arabella Parks and her mother. Lady Antonia was there, sitting on the groom's side of the church. Honoria and Adele were there too, sitting on either side of their father. Even J. Albert was there with his mother, not brave enough to have scorned the marquis and not shown up. Last, to her surprise, Mrs. Myers sat with old Widow Tannahill.

Terrified, her eyes lifted to the front. In the first pew, Evvie sat with George, who looked positively dazzled by the sight of his beautiful sister. But nowhere did she see Ivan.

Unable to stop herself, she felt her legs begin to buckle beneath her. He had not shown. *He had not shown.* The trick had been played, the revenge completed.

Holland supported her and kept her standing but suddenly she didn't care. Her heart was shattered. The enormity of the situation was upon her but she couldn't feel anything except anguish and regret. With sudden and ferocious clarity, she knew that without Ivan, her life was over.

Her future was now only a living hell to endure until she
was blessed with the reprieve of death.

"Look up, Lissa," she heard Holland whisper. She
turned her eyes to him, then followed his gaze. The door
to the parsonage opened and Lord Kovel appeared. She
almost half expected him to make the announcement that
Ivan was not to show, but he didn't say a word. He merely
stepped aside and let the marquis precede him into the
church.

Her hands moved to her lips and she muffled her sob
of relief. She could hardly believe it was true as she
watched Ivan and Kovel move to the front of the minister.
When they were in their respective positions, they turned
to face the bride. Her gaze met with Ivan's and suddenly
there was no one in the church but the two of them.

He had come. Relief and joy swept her brow. All that
he had said to her was true. There were no more lies. The
past had been played out. Though she hardly dared to
believe it, it seemed that finally their fates were to entwine
as she had always prayed they would—in contentment and
love.

She wiped her cheek and found it damp. She was
crying, yet this time it was not from anguish. She had
never felt so utterly happy as when she looked at her bride-
groom. And when she saw how he looked at his bride.

Ivan's eyes gleamed with admiration of her in her
finery. But there was another emotion in them as well, one
that she had seen before, yet had never quite understood
—until this very moment. With tears streaming down her
face, she glanced down at her engagement ring still on her
hand. "Love me" it asked, as he was asking now. She
smiled through her weeping and without doubt or fear,
silently answered, "I will." She looked up and saw that he
held out his hand for her. When Holland began their walk
down the aisle, it was all she could do not to run shamelessly into her love's arms.

. . . Oh my soul, so may thy face be by me when I close my life indeed; so may I, when realities are melting from me like the shadows which I now dismiss, still find thee near me . . .

David Copperfield to Agnes,
Charles Dickens